What people are saying about

Red Dr...

Having been a therapist, j[...] years, I have had a rather deman[...] ...nd I met Bridget when she came to train with me as a hypnotherapist. Her ability to learn very quickly made it easy for her to take on the complicated issues of her clients. It was obvious from the start she had a knack for working with people's minds.

Bridget's ability not only to tell her stories but also to write with such a natural flow is a rare combination, which sets the stage for a fascinating book. Once I started reading her book, I could not put it down, as it's a compelling page-turner. I am already looking forward to her next one, as I know there will be.

We became friends over the years as I watched her intriguing life unfold. In my experience, there are a few people who have the most adventuresome lives. In fact, as an author, this is the type of person we look to interview for our own books. Bridget is definitely one of those people.

Valerie Austin, International Therapist, Journalist and Filmmaker

Engaging, light-hearted and deeply touching, this book deals with universal themes: alienation, exploration and the quest for reconciliation - with who you were, where you are and what you want to be.

Jane Bailey Bain, Author, *Lifeworks*

A story of awakening. Deeply relatable for anyone who has felt the inexorable pull of the search for greater meaning. This book explores the uncomfortable, magical journey into an expanded version of ourselves. Poignant, vulnerable and real - I was

gripped as if by the telling of my own story.
Helen Ludwig, Conscious Leadership Consultant

Bridget's book takes you on an engaging romp through the protagonist's spiritual and personal transformation. As a behavior specialist, I found her characters to be relatable and authentic. As a reader, I found myself hungry for more...
Marc Cooper-DiFrancia, CEO and Founder of Creative Self Mastery.com

Red Dress

A Novel

Red Dress

A Novel

Bridget Finklaire

ROUNDFIRE
BOOKS

Winchester, UK
Washington, USA

First published by Roundfire Books, 2021
Roundfire Books is an imprint of John Hunt Publishing Ltd., No. 3 East St., Alresford,
Hampshire SO24 9EE, UK
office@jhpbooks.com
www.johnhuntpublishing.com
www.roundfire-books.com

For distributor details and how to order please visit the 'Ordering' section on our website.

ISBN: 978 1 78535 560 8
978 1 78535 561 5 (ebook)
Library of Congress Control Number: 2020940134

A CIP catalogue record for this book is available from the British Library.

Design: Stuart Davies

UK: Printed and bound by CPI Group (UK) Ltd, Croydon, CR0 4YY
Printed in North America by CPI GPS partners

We operate a distinctive and ethical publishing philosophy in
all areas of our business, from our global network of authors to
production and worldwide distribution.

Lokah Samastah Sukhino Bhavantu

May all beings everywhere be happy and free, and may the thoughts, words and actions of my own life contribute in some way to that happiness and to that freedom for all.

Chapter 1

September 20th, 2008

Katy sat in the garden on Saturday morning, snatching five minutes to herself. The roses were fading, she noticed, wrapping her gown against the autumn chill. She didn't know then that three days later she would do something unexpected. The impulsive decision would seem like nothing, yet this one small act would set in motion a domino effect that was to change her life forever.

The weekend flew by in a flurry of chores, finishing abruptly on Sunday evening. The Stone family slept through the night to the rhythm of Richard's snoring. Katy lay awake in the darkness, listening to life. It was calm in the well-groomed suburbs of West London with its parks and leafy streets, but still there was the rumble of distant traffic, a night bus idling at the lights, revelers in the street, their loud slurs deadened by the tall, terraced buildings. Far away a late train rattled over its tracks, a fox rummaged in the bins, and a 747 followed the river as it descended towards Heathrow. London: continually alive with diverse people making their way through its veins and arteries, she thought. Her favorite place in the whole wide world.

The digital clock read 03:03 when she rolled over, catching its neon figures in the gloom. She couldn't remember the last time she'd had a decent night's rest. At this rate, she'd be tired tomorrow, and she had to get to Terry's by 11 am. Her mind raced off in another direction. If only she could sleep! It was the stress, she supposed: mother, wife, self-employed therapist and homemaker. It wasn't easy for anyone, the pressure of living in the time-starved, work-weary, money-guzzling, glorious capital.

* * *

Damn, thought Richard, wrenching himself from the thrilling dream that cleaved at him, his body aroused, nerve-endings tingling. His hand groped for the alarm before it woke everyone. Lucky cow, he thought, looking over his shoulder at his sleeping wife. He watched Katy as she let out a groan, frowned and pushed her earplugs tightly in place before rolling over. A tangle of dark auburn hair sticking out from the top of the crumpled duvet was all he could see.

Still fancy her, he thought, picturing the face he'd woken up to almost every day for seventeen years. Piercing blue eyes and full cherry lips, she was his little prize. He couldn't think exactly what was missing, apart from the obvious! He was lonely, he supposed. Empty. It had gone wrong somehow.

He shuffled into the en-suite in his dark striped pajamas. The ones she hated.

"Why don't you just go without?"

"It's cold."

"Wear a t-shirt and boxers then."

T-shirt and boxers. Who did she think he was?

After adjusting the mirror, and brushing shaving foam over his greying stubble, he let out a sigh and gritted his teeth. Another day in the jungle. He hoped he didn't end up punching someone. He'd like to wipe the smile off some of those faces, he thought, scraping the edge of the razor across his square jaw.

Richard's thoughts turned back to his dream. They'd had hardly any sex since the children were born and that was years ago. The blood was coursing through his loins, but she was always tired. Always some bloody excuse. Frigid. That was the word, she was fucking frigid. Stepping into the steamy shower, he contemplated the erection his wife didn't want and girded his tall, muscular frame against the force of the water. A while later, feeling refreshed, he stepped onto the duckboard and grabbed a thick white towel from the wooden stand.

Katy scrunched up her eyes and sighed unhappily, roused from her sleep by the noise of the pelting shower. He was doing it on purpose, she thought. He'd changed. The truth of it was, she didn't fancy him anymore. He was cold, angry and controlling. She hated the rotten smell of his morning breath, and those ridiculous 'old man' pajamas! What a city gent wears, she mocked silently.

Her mouth curled up at the corners as she thought about the cocky young man in a white t-shirt, an old guitar slung over his shoulder. The one in the photographs, the young Richard, Rick as he was then. What a contradiction, loving literature, poetry and the thuggish game of rugby! She imagined him sitting in the Student's Union reading D.H. Lawrence and wanting social justice and rock and roll. He'd have campaigned for worker's rights, and written an album of protest songs and a seminal novel. Of course, she'd missed his best years, having met him later when he joined the corporate world. But there was still a trace of the revolutionary back then.

Ambition had taken over now. He'd watched other people feather their nests with lucrative deals, and he liked what he saw. Greed, finance, and spin. The City had become his tribe. The jungle, he called it. He'd elbowed his way up the ranks to senior partner, subtly, of course, the seemingly suave advisor. Persuasion, manipulation, raw intelligence, and a dollop of charm. That's all it had taken, but he'd lost himself in the process and was losing her along the way.

Richard surveyed himself in the bathroom mirror. At least I'm not bald, he thought, slicking back his dark hair and splashing Trumper's cologne over his face. Dressing as quietly as he could, he buttoned a fresh Pink's shirt. "For fuck's sake!" he muttered, fiddling with the silver bulldog cufflinks. Adjusting the knot of his Hackett tie and smiling into the mirror, he gave himself a wink. He had to look the part if nothing else. Straightening his suit jacket and folding a crisp, white handkerchief into the top pocket, he took another look in the mirror before examining the shine on his black leather Loakes. The deliberate clomping of his shoes across the stripped floorboards woke Katy at last.

"You off?" she murmured.

"Yes. Bye, Kittykat," he said, bending over to kiss her, the stale taste in his mouth still lingering beneath the toothpaste. "See you this evening."

He closed the bedroom door behind him before thudding down the stairs to the tiled hallway. Narrowly avoiding the clashing jangle of metal, he edged through the half-opened front door. "Wretched wind-chimes," he muttered as he hurried into the cool morning air. Bloody Feng Shui bullshit.

As he strode towards the station, he noticed curtains opening one by one as sleepy Turnham Green woke up to another grey day in the Capital. He passed row upon row of Victorian and Edwardian terraces and semis, with clipped olive bushes standing in Grecian planters like threshold guardians. Inside the sumptuously furnished houses, he imagined walls knocked through to expensive glass extensions. Neat, 'farrow cream' painted, wooden shutters covered the wide bay windows. It all stank of money and snobbery. He secretly despised what he'd become. Occasionally there was a rundown house with a badly painted door, old fashioned wallpaper, faded curtains and weeds peeping through the cracked paving. Must be old bags living in those, thought Richard, forgetting his own humble beginnings. Pop their clogs and someone'll snap the place up and make a fortune! The cynicism was rotting him from the inside out.

Men in grey suits strolled down perfectly tiled pathways, marching purposefully to their toil with hard briefcases, like worker ants seething out of the nest. He'd like to smash their smug faces.

Arriving at the station kiosk, Richard nodded at the sickly-looking man in attendance. "Financial Times and a packet of sherbet lemons."

"Two pound sixty, mate."

He handed over the coins, folded the newspaper and thrust it under his arm. The train was packed. Barging his way through the doors onto the already heaving carriage, he squeezed his tall, sturdy frame into the crowd and bent his head to avoid the curvature of the door. Sighing, he looked down at the dandruff on the collar of the man in front and sneered.

* * *

"I don't know what's wrong with me, Terry," said Katy, looking up at the quiet, wiry man who sat in front of her that morning.

"Is it work?"

"I don't know." Katy gazed out at the elegant buildings opposite, their outlines distorted by the uneven glass of the window. "I don't think so." She pulled her manicured eyebrows together in thought. "I'm exhausted. It's a challenge, dealing with people like Seamus and everything he's been through, but it's rewarding."

"From my perspective, you're doing well!" said Terry, glancing down at his notes. "You've got most of your clients under control, and you're a good therapist." He clicked the top off his pen and made a note in the margin. "Okay, so there's one or two cases that stump you sometimes, but by and large you deal with it. Even Seamus!"

"Thank you," she said, brushing aside the compliment. "I love Harley Street and it's going well..."

"But?"

"I'm wondering if I should have a few sessions of private counselling." Katy fiddled with her left earring as she crossed her legs and leaned forward, folding her right arm in front of her. Defensive, she thought. He'll have noticed.

The consulting room was quiet and comfortable, furnished

the old-fashioned way, with buttoned leather chairs and a shiny mahogany desk. A wooden standard lamp lit a dark corner with its pale, yellow light. Outside, faded red geraniums hung from the window boxes, oblivious to their urban dwelling. Terry Slater was an experienced psychotherapist and mentor. He was her sounding board and her supervisor. He understood her clients and made helpful suggestions when the going got tough. She trusted him.

"With me or with another therapist?"

"With you, if that's okay? I'm not sure of the rules."

"Yes. It's fine. It's all confidential anyway," said Terry, opening his large, leather, desk diary. "I could fit you in tomorrow if you like. I had a cancellation at 12 pm."

"Perfect!" said Katy, checking her schedule, "I'll see you then." Her face softened with relief. She knew she was doing the right thing, however scary.

Rushing from the peace of Terry's room into the crowded street below, she hurried towards the tube station. Jostled by the masses squeezing themselves onto the carriage, she was surprised to find an empty seat. As the train lurched, she thought about the rest of the day that loomed ahead. A grid of rigid one-hour segments filled the pages of her diary. She'd left a gap tomorrow, around midday, to draw breath and take stock, and another at 12.30 pm for sandwiches and a cup of tea before the onslaught of clients. Funny how the gaps filled up, she thought, but lucky that Terry could see her. She'd better finish on time tomorrow, or she'd be rushed as usual. Her stop. She fought her way to the door. The underground was dirty, dusty, windy. She held her jacket around her and squinted as she trotted up the escalator, tousled hair blown backwards by the blast. She'd better get her head around this afternoon's clients if she wanted to give them her best shot.

September 23rd 2008

It was midday in the quiet comfort of Terry's consulting room and Katy sat once more in the sumptuous chair, straightening her skirt as she crossed her legs.

"So," said Terry, pouring two large glasses of water and handing one to Katy. "What made you want to see me?"

She took a deep breath. "I don't know, exactly! An inkling, I suppose."

He waited patiently.

"I feel..." She bit her bottom lip and looked up at the moldings on the ceiling. "I can't describe it. Something's not right." She paused, trying to locate what it was. "I'm worn out, I think!" She took her gaze back to Terry, who was making notes with his fountain pen, the nib scratching across the paper. "I feel empty, arid and..." She stopped.

"And?"

"I don't even know if I need therapy." Katy uncrossed her legs and re-crossed them again. She'd forgotten how uncomfortable it was to be in the patient's seat. It took courage to admit there was a problem – to see a therapist, she thought, recalling what she said to her own clients.

"After all, I lead a privileged life, don't I?" She raised her eyebrows as if awaiting an answer to the rhetorical question. "It probably looks like I've got it all." She looked down at her hands, loosely folded in her lap. Her thumb nail needed filing and she picked at it nervously. "But it feels like I'm living a lie." A lump was forming in her throat. "I can't work it out, Terry! I should be feeling on top of the world!" She composed herself and marshalled her thoughts. "Don't get me wrong, I'm grateful..." She faltered and checked herself, not wanting to cry or sound like a whining bitch. She was acutely aware of being judged – not by Terry, but by herself. She was supposed to know what she was doing, have it all under control! What would he think? "All those clients who can't have children or struggle with an addiction or feel alone in the world." She swallowed. "Then there's the broken cases – the 'hole in the soul'. I've got nothing like that to complain about!" She shuffled in her seat and took a deep breath.

"Go on."

"I'm sorry, Terry," she said, taking a packet of paper tissues from her bag. She looked away, mortified. "People think I've got a great life, and I have!" She dabbed carefully under her eye, mopping up a stray tear before it ran dark rivulets of mascara. She didn't want people to know or to see. "I struggle to get out of bed in the mornings. Wish I could lay there all day and sleep! And I'm feeling so tearful. It's not like me." Diverting her attention away from her thoughts, she glanced back at Terry. "I can't face Richard, either. He's draining. He doesn't understand and he won't listen. I can't talk to him about anything."

"Have you tried?"

"Yes. He turns, like a mad dog, barking and snapping. Takes it all personally, thinks I'm criticizing him. He makes it all about him – just like my mum and dad did."

Terry pursed his lips slightly and made a note on the page.

"Why do you think Richard's acting like the wounded party?"

Katy wiped the end of her nose with a fresh tissue. "I don't know, but I'm the one who ends up consoling him and making it all better."

"Like the caring person you are, but what's actually going on here, Katy?"

She blushed. "He's so distant and angry, and I don't know what to do."

Terry was looking straight at her.

"I guess he's in denial and deflecting criticism by projecting."

"And where have you seen that pattern before?"

Katy ducked the question. "It's not just Richard. I feel as if I've lost something valuable. This terrible feeling of loss and panic. I feel trapped, somehow. Like it's all closing in on me."

She didn't want to admit it to herself, let alone Terry. "It's easier to put on a brave face and pretend everything's fine. Just carry on. Stay positive. Keep passing 'go' and all that."

"What are you avoiding by pretending?"

Katy changed the subject. "One of my clients complained the other day that their life was like chewing an old piece of gum – all action and no flavor! I know that's how Richard sees it." She thought of the home she'd built, the family she'd created, the children she'd nurtured through sickness and health. "I told Rich I've got too much on my plate, but he doesn't get it. He thinks I should see fewer clients, but my career keeps me going! It's juggling everything else that's wearing me down."

Terry smiled. "Could you be mirroring each other to some extent? Has your life lost its flavor too?"

"Yes. I think it has, and I need your help to get it back." Her stomach knotted. She'd hated saying that. It was a weakness, needing support. Helping others was easy, but she was awkward when it came to being helped. "I need a safe sounding board and a place to work it through."

I want to be happy, thought Katy, smiling to herself. That's what lots of clients said. Katy would ask them "What would make you happy? How will your life look when you're fulfilled? What will you be doing differently?" The answers were usually simple. I'll have a girlfriend. I won't be fat. I won't have these panic attacks. Did that bring lasting happiness? Katy wasn't sure. Nobody's life could be happy all the time, and didn't contentment come from within? Perhaps it was *meaning* that was important in life?

"I think you're working too hard. When was the last time you had a break?" said Terry, snapping her out of her reverie.

"Recently – July!"

"What can you do to slow down, do less?"

Katy could feel the resistance pressing against her. She

couldn't possibly slow down. There was far too much to do. The last thing she wanted was for it all to come crashing down. It had taken too much to build.

"Can you take some time out for yourself? A small break in your day? That's what I'd like you to do between now and our next session."

At around 3.30 pm, Katy was barging through the front door of number eleven Sycamore Road, the wind chimes ringing out in celebration. 'Welcome home,' they seemed to be singing.

"Tea!" she said to herself, reaching up to the top shelf for the Earl Grey. Sipping at the hot liquid, she sighed contentedly as she sat back in the kitchen chair, reflecting on her session with Terry. Time out for herself? Huh! Two minutes with a cup of tea before all hell breaks loose! She savored the moment, then made a mental note of the afternoon's chores. Meet the kids in town, new rugby boots for Freddie, school blouses for Tilly and a quick dash around Waitrose. There was nothing to eat in the house.

It was seven o'clock by the time they returned. "Can you lay the table, Freddie? Dad'll be home soon." Katy was unpacking the bags and trying to take her jacket off at the same time. "I'll heat up the chicken. Tilly? Tilly? Where are you?" I'll do it myself, she thought, pulling open a packet of salad leaves.

The wind chimes rang out their warning as Richard thrust open the door. "Train stopped at Earl's Court for ages," he grumbled. "What's for tea?"

"Hello, Darling," muttered Katy, thinking – it's supper, not tea. Tea's at 4 o'clock with sandwiches and scones. He probably hadn't heard her and probably didn't care. He was rushing upstairs to change.

"It's ready!" she called a moment later, adding oil and balsamic to the salad. Katy looked across the kitchen table at her husband as he helped himself to chicken. He was good looking, maybe that's why she'd married him? She'd loved him once: wanted to get hitched and feel settled. All those chemicals churning around, the great romance, the thrill of the chase! He'd swept her off her feet, the smooth-talking man in the dark suit.

Richard was reading the Evening Standard as he slid a finger over the plate and licked off the juices. "You okay?"

"Yeah. I'm fine."

Katy picked at her lettuce, her thoughts still rumbling around. He often said, 'I'm a good catch', and she supposed he was. He'd always provided for them. She tried to focus on the positive. The crux of Cognitive Behavior Therapy, she reminded herself, was to see things from a fresh perspective: to reframe.

Clearing the plates and packing them into the dishwasher, her thoughts rambled on. She could trust him – she knew he was reliable. Not like Adrian who was a totally irresponsible git or Nick who was a bloody alcoholic. If only she'd been trained! She could have helped Nick! Jeez! His childhood was a mess. When she thought of it now, she realized how stupid she'd been, wasting her time, trying so hard to be the one who changed him. She'd put so much love into that relationship and nothing had shifted. But you have to want to change, she thought.

Wiping the table, she looked up and smiled at Richard. He had all the qualities her parents had wanted for her in a spouse: tall, dark, handsome, with an education and a good job. They were companions alright, but the passion had fizzled long ago. And it was all her fault.

"Thanks, Mum," said Freddie, pulling back his chair with a scraping noise and heading off to his room.

"Homework?"

"Yeah. Tons of it." He groaned.

"What about you, Tilly?"

"What's it to you?" she said, slouching in the chair, kicking a foot against the floor, and giving her mother one of her withering looks.

I don't know where I went wrong with that girl, thought Katy, I've done everything to support her and this is how she repays me.

Richard paid no attention. His nose was buried in the newspaper.

There's no spark, she thought, watching her husband as he read the sports page. We keep up appearances, but inside we're chalk and cheese. I've been papering over the cracks for years. I wish we could go back to how it was in the beginning.

"Rich, can I talk to you about something?"

"What?" snapped Richard, "I've had a hard day at the office and I just want to unwind with the paper."

Katy twiddled her left earring before returning to the dishwasher, clunking the door shut and switching it on. It was never the right time, not for Richard anyway. Last weekend he'd been too tired, on holiday he'd wanted to get away from it all, and last night he'd wanted to watch *The West Wing*. No matter what moment she picked, it was wrong, and he'd have a rebuff lined up.

"I'm feeling a bit overwhelmed," she said as Richard turned the page and took a gulp of red wine from the generous glass he'd poured. "When would be a good time to chat?"

"Don't come at me with your therapy-talk! I told you before – see fewer clients!"

"It's not the client work, Rich, we've been over this!"

"Then what the bloody hell is it?" He slammed the paper onto the table.

"It's okay. We'll talk another time, when you're not tired."

"You've disturbed me now, you may as well carry on."

"It's a big house to run, and the kids still need me, even though they're more independent, and—"

"For God's sake, Kit, get a housekeeper!" He picked up the paper and returned to the sports page.

She didn't want a housekeeper. She wanted a husband who

cared and children who appreciated her. She'd had to help out at home when she was young. She might as well be a housekeeper herself, she thought, at least she'd get paid and be able to take leave!

"But I don't want a housekeeper! I just want a bit of support. You could help me load the dishwasher or book the car in for service or organize a holiday! Anything!"

"You don't think I support you? Look at all this," he said, holding his arms up and gesturing to the large modern kitchen with its black, granite worktops and taupe-painted cupboards. "You don't get this on a therapist's salary!"

"I know, Rich," she said, "I didn't mean—"

"What the hell did you mean?" His nostrils flared as his jaw tightened, a small muscle twitching at the corner.

"Nothing, Rich. Nothing," said Katy, turning to the stove and rubbing at a spot of burnt-on food. She pushed the chairs back under the table and caught his wild, indignant eye. "We do need to talk and you're running away from it. In therapy we call that 'denial'." She backed away, thinking he might just lash out, but he restrained himself and went back to the paper, flicking it sharply as he turned the page.

"I've got a few post-session notes to sort out," said Katy, boiling the kettle and making herself a cup of mint tea. "Could you leave a small glass of that for me?" She nodded at the bottle of Valpolicella. He glared at her before taking himself and his paper off to the sofa, his eyes firmly fixed on the TV page.

He's not listening, she thought, looking over at Richard, now slumped on the couch with the remote in one hand and a refilled glass of red in the other. He never listened.

It wasn't just him. Tilly and Freddie were just as bad. At least Freddie was cheerful. At their age, Katy was already proficient in the art of domestic drudgery. It was different nowadays, she thought, and just as well: she didn't want her kids to have the life she'd had. She wanted to redress the balance, break the pattern, help and encourage them, nurture them. But it was a one-way street.

Katy lugged her briefcase upstairs and checked in with Freddie, who was sitting at the desk in his bedroom. "How's it going?"

"Okay."

"Need any help?"

"No. I'm alright, Mum." He turned and smiled as she ruffled his hair and gave him a hug.

Tilly was reciting lines for her school play, and flashed a look of thunder as Katy approached, as if to say, 'Don't you dare disturb me!' Katy nodded and backed away, shutting the door to her daughter's room.

Another flight of stairs led to the top of the house where Katy's office overlooked a tree-lined suburban street. It was peaceful there, and walking in, she breathed a sigh of relief. She saw a few clients here, answered emails, paid bills, ran the family finances, and booked holidays online. There was a lavender-colored massage couch in the corner, where she gave the occasional healing. She'd trained as a Reiki Master some time back. It was a swap with a friend, otherwise she'd never have considered anything like that. Shanti had trained her, and in return, Katy had counselled Shanti through her divorce. It turned out that she loved Reiki. And she loved this room with its calming blues and violets and its one indigo wall. A stack of white shelving was lined with books, crystals, relaxation CDs, aromatherapy oils, candles, and a wooden statue of the Buddha. There were small pictures of sacred geometries and Indian deities. Her qualification certificates were framed and hung above a small, iron fireplace with patterned blue and white slip-tiles either side. Psychotherapist. Advanced Hypnotherapist. Reiki Master. Under the couch was a pale-blue, Zen meditation stool.

Better get this done, thought Katy, sitting at her desk and opening her leather briefcase. It was just gone 9 o'clock. She became absorbed in each case, her analytical mind pulling together all the pieces of the jigsaw until she could see the bigger picture from the details she'd gleaned. Writing a few well-chosen words at the end of each file enabled her to remember what ground had been covered, what she'd understood of the case, and which direction to take. She was totally absorbed, giving each one her undivided attention, turning over the details in her mind so she could see every angle. Everything neat and in its place, she filed the notes and locked them safely away before tackling her emails.

A weariness tugged at her as she pondered her clients and their heart-rending stories. Staying detached was important if she wanted to help them, but it was difficult at times. She shook off the melancholy that crept around her like a ghost but couldn't shake off the analytical mind that continued to whir.

It was almost eleven o'clock when she went downstairs to say goodnight to Tilly and Freddie. Tilly would probably push her away as usual. Richard was snoring on the sofa in front of *Newsnight*, Jeremy Paxman's voice rising into the darkness as he interviewed his prey. Gently taking the remote, she silenced him. Richard jolted himself awake. "I was listening to that!"

"You were asleep!"

He scowled at her. "I'm off to bed."

Katy crept back to the study. It had been a long day. She had too much on her plate, but nobody seemed to care. Her thoughts turned to her homework from Terry: this was the only time she had to herself, the house quiet and everyone sleeping.

Pulling out the meditation stool, she sat upright, her hands resting in her lap, right palm holding the left and facing upwards, the thumbs lightly touching. Her eyes closed but her head wouldn't stop. The point of meditating was to still the mind, but this was the only time she had to think about her life – when there were no demands, no interruptions, nothing to do.

Stop Katy! Don't get attached to the thoughts. Acknowledge

them, then let them go!

They tugged at her. There was so much to reflect upon: clients, children, life. There was no time to stop or contemplate, and no time for pleasure. Perhaps the monkey mind kept her busy so she couldn't hear the whisper of her heart. Katy thought about Terry, then Richard. She considered Tilly, then Freddie. They could do what they wanted in their spare time. Spare time, huh! She wished she had some. It was all doing, doing, doing with no time for being!

Her mind turned to the couples counselling that she'd forced Richard into a couple of years ago: it hadn't made any difference. He was stubborn, controlling and manipulative. Of course he was never going to let anyone in! She recalled him charming the pants off the woman, who'd fallen for his quick intellect.

The thoughts stopped for a brief moment. She'd made a mess of things but couldn't work out where she'd gone wrong. She'd tried her best, done everything that was expected of her. Tears rolled down her cheeks. Having fearlessly worked through her demons, she'd painstakingly rebuilt herself, and here she was, married, with two children, living in a desirable residence and excelling in a career she loved! She'd worked hard for her treasures, but they didn't seem to be glittering. Be positive, she told herself, have gratitude. Focus on the breath. Cool in the nostrils as you breathe in. Warm as you breathe out. Relaxed awareness, expectant gratitude, following the breath, focusing on the Hara, three fingers width below the navel.

The restless thoughts began to subside. The breath became shallow and slow. Her shoulders dropped.

She'd been meditating almost every night for about nine years and it had become the most important practice in her life. She couldn't imagine how she'd cope without it. Katy's mind became still. Her whole being expanded outwards and upwards into nothingness and nowhere-ness. It felt as if the sun were shining on the inside. Warm, loving, radiant. She was the silent witness.

Beyond the self: big and luminous. Peaceful and eternal.

Ooh! I'm not thinking. Bugger. That's a thought.

Breath. Hara. Silence.

It felt as if she was being held. A loving presence was there, inside her, surrounding her. She wasn't alone.

Focus. Breath.

She wondered if that might be God? Katy winced. *God*? But she wasn't religious! Maybe Shiva, Source, The Divine, or even Yahweh like the U2 song? That sounded better. God wasn't very cool, was He? Funny that. Even the spiritual people didn't like using the 'G' word! It was very old-fashioned. She squirmed. Too many negative connotations.

He was omnipotent, wasn't He? That meant all-powerful. Yes. Potent. Powerful. What were the other two? Omnipresent – everywhere at once – and omniscient; all-knowing. He knew everything. He's a 'know-all', she thought, the corners of her lips curling upwards into a smile. I wonder if He's really a She? But that would be Goddess!

Breathe. Hara.

She giggled. So, He knows I'm sitting here laughing at Him. He knows my life's a mess and He probably knows why, because He knows everything! He's got all the answers! And if He's everywhere, it means He's here with me right now! And He has the power to do anything! Or She has. Maybe She's both – beyond gender.

Breathe, Katy. Breath. Focus on the Hara, and let go of the stupid thoughts!

She should hand her life over to God! He couldn't screw it up any more than she had! She spent her life solving other people's problems but couldn't sort out her own! Maybe it took her mind off... She paused. Maybe being busy stopped her sinking. Stay positive! What was it they said? If you fake a smile you produce all the right neurotransmitters? Fake it till you make it!

Katy adopted a positive attitude. There was a solution to

every problem. Damned if she could find it, though!

"I hand my life over to God!" It just came out, unexpectedly, as if someone had pushed an invisible button. Perhaps it was her true self, the one buried beneath domesticity and keeping up appearances!

Oh well, let's see what happens, she thought, see if He does exist, if He really is omni-all those things!

Breathe. Hara. Silence.

Expanse. Stillness. No time. No thing.

A loving, distant Voice – a male voice – spoke softly, tenderly inside Katy's head, as if just above and behind:

"The road is long and boring at times, but then a beautiful vista. It twists, turns and rises, and leads occasionally to dead ends. There are obstacles, and steep and jagged byways. It's frustrating, but the challenges are there to strengthen you. It's all there for the learning. You think you've taken a wrong turn or ended up in the wrong place, but the truth is, it's just an experience. You created it from the choices you took. You're growing. You can always let go and choose something different or respond differently. Everything happens for a reason. The soul has planned it – for your edification. That's the purpose of the adventure you call life, this schoolhouse called Earth. You face and transcend the difficulties, empowering yourself as you go – else you're stuck in the cul-de-sac you've chosen, pulling yourself in to hide in small, safe spaces. See through the illusion. Grow wise and detach from the turmoil. Advance through the maze of opportunities and learn to rise up! See the full panoply of possibility from a higher vantage point! For every steep hill there's a breath-taking view. For every arduous step there's an epiphany. For every sadness there's a joy. For every fear there's a strength. For every loss, there's a gain. Most people stay in the comfort of their own cul-de-sac. What do you choose? Safety or the courage to take flight? Limited life or limitless light? You have free will."

Chapter 2

October 2008

Sessions with Terry were going well. He'd given Katy tasks each week and she'd diligently applied herself, despite initial resistance and panic. She'd carved out ten minutes during the day, giving herself permission to do something other than client, business or domestic work. She'd started to read again, catch a program on Radio 4, or listen to a self-help CD. Sometimes she'd browse around John Lewis on the way into work, feeling guilty afterwards if she'd bought something. Some days were still too busy to find time out, but, on Terry's recommendation, she was walking in the park for twenty minutes every other day. Yoga extended to an hour at least three times a week. She was eating fresh organic meals where possible and took supplements each morning. At the weekend, she began to pursue her own interests, diving deeper into spiritual teachings and meeting new people along the way. Her mood was shifting but she was still worn down, and now feeling guilty as well.

To the chattering classes of West London, Katy was becoming an anomaly. "She's probably having a mid-life crisis," she imagined them saying. "Look what she's wearing now!" Katy was bored with the tribal uniform of Boden, White Stuff and Sweaty Betty. Never really liked it, she thought. It was like dressing up and pretending to be someone else. She'd taken to wearing chic little jackets from the high street chains, chunky ethnic jewelry and tailored trousers with sexy shoes. It was Richard who wanted to belong. It made him feel successful, donning ridiculously expensive sweatshirts and boating shoes, as if he'd gained access to some exclusive club.

The mothers in the book circle crowed as they played their obligatory game, gathering each month in plush sitting rooms designed to impress. Each host competed with the last, it seemed:

costly Persian rugs, elegant sofas, centerpiece coffee tables replete with big, arty books. There might be an extravagant scented candle burning in a glass jar, sending out sickly fumes of Oud or Bergamot. Thick feather cushions plumped to perfection stood as sentries, daring you to sink into them. "The villa in Tuscany was simply, divine," said one of the circle of ladies, taking a sip of cheap Chianti, "William and the children loved the pool and I have to tell you, the pool boy was—"

Someone interrupted, "Oh the spa at The Lensbury is an absolute *must!* There's a gorgeous hunk running the gym next door. We went last week, you should try it, darling!"

"Really? It's a bit of a schlep. We're at the Hogarth."

"This Chianti's not bad, but I prefer Merlot. Sainsbury's has a great Chilean one on offer at the mo."

Katy didn't like either very much. How could they show off their wealth then drink cheap plonk like this?

"Where did you go in Tuscany? We rented a superb house in one of the vineyards last year."

Katy rolled her eyes and interjected before the woman had chance to answer. "Did anyone read the book?" They all looked at her blankly for a hesitant moment before continuing with their conversation. "A little place near Lucca. Did Harry get into Latymer? It really is the best of the local privates." Katy sat in silence, watching the topic move from who had the most impressive holiday, to which was the best private school, to who had a booking at Nobu. She watched them scoff at the lower income families who couldn't afford private education and had never been to The River Cafe. She hadn't had time to read the book, and in any case, she didn't much care about the latest fiction. She wanted to read Conversations with God or Power Versus Force – something that might enlighten her. She'd bought The Artist's Way and The Art of Happiness, but they sat on the coffee table collecting dust while she battled with running the house, her practice, and the family. It was difficult enough juggling life without pursuing the mystical, but it was pulling her, and she wanted more.

"Lovely to see you all again," she found herself saying, as if a small hidden part had suddenly plucked up the courage to step forward. "But I really do have to dash!" The lively banter stopped. "Sorry..." said Katy. "I've been busy and I'm tired. I'll come back at some point, I'm sure." She didn't feel sure, but the words had left her mouth before she could sensor them.

"Oh! Such a shame, Katy, we were about to get going."

"Bye, darling!"

"Send our love to the gorgeous Richard!"

A crescendo of chattering and laughter could be heard as she closed the front door behind her and walked into the crisp, clear evening. If they only knew the real Richard! Looking up at the night sky, she took a deep breath and noticed the stars seemed brighter than usual. A smile crept across her face as she walked home breathing in the cool of the night, her mind perfectly still, in awe of the expanse of velvet, inky blue above.

With the book circle and the gossiping mothers out of the picture, Katy was free to read what she pleased and connect with more open-minded people.

* * *

Tara was a friend of Shanti's that she'd met at *Alternatives* in Piccadilly. Having been a nurse, she had a sensible, grounded approach to personal and spiritual development. She'd survived cervical cancer and against all odds, and the advice of her doctor, had managed to fall pregnant. Twice. She and her husband, Ben had taken a complementary approach and it had worked. Katy had got to know her when she'd recommended her colleague, Fran, for hypno-birthing. They sat now, with a few other friends, in the lived-in kitchen of Tara's Streatham home, eating gluten-free cake and sipping yogi tea. The book circle seemed a million miles away.

"Tara! Tell Katy about your soul contract!" said one of the bright young things, sending her child out to the sandpit to play.

"Oh yes! You must!" said another.

Katy wasn't listening. She was preoccupied with her own existential struggle and her need to fit in. I wish I'd worn something different, she thought, looking at the jeans and t-shirts. She loosened her silk scarf, slipping it covertly into her leather handbag.

"I went to see this amazing woman called Dinah," said Tara, brushing a crumb from her mouth. "She's up in North London – not far from Stoke Newington. She does soul contract readings! I think you'd like her."

Katy smiled. "Mmm?" She watched the way Tara's glossed lips moved as she spoke. It reminded her of someone, but she couldn't think who. Perhaps it was a client? Her mind began its search, and along the way lost track of what Tara was saying. She had to forcibly bring her concentration back. It was second nature to act as if she was engrossed while actually thinking about something else. Maybe she'd learned it from her mother, or perhaps it was the sheer effort of staying present with clients that gave her the self-appointed right to switch off socially? Katy felt bad and made a mental note: listen properly to friends. Often, she'd be comparing what they said with her own views, wondering what others might think, and calculating what time to leave to avoid the traffic. Her mind was so distracted these days and her friends deserved more.

"...and I'm not joking, it was so accurate," she heard Tara say. "And it'll give you the bigger picture."

What bigger picture, thought Katy? "Oh, that sounds great!" she said, hoping Tara wouldn't notice but it was obvious from her expression that Tara saw right through it. Katy blushed. "Sorry. I was miles away – too much going on in my head!"

Tara gave her an understanding smile. "No problem – been

there, done it – ticked the box! Here, I'll write down her details for you. Have a look at soul contracts on the internet, I think you'll get it."

"Thanks." Katy smiled, still lost in her thoughts. If the content of a conversation fascinated her, she would be captivated and give it proper attention, but often she dismissed things with a healthy dose of common sense. The inner sceptic would mock silently in Richard's voice, or was it Father's? Difficult to tell. 'What a load of rubbish,' she could hear them say inside. The outer persona smiled and took the slip of paper with a polite, "Thank you." Somewhere in the middle, the real Katy was caught between the two, like a rabbit in the headlights, fraught with indecision.

If a quirky idea or an offbeat book came across her path three times, Katy would take it as a sign that she should investigate further and ignore the inner critic. This was the first she'd heard of soul contracts. She made the right noises and forgot about it – until three days later, when she ran into Ben at Earl's Court tube station. "Did Tara tell you about the soul contract lady?" he said.

"Yes! She did!"

"Oh my God! It was amazing," he said, his face animated, his hands gesticulating. "We had our relationship contract read as well, and it was all there in black and white!"

"In black and white?"

"Yes. You get a chart and a recording. Didn't Tara tell you?"

The train timetable flickered as the information shifted. A platform change was announced over the Tannoy. "Yes, she did! She did indeed… That's my train, I've got to dash! Sorry! Give my love to Tara and the kids!"

It would take another chance meeting three days later before the message hit home, this time from their mutual friend, Shanti Kapoor, Reiki Master, Healer, Yogi and manager of the Rainbow Emporium in Covent Garden. "Oh my God, Katy, you've got to have it done. I'm telling you, it's amazing!"

Soul contracts: Katy had never heard of them until six days ago. Six months prior, she'd have dismissed them as ridiculous twaddle. Now, here she was, sitting at the top of the number 93 bus with Shanti, discussing the importance of a reading.

"I think it might set you on the right path, give you direction."

"What do you mean?"

Shanti touched Katy's arm and held her gaze, "You know I'm psychic? I pick up on things. See things other people don't notice."

"Like what?"

Shanti smiled and patted Katy's arm. "It's okay. I'm not judging – just being a friend! I'm here if you need me."

"I appreciate that, Shanti, but I'm not sure what you're getting at?"

"We all need friends to tell us what we don't want to hear! Maybe it's time to let your hair down a bit? This is my stop. Get the contract done, Katy – here's her number."

Katy stared at the scrap of paper and tucked it into her handbag. It took another 30 minutes before she was home.

"I'm thinking of getting my soul contract done," said Katy over supper.

"Whatever makes you happy, Kittykat."

Richard wasn't interested. He was reading the paper and probably didn't give a damn about soul contracts. "I'm happy to let you dabble in this world of make-believe," he said. "As long as you don't end up driving an orange VW Beetle!" He turned his paper over and chortled. "You'll be hugging trees next!"

Tilly rolled her heavily kohl-lined eyes and left, intent on making as much noise as possible by banging down her cup and stomping up the stairs.

"Do you want yours done too?" asked Katy, studying Richard's face.

"What?" He looked up with a frown. "Go and do whatever

you want, Kit, if it keeps you out of mischief," he said, letting out a snort and returning to the sports page. Freddie grimaced and got on diligently with the business of eating the last meatball. Richard's tone would have upset her before, triggering vague childhood recollections of being teased and humiliated, but she'd grown a thicker skin and was shifting her perspective – rising above. There was a bigger picture, so she let it go, rather than let his little dig get to her. "There's more to life than our five senses, you know," she said, pushing her palms against the table and standing up.

"Yes. There's logic and critical thinking for a start!" Richard flicked over the page, absorbing himself in an article about the best places to network in the City.

"And sixth sense, Rich, even you follow your hunches and your gut instinct sometimes!" she said, clearing away the plates.

"That's different."

"But how?"

"It just is."

"I want to know more, Rich! I want to understand energies, forces, unexplained phenomena—"

"Yes, dear."

She loaded the dishwasher, secretly longing to share her fascination with the metaphysical world, wanting to discuss paraphysics, psychic channeling and miraculous healings. She filled the kettle and thought about crop circles, the Philadelphia Experiment, and the Bermuda Triangle. Nobody would be interested. "I'm going upstairs," she said, taking a mug of chamomile tea up to the office.

She was searching for something and the further she explored, the more challenging it became. With every step, her awareness expanded, forcing her to rethink how she saw the world. New levels of understanding were being integrated as she shifted perspective. Accepting what her former self would have condemned as nonsense, she picked up the office phone and dialed.

"I'd like to book an appointment to have my soul contract read."

The lilting voice at the other end of the phone was ethereal and other-worldly.

"Yes. Three-thirty, ninth of October is fine," said Katy.

"Can you email me your date of birth, the full name on your birth certificate and any names you've had since then. Could you get those to me this evening?"

A soul contract, it seemed, was exactly what it said: A contract your soul had entered into before incarnating, detailing what you were here to do and what you had come to learn. It would give you an overview of your soul purpose and the dynamics of any key relationships with significant others. Katy had given Dinah relevant information for Richard, Tilly and Freddie.

October 9th, 2008

Dinah's North London flat was furnished with artefacts and wooden carvings from Asia and India, offset by stark, white walls and floorboards. A joss stick sent a wisp of sweet-smelling smoke into the center of the room. Dinah's caramel skin shone with health, her dark hair swept back into a perfect, thick, coiled plait, accentuating a classic oval face and almond-shaped, brown eyes. Her fine ankles tinkled with the sound of tiny bells on a silver chain. Deep red nail polish, perfect in its execution, adorned the toes of her dainty feet which danced lightly across the floor, the blood-like pools of crimson caught between the white of the floor and the brown of her feet. Katy had an urge to cry and stifled it. The scene reminded her of her past – pre-Richard, when she was single and living near Archway in a Bohemian flat. She missed it. It seemed so far away and out of reach, so at odds with her sleek new existence. She'd adopted the role of WASP wife and lost who she was. Out of place and out of time, she'd mislaid herself. Creativity, individualism, and playfulness were missing. She'd been swallowed up by faded-grey, classic lines and metropolitan suburbia.

"Take a seat," said Dinah, bringing a jug of water and two glasses from the small kitchen. Katy took a notebook and pen from her bag. From a carved Moroccan cabinet, Dinah pulled an old tape recorder and a blank cassette. Katy stared in disbelief at the antiquated machine. Slipping the cassette into the player, Dinah pressed two of the chunky buttons and it began to hum. "Soul Contract Reading. Katy Stone. Ninth of October two thousand and eight." The session was recorded but the cassette was never to be heard. There was nothing Katy owned on which to play it.

"These are the Moses Codes," said Dinah, showing Katy a sheet of paper with strange symbols. "They're derived from your date of birth and your birth name. You also have what we call an 'overlay' name. When you married Richard, you changed your name to Katherine Alison Stone and that brought in a whole new vibration and path."

"What does that mean?" asked Katy.

"That's what I'll be explaining over the next couple of hours. See this diagram? It's like a Star of David, or two intersecting triangles. The upward pointing triangle is your physical life, the downward is your spiritual life. The center point is your ultimate soul-purpose. Think of it as a destination. You've got to work through the other six points first."

"Oh," said Katy, scribbling furiously in the notepad.

"I'll show you the karmic debts, the obstacles, the challenges, the opportunities, and we'll also talk about the implications of your name change to Stone, as well as the relationship dynamics with Richard, Matilda and Frederick."

Katy became engrossed in the symbols, signs and meanings which were based on numerology – the numbers in her date of birth and the numerical value of the letters in her name, with *A* being one, *B* two and so on up to *I* which was nine, then *J* which started back at one.

"Nine is a very special number. There are only two letters of the alphabet which represent nine: *I* and *R*. Everyone wants nines! That's why Danii Minogue added that extra *I* to her name! I don't think you realize the importance of it! You've got six nines in total in your name and your birth date adds up to nine. Nine is unique, mathematically speaking – multiples of it, added together, always come to nine."

"What do you mean?"

"Well. Two nines are eighteen. Add the one and eight of eighteen together and you get nine. But it carries on like that. Let's take a random number."

"Thirty-six," said Katy.

Dinah scribbled down some calculations. "Thirty-six times nine is three hundred and twenty-four. Add together three, two and four and you get?"

"Nine!"

"It's the last of the single digit figures. Ten has two digits, so nine is the completion of things. It's a highly spiritual number and happens to be your life path. You're here for high level spiritual work and it's probably your last incarnation. By the way, your chart shows you're very psychic."

Katy was reeling with disbelief. Could this be true, or did she say this sort of thing to everyone? She couldn't take it in, wasn't it just pie in the sky? Put it down to experience, she told herself, we live and learn.

"You okay? Do you need a break?" Dinah halted recording with a clunk, resuming after a short while and taking a fresh sheet of symbols from her folder.

"When you married Richard," she said, "you changed your surname, and that brought in a whole new vibrational overlay. I can see how it must have catapulted you into motherhood and domesticity at such a rate that you barely had time to consider."

Katy stopped writing and stared at Dinah. "It would have forced you to become family-oriented and shift your values," she continued. Katy opened her mouth to speak, but hesitated, letting Dinah carry on. "It also doubled your workload and stress! See?" she said, pointing to a pair of squiggles. "It's a karmic knot."

"What does that mean?"

"There must have been karma from a past life for you to work through, a life-lesson if you like?"

"What sort of lesson?"

"I can't tell, but it has a 'doubling' effect. You'll have ended up doing twice as much as you did before."

"And getting horribly busy?" asked Katy, watching carefully for a reaction.

"Yes. You probably feel overstretched."

"That's exactly how I feel! Overwhelmed!" she said, focusing fully on Dinah now and wondering how she could possibly have known any of this. "I look after everyone – Richard, the kids, the house – not to mention my clients. I do my best, but the responsibility weighs me down. I can't break free of the mounting workload!"

"You feel trapped? Suffocated?"

She'd nailed it precisely. "It feels like it's all caving in!"

"Yes. I see that in the charts. You're so busy, you don't know who you are anymore."

Katy edged forward, leaning in towards Dinah. "Carry on!"

"Let's get to the point of it all, your soul purpose, which is at the center. I think you'll like it! See this?" She was pointing at a symbol. "It means you were born to talk!"

Katy tipped back her head, laughing. "Everyone's been telling me that for years! Even on my old school reports it used to say, 'Katherine talks too much'. I was always getting into trouble!"

A hundred and fifty pounds and a whole afternoon for something she already knew! Suddenly, she became aware of a life-long struggle between the desire to talk and the need to keep herself in check and be quiet. A counsellor needed good listening skills, but she'd opted for approaches that involved speaking to her clients: Hypnotherapy, Cognitive Behavior Therapy, NLP.

"It's not just about talking, Katy, it's about speaking!"

Katy came from a boisterous family, most of them older than her, and all very chatty. They would talk in unison, each hoping to be heard above the din of the others. Her mother spoke the loudest, slicing through them all like a Spanish Galleon in full sail. Only her father was able to usurp her position. Katy's tactic was to gabble quickly, in the hope of fitting in what she wanted to say between everyone else's chirping. She'd always felt that nobody was listening anyway. They were thinking about themselves and the importance of their own contribution. Speaking? Who was going to listen to *her*?

"Public speaking," said Dinah, leaning forward and raising her voice slightly to get Katy's attention. "You're going to be talking to big audiences. Teaching them."

Katy stared at Dinah, her mouth slightly open, her eyebrows raised. What on earth would she be telling them?

"It's your soul's purpose! Speaking from a stage, leading by example, pioneering a new evolution in consciousness!" said Dinah, her voice rising with excitement, her words tumbling out.

"What? Me?" Katy became animated, warming to the idea yet at the same time overwhelmed by it, a thrill running down her spine. The stressed mother, wife and therapist was happy to exchange roles and bask in the limelight for once, but the thought of standing on a stage in front of all those people petrified her!

"You'll be sharing your wisdom publicly. Remember, it's the potential we're looking at. You'll have to want it, claim it, and work for it. It's a life-time goal, but what a goal!"

Katy suddenly felt small. There must be some mistake. The vision both thrilled and terrified her at the same time.

"But I'm not sure – I mean – are you certain you've got it

right?"

Dinah laughed. "Yes! I'm sure! You're likely to face a few challenges along the way, but that's what the symbols are telling me loud and clear, and they don't lie!" Her face grew more serious. "The only thing is, you're going to have to change your name."

"What?"

"You definitely can't do it with your present name."

Katy's bubble burst, her shoulders visibly slumping. "But I can't do that!"

"I used to be Diane but I tweaked my name to shift the vibration. It was a game-changer. It's all been unfolding beautifully since then."

"I'd feel like a fraud."

"Have a think about it. Tree used to be called Simon. He's my mentor and heads up the UK. Went out to California to study, changed his name and his whole life turned around! I promise you! It's magic!"

Katy suppressed the urge to laugh and blurt out something sarcastic. She could hear her cynical self, mocking in Richard's tone. What sort of person calls themselves Tree? It's not even a proper name. She can't be serious.

"But I don't want to change my name. There's no way I could be called Cloud or Kali or whatever, it would be ridiculous! I'm Katy or Katherine. Even Kittykat drives me nuts!"

"You could change your surname? Think about it. I'm sure you'll find a way," said Dinah, sipping at her water. "And it would be a pity not to fulfil your role… otherwise you'll have to come back again."

"For another reading?"

"No. For another incarnation."

Sitting on the train home, Katy kept going over the session in her mind. She looked at her notes and the charts that Dinah had given her and wondered how she was going to listen to that cassette! It was easier to think about something small and technical than to contemplate the bigger picture. She reflected on how marrying Richard and taking his name had thrown her into domestic chaos and overwhelm. She pondered the significance of the number nine. Her lucky number was three, she remembered, and three threes were nine! The train lurched into Turnham Green. The sun emerged from a tiny hole in the dense, drizzling cloud and cast a brief rainbow over the grey. What was she going to give them for supper? They'd be hungry.

Katy's evening meditation extended to almost two hours. It was the thoughts – they wouldn't stop: the unwelcome suggestion of changing her name, and the concern that she'd wasted her money on an elaborate ruse. Behind that was the worry that the reading might be true, and that she might not be able to fulfil her soul purpose. What if she wasn't up to it? Then there were the doubts about the purpose itself. What if Dinah was mistaken? Toying with the idea of linking her name with Richard's, she muttered them aloud, as if trying them on for size. "Katherine Fralinski-Stone," then "Stone-Fralinski." No, it sounded like a firm of accountants. She sheepishly whispered out into the night. "God? Are you there? Can you hear me? Do you exist?"

What the hell would people think? What would Richard say? It had gotten out of hand and gone too far now! The therapist within pronounced it a fantasy, an escape from the stresses of reality.

Breath. Hara. Focus, for fudge sake!

The thoughts cranked up again. It had been fun, this spiritual odyssey. It had injected some excitement into her life, and for a while she'd thought she knew who she was, thought she belonged. Well it was time to stop! It had run its course.

Breath. Watch the breath and focus on the Hara.

A minute or two of silence, then a distant, gentle Voice. Was it inside her head, or just above and behind?

"This Stone isn't rolling, it's gathering moss."

If she remained a Stone, she'd be anchored where she was. To continue along the course she'd set, she'd have to change her name. Straining towards the soft Voice, she breathed, "Give me a name I can live with that fits the bill. I don't want to sound phony or be humiliated." Sitting motionless, hardly daring to breathe, she waited. Nothing came. Perhaps it wasn't meant to be, she thought, with a sigh of relief.

An uneventful weekend passed and still there was no inspiration. By Monday morning, she'd given up. On Monday evening, as she flicked through her emails, she noticed a message from Dinah:

I've got good news! Called Tree on Friday after our session. Knew you wouldn't mind! Sent him the charts and he says your maiden name is perfect! Go with that. At least it won't be too much of a change for you! Om Shanti, Dinah x

Katy's heart was racing. Her answer had come, and it was real! A name that she could live with that fulfilled the criteria. Should she call a halt now or plunge headlong into it? Do or die? Fralinski was reminiscent of the care-free boho girl she desperately wanted to revive. It could work, but she'd have to float it past Richard first. Her insides knotted and her mouth went dry. It would be okay, she told herself, he loved her, didn't he? She'd been Fralinski when they met and at least it wasn't a total name change! She sighed with relief, then froze at the next thought: Telling him wasn't going to be easy. She'd have to choose her moment, and she'd better get her argument straight.

Freddie and Tilly were out the following Friday, and Katy seized her opportunity. "Fancy a glass of decent red?" she asked. A bottle of Brunello and two expensive glasses sat on the granite counter.

"What are you up to? Not another one of your expensive

courses?"

She poured the dark liquid, her hand steady so as not to disturb the sediment.

"No, not a course," she said, smiling and handing a glass to Richard. "I thought I'd take the weekend off. Go for a walk along the river with you, maybe go to the cinema, if you like?"

"Cut to the chase, Kittykat. What do you want?"

"Don't be cross, Rich."

"What is it?"

"I need to change my name."

Richard furrowed his brow, turning to her with a quizzical look.

"It's okay, I'm not changing it to anything daft," she said, swallowing a mouthful of aged Brunello. "I thought I'd change it back to Fralinski."

Richard stood up, walked over to the French windows and stared into the garden. The day was fading. Katy sensed his thoughts before he did – anger, confusion, rejection.

"What the hell's got into you, Kit? All this so-called 'spiritual' stuff?" he said, spitting flecks of wine in his frustration. "It's gone too far. We've been married for sixteen years, for God's sake! Hasn't Stone been good enough for you?"

She took a step towards him, instinctively reaching out, but withdrawing her hand before it made contact. "I was Katy Fralinski when we first met and it was all fresh and exciting, then, remember?" She let the thought take root, watching him as he fixed his attention on the gloom outside. "It might rekindle what we had!" It was a long shot, but she had to think of something to convince him. "Come on, Rich, it might inject some life into our marriage? Resuscitate it."

"So, you think it's moribund?" said Richard, his face slackening as he turned back towards her.

"We're still us! We're still married, aren't we?" said Katy, gesturing with open palms, her eyes widening. She held his gaze and his face softened as he swilled the ruby nectar around his mouth and swallowed. "Fine, but I don't really understand why!"

"I think it would be good for Harley Street, too, having an unusual name that stands out."

"I don't get you, Kit. I don't understand what's happening... or how changing your name's going to solve anything." He stepped towards her, placing an outstretched hand on her shoulder and looking into her piercing eyes.

She flung her arms around his neck, nearly spilling the Brunello in the process. His body was shaking almost as much as hers. "Thank you, Richard. It's important to me... To us."

"Go on then, but you've got to tell the kids first, then your bloody parents, and our friends. What are they going to think, Kit? Have you factored that into your equation?"

She had, and it filled her with horror.

The task of telling everyone and reverting to her maiden name was less problematic than she'd thought. The kids didn't seem to care, her parents disapproved of whatever she did anyway, her old friends thought she was going off the rails so what did it matter, and her new friends were fully behind her!

The first opportunity to make an official change came the following week at the bank. She'd been waiting in the queue for some time, agitated by how languorous the service was. She'd have gone under as a therapist if she'd had that attitude! Shuffling her feet, she checked her watch for the umpteenth time.

The problem, she thought, was that nobody was motivated! Coughing loudly, then tapping her fingers against her handbag, she drew attention to herself and looked away. Her jaw clenched as she dug her stiletto into the logo on the carpet. "For God's sake," she muttered, visibly rattled by having to wait. She wanted to shriek 'You're wasting my time!' at the top of her voice. Her heart was pumping and her limbs trembling. She was going to be late. A muscle twitched on her temple. This level of stress was out of all proportion, she realized. It must have been the pressure taking its toll. She'd crammed her days so full there was no room for maneuver. Agh. Now the teller was chatting to that woman, and she was in a hurry, for God's sake! She held herself back from causing a scene, wincing at the thought of losing control. That's what mother used to do – manipulate with drama. Inside, Katy felt like crying, or running down the street screaming and shouting.

Collecting herself, she noticed the utter tiredness behind the impatience. Perhaps she'd leave it till another day? But then she'd have wasted the last fifteen minutes. The guy in front left. It was her turn next. It would be a muesli bar on the train for lunch, at this rate!

"Oh, are you getting divorced?" said the young assistant in the sing-song voice of a nine-year-old. "Because you've got a joint account and it'd be better to separate it now, before proceedings." She pushed her spectacles up with a chubby finger, and peered at Katy, who, by now, was losing her composure.

"No, I'm not getting divorced!" she said, the force of her voice taking them both by surprise. Katy clenched her fists inside her jacket pockets, digging her nails into the palms of her hands. "I'm changing my name because—" she gritted her teeth as the thought hit her. *Because I've had my soul contract read and a woman in Stoke Newington says I've got to change it if I want to be a leader for a new evolution in consciousness.* Her face reddened as she looked down at the floor. "For professional reasons," she said, smiling weakly at the assistant.

Katy told everyone the same story. "I want a more unusual name than Stone. Something that'll stand out in Harley Street." It was a convincing lie that she hid behind as she tried to forget the original impulse.

Katy felt out of kilter, unbalanced, as if she wasn't there. Was this madness? It felt as if she was witnessing her life at a distance and through a haze. "I feel like I don't have a body sometimes!" she told Terry. "Like I'm drunk or stoned. The world's gone a bit fuzzy and I'm living in my head."

"And why do you think that is?"

"I don't know! I'm not myself. I'm usually so in control!"

"Perhaps it's a good thing to be less controlling?"

"I don't mean it like that. I'm not as efficient as I was. I can't make decisions like I did."

"That could be adrenal fatigue – you're always on the go and your mind's never at rest."

"Yes it is! When I meditate!"

"For half an hour a day?"

"But I've always been like that. It makes for a good therapist, having an analytical mind!" Katy's voice was rising as her body tensed. She was gripping the arms of the chair with her hands.

"You'd be even better if you could switch off and let things percolate," said Terry, leaning back in his chair and steepling his hands.

"I can't make up my mind – about ordinary things, like whether to buy lamb or chicken."

"Is that important?"

"I get easily swayed by other people's opinions and I'm thinking things through too much," she said, picking at her nails. "I need to make instinctive decisions, but I can't!" She furiously fiddled with her earring, then ran her fingers through her well-groomed hair. "My mind's elsewhere, as if I'm absent from my own life!"

"You sound lost."

"And I keep losing my temper, which isn't like me! I got angry with the woman in the bank the other day. She was only doing her job, but I could feel this aggression spiraling from nowhere."

"Adrenal fatigue. You know the score – fight or flight. You're either going to get angry or jittery or both," said Terry, his warm eyes searching for signs of recognition. "Tiredness is tracking you down, isn't it?"

Katy's eyes began to well up. She was cross with him for being right and she felt like a fool. Fighting to get a grip on her emotions, she realized it was useless trying to control them. For God's sake, Katherine, this is so unprofessional, she told herself, looking furtively at Terry with his kind eyes and open face.

"You don't need to feel bad, Katy. Guilt demands punishment but what have you got to feel guilty about? Being human? Showing emotions? It's only adding to your already stressful load!"

"I know. It's just that everything seemed so fixed and solid and now it's giving way."

"And how does that make you feel?"

"Uncertain. Disoriented. Like I'm sliding on a slippery surface."

"And you hide it stoically?"

"Yes," she said, her head bowed, her body curled forward. "I suppose I'm keeping up appearances."

"Maintaining a shiny veneer?"

She nodded.

"What about the real you? What's happening on the inside, Katy?"

"I don't know." She lifted her head, her pursed lips smiling, her watering eyes betraying her.

Meditation was keeping her sane, bringing down her rocketing stress levels, and giving her time to reflect. It was almost a week later, around midnight that she sent a message to Dinah.

"Is it possible the name change is disrupting my life? I can't concentrate and I'm feeling angry and anxious. I'm not myself. Just want to burst into tears. Do you think I've made a mistake? Could you double check the details? You did get the spelling of my name right?"

Dinah's answer came back:

"All the details are correct. It's usual for people to experience

disruption when they change their name. You're altering the vibration and energy of who you are. If you want to transform your life, you have to let go of the old way of doing things. You have to release who you've become, so you can be who you're destined to be. The old has to break up to give way to the new.

Ground the vibration of your new name. It's tipping you off-balance as the energies come in. Bring them through and root them. You're drifting in no-man's land between Stone and Fralinski. Be gentle with yourself."

How the hell was she going to do that!

Chapter 3

It was a clear night as the first chill of autumn descended over the fields. A waxing moon cast an eerie glow across a long gravel drive, at the end of which stood a lonely house with gabled roof and leaded lights. Apart from a distant car and a soft rustling in a hedgerow, everything was deathly quiet. Red roses had faded long ago as summer slipped away, their desiccated petals lifeless along the path to the front door. Heavy curtains, designed to shut out prying eyes, hung at each window. A child dreamed sweetly in her bedroom, pretty in pink, while the lady of the house, slept deeply under a sumptuous duvet, her long dark hair splayed over the pillow, the capacious sleigh bed dwarfing her tall, rangy figure.

A single flickering light shone from the attic window where a balding man was silhouetted, a bead of sweat catching the moonlight on his pate. Glassy eyed, he stared at the screen, trawling the internet, one hand on the mouse, the other in his lap. He'd locked the door and plugged in the earphones, but his heart was racing nonetheless. He took a generous gulp of brandy from a crystal cut glass. His breathing quickened, his prey was in sight. Almost there, tracking it down, this one thing that numbed his miserable existence. He watched the naked bodies writhe on the screen as he fumbled with his right hand – the only relief from a life in which he felt so trapped.

He fretted, mopping his brow with his handkerchief then casting a worried look at his watch. Burying his face in his hands he leaned forward, his elbows on the desk, his torso bent over. Tomorrow he'd be in London. Maybe he should see someone – a professional who could help. He just wanted a relationship that worked. Recovering his composure, he punched 'psychotherapist central London' into Google.

* * *

At number 11 Sycamore Road, Richard was already snoring when Katy tip-toed her way upstairs with a cup of cocoa. Passing the large mirror at the top of the landing, something caught her eye. Must have been a shadow, she thought, glancing back at it. "I'm sure I saw something – a flash?" She scrutinized her reflection.

A soft Voice made her jump. "Good Evening!" it said.

Holding her breath, her eyes widening, she gingerly looked around. Nothing. The Voice, gentle, loving, spoke again. "It's okay – you're perfectly safe." She had the crazy feeling it was coming from the mirror. Turning, she observed her image gazing back at her, looking quite normal. But wait! There...something glimpsed from the corner of her eye. When she looked straight at herself, she saw only her own striking features staring back. And another thing, she sensed it in the mirror, but it sounded as if it came from behind her, or maybe above. It's in my head, she realized.

"Hello, Katherine!"

The Voice filled her now with a mixture of fear and warmth. It seemed strangely familiar as she listened, lifting and comforting as it rose and fell with easy, confident intonation. "I'm here to help you. Are you ready?"

"Ready for what?" asked Katy, trying to keep her wavering voice calm. "And who are you?"

"Are you ready to learn what I've come to impart?"

"Depends on what you're imparting!"

"Wisdom."

"But who are you? And where are you?" she said, her eyes darting from side to side.

"I am that I am, but that matters not. I'm here with you. I'm part of you, as you're part of me. I exist but not as you would understand existence."

"Good God! Are you going to carry on talking in riddles with that 1930s accent?"

"Does it displease you?"

"No… It's just odd!" said Katy quietly, not wanting to be overheard. "This could be dangerous – what in God's Name is happening?"

"Quite the contrary. It's perfectly safe and most definitely in God's Name. Would you like me to continue?"

Katy's eyebrows shot up as she instinctively took a step back. A therapist hearing voices in her head – what if it got out?

"It won't."

"How did you—?"

"Thought communication. That's how I'm talking to you."

What if it's all nonsense?

"It's not nonsense. It's very real."

Hearing the voice of Wisdom? This was madness!

"Not at all," the Voice replied patiently. "I'm communicating with you directly from a Higher Plane."

"I see."

"I don't think you do. Can I begin?"

"How long's it going to take? I was about to meditate!"

"Oh! Meditation! That's wonderful. I'll talk to you while you're meditating."

"But…"

"It's okay, there's no such thing as time where I come from, so you'll still have plenty of earth time to meditate and get to bed before midnight."

"Oh."

Katy walked uncertainly into her office, not daring to look back. Fishing out her meditation stool from beneath the couch, she positioned it in front of the window. Kneeling down in the thin, pale moonlight, she drew her cardigan against the chill of the autumn evening. Her eyes closed, her breathing steadied.

"You know you're a powerful creator, don't you?"

"I can create a hell of a scene with Richard, if that's what you mean?"

"You were made in the Image and Likeness of God!"

"So, He's up there in heaven, trying to stick to his low-carb diet and get to yoga three times a week?"

"He?"

"Does He sneak off on Friday evenings for a naughty cigarette and a glass of vino with the girls?"

"God is beyond gender – He, She, It, They – because the Godhead is collective too – the many and the one – the different facets of the same diamond, so to speak. We'll call Him 'Father' because of the fathering principle in creation – the yang – the 'doing', the 'externalizing', the 'administering'. 'He' is more useful in conversation don't you think? But He's by no means limited to the masculine. He's Supreme, Ultimate and Absolute. Three-in-One."

"What do you mean?"

"He's not some old fogey with a long white beard, sitting on a fluffy cloud like a saintly Santa, giving presents to the ones who've been good."

"Richard's told me about the Catholic God of hell and damnation – thinking up penances for people who've broken the speed limit or coveted their neighbor's ox or diddled their tax return. No thank you, that's not my idea of a Divine Being!"

"Nor is it mine."

"Cut to the chase, will you?"

"God's a powerful creator and made you in His Likeness."

"I get it. He's just like me."

"No. You're like Him. You create everything in your life – the good bits, the bad bits, the things you know about, the things you don't know about."

"What do you mean?"

"You're a powerful creator, just like the One who created you."

"I thought God was a light within?"

"In a way He is, but that's not the entire picture. He's everywhere and everything, inside, outside and beyond. In fact,

He's more of a verb than a noun!"

"Huh?"

"He's a Divine Creative Eternal Force, constantly creating and re-creating. A Thinking Intelligence, powered by Love and Light. He's beyond gender, beyond time, and beyond explanation."

"Why are you saying it like that? *Love* and *Light?*"

"Because it's not just the love you feel for your children, or your dog, or dark chocolate, it's a much Higher Force in the Cosmos. The Light is way beyond the limited spectrum of the light you have here, so I'm trying to distinguish…"

"Oh… I've got to meditate now. I'll be tired in the morning."

"Time is suspended while we're having our little chat, but if you'd rather I stopped…"

"Just finish your point, then let me be."

"God is beyond description – ineffable – you can't really comprehend! But what I can tell you is that humans are part of a vast, never-ending, Divine, Intelligent, Creative Energy. A Divine Mind, if you like. A Higher Thought Process. The Godhead, or more precisely, Elohim, created you humans from itself, from its own emanated coding of Love-Light-Life. You're made of God's Thought Forms, made of Love, made of generative Light – everything is. And your minds are connected to a much Greater Mind Force than you can possibly imagine."

"I see."

"I doubt it. Think of what you can do! You're plugged into it all like a laptop on the internet, only you can do a great deal more and it's infinite."

"Really," said Katy, with a rather flat tone she hadn't intended.

"Whatever name you give The Most High and all His myriad emanations – masculine, feminine, plural – whatever your religion, whatever your Word – the Truth remains."

"What truth?"

"God is a cosmic, ever-present, all-powerful, all-knowing, ever-evolving, loving intelligence. He formed all things and is in all things and connects all things – known and unknown – including you. And the unknown is far, far greater than the known. Think of it – no beginning, no end, infinity, everywhere, always was, always is, always shall be – can do anything, and you can access it! Makes the human mind boggle, doesn't it?"

Katy opened her eyes and stared out at the moon in silence. A small, golden spanner had been deftly lodged in the workings of her mind, causing it to seize for a second.

"Big, isn't it?"

Katy took a deep breath, blinked, and closed her eyes, hardly daring to think, let alone speak.

"That's the thing," continued the Voice, "I'm not telling you anything new. But people don't take these Truths on board. They hear them, dismiss them, and think about something much easier like, 'when are we going shopping' and 'what are we having for supper'."

"Those things are important!"

"They seem important."

There was a long pause before the Voice started tentatively again. "All this wisdom is lost on humankind. The Words fall like autumn leaves then turn to dust, only ever skimming the edge of the intellect. They aren't experienced or embodied. There's no true knowing. Humans log the mysteries, file them in their minds under 'things – useful to know' then carry on with what's pressing. You're not listening, are you?"

"I'm trying to, but it's not easy listening to a disembodied Voice at the end of a long day, when all you want to do is slip between the sheets and drift into nod land."

"I understand. Should I go?"

"Finish. I get the feeling there's more," said Katy, sighing.

"Humans don't experience themselves as embryo gods. It all seems too bonkers, too abstract, too unreal – un*real*ized. It's simply not scientific, not logical. You think it's all a metaphor – the scriptures, I mean – a little story for Sunday School. It seems to me you mostly think church is a quaint old-fashioned thing for getting married and naming your babies. And perhaps it is!" The Voice chuckled. "You don't realize the power that you hold. You carry on living your modern lives, struggling for control, and trying to grab what you can in the process." There was another pause. "I don't know where we went wrong," the Voice said, a sad dismay replacing the jovial tone. "Humanity's fallen asleep! Completely unaware of what they're capable of! Forgotten who they are, what they're here to do!"

"I'm sorry," whispered Katy and with that the Voice was gone.

Climbing quietly into bed after her meditation, Katy glanced at Richard, a shallow scowl was etched across his slack features. Even in sleep he wasn't at peace, she thought, lying on her back and staring at the thin sliver of moonlight that made its way through the gap in the curtains. She was pondering the experience with the Voice before she drifted into a fitful sleep. Vivid images roused her at around 3.30 am. Still haunted by the lingering dream, she got up and shuffled to the bathroom. She needed to write it down – it would be useful for Terry. Retrieving a notebook and pen from the desk drawer upstairs, she put them on her bedside cabinet and scribbled down a few notes. Richard rolled over, half-opening one eye with a frown on his face. "I had the weirdest dream," she explained. "Just writing it down before I forget!"

* * *

Three days later, in the easy surroundings of Terry's consulting room, Katy took out her notebook. "I've been having some vivid dreams," she said. "Unusual ones."

"Interesting." Terry nodded.

"Shall I share them with you? I noted them down."

"Please do."

"I dreamt the world was a big training ground for people to come and learn things, except we weren't learning – we were just copying."

Terry raised his eyebrows as he stared straight at Katy.

"Children were copying from their mums and dads and the people around them – mimicking them – and we know that's true from therapy, don't we?"

Terry smiled and bobbed his head in confirmation.

"Then they went to school and copied what the teachers said and what the books said…"

"Go on."

"In the dream it didn't stop. People carried on copying all their lives! They copied the professors at university, the bosses at work, their colleagues, their predecessors."

"With no variation?"

"Personal tweaks, but nothing fundamental."

"What sort of tweaks?"

"Sometimes they stumbled on something useful or better, and there were a few bright people thinking up fresh ideas, but mostly it was just the same old same old," said Katy, a frown on her face as she pieced it all together. "So, the personal tweaks were just peripheral things. Superficial. Like changing the color or moving the furniture in a room. It makes it look different but really it's the same furniture and the same room."

"And what do you think it all means?"

"I was hoping you'd tell me!" said Katy, letting out a short burst of nervous laughter. "I don't think we're supposed to just copy and move the furniture around – metaphorically speaking – I think we're meant to work things out for ourselves, progress, conjure up new ideas."

"Like Leonardo da Vinci or Picasso?"

"Yes! They thought outside the box, didn't they?"

"They were geniuses."

"I suppose," said Katy, troubled somehow by the response.

"But don't we all have the potential inside us?"

"Carry on telling me about the dream," said Terry, making notes on his pad of crisp, lined paper.

"It was like a big sausage machine."

"What was?"

"The world. Humanity. We were all just learning from the last person, so we knew how to perform – like circus animals being trained to jump through hoops to rapturous applause," she continued, grappling with the ideas that were forming in her head. "We were training ourselves to do what was expected – it was like a people factory."

"And who was doing the expecting?"

"Society. The authorities. Our elders. 'Them'."

"Anything else?"

"Yes. It went a bit weird, you know, how dreams do?" said Katy, the glow in her cheeks reddening. "Everyone was copying and doing what they were supposed to do, so they could earn money and afford to live a sort of mechanized life like everybody else!"

"Carry on." Terry was scribbling.

"It went into a thing about boxes," she said, pausing to look at her notes and gather her thoughts. "I realized, in the dream, that all of our lives are lived through boxes. All compartmentalized."

Terry nodded. "Just like the psyche. We compartmentalize. The furniture is the same unless we dig into the shadow – into the deep subconscious – then integrate."

Sitting up straight and with new vigor, Katy continued. "In the dream people did what they had to, so they could earn money to buy a big box in a safe area, then decorate it the way they wanted – well not really how they wanted, but how the interior design magazines dictated. Everyone in the dream had some sort of box – their home – and it was like watching ants marching to and fro. All regimented and organized. All overseen by the Queen."

Terry raised his eyebrows, dragging the nib of his fountain pen across the page.

"They all left their boxes to get into shiny, smaller ones – cars or buses – to go to another, much bigger box."

"Work?"

"Yes. You get the drift," said Katy, dropping the explanations. "If they were lucky, they got to meet another person from another box and share a new box and have a couple of lovely kids. At the weekends they all went to big, bright boxes, full of little boxes filled with trinkets. They could buy things they didn't really need, then maybe go to another big, dark box to watch a flickering screen of somebody else's life that was better than theirs."

"Sounds like a dystopia!" said Terry.

"I know. But we do watch feel-good movies about people living the lives we'd like to live, don't we? It's part of the escapism from the drudgery of life."

"That's quite a dim view, Katy."

"I know. It's reflecting the state of my mind isn't it? All drudge and no thrill. I saw people living out this 'box' life: Restaurant boxes for special occasions, pub boxes for drinking. Kid's telly boxes to keep them quiet, Xboxes, or whatever they're called, to keep them entertained. Everyone was trapped by their little mobile phone boxes. They were all disconnected, living a grey, mechanized life, on treadmills they weren't even aware of!"

"Sounds like The Matrix." Terry smiled. "Do you feel boxed in?"

"Yes," she said, her heart thumping with the admission. She'd been trying to avoid that one.

"The subconscious always finds a way to let you know," said Terry, frowning.

"It was a box structure for guaranteed achievement!" said Katy, wondering where that revelation had come from. "If they stayed inside the box formula, they had a tried and tested road to success which could be measured by the size and luxury of the boxes. Except it doesn't always work in real life does it?"

Terry nodded as he leaned back in the chair and replaced the lid of his pen with a click.

"I could see in the dream it was more about control than achievement!" She was on a roll now, ideas flooding in and joining the dots. "We measure success by how well we're doing in the maze of boxes and what sort of boxes we have! There's no freedom of movement, no freedom of expression! It's impossible to do things differently!"

"Are you talking about the dream or your own life?"

"The dream...but it's a reflection of my real life, isn't it?"

"Yes." His gaze met hers. "What about the people who've opted out?"

"Tramps, gurus, self-sufficient-off-the-grid types? They're outside the system, aren't they? But they're shunned by society. If you're inside the system you can't fully express yourself. Actually, you don't even know yourself properly!"

"It was a dream, Katy – you don't have to live it – you have the power to change it!"

"It felt so real, so suffocating."

"Tell me more about what you felt."

"Squashed by the system. Insignificant. I couldn't be me. I couldn't be authentic or do what I really wanted to do. I felt hemmed in."

"Be with the feeling. Just allow it. Carry on."

"We're all on a treadmill. Pacing forward but going nowhere."

"YOU are on a treadmill?"

"Yes. And it's going too fast. I'm trying to catch up but the schedule's too tight. There's not enough time or space for me. I feel pinched off."

"From what?"

"Real life, living, me. I don't feel alive!"

"And?"

"I'm trapped in my fur-lined, gilded box. The door's unlocked but I stay inside."

"Why?"

"Because it's safe."

Terry nodded and gestured with his pen for her to continue.

"I don't know what's beyond the boxes."

"Many people fear the unknown, Katy, that's why so few opt for therapy! But the subconscious will find a way to nudge you into it. That's how we grow!"

"I'm scared."

"It's okay to be scared and brave at the same time," said Terry, his voice measured and confident. "They say the magic happens outside of your comfort zone – outside of the box!"

"I'm fed up with the box, Terry, it's stifling me! I feel like a wild animal trapped in a small cage. A cheetah, say! First, she was angry and spat and clawed, then she got anxious in case she couldn't escape, and eventually she calmed down and surrendered. I guess that's where the listlessness began. There's more, but I think we've run out of time."

"Yes. Time waits for no man – or woman."

"I'm always running out of time."

"I'd like you to carry on with your dream diary this week and take a look at what's draining your time. Start to become aware of where it's going."

As Katy left the consulting room, she heard the old-fashioned telephone ringing from Terry's desk, his quiet but confident voice answering.

"Yes, this is Doctor Slater... No...I'm sorry but I can't take on any more clients at the moment. But I can recommend someone else?"

Another pause, then, "If money's no object, I can highly recommend The Priory Clinic in West London for addictions. I'll give you the number. I recommend you talk to Dr. Erasmus Watkins or his secretary, if you can."

Chapter 4

Richard opened the middle drawer of his desk and dipped his hand into the rumpled packet of sherbet lemons. There was something about the acidity and the sudden fizz as the sherbet broke through that gave him a moment of pleasure.

His phone rang and he tucked the candy into his cheek. "Richard Stone," he said. "Oh yes. Thank you for getting back to me. I wanted to know how much you charge?"

"Depends on how long and what hours, mate."

"I was thinking just a bit of tracking, Monday to Friday, about 9 o'clock in the morning till nine at night."

There was a sucking in of air on the other end of the phone. "That's gonna set you back a few spondulis."

"How many 'spondulis' exactly?"

"Depends on how many weeks and where."

"Just a couple of weeks. All London based."

"And what's the err…extent of the assignment?"

"I just want to know what she's up to. Where she goes, who she meets, what she buys."

"Think it's another geyser then?"

"No. I just want to know her movements."

"Okay, Boss. We'll settle the details and I'll get on the job Monday. That's two grand each for the two weeks. Four big ones in total."

"No cock-ups, okay? Discreet's the word."

"Discreet's my middle name."

Richard's sumptuous leather chair let out a puff of air as he leaned back, swiveling it around so he could look through the huge picture window towards the river. Weak sunlight was catching the occasional ripple of brooding grey, while the shining skyscrapers at the water's edge pierced the threatening clouds above. A seagull swooped down towards an overflowing waste bin, picking at a half-eaten sandwich with its long, orange beak. The sherbet exploded in Richard's mouth, bringing him back from his machinations. He just wanted enough power and money to be happy and secure. She'd have a fight on her hands if he found anything out. He didn't think it was another man, but you never knew with her these days. She was his wife in any case and needed to tow the bloody line. All this spiritual bollocks! He'd talk to the kids later – a bit of charm and manipulation wouldn't go amiss – power in numbers – get them on his side. Maybe they should all go away for the weekend – somewhere plush – a boutique cottage in the country. They could play Monopoly or watch a film, go for a walk on Sunday and swing by a pub for lunch. Yes. That's what he'd do. Women always fell for power and control. He rang through to his secretary. "Helen. Find me a luxury cottage for four, within an hour's drive of Turnham Green, will you? Something out in the sticks. Make sure it's got a good country pub nearby. Can you book it for next weekend? Thanks, you're a star." He unbuttoned his suit jacket, took another sherbet lemon from the drawer, and picked up a dossier before leaving his office for the boardroom.

* * *

In another part of London, a small, bald man in civvies took his position at the negotiating table in Whitehall – a Ministry of Defence, confidential, strategic meeting. He'd be back at High Wycombe later, where there was a room waiting in the mess, and a roast dinner in the oak dining room. He'd wash it down with a decent claret. He salivated, his eyes glassy and distant. A tall official next to him fidgeted in his seat, pushing aside a starched white cuff to take a look at his Breitling before sighing. The bald man fiddled with a piece of paper in his left pocket, his heart racing. He twitched slightly, then froze for a moment, like a rabbit in the lights. The meeting ticked through the neatly titled increments of someone else's agenda. Nobody asked his opinion and he kept quiet apart from the odd 'yes' or 'no'. His superior would be pleased with him. He'd kept his head down and it had all gone smoothly enough. At least they hadn't cut the budget – that had been their biggest concern.

Out in the cool air he marched, briefcase in hand, towards the Red Lion for a little post-meeting refreshment. Sipping at a reasonable glass of Côtes du Rhône, he reached into his jacket pocket and pulled out the folded paper. Three names, two numbers and an email address. The Slater bloke couldn't take him on. His eyes hovered over the names. He had to do something, it was getting out of control. Of course, his life looked great from the outside – the big country house, the trophy wife, the rank – but it was all slipping through his hands as he spiraled into a hell of his own making. He hung his head, shaking it slightly, his back bowed down by the weight of his thoughts.

The barman smiled at him as he downed the red liquid. "Cheer up mate! It might never happen!"

"That's what I'm worried about," he said, slamming the empty glass on the bar before walking out into the street. He dawdled across Westminster Bridge, glancing down at the cold murky water of the Thames. Thank goodness he was staying at High Wycombe this evening. He couldn't face the commute home, and worse, the facade of domestic bliss that would be waiting. A sick feeling welled up in his stomach. He grimaced as he walked down the steps to the tube station and onto the train. After grabbing the last empty seat in the carriage, he put his briefcase on his lap and stared down at the dirty floor where thousands of feet would jostle for space in an hour or so. The acrid smell of sweaty humanity crammed into a small, airless space seemed to linger on the upholstery. He wondered how many tramps had sat on the well-worn fabric. A bad taste sprang into his mouth and he wrinkled his nose.

Back at the mess, a lackey took his briefcase and small overnight bag to his room and turned down the sheets before saluting and leaving the room. "Sir!"

The small, bald man loosened his tie, undid his collar, and flopped into the armchair. He reached for his briefcase, extracted a laptop from among the papers and switched it on. His hands hovered over the keyboard ready to compose something, but his jaw clenched. Where should he start? Instead, he unzipped his flies, launched the browser, and pulled up his favorite website. He shouldn't. He mustn't…it was becoming an obsession…but he couldn't stop himself. Everybody does it, he told himself! Every, damn, hot-blooded male with a pulse! But not like this, not to this extent, not when they had a smoldering brunette wife at home, who was longing for intimacy.

He'd fallen asleep in the chair and was now jolted awake by the sound of footsteps in the corridor outside. Scrambling to change the website and clean up, sweat pouring down his high forehead, he remembered the piece of paper in his jacket pocket. A lump was forming in his throat, his heart thumping now as he unfolded it and studied the names. Reaching for his phone, he dialed The Priory. A recorded announcement struck up its monotone voice and he left a hurried message, hung up and dressed for dinner.

A large plate of roast beef with two Yorkshire puddings and a bottle of Claret later, he staggered to the bar for a postprandial. "A *large* brandy, for God's sake, man!" he said to the sheepish barman. "Yes, Sir. Right, Sir. Here you are, Sir."

It was almost midnight by the time he staggered back up the corridor to his room. The small folded paper was sitting unfurled on the desk where he'd left it. Noting the email address, his hands skipped over the keyboard. "No time like the present," he said aloud, tapping out a short message before mustering the courage to send it, his hand hovering over the mouse as he did battle with himself. "Hit send, you bastard! Send it! It's your one last chance at something good!"

No, he thought, it'll be censored, it's my MoD email. I can't risk it – and Lauren'll have her nose in my personal account. He typed the therapist's name into Google and found the website again. There was an enquiry form, he reminded himself, yes, that would be a safer bet.

* * *

Several miles South-East of High Wycombe, Katy was slipping into bed. Richard was dozing as she gingerly lifted the covers, hoping not to disturb him. There was a bitter taste in her mouth as her body recoiled slightly with the thought of his touch. Richard stirred as she pulled the duvet close. He rolled over, leering at her, his needy hand reaching towards her.

"I'm sorry, Rich, I've got a hell of a headache!"

"The oldest excuse in the world, Kit, what the hell?"

"And my back's been playing up," she said, turning away from him and clinging to her side of the bed, her stomach knotting and her jaw clamped tight. Her whole body was taut with tension as she lay unmoving, pretending to sleep. As soon as the rhythm of Richard's snoring steadied, she tiptoed downstairs to the drink's cabinet, where she poured herself a generous whisky. Around one o'clock, back in her bed and still wide-awake, she remembered some breathing exercises she'd taught her insomniac clients. Breathe in for the count of seven, and out for the count of eleven, then relax each part of the body. She was asleep within ten minutes, and within another twenty, her mind was skimming in and out of a lucid dream. Boxes everywhere, then a treadmill, going faster and faster, then flashes and images and thoughts darting into her mind.

She woke up in a sweat. Reaching out to sip some water from the glass by her bedside, she noticed the notebook. Taking up the pen and holding a torch in her mouth, so as not to wake Richard, she wrote:

They're on treadmills that keep going faster and longer till they're exhausted. They're doing it for money. The reward is two weeks off. They get on a big tube with wings (a plane?) and go to another part of the planet where the boxes are a bit different. I can see beaches and mountains. There's a forest with waterfalls. Fresh water. Thirst quenching. Drink it all in. Plump up and expand. Unwind and uncoil. They're pale and desiccated. Thirsting – not just for the water. They're looking for something real and warm. They're looking for happiness, kindness, something nurturing. They're joyful and alive for a moment, talking to the locals and envying their simple way of life.

After putting down the pen and book, and switching off the torch, she snuggled under the covers and closed her eyes. The dream resumed: The box people returned on the tubes with wings, oblivious to their treadmill lives. Behind the beach and at the edge of the woods, there were piles and piles of rubbish – stinking, rotting trash. The sea washed up water bottles, drink cartons and suntan lotion tubes, all covered in black tar. At the other side of the mountain was a gigantic gash – a massive quarry or mine, so big it made the people look like ants. Someone or something had been mining minerals, metals, gemstones, coal, oil – you name it and they'd plundered it, hoarding it away in cavernous storehouses. It was a wholesale ransacking of the planet, the great mother, Earth, which seemed to be alive and crying like a person. She was collecting discarded boxes in her arms, stuffing them into her vast apron pockets. Plumes of noxious smoke belched from a factory which was pumping out shiny new boxes at an alarming rate. Katy roused herself from the scene to write it all down.

"Competition, acquisition, consumption," said the Voice.

It took her by surprise. She'd thought it had gone.

"Would you like me to continue sharing Wisdom?"

"Sshhh! You'll wake Richard."

"He can't hear me."

"I thought you were confined to the landing mirror and my office! This is my private space, for God's sake!"

"I'm sorry. We can resume tomorrow evening when you meditate."

"No. I'm wide awake now, what do you want?"

"You're seeing where this 'sleeping' human consciousness – this unthinking way of living – ultimately leads, aren't you?"

"I think it's just a reflection of my own psyche, actually. All the symbols are parts of me. I really relate to the planet – all my resources being drained while I take on other people's shit – I mean rubbish—"

"It's okay."

"I'm taking on other people's stuff – not just client's, but Richard's as well!"

"As within, so without! Your own psyche is a reflection of the outer world. Humans use Earth's bounty as if it were boundless, turning a blind eye to mounting problems and hoping she goes on swallowing your detritus."

"Hadn't thought of it that way…"

"Out of sight, out of mind – but it's happening, Katy!"

"Are we creating it? This modern box myth where we keep learning from somebody else and carrying the baton onto the next treadmill?"

"Yes. But you could create something else."

"How?"

"Stop seeing life as something you have to get through. It's not a game you have to win. It's not Monopoly, you know – you're not here to learn the rules, shake the dice, pass go and pick up £200! It's not about trophies and trinkets and possessions or how much you can get. You don't shuffle off this world saying, 'Thank goodness we got through it, with our pension and nest-egg intact!' There are more noble reasons for life!"

"Like what?"

"You have a Divine Self – a Greater Self – which chose to come here to explore, learn, expand, become more aware and grow! You all have it! It's waiting for you to wake up and fully express your true essence. It wants you to follow your bliss – not a spa package with a scented steam room but your soul's joy, the thing that makes you alive with enthusiasm!"

"Isn't that a bit selfish?"

"On the contrary – it's a service to humanity and the world. You're each a piece of a larger jigsaw. When you follow your soul's purpose you're contributing! And joy is the best contagion there is!"

"How do I follow it?"

"That's what I'm here to share with you. But not now. Richard will be awake in precisely nineteen minutes and you need your sleep."

"But..."

The Voice was gone.

Chapter 5

Dr. Erasmus Watkins' secretary was a large lady, no nonsense and kind, with a jolly and booming voice. "You left a message last night?" she bellowed down the phone.

The small, bald man held the phone away from his ear, glad he was alone in his room. It was 9 am and he was in no hurry to get back to Brize Norton.

"I, I, err, I, um…" He couldn't seem to get the words out.

"It's okay, no need to be shy."

"I think I, well, I think I might have an addiction. Dr. Slater recommended you – well the clinic – he told me to talk to you – well, Dr. Watkins."

"Have you looked at our treatment programs?"

"Yes. I've seen them on the internet. I don't think I can do the residential. It's my wife. Don't want her to, you know, *know*."

"I see, that's fine. It's all confidential – the one-to-one sessions with Dr. Watkins, group therapy, art therapy, extra-curricular classes and, of course, the twelve-step program which forms the core of our treatment. The first thing is to come for an initial assessment. How's the 22nd? We have a slot at 11 am."

"This month? Yes. I can do October 22nd. Thank you… There's something else… I'm having trouble, er, 'performing'…with my wife…" he hesitated and gave a short, high-pitched laugh, "b– but not when I'm 'flying solo'."

"Impotence? Most patients find it all falls back into place once they've worked through their addiction."

"I hope so…is there anything I need before 22nd?"

"I'll send you the relevant forms."

* * *

Katy trudged upstairs to the office in her dressing gown, a mug of hot tea in one hand and her phone in the other. It was 9 am.

She'd fallen back to sleep after getting up for breakfast with Tilly and Freddie. Thank goodness she didn't have any clients until later that afternoon. It would give her time to catch up on emails and session notes before heading into town. Yawning, then giving her face a gentle massage to wake up, she sat at her desk, her laptop flipped open, watching it whir into action. She should get a new one, this old thing was taking ages to load. She wondered how much time she wasted waiting for it! Sipping at her English Breakfast, she stared out at the street below. The trees were just beginning to lose their leaves and it was quiet after the usual flurry of morning activity.

As the expected page of new emails filled the screen, one in particular caught her attention.

Just thought I'd check in with you! I know you've been off balance with the new name.

Popped into my head the other day that an Aura Soma consultation would be perfect. There's a great practitioner out in Hertfordshire – lives near a forest – her name's Lavinia Montgomery. Suggest you see her asap. Will text you her number – don't have it with me now.

Love & Light

Dinah x

Katy started deleting circulars and mailers from the long list, marking invoices with a yellow star – she'd look at those later – and passing over a deluge of unimportant messages. There was a three-line whip from her brother about Mother's birthday party, which she was compelled to read, three client emails and three website enquiries. She started with the enquiries, one of which she read twice, a smile spreading across her face. "Bloody hell!"

* * *

Richard arrived at his 9 am meeting. He wasn't exactly part of the City and yet he was: not a stock-broker or a corporate lawyer, either, but an advisor – a bit of a spin doctor – a PR supremo with a head for figures, strategy and manipulation. He liked the City. It was all numbers, old-boy's networks, East Enders made good and calculated risks. Locking antlers in the boardroom and drip-feeding massaged information was his stock in trade. He'd carefully carved out a territory in this bravado world of patriarchal testosterone, and he guarded it fiercely. Surveying the room full of interested parties, his thoughts turned to a David Attenborough program he'd seen about a troop of baboons. They kept fighting to keep rank while the big alpha male beat his chest, barking the loudest and reclaiming his position at the top. This troop would soon fall into place and he'd have them eating out of his big fat hand. The battle for supremacy! Yes! It was the power and authority that fascinated him. Only Westminster with its seductive seat of political clout glittered more golden than this. Perhaps he'd become an MP later in life, or a political strategist. For now, he was stockpiling his assets and lining the nest. Those sorts of ambitions took careful funding, but it would all be worth it! Ultimately, it would change his life, give him the power he craved. His colleague, swan-necked and elegant in her stilettos and Austin Reed suit, flashed him a smile from the doorway as she entered the room. A waft of Chanel accompanied her as she strode towards her seat. The meeting began.

Chapter 6

"Hello? Is that Lavinia Montgomery? I'd like to book an Aura Soma consultation," said Katy. Sipping at a mug of peppermint tea, she listened to the clipped vowels of the older woman the other end of the phone. "Dinah gave me your number... Yes, eleven o'clock tomorrow would be perfect. What's your address?"

She'd better find out more, thought Katy, typing *Aura Soma* into the search engine. Ooh! Nice bottles! The chunky square design reminded her of Chanel No.5, except each of these – there must have been a hundred or so – were neatly bisected with a different shade above and below. They were called 'Equilibrium' bottles. Well, that made sense, thought Katy, the top bit must be oil-based and the bottom bit water – otherwise they wouldn't stay like that! Did it say what was in the bottles? 'A unique vibrational process.' Katy assumed it must be herbs, coloring – maybe aromatherapy oil. They had names like *Arch Angel Michael*, *The Essene* and *Birth of Venus*. Ah, there it was, *'Harnessing the vibrational powers of Gaia. The bottles are a system of color, plant and crystal energies that bring you closer to self-understanding.'* Sounded intriguing, if a little bizarre. She read on, *'Aura means light, Soma means body, the colors you choose will reflect the needs that are hidden within.'* Katy frowned slightly and pursed her lips, but beneath the mistrust, a lightness was rising within her that broke into a thin smile.

Having finished her preparation, she slipped the files into her briefcase along with her old-fashioned desk-diary, and left for Harley Street. She loved that diary, with its client appointments, 'to do' list and notes. It was her way of dealing with stress. Planning ahead, writing things down, and being organized, kept her from feeling overwhelmed. It was a strategy that had helped her make sense of a chaotic childhood, and it continued to serve her now.

At precisely 8.55pm that evening, her last client paid and left the building, shortly followed by Katy, lugging the heavy briefcase into the damp evening air. Oxford Street station was less crowded at this time of night and the train was half empty. Taking the first available seat, she flopped down and let the gentle swaying of the carriage lull her into a light sleep. An abrupt stop accompanied by a robotic female announcement roused her and she hurriedly gathered her bags. Stepping across the platform to the District Line, she caught the next train towards Richmond. At Turnham Green, she pulled herself to her feet, trying not to think about the nine-minute walk that lay ahead.

The windchimes sang out their welcome as she pushed through the door to hear Richard's voice calling from the snug.

"Thought you were leaving something in the fridge!"

"Rich! I was busy!"

"Had to get a sandwich."

"Well, I'm sorry!"

Rolling her eyes and taking a deep breath, Katy set her briefcase on the bottom step, hung her bag over the newel post and unbuttoned her mac.

"Don't know what I pay you for!" said Richard, sniggering at his own joke as she moved into the snug. "Sit with me and watch the news!" He patted the cushion next to him and her aching body buckled and folded to his bidding. She sank onto the sofa, giving him a cursory peck on the cheek. He smelled of sickly sherbet lemons and stale breath. The television flickered as they sat in silence, her mac over her arm, her red high heels pinching, her head swimming with clients. "I'd better get my post sessions notes done."

Richard pursed his lips and flared his nostrils.

"It'll only take a minute."

He gave her a dismissive wave. Katy felt a shot of guilt as she wrestled with herself. "It won't take long," she said, giving him a sideways glance. "I'll meditate later when you've gone to bed."

If she didn't get the notes done now, she'd forget the details.

Richard was flagging by the time she'd finished.

"So, how was your day?" she asked, putting on her brightest client-smile, straightening her skirt and running a hand through her hair.

"Bloody big meeting. Can't tell you!" he said, tapping the side of his nose with an index finger. "Insider trading and all that. Did you have Seamus today?"

"No. Seeing him tomorrow. The usual stuff. Can't tell you," she said, winking and putting a forefinger to her lips. "Client confidentiality!"

"Come on, Kit, give us a bit of dirt!"

"I can't!"

"Swap? Tit for tat?"

"Richard!"

He leaned in as he nudged her gently with his elbow. "Go on!"

Katy turned towards the television and changed the subject. "What's happening in the world, then?" The news items rolled over her as she stared at the shapes on the screen.

"I'm off to bed," said Richard, pointing the remote at the television. They ambled upstairs in silence, Katy giving him a perfunctory kiss outside their bedroom before heading up the second flight of stairs to her office.

She stopped fleetingly at the long mirror on the top landing.

"You create with your mind, you know," the Voice whispered.

"Do I?" she replied, slumping forward.

"If it's not convenient?"

"It's been a long day."

"I'll leave you be."

"No!" She was standing right in front of the mirror, searching for the source of the Voice.

"The human mind is born of the Great Creative Mind. It's part of the Divine Intelligence that flows through and connects all things...not that anyone seems to be interested."

"People don't really believe in that stuff."

"That's the trouble. I can't get anyone to take me seriously!"

"Does that surprise you?" Her eyebrows drew together, and a smile lit her face.

"The mind is powerful! People are always forming the path ahead, but most of the time they're doing it on auto-pilot."

Katy stifled a yawn.

"So few understand the mechanisms at play!"

"What mechanisms?" She could tell she was in for a long night, but before the Voice could 'say' anything, she remembered that time stood still during these bizarre conversations. She resigned herself and sat cross-legged in front of the almost floor-length mirror.

"The mechanisms for creating and manifesting."

"All that 'cosmic ordering' rubbish?"

"No. True creation starts with an idea, a thought and a contemplation."

"And then you've got to work out how you're going to do it."

"No. That's the thing. There's very little you have to work out."

"You believe that bullshit about the universe delivering everything you want? I haven't noticed much being delivered – except bills!"

"You have to play your part but when you create on purpose – according to your soul's purpose – it all falls into place."

"How? We just ask for something and that's it?"

"You need to think about it, visualize it, feel it."

"And then?"

"Intend it, and bit by bit the universe will conspire to help you!"

"Why would it do that?"

"Because you're part of it, and it's bound to support whatever you're creating! You just have to take the right inspired actions."

"And what exactly are 'right inspired actions'?"

"You'll encounter opportunities and synchronicities along the way – signs that let you know you're on the right track. You take the first step and the next one shows up. It means you don't have to work it all out in detail. In fact, it's better if you don't! Let it unfold like the petals of a flower!"

"Huh?"

"If you can stick with it, you'll be open to inspiration, to thinking outside the box! There's room for the Universe to maneuver when you don't have it all set in stone."

"Like an artist serendipitously creating a better piece than she'd imagined?"

"Yes. Things emerge, and what you thought was impossible becomes possible."

"Like walking upstairs in the dark. You don't have to see the top step, you only have to see the next one."

"That's a fair analogy, but think of a multi-colored, multi-level stairway! You could still get to your destination, the top, but there would be myriad routes to choose from."

There was a soft swoosh below as a pajama-clad Richard opened the bedroom door and called up. "Everything okay up there? Who are you talking to?"

"No-one! Thought you were asleep."

"You coming to bed soon?"

"Just going to meditate."

Katy glimpsed her face, pale and frozen in the mirror.

"Remember I can read your thoughts. You don't have to whisper for me to hear," said the Voice.

Katy thought she saw something flash in the mirror.

"Why's life so stressful then?" she thought, imagining she was talking out loud. "Passing go and collecting £200 so we can live in a better box – working our arses off to pay the flipping mortgage."

"That wasn't the original plan. You've heard the expression

'where your attention goes, energy flows'?"

Katy nodded before remembering nobody was watching.

"I can see you're nodding," said the Voice. "A lot of people allow their attention to flow to their problems or to doing what's expected of them, living in a better box, so to speak, in the belief that it will bring happiness." There was a pause. "Or avoid calamity."

"And it might not."

"Quite so. What you focus on grows, but most people don't know what they're focused on. Sometimes they can't decide what to give their attention to! In fact, many are preoccupied with the very thing they're trying to avoid!"

"Because it's habitual?"

"It's often unconscious, yes. Could I give you an example?"

"Please do."

"Let's say you're trying to put on weight."

"Put on weight? Why would anyone want to put on weight?"

"Well, you're a little below your natural weight and so are many of the women you admire."

"I happen to think I look good." Katy smoothed down her clothes with the palms of her hands, appreciating the outline in the mirror.

"Okay. Let's say you want to lose weight, but for the life of me, I don't know why! It wasn't like that before, you know!"

"Well it is now! Go on, how do I lose weight?" She was eager to hear, ears pricked up, leaning into the mirror.

"Well, there you are, thinking you're focused on losing weight. That's your conscious thought, that's where you think your attention is, but it's not where it really is."

"You've lost me."

"What's the first thing that comes to mind when you think of losing weight?"

"My big bottom. I wish I could lose it from there, not my bust."

"And then?"

"I'll have to stop eating sandwiches and have salad instead."

"And?"

"My jeans are too tight, and I'd love to get into a size six."

"So, what you're really thinking about, is your big bottom, delicious sandwiches, your tight jeans and how you can never get into a size six."

The Voice was right, but she hadn't thought of it like that.

"And that's what you create. You lose the weight from your bust, your jeans are still tight, you crave sandwiches and your bottom is still a very nice, if I may be so bold, size eight...or ten, depending on the cut and the brand."

Ignoring the final comment, she thought it through. "And after three days of salads, I give up."

"Exactly!"

"And look longingly at the size six jeans and the girls who can fit into them."

"Yes, and you feel despondent. Ultimately, your preoccupations are bringing you angst."

Katy groaned and rubbed her eyes. The Voice was yet to tell her how to get into a size six, albeit a designer six, which was really an old fashioned ten.

"For the most part, when people think about something they want, they're actually thinking about the opposite, because it's all a sliding scale."

"What is?"

"Weight, for example."

Saints preserve us! thought Katy, before remembering the Voice could read *all* her thoughts. "Indeed." The Voice continued. "But weight's like 'temperature'. Cold and hot are just opposite ends of the thermometer. Where does one begin and the other end?

"Is this one of those fad diets where you have to walk about in a plastic onesie and sweat off your excess pounds?"

"Good Lord, no!" said the Voice, a chuckle curling its way around the words. "Heavy is one end and light is the other. Your conscious focus is on losing weight but your unconscious attention is on what you currently weigh, what you don't want to weigh, what jeans size you are and how tight your jeans are – so you end up manufacturing more of the same, and as a result, you feel dissatisfied."

"And work even harder to lose it by going to the gym and trying in vain to cut out dark chocolate."

"Yes. And even if you did create a size six, you'd struggle to maintain it, because it's not your natural equilibrium. So ultimately, the preoccupation with weight is unsatisfactory. Either way, it brings misery." There was a pause. "And if you're overweight, like half the population of the Western World, it's even worse! You're desperate to lose weight, you're obsessed with calories, diets, exercise, cravings, and on top of that, what else?"

"The fear that you'll never lose it. I've seen that in clients, it's all-consuming. Then they comfort themselves with the wrong foods. It's a vicious cycle!"

"Yes. Whatever you're preoccupied with is the thing that's paving the way to your future, and most people notice what already exists – either around them in reality, or within their own psyche – so they recreate it over and over."

"Tell me how to stop!" blurted Katy out loud. Clamping her hand over her mouth, she froze, and listened carefully for signs of Richard. Nothing.

"Move to a higher vibration."

"Hang on. I need a pen and paper."

"You'll remember, but if you insist..."

Katy moved into the office, retrieving a pad and pen. The Voice followed her to her desk. "Move to something bigger, more noble—"

"Than my desk?"

"More noble than weight."

Katy was wondering what 'more noble' meant in this context.

"Health, for example," said the helpful Voice. "Focus on health and your weight will take care of itself, because you'll be a healthy weight. And, of course, if you're a healthy weight you'll be happier."

I'm not convinced, thought Katy.

"Shall I use another example then?" Katy had forgotten the Voice was able to hear private asides.

"What if you're not healthy?"

"Think about what you'd love to do! Better still, think about joy. Did you know that joy, laughter and fun are the best cures for most modern ills?"

"It's quite hard to have fun when you're sick!"

"Actually, it's often the lack of fun that *makes* you sick…"

The Voice had caught Katy's imagination. "What about the C word?" She instantly blushed. "Cancer, I mean!"

"Eat healthily, rest well, sleep properly, stop worrying, let go of anger and start having fun – and cancer won't visit you… Unless you live under a mobile phone mast, or you're subject to other man-made pollutants or Electro-Magnetic Fields. There are some souls who signed up for the experience in order to learn, but for the most part, you have a choice."

Katy hadn't written a single word. The pen was still poised. The Voice gave her a moment, knowing precisely when to start again.

"What you *consistently* rest your attention upon – or think about, do, and talk about – is the thing you create. The rub is that most people rest their attention upon their troubles – the *opposite* of what they actually want – or upon the fear of not getting what they want!"

"So, they keep on recreating the same thing!"

"You're getting it, Katy! By Jehovah, you're getting it! The things that bother people are the things that occupy their minds.

Those are the things they think about, talk about, tell their friends about, tell themselves about, worry about. They recreate those things over and over in thought, in feeling and in word."

"And those thoughts, feelings and words become reality?"

"Quite so... And the 'reality' which they create 'proves' to them that the original thought, or fear, was real!"

Katy was staring out of the window at the streetlight opposite.

"You're absolutely right – I see that in my patients all the time."

"You're teaching them to look at things differently – to change their *perception* of things and think 'outside the box'."

"And because of that, they get different results."

"Precisely. They experience something else." The Voice let it percolate for a moment, giving Katy time to assimilate.

"Even when we're trying to do something positive, we're thinking about what could go wrong," she realized.

"You've got it, Katy!"

"Like when you're buying a house. You keep thinking of all the hurdles you've got to jump, so you don't get your hopes up in case it all falls through." She paused, catching her breath with the insight. "You're not thinking about how lovely it will be when you're living there – you're worrying about how awful it will be if you don't get it."

"Is it not so with many things, Katy?"

"Yes." Katy was wide-eyed, imagining the impact of this realization. "We're engrossed in the fear of not getting what we want!"

"Correct."

"How do we change?"

"Become aware of your thoughts by observing them. Change your mind, so to speak, and you'll alter your life or at least your experience of it!"

"But how?"

"Spend some time day-dreaming about the things you *really*

want, the things your deeper, noble self wants. Be playful and catch any fears, simply acknowledge them, then let them go. Tell yourself a different story."

"That's easy to say!"

"You say that to your clients!" The Voice chuckled. "Have faith, Katy! Choose your dreams. Intend them. Ask for them – ask and ye shall receive. And choose your thoughts, your actions, and your words. It's just a matter of sticking with the dream, working towards it, and receiving the opportunities that come along."

"Like booking the removal van and setting up the mortgage."

"Or trusting that if this house falls through, there's a much better one waiting for you!"

"That's true! But how do I know what I *really* want? What my 'deeper self' wants, whatever that is?"

"Do you want to eat a packet of delicious biscuits every day or do you want to be healthy?"

"Be healthy."

"Why?"

"I'd feel happier in the long run."

"Exactly. What your deeper self wants is positive and lovely. Ultimately, it's beneficial and fills you with joy! It's something you become so absorbed in that you lose track of time. Did you know that truly giving, because you want to contribute, brings people the most joy of all?"

A smile spread across Katy's features, her eyes twinkling as a lightness enveloped her. The Voice gave her a moment.

"That's what 'following your bliss' means! It's making the choices that truly delight and serve! It's taking the path that consistently nourishes and gives to the whole."

"Otherwise you're chasing the short-term high of the packet of biscuits."

"Or the immediate gratification of buying new things and 'having' them."

"Which fizzles out very quickly."

"It is truly God's Will that you follow your bliss!"

"What's God got to do with it?"

"Everything. Think of Her as a kind and loving parent, just wanting the best for her children.

In fact, think of Her as love in action. As I think I mentioned before, She's more of a verb!"

Katy drew her eyebrows together. "I still think of Him as a He!"

"He's a Trinity, actually – Three in One – Father, Daughter (or Son), and Holy Spirit or *She*kinah in Hebrew. Or Osiris, Isis and Horus if you prefer?"

Katy was deep in thought. "Father, Mother and Child? But I can't visualize three in one."

"Think of the three primary colors making one white light."

The Voice prompted her. "What do you want for Tilly and Freddie?"

"I want them to be happy."

"Exactly. That's what The Most High wants for you! He wants you to be happy, be joyous, have fun."

"Sometimes the thing that fills me with joy is seeing a client heal and move on."

"Yes. It's a win-win. You're happy, the client's happy, you get paid and your client gets better. Contribution isn't about giving everything away for free, though of course, it can be."

The Voice retreated and she fished out her meditation stool. Breath. Hara. Expansiveness. Light.

* * *

At around 10.40 am the following morning, Katy was driving through a busy Hertfordshire town, watching it stretch out neatly in all directions. It was well groomed, and laid out in pleasant, inoffensive style with clean streets and shiny buses. It seemed a million miles away from London, yet it had taken just under an hour to get there. Driving out towards the countryside, she turned left then swung into Lavinia's cul-de-sac. It wasn't exactly a forest, more of a leafy glade. Katy had imagined a Hansel and Gretel cottage tucked away from the world, but Lavinia's house was comfortable and detached with a large conservatory to the side and an English country garden set with lawns and herbaceous borders. It was about fifteen minutes' drive from a large supermarket and the usual small-town amenities. Katy parked in the sweeping cobbled drive which ended in a small round-about affair with a cherub-clad stone fountain at the center. She picked her way through autumn leaves to a large porch with a small topiary bay tree either side. Pressing a highly polished brass button with her index finger, she heard an old-fashioned bell ringing somewhere inside. A smartly dressed, middle-aged woman opened the door. The smell of floor polish wafted across her light floral perfume.

"You must be Katy!" Her coral lipstick was shimmering as she spoke, "I'm Lavinia! Come in, come in!"

Katy stepped into a large, tiled hallway as Lavinia opened her arms, embracing her as if she were a close friend.

"Coffee?"

"Do you have tea?"

"Earl Grey or English Breakfast?"

"Earl Grey please!"

"Come on through. Make yourself comfortable. I won't be long. The kettle's almost boiled."

Katy sank into a wicker conservatory chair overflowing with plump, leaf-motif cushions. This must be her consulting room, she thought, taking in the light, airy space with its white shelves and glass coffee table. Cream walls were the perfect foil for heavy green foliage and floral displays – cheese plants, rubber plants, ferns, an exotic looking red flower, a miniature powder-pink rose and a variegated purple orchid in full bloom. There was a small aquarium on one side, with bright, neon fish darting about among fronds of weed. The French windows opposite opened onto a huge lawn which stretched towards a copse of mature trees beyond.

"Earl Grey," said Lavinia, bustling in with a smile and setting a tray down on the coffee table. She poured into old-fashioned cups, complete with saucers, from an ornate gilt-edged teapot. "Sugar?"

"No thanks, just as it comes."

"These are the bottles," she said, sipping at her tea and motioning towards a huge white bookcase. She flicked a switch at the side and its glass shelves lit up, illuminating 108 bottles sitting in neat, serried rows. Katy stared at the display, mouth open, an uneasy feeling rising inside. Richard was going to laugh like a drain, if he ever found out!

Lavinia picked up a clipboard and a slim, gold, ballpoint. "Let's get the nitty-gritties out of the way. Full name?"

"Actually, I've recently changed it back to my maiden name – Katherine Alison Fralinski."

"Ah! That's why you're here," said Lavinia, softly raising her eyebrows. "You need to ground the vibration of your new name."

"But I had it before…"

"Not purposefully, as part of your path!" Her head bobbed up from the page as she looked at Katy. "I can tell you're spiritual through and through, you're like a stick of Brighton Rock!" She was waving the pen at her.

"You've been sent here, Katherine!"

Katy uncrossed her legs and sat forward, shifting in her seat, absent-mindedly checking her handbag while Lavinia waxed lyrical about Aura Soma and spirit guides, Archangels and chakras.

"What you need to do now, Katy, is take a look at all the bottles and choose four," said Lavinia, motioning with her pen towards the shelf. "Choose the ones that you're drawn to – the ones that speak to you. It's not about guessing what they mean or going for your favorite colors."

Katy furrowed her brow and stared at the shelves.

"Just allow yourself to be guided," said Lavinia, a kind smile lighting up her face.

Trying to ignore the doubts that were creeping in and the voice that was telling her it was nonsense – was it Richard's or Father's? – Katy stood up. She'd come a long way, and not just the distance from London! Shanti had been proud of her accepting angels as things that really existed, seeing extraordinary healings as part of everyday life, reading authors who professed to be having conversations with God. She'd baulked at Shanti's insistence that there were people who'd lived past lives on other planets, but that was Shanti. She'd believe anything. What about this? Bottles of colored oil and water which were going to help her if she chose the right ones. Was it for real, or was she just being gullible?

"It's okay!" said Lavinia, breaking the silence, "I can sense you're torn. That's what happens when you change your name. You're pulled two ways!"

Katy was indeed torn; part of her was excited and intrigued, while the other wanted to laugh and dismiss the whole silly charade. She was normally decisive, sure of herself, in control of her own mind, but recently she'd been flustered, baffled and doubtful. "I feel a bit overwhelmed!" said Katy, her heart beating, her mouth becoming dry. Sipping at her Earl Grey and collecting her thoughts, she spoke deliberately. "I usually pick things straight away, but..."

"I know. It's okay. Take your time, my dear."

Katy took a long, slow breath and ran her gaze along the shelves of colored jewels, her eyes darting from side to side. Getting things right had been her hallmark, but she didn't know what 'right' looked like at the moment. Clenching her hands slightly and holding her breath, she started second-guessing. I can't afford to get this wrong, she thought, stepping towards the shelves and opening her palm to sense the bottles.

"Don't touch them!"

"Oh! Sorry!" Katy could feel her cheeks burning as she backed off. Her eyes widening, her mind trying not to think of what the hues might mean, she ran her palm a distance away from the shelf, trying to sense the energy, and at last picking out seven bottles. She could whittle it down later.

"Is that the order you chose them in?"

"Oh," Katy's eyebrows shot up as she took a step back. "I didn't realize that was important." Come on, Katy, she told herself, how difficult can it be to pick out four colors in order of preference! It's not rocket science and your life doesn't depend on it. Just do it.

"It's a huge undertaking," said Lavinia, taking off her spectacles and letting them dangle on a gold chain around her neck.

"Choosing four bottles?"

"No dear! Changing your name!" The frames were resting on her salmon, cashmere sweater as she spoke. "Your name is your vibration and it takes a lot of grounding."

"What does that mean, exactly?"

"It's got to come through you, like a signal coming through a radio. It's going to alter the course of your life!"

"Oh!" Katy had a dream-like sense that none of this was actually happening.

"In the beginning was the Word, you see?"

Katy shot her a puzzled look.

"Words are vibrations and they carry codes, sounds, colors, shapes and energies – do you get the enormity of it? This name is going to reset you, recode you – put you on a new path."

Katy hadn't thought of it that way. Clearly, she hadn't thought it through at all. "I can't even choose four bottles in the right order!" she said, fumbling with her left earring. Lavinia carefully lifted each of the seven bottles by the cap, bringing them forward to the front of the shelf where they stood proud of the others.

"Now. Stand back. Breathe. Go intuitively – the very first thing that pops into your head before you start overthinking."

Katy stared at the seven bottles, trying to clear her head of conflicting chatter, swallowing her embarrassment, and wishing she knew what to do. Lavinia must think she was stupid. She stepped forward to push one of the bottles back.

"No!" shrieked Lavinia. "Don't touch! Lift them by the cap, or you'll imprint your energy."

Noticing Katy's worried expression as she whipped her hand back, she added, "Sorry to shout, dear, just so important!"

Katy carefully lifted one of the bottles by the lid, watching the oily layer moving over the watery one, dividing the bottle horizontally, no matter at what angle it was tilted. There was something satisfying and captivating about it. Most of the bottles had two distinct hues but some, she noticed, had the same top and bottom, the oily layer looking richer. Which was she supposed to choose, and in what order? For God's sake, it was only a bottle of colored water! It couldn't be that important, could it? Somehow it was. Carefully placing the bottle back in line with the others, she'd made her first decision. She let go of the breath she'd been holding. But what if she'd made a mistake?

"It's okay. Take your time!" said Lavinia, clasping her hands loosely together, her brightly varnished nails settling among her gold, jeweled rings.

It was a slow and painful process, like being stuck in a supermarket queue with a trainee cashier. Katy chewed her bottom lip, closed her eyes, and opened them again. Shifting her weight from one foot to the other, she eventually turned around to face the garden, then spun back, her eyes catching a lime green and magenta bottle. She lifted it by the cap, setting it back in line with its neighbors, before changing her mind and snatching it back. Lavinia intervened, taking all six bottles in her manicured fingers and placing them on a small white table to the left. Katy watched, as she absent-mindedly turned her bracelet around and around. "I'm sorry! I'm not usually like this! I'm wasting your time, perhaps..."

"Not at all!" said Lavinia, a warmth exuding from her pale-grey eyes as they wrinkled at the corners.

Katy gave a feeble smile. "Take that one away, the black and jade."

Five bottles remained on the table.

"Two of these are similar. They both make pale olive if you shake them, see?" She demonstrated. "We'll take that as *one* bottle. You're going to work with them both at the same time. Now, which was the first that caught your eye?"

Katy struggled to place them in order while Lavinia slid her glasses back onto her face and peered at the bottles in front of her. At last, they were in order.

A torrent of information poured forth from Lavinia. "Hang on! I need to write this down," said Katy, reaching inside her bag for a small notebook and pen.

Lavinia told Katy the name of each bottle, its number, what the number meant, what the bottle was going to do, why she'd chosen it, what it said about Katy, how to apply each one and when to apply it. Then she elaborated on which Angel or Master she'd be working with, which chakra it would be healing, which order they must go in and why. It was a stream of consciousness which Lavinia said had 'come through her from her guides'. Katy was struggling to get it all down and forgot to be skeptical. It was a mesmerizing monologue and she did her best to nod in the right places. Lavinia finally stopped and took off her glasses, letting them hang over her pale-pink bosom.

"Take them all and start with the two green ones – in fact, put them on right now and then again at bedtime."

"Do I keep going till it's all gone or do I rotate them?"

"One at a time. Don't go onto the second until you've completed the first. You might need another bottle if you're not quite finished!"

"How will I know when I've finished?"

"Oh, you'll know! You might even finish before the bottle's empty!"

"What do you mean when you say 'finish'?"

"The bottle will have done its job."

Great, thought Katy, her mind searching for something more solid. How would she know when it had done its job?

Lavinia picked up on her thoughts "Your intuition will tell you. Move on when you intuitively know the bottle's done. Now, let's pack these up for you. That'll be £250, please, dear."

Blimey, I hope it works, thought Katy, counting out the cash from her purse.

"Oh! I almost forgot – you need to take an SRT course, Spiritual Response Therapy, they're telling me it'll help you clear the blockages!"

"They?"

"My guides!"

"What blockages?"

"They didn't say, but I can recommend a brilliant teacher! She's in Brighton – Jane Joyheart – she heads up the UK and I've worked with her before."

I wonder what she changed her name from, thought Katy, probably something perfectly ordinary, like Smith.

By the time she'd arrived home, Katy was craving the color green. Out went the uniform of black, navy and cream, and in came a dark olive jacket she hadn't worn in ages.

That evening she spent an hour going through her wardrobe, retrieving anything olive, sage or forest – and digging out an old pea-green yoga top she'd bought in the sale and never worn. It had always been a shade too green, but now it was perfect.

Taking off the olive jacket, she replaced it with a bottle-green hoodie over the pea-green yoga vest.

"Just checking emails and I'll be with you," she called to Richard, who was laughing at something on the television.

Upstairs in the office, she opened the laptop and stole another look at the enquiry form from last week. She ought to have replied by now, but something had stopped her. She deliberated again. A note from Shanti caught her attention instead.

Hi Katy

How's the name change going? Just been chatting with a customer about an amazing training. Thought of you immediately! You'd love it! SRT. There's a woman in Brighton who teaches basic and advanced – Joyheart – Look her up!

I'm off to Richmond Park next Sunday if you want to join me?

Love

Shanti xx

There wasn't much point in hanging around for a third mention. Katy tapped 'SRT Brighton Joyheart' into the search bar. It came up immediately: Jane Joyheart, SRT, Spiritual Response Therapy – Teacher, Consultant and Practitioner. The website was green, she noticed as she wrote the phone number into her diary.

Hi Shanti

All going okay with the name. I'll call Jane Joyheart tomorrow. Found her number online. Can't make Richmond Park – spending time with Richard. You know how he is! Enjoy!

Love

Katy xx

Richard's voice was booming up the stairs. "Where are you, Kit?"

"Coming!" She hurriedly closed the laptop before skipping down three flights of stairs.

"Blimey – what are you wearing?"

"I'm working with this Aura Soma stuff and I feel compelled to wear green."

Richard screwed up his nose.

"I'm sure it'll pass," she added.

"I bloody hope so!"

Katy was restless. Richard had been asleep for hours as she dipped in and out, her mind jumbled, the bedding twisted as she struggled to find repose. At around 3 am, she rolled onto her back, opened her eyes, and stared up at the ceiling.

"You'll get there!"

"Shhh!"

"Richard can't hear, remember?"

"I can't sleep."

"Your mind's ticking over, thinking about the day, the Aura Soma, the SRT."

"How do you—"

"I wanted to talk to you, but you didn't meditate tonight."

"Decided to spend time with Richard."

"Guilt?"

Katy grimaced. "I feel bad. I've been away on a lot of courses recently."

"They're old enough to look after themselves you know, Katy."

"They might not see it that way."

"And what about Richard? Is he not their father?"

"I suppose."

"Isn't it time you gave to yourself as well as others?"

"But they're my family."

"And you've been there for them."

Katy sighed, pulling her hands from beneath the duvet to expose her arms to the cool night air.

"May I speak with you?"

"You might as well – I'm wide awake!"

"Have you ever noticed how one person might struggle with health while another has problems at work and yet another finds relationships the big challenge?"

"Yes! I see it all the time at work! It depends on what's buried in the subconscious."

"And you're able to help them understand what they're blind to?"

"What's hidden in the shadow, yes. But it's always easier to see the solution to somebody else's problem."

"That's true. But as a therapist, you could observe your own problems and patterns, couldn't you?"

"By seeing them mirrored in other people?"

"Projection is perception. What you see in your clients, you can heal in yourself."

Katy stretched her hands out, then clasped them behind her head. "What I'm projecting from inside of me, is mirrored back by the outside. Classic psychotherapy. What's hidden in my subconscious is there for me to see in my client, or anyone else for that matter."

"Or in the environment. You project out, and the world reflects back. What you see is not reality, but a projection of your *version* of reality – your *perception* – of what 'reality' is to you."

"Some people will see a mouse as a sweet little creature, while others will be terrified of it. It depends on their perception – what they're projecting from their past experiences, which are buried in the psyche. We're all looking at life through the lens of our experiences."

"Absolutely. And you can get an inkling of what's buried if you observe what your reactions are. That's mindfulness, detachment. Watch and don't act automatically."

She lifted herself onto her elbows. "Ah! I see what you mean! If I'm triggered or have a strong reaction to something, it's telling me about my hidden self?"

"Good Lord in Heaven above, you're getting it!"

"And if I dig a bit deeper, unpack what's behind the reaction, I'll be able to see it for what it is."

"And once it's revealed, you can examine it, understand it, look at it in a different *light*."

"Just like therapy, but I'd be both the therapist and the client."

"It's just a matter of noticing what upsets or angers you, then digging beneath to see what's *really* causing it."

"Rather than what I think has caused it," she said, lying back on the pillow again.

"Precisely. But you can only do that if you step back from the emotion. It's catching the moment between cause and effect, between the trigger and the reaction."

Richard turned over in his sleep, letting out a small fart as he went. Katy froze for a moment, watching him carefully in the darkness.

"He can't hear us," the Voice reminded her.

"Oh yes."

"The thing you criticize the most in others, is the thing that tells you more about yourself!"

"Another effect of the mirror."

"And if you can heal it, then next time you'll have a different reaction! The mouse will be a cute pet."

"Which means you're creating a different reality?"

"By Adonai, you're there. You're already doing it for your clients, and you have the skills to do it for yourself."

Katy rolled away from Richard, sliding an arm under the pillow and closing her eyes.

"Now." The Voice spoke softly. "Imagine you're completely relaxed, at rest, nothing to think about except to let go, every part of you on holiday, lazing in the sunshine, the sea gently lapping against the warm silver sand. A boat gently bobs on a cool, calm quilt of shimmering blue, rocked tenderly by waves of warm, comfortable feeling, deeper and deeper asleep."

* * *

"Is that Jane Joyheart?" Katy clamped the phone tighter to her ear.

"Speaking. How can I help?"

"I'm calling about the SRT course."

"You've phoned at exactly the right time! I'm running the basic workshop next weekend and one of my students had to drop out. The place is yours if you'd like it...ooh, the hairs on my arms just stood on end – you're obviously meant to be here. You must be part of this particular soul group!"

"That's short notice – let me check the diary." Katy flipped over the pages knowing there was bound to be something booked in. The following weekend was blank. A strange tingling ran the length of her arms and legs, almost a shiver.

"When's the next course you're running?"

"Not until March next year. Where do you live?"

"I'm in West London."

"My colleague, Brenda, is closer – she's in Teddington – I think she's running the basic soon. Hang on..." There was a rustling in the background. "November 21st, 22nd and 23rd."

"Oh...I can't do that weekend." It was Mother's birthday and she'd never hear the end of it if she didn't go.

"I don't want to influence you, but it seems so synchronistic! Gill only cancelled half an hour ago, and I knew someone would step forward to take her place!"

Chapter 7

Richard sank back in his chair, hands clasped behind his head, long legs stretched under his desk. The phone buzzed. "Put him through, Helen." He unlaced his hands, leaned forward, and lifted the receiver to his ear.

"Not much to report, Guv. Watched 'er for two weeks, per your instructions. Home, Harley Street, Waitrose, 'er friend at number 36, her whacky friend on the bus, a visit across the river to Streatham and the usual shops, cafes, coffee shops. Let me see... Bought an expensive dress in John Lewis on Wednesday, eats that 'orrible bitter chocolate when she thinks no-one's looking. Bought four bars."

"Anything else?"

"Well—"

"What?" Richard leaned forward, switching the receiver to his left ear, and picking up a pen.

"There's this one geyser she seems to be seeing regular, like!"

"Details?"

"Some bloke by the name of Slater. Terry Slater. Sees him at least once a week at his posh house."

"Thanks. Consider the case closed."

"You don't want me to follow up?"

"No."

There was a knock at the door. "Yes!"

Helen shuffled in with a file of papers. "I've managed to book the cottage."

Richard peered at her.

"The one near Ashdown Forest. You just need to confirm what time you'll be arriving."

Richard scanned the details. Perfect. He'd confront his wife about this Terry bloke then whisk her away – surprise her – she was bound to come to her senses and realize he was still a good catch. It was about time he had her to himself! Hopefully, without the bloody green outfit, the flipping angel cards and the latest rubbish she'd been reading. He needed to get her back on the straight and narrow, take control, get things back to normal.

Richard swiveled his chair towards the window, lost in thought. The City, Westminster, then he'd be free. Only another eleven years and he'd be able to retire. Idyllic England beckoned whenever he felt uncertain. His carefully airbrushed dream of the future kept him alive: he and Katy, sitting in striped deckchairs in an English Country Garden. Geraniums in ornate stone pots on a large weathered patio, lawns, delphiniums, hollyhocks, and an old iron seat around an equally old oak tree, somewhere at the bottom of the rolling garden. He'd employ a gardener and read all the books he'd missed in his time-starved plan to get to the top. Sauntering hand-in-hand with his wife, they'd sit on black, shiny, park benches, feeding ducks on the river or seagulls at the beach. There'd be luxury resorts and temperate climates, spas, pampering manservants and obliging handmaidens. Richard's vision of retirement – a genteel England that never really existed. He'd sit in his silk, paisley, smoking-jacket and write his novel on an old-fashioned typewriter in the mornings. After luncheon at the club, he'd take grand pianoforte lessons – he'd always wanted to play – and Katy would slow down at last and sit with him. It was a hackneyed vision but one that gave him hope, one that spurred him on.

Just beneath the carapace of corporate life, he was breaking apart – rotting from the inside out, extinguishing his past, uprooting his origins, discarding them for power, security, and a very middle-class pension. He hated what he did, hated himself if he were honest, which he tried not to be. He could almost smell the stench of self-betrayal.

On Sunday evenings a brooding darkness would engulf and follow him like the ghost of the self he'd killed. Katy accused him of casting a gloomy depression over the entire household. Every Monday he would shake it off as he gritted his teeth, pushed on by the dream, seduced by the day when he'd have accumulated enough. His patient tenacity would pay off, he knew it.

Later that evening, from the vantage point of the sofa, he watched his wife fussing in the kitchen. Why the hell couldn't she leave the washing-up and indulge him? Some kind of Indian mantra was playing softly in the background – over and over it repeated itself. He'd seen Katy lose herself in pet enthusiasms before. The novelty always wore off: Feng Shui, favorite restaurants, step-aerobics, authors, music. She seemed to immerse herself and guzzle at the new until sated, chew the fat till there was nothing left, then discard the bones and move on, realizing it wasn't what she'd wanted after all. Her endless search, for what, she didn't know and nor did he: careers, houses, friends – he'd seen them come and go – and it would be the same with this latest fad. He'd get his Kittykat back, he knew it. He'd bide his time for now and play along. She was bound to realize it was all nonsense, and then she'd be running back to him for a reality check.

"One of these days you're going to dematerialize as you wash up!" he said, with a forced laugh. She turned to him and smiled.

"I've got a surprise, Kit, how do you fancy going away for the weekend? Ashdown Forest, the place that inspired AA Milne and the Hundred Acre Wood." He was beaming from ear-to-ear as he played his trump. He knew she loved Pooh Bear. She'd read the poems to the children when they were young.

"You're joking? You never book anything!" she said, dropping her smile.

"Well, there's always a first."

"Next weekend?" Katy was wiping her hands on a tea towel.

"Yes! Just you, me and the kids!"

"I can't, Rich! I'm booked on a course in Brighton!"

"Why the bloody hell didn't you tell me? I thought you were taking the weekend off?"

"Changed my mind!"

"I thought we were going to spend some time together?"

"I'm sorry, Rich! This course came up spur of the moment!"

"Then cancel it!"

"I can't. I've paid! I always book the holidays and I always check with you, first! Why didn't you check with me?"

She was being ridiculous now.

"Then it wouldn't be a bloody surprise, would it?"

"I'm sorry! I didn't know! Plans change – just like they do with you sometimes!"

It was typical of her to twist it around. She was walking towards him now, arms outstretched, palms open.

"I don't know what the hell's got into you, Katy Stone." Richard's face was thunder, his voice booming now as he stood his full six feet two, flecks of spit leaving his mouth as she came closer. Throwing down the paper, he marched hurriedly past, pushing her out of his way. She was saying something softly to herself.

"Fralinski. It's Katy Fralinski."

He stormed out into the cool evening air. It must have been this Slater chap that had gotten to her. He'd have it out with her right now.

The chimes jangled as he barged back in, knocking them almost off their hook. "And another thing!" He snorted. "I know all about your little tête-a-têtes." He jabbed a finger at her and slammed the door behind him, rousing Tilly and Freddie from their bedrooms.

"What's going on?" they chorused.

"Nothing. Go back to your rooms," bellowed Richard.

"Calm down, Richard. They can hear us."

"I am calm," he shouted. "Do you think I'm stupid?"

"I don't know what you're talking about!" He could see her eyes darting from side to side as she tried to think of an excuse.

"Does the name Slater mean anything to you?"

"Yes, he's—"

"You've been seeing him, haven't you?"

Katy put her sleeve up to her mouth, trying to cover what looked suspiciously like a smile.

"Richard! He's my supervisor! My clinical supervisor!"

"But you only need to see a supervisor once a month – you've been seeing him every week." He wasn't going to let her get away with it. He could see she was rattled.

"And how the hell do you know?"

"You've been spotted, Katherine."

His wife took a deep breath and closed her eyes. She was probably getting her story straight.

"I've been seeing him for a few extra therapy sessions."

"What?"

"I've been feeling a bit," she searched for words, "*low* recently and I thought it would be a good idea to talk it through."

"Why didn't you talk to me about it?"

"You never want to! I tried! And anyway, I needed a professional perspective, Rich, that's all. I swear to you, there's nothing in it!"

Richard stared at her, unflinching, searching her face, the muscle in his jaw twitching.

"Have you seen what Terry Slater looks like?" she said, the beginning of a smile curling at the sides of her mouth.

"I don't care what he looks like, you're not seeing him again." There. He'd put his foot down.

"Rich! He's an old-school psychotherapist and happens to be my clinical supervisor!"

Chapter 8

A small, bald man, impeccably dressed in a stylish suit and polished black brogues, stepped off the train at Paddington station. He made his way across the concourse, stopping at one of the kiosks for coffee and Danish. At the taxi rank outside, he hailed a cab. "The Priory, please."

"Roehampton?"

"Yes."

Forty minutes later, a black London taxi swung into the car park of the Priory Hospital, depositing its bald occupant in front of a large, arched reception door. The man stared up at the iced-cake concoction of white crenelated walls, turreted chimneys, and mullioned windows. Straightening his Italian silk tie and pulling his jacket sleeves down over his solid silver cufflinks, he straightened himself up and mounted the wide, shallow steps to reception.

Opulent chairs, a plush carpet and an antique chandelier did nothing to hide the institutionalized smell of disinfectant. A polished maple table, laden with shiny copies of Country Life, Harper's Bazaar and GQ magazines dominated the room. Rifling under the latest editions, he found an old copy of Esquire and sat waiting to be called.

Following his initial visit, he was about to experience his first one-to-one session with Dr. Watkins. He would be 'taking his history'.

After some preliminaries – name, date of birth, occupation – the questions began to probe a little deeper.

"Tell me about your parents."

"Dad's not around much. He's Italian by birth but moved here as a young man – that's how he met my very British mother. Mum died almost a year ago. Lung cancer."

"I'm sorry for your loss. How are you coping?"

"Gave up smoking on the spot! I loved Mum. She was decent.

Put up with a lot of shit from Dad. He wasn't exactly the loyal husband."

"Go on."

"The hospital told us we grieve in different ways. We weren't that close – not as close as I'd like to have been. She wasn't that sort of Mum. She was quiet but firm. Brought us up strict Catholic. Had a keen sense of right and wrong."

"And have you inherited her sense of right and wrong?"

"I'm not sure what you're getting at?"

"Just asking if you're like your mother in that regard?"

"Do you think I've done something bad?"

"Not at all," said Dr. Watkins, making a note on his pad. "What would happen if you had done something bad?"

"How do you mean? Are you accusing me?"

"Not at all! Just asking how you'd feel?"

The bald man stared down at the edge of the desk, hesitating for a moment. "Afraid, I guess." He paused. "And guilty."

"And Father? Were you – are you – close to him?"

"In many ways, yes. I didn't inherit his Italian looks – I've got my mum's pale coloring – but I've got his quick temper – and definitely his Latin libido!"

"Is that why you're here?"

The bald man blushed, lowered his eyes to his lap and fiddled with his left cufflink. "Partly."

"We'll get to that in good time. Let's continue with your childhood. Any siblings?"

"My sister, Maria, she's two years younger than me. After she was born, my Dad was away a lot and their marriage fell apart. They slept in separate rooms. It was a bit of a pretense but they stayed together. Dad's still in the house – with his new fancy woman."

"And what about your sister?"

"Married with two kids, lives in South London. She's a teacher. Happy enough. We get on well, not when we were kids though. We used to fight. She gets cross with me sometimes. Just doesn't get me."

"In what way?"

"Opposite views on the world, that sort of thing – but we've learned to accept each other. Mostly."

"Tell me about your childhood."

"When I was young, we lived near Southampton. But I spent most of my childhood in Surrey, in a small market town. Dad was away a lot. We didn't see him much. Mum was the usual housewife. I think she was depressed. We were close, but she wasn't very cuddly – could be a bit of a moral compass. Nagged sometimes, but she was always there for us. She was the one who made me change schools. That's why we moved in the first place, actually."

"Tell me more about that."

"I was almost albino as a kid – and small. The other boys used to bully me, call me names, tease me. The usual nonsense. I got beaten up in the toilets once. Not badly – but enough to make me scared of school."

"I'm sorry to hear that. Tell me more." Dr. Watkins' soft, dark eyes watched him, holding him in their encouraging gaze.

"Mum tried to help me but those bastards weren't going to give in that easily, were they?"

Dr. Watkins nodded. "What happened next?"

"We moved. Mum found me another school. I realized I was quite bright and if I got my head down and tried, the teachers would respect me, but I needed to get the other kids on board." The bald man stared at something invisible, slightly to his right.

Dr. Watkins watched the bald man's eye movements, his facial expressions, his body language. The man had his knees together, his toes pointing inwards, his feet raised with the heels stretched upwards. He was burying his clamped hands between his thighs and leaning over, his back slightly bent, his shoulders slumping forward, his high forehead wrinkled. Dr. Watkins waited as he noted the signs.

"When I was older, at secondary school, I started to rebel a bit – found the hot Latino blood in me! I got into trouble. Nothing drastic. Bunking off, pranks, scraps with other boys, lifting girl's skirts – petty stuff like that."

"And how did you manage the scraps?"

"My dad had given me some weights to play with in the garage. I started cycling as well – my old man loved watching bike races, he still does, that's how I got into it. I started doing press-ups, too, and learned how to defend myself. I still cycle by the way. Keeps me fit."

"So, you spent some happy times with your father?"

"When he was there, yes. Mum used to moan we were two peas in a pod."

"What did she mean by that?"

"Drinking, smoking...dirty magazines."

Dr. Watkins inadvertently raised an eyebrow.

"The usual 'top-shelf' stuff they had in those days. Quite tame really," said the man.

"How old were you then?"

"About fourteen, I guess. That's when I started to fill out, grow hair – raging hormones and all that. I was a looker in those days, and I knew it!"

Dr. Watkins scribbled some notes while the man reached for his glass of water, almost draining it in one go.

"Carry on."

"I learned how to seduce women. Copied my dad. He was a charmer with the ladies. Watched his style and emulated it."

"So, you were popular with the girls?"

"In those days, I could probably have had more or less any girl I wanted."

"That sounds very confident for a fourteen-year-old?"

The bald man's mouth stretched into a wide smile as his mesmerizing blue eyes twinkled. His knees opened, his heels dropped to the ground and he leaned back in the chair, the flats of his palms on his strong thighs.

"I was about fifteen by then. Something happened. I just became popular – with the girls and the boys, not *that* way, I mean, they saw me as cool – and it somehow made up for the years of being shunned."

"What happened next?"

"It got out of hand. I could charm the pants off the girls, and it became a sort of game. How many could I chase down? How many would capitulate, if you get my drift?"

"And how many did 'capitulate'?"

The bald man laughed. "Not many in the early days, but I got better with practice. And as they got older, you know…"

"There were more substantial conquests?"

"I got my rocks off more often, if that's what you mean – and I got good at it too!" he said, widening his cobalt eyes as he smiled broadly.

"And how did that make you feel?"

"How would you feel? Bloody powerful!"

"Happy?"

"I was never happier than when I'd won a conquest."

"And afterwards?" Dr. Watkins probed further.

The bald man hunched over slightly, his knees pulling together, revealing the outline of sinewed muscles beneath his suit. He stared at the floor for a moment, deep in thought. "It was never enough – the thrill of the chase, the sex, the girls. I probably felt a bit guilty. Felt bad."

"And how did you deal with that?"

"Not confession, that's for sure! The Catholic Church had lost me. I just kept going! Every time I got a new girl, I felt better. Funny really…"

"Why?"

"I hated girls before. They'd stood around giggling in their silly frocks and plaited pigtails – laughing at me while some

brute was pushing me around in the corner of the playground."
The bald man frowned and sat up straight. "I suppose I felt
powerful over them in the end. I could do what the fuck I liked!"

"*Anything* you liked?"

"I never abused anyone. Never forced it. I didn't have to.
I could twist them round my little finger most of the time. I
learned to treat them a bit mean to keep them keen, but only so
far…that was the trick. Be nice, be easy-going, don't threaten,
then be a bit mean."

"In what way were you mean?"

"Not calling them when I said I would, not making any
commitment, looking at other women – that sort of thing."

"And did that continue?"

"For a while. I was into dirty magazines and learning about
women and what they liked."

"From the magazines?"

The man's head nodded. Dr. Watkins opened his mouth as if
to say something but must have thought better of it.

"I did feel guilty though. I hadn't been to confession and I
was, you know, relieving myself a lot as well as doing it with
girls. Part of me knew it couldn't last and I'd end up burning in
hell!"

"And did you?"

"In a manner of speaking…"

"What happened?"

"When I got to university, I realized I had to sober up. I
couldn't go on playing the field as hard as I had."

"You were drinking too?"

"Drinking, smoking, magazines, girls."

"Carry on."

"I was growing up, I guess. Realized it was a teenage thing,
except that was the problem, I was acting grown up but the
teenager was still coursing through my veins. Then disaster
struck." He hesitated then lowered his voice. "I started losing

my hair at the age of nineteen."

"That must have been difficult for you. How did you handle it?"

"I panicked. It was falling out fast. By the time I was twenty, I was bald. Thought it was Divine retribution." He finished the water in one large gulp before setting the glass down and continuing. "I didn't think I could get girls anymore. I mean, who would want to go out with a short, bald man? I hid in my room for months. Felt terrible."

"Did you tell anyone? Was there a college counsellor?"

"Nope. Kept it to myself. That was my annus horribilis."

"Did you continue with the magazines?"

The bald man's face turned a pale shade of pink as he shuffled in his chair. "And worse."

Dr. Watkins raised both eyebrows before recomposing his neutral expression.

"I developed a predilection for prostitutes."

"Tell me more about that."

"Not much to tell really. A few times with a couple of different girls. Nothing *too* kinky." He said, running a finger beneath his collar. "Quite an exciting experience for a young man."

"Anything else that you feel is important?"

The bald man cleared his throat. "I had an air of mystery surrounding me, and some of the ladies that I'd chatted up before got curious. In the end, I found that being bald didn't make much difference. Of course, at that age, quite a few of them wanted classic good looks, the tall, dark type, but the sensitive ones – they were all over me."

"And then?"

"I knew I had to settle down, so I started going steady. It was the first time I'd had a relationship that lasted more than a few weeks."

"The swing of the pendulum."

The man looked up at Dr. Watkins, his brow furrowed.

"You swung from playing the field to the opposite – settling down at an early age. We often find personalities swinging from one extreme to the other. It's a way of compensating for perceived deficiencies. But what triggered this turn of events?"

"I don't know – I had the feeling I had to conform! My dad was annoyed with me and my mum was disappointed. They always thought I'd amount to nothing – piss it all away – the charm, the intellect. I had to prove them wrong."

"And how did you do that?"

"I signed up for the Royal Air Force after graduation. Mum and Dad couldn't believe it. Didn't think I'd have the staying power. But I proved them wrong."

"Carry on."

"I stayed! Did well, then got married in my early twenties. It seemed like the right thing to do. The RAF like a married officer. See it as a stable influence. It means you get a nice quarter to live in."

"And how was married life?"

"Disastrous, if I'm honest. We were young and came from different backgrounds. It was never going to last. We were miserable."

"What about the sex life?"

"I lost interest pretty early on. Went back to the magazines. She didn't seem to mind. I don't think she even knew."

"And the prostitutes?"

The bald man nodded. "Only once or twice, and not at home – only when I was away with the Force."

"Divorce?"

"Yes. Then threw myself into my career and worked my way up the ranks."

"Still single?"

"No. Married my second wife, who was friends with Caroline."

"Caroline?"

"My first wife." He paused. "My second wife was the ex of one of my colleagues, so she knew what it was like to be an RAF girlfriend. She'd always fancied me, she said. Actually, she made the first move! That was a turn up for the books! Someone chasing me! I fell for her. Who wouldn't? A powerhouse of a woman who's never satisfied. Tall, slim, model's legs, long dark hair, works in the City."

"Never satisfied sexually?"

"Never satisfied with bloody anything – especially me! I sometimes think she's got me under her thumb."

"And has she?"

"I don't know. Put it this way – we're together. Just. It's been ten years now. We've got a daughter."

Dr. Watkins seemed to sense the tone of voice, the marginal turning away of the head, the slight pursing of the lips.

"Tell me about your daughter."

"She's a sweetie, but she's hard work. Don't get me wrong – I love her to bits. She's got ADHD and she's dyslexic. Struggles at school. Her mum's not really there for her – she went back to work when Amber was just a few weeks old. I try my best, but I have to work, too, you know?" The bald man buried his head in his hands and leaned further forward. Dr. Watkins noted the genuine emotion, the love, the despair, the longing to be able to do something.

"How old is she?" he asked in a soothing tone.

"She's a millennial. She'll be nine next year."

"And what about your wife?"

"She's younger than me."

"Tell me about your relationship."

"She's high maintenance, terrifying at times. She's taller than me, dresses in Austin Reed, and is totally unapproachable! She's a woman in a man's world – works at a big merchant bank in the Square Mile. They call her 'the Ice Maiden'."

"She refuses you sex?"

"No. Quite the opposite. She demands sex, but she's not very loving. The ice maiden suits her. She's cold, emotionally, a ball-breaker of a woman, and well…"

"Do you feel emasculated?"

"More like castrated! I can't always get it up, and when I can, I can't finish the job. She gets angry with me and I get sore – or limp – and it makes the whole thing worse."

"And is that why you're here?"

"No. She says I'm an alcoholic. I disagree. We drink a lot in the mess and I love my fine wines and brandies. It's a drinking culture, but I'm not an alcoholic. She asked me to do something about my addiction, but she doesn't know I'm here. Personally, I'm more worried about the porn, and the sex – or lack of it. With the internet, I've progressed from dirty magazines. I read an article that said you become desensitized to the real thing. Did it initially so I could get it up, but got carried away. Look, it's nothing terrible. I'm not some kind of pervert, but I'm looking at the sites more than I should. At least once every evening, most mornings, and often in the day as well. I feel bad. She's making demands, I can't deliver, but in the privacy of my study…"

"And if things were more harmonious between you and your wife, would you still be resorting to this pattern?"

"Not to the extent that I am, I don't think."

"And how long have you been using pornography in this way?"

"Since my daughter was born. I didn't feel the same about Lauren, and when she abandoned the poor kid and went back to work full-time, something inside me broke."

"And how do you feel about your wife, Lauren, now?"

"I hate to admit it, but I feel used. Hen-pecked, even. I'm just her lackey – fixing the house, taking her places, looking after our daughter."

"Have you been for counselling?"

"We tried but her job's demanding and she missed one of

the appointments. My heart wasn't in it, so we quit after three or four sessions. She accused me of not taking it seriously – and never tires of reminding me that she paid for it all!"

"She makes a big thing of money?"

"She's the big earner. I do what I can to contribute."

"It sounds as if it's not working between you and your wife. Could that be the cause of your issues?"

"I don't know. Sometimes I think it is, other times I think I've got a problem. I have to steel myself against sitting in front of that screen more often! It could easily slip into four or five times a day!"

"We'll get to the bottom of it. That's why you're here." Dr. Watkins hesitated before closing the session. "Was there anything else?" The bald man seemed to have had an insight and Dr. Watkins sensed it.

"Yes. I can't help thinking that if I were in the right relationship, the sex, and everything else, would take care of itself!"

Chapter 9

November 2008

Katy stood on the top landing in front of the mirror, her hands in her pockets, looking at the space around her reflection. She took a deep breath, leaned in slightly, and tentatively whispered. "Just to be clear. Do we create our experience of life mostly from unconscious thoughts that we're projecting?"

"Not all of your experience, but a good deal, yes. That, and habitual patterns," said the Voice.

"And they mostly stem from childhood?"

"Generally, yes."

"Hang on – we're constructing our lives based on the beliefs of a toddler?"

"More frequently than you might imagine."

"So, Freud was right, we're conditioned in the first five years of life?"

"Yes. Have you seen the film, *The Matrix*?"

"What's that got to do with it?"

"It's not far from the truth. You're mostly living an illusion, but one that you've created, along with those in positions of power."

"That's what the Eastern Philosophers said."

"People reproduce what already exists – either through habit, or because they notice what's currently there."

"And if it's there, we believe in it."

"Yes. It's a self-limiting behavior."

"We're limited by our own beliefs. I've heard that before. So, we're trapped in a reality of our own making?"

"And that leads to the question 'what is real?'" the Voice had a mirthful quality. "You think things 'happen' to you, but mostly it's you that has set it in motion."

"Aren't there exceptions? Surely some things just happen?"

"There are collective creations, like pollution, or crime. And then there are karmic ones from past lives!"

Katy grimaced. "Paying the price in this life for something you did in another?"

The Voice carried on. "Sometimes your soul engineers a situation, to grow from it."

"Like Neo in the Matrix, learning from Morpheus?"

"Yes."

"Is that why things happen over and over?"

"If you don't understand first time, you'll get an alternative setting and different characters."

"But the same pattern until we finally twig."

"Then it goes away."

"And it's always something about ourselves? We're made aware of an unconscious pattern so we can resolve it – that's how therapy works."

"And that's why you can overcome your challenges and re-write the screenplay of your life. Think of it as a film. You're the writer and the director. You can change the ending."

"How?"

"Your childhood programming wasn't your responsibility – but how you resolve it, and what you make of your life as an adult, is."

"That's interesting…" Katy sat down in front of the mirror.

"Notice the story you're telling, the things you say often to self and others."

"Neurons that fire together, wire together. But what's the new ending to the story? How do I know what to go for?"

"Dare to dream, Katy. Choose the greatest of your visions, your good imaginings, the ones you see when you're not thinking, the ones that feel impossible, those that thrill you – and stick with them. They're the new ending."

"But …" She was about to ask where the ideas would come from.

"Sit in silence or walk in nature, take a shower or chop wood! When you stop thinking, the answers come."

Katy frowned. "But I'm too busy to rewrite the future!"

"Have you decided life's busy? Is that what you think and say?" The Voice paused. "In a literal sense, you're making it so! You're forming a neural pathway in the brain that links 'life' and 'busy' with 'overwhelmed'."

"Oh my God, you're right!"

"I AM. You've heard of neuroplasticity? Rewire yourself! Start associating 'life' with something else – 'fulfilling', 'exciting' or 'peaceful'. And whatever you decide to do, for goodness' sake, do it because you love it and want to do it."

"What do you mean?"

"Do things because they bring you joy and make you feel good – because that's what you came here to do."

"But..."

"Mankind creates good things, too, but many people are unwittingly pessimistic."

"Why?"

"You're subject to negative influences that are constantly bombarding you."

"The collective unconscious? All the fearmongering? We worry about the petty stuff and the things that are wrong, rather than concentrating on what's good and what's right!"

"It's human nature."

"What can we do about it?"

"Choose which thoughts to cultivate, and which to ignore."

"Are we talking about designing things? We can't influence everything in our lives, can we?"

"From the wheel to the iPhone, from Bach to Bob Dylan, you are creators. Whether that's inventions, art or music, or whether that's circumstances, relationships, opportunities or challenges. You generate it all!"

Katy was staring into the distance, trying to fathom it all.

"Discover yourself, who you really are, not who you were conditioned to be," said the Voice. "Then you'll know the ending you want for your film." There was a pause. "Understand there are Greater Powers and Forces in the Universe. Harness the quantum field. Everything is energy and vibration, including the activity in your brain."

"What does that mean?"

"It means you can influence reality."

"Mind over matter!"

The Voice chuckled. "And you can use your mind to survive your box life or to seek something more noble and fulfilling."

"Noble? Like what?"

"The evolution of the soul, of humanity itself!"

"That's profound." Katy fell silent as her mind knitted it all together. Leaving the mirror, she shuffled into the office and pulled out the meditation stool.

"Tell me how it works."

The Voice had followed her. "Think of a gardener." There was a pause. "She plants a seed but has to wait for it to sprout. Maybe the roots are delving beneath the surface. She sees nothing but knows it's growing. Each day, she waters and waits. If she plants an apple pip, a tree will eventually grow, and providing she tends to it, she'll reap many apples."

"Hmm. It'd take years, though!"

"And while she's waiting, she can plant carrots, herbs, strawberries, pansies – things that grow quickly!"

"Hmm."

"You reap what you sow and it's the same with ideas. You play your part and creation collaborates. The pip won't grow without mother nature, and it won't thrive unless you plant and water it."

"I see what you mean," said Katy. "And no amount of tinkering or worrying is going to make any difference – or make it grow faster. You've got to plant it, give it what it needs and have faith it'll grow." It was starting to make sense now. "And you know it's going to be an apple tree, even when it looks like a stem and a couple of leaves."

"Quite so. Think of your dreams as seeds being planted in the womb of time. You nurture them, tend to them and let nature take its course."

"But they'll come to fruition in their own time and in their own way? Like a baby taking nine months in the womb – you can't make it come sooner?"

"Pretty much."

"Otherwise you're trying to open a rosebud with your fingers, rather than let it unfold in the sun. I use that metaphor with my clients sometimes."

"I know…and it's a good one. Many people are either planting seeds then forgetting to water them, or losing faith when you don't see immediate growth, or planting what's already in the garden!"

"Or letting it self-seed! What about the weeds? They just keep growing!"

"If you're spending all your time weeding, the apple tree isn't going to get planted, let alone come to fruition!"

"What are the weeds, metaphorically speaking?"

"All the thoughts that sabotage you – mostly fears and doubts. But some weeds condition the soil. Pull out the big thistles and thorns but leave the rest."

"And if you ignore the weeds and plant a tree, you'll get fruit." She laughed. "The weeds will grow, but who cares when you have an apple tree?"

"Less so when you have a whole garden of beauty! Some people swing between the thing they want, and the doubt they'll get it!"

"Big weeds and a small apple tree?"

"Yes!" the Voice chuckled, "They plant a good idea, the doubts creep in and it withers, so to speak. You need consistency."

"And I guess you have to give things time and space to grow. It takes a while to cultivate a mature garden."

"And don't forget to enjoy the process! A tree doesn't strain and flowers don't stress!"

"Don't try too hard?"

"Take delight in each stage, in each season, in each cycle, just as a child does, just as the gardener does!"

* * *

"Blimey, Kittykat, you look like the Jolly Green Giant!" said Richard, leaning in to peck her on the cheek. She looked down at her outfit. Olive, linen trousers, spring-green t-shirt, and a sage, wool jacket with a bottle-green and lime scarf.

"I should be back around eight-ish. I've left a lasagna in the fridge. Tilly can heat it up and steam some veggies. Freddie's seeing Tom later – his mum's collecting him after rugby, and he'll get the bus back."

"Drive safely, Kit – I know what you're like with the loud pedal." Richard smiled, more at his own wit than at Katy.

"I will. Thai takeaway later? I won't have eaten. They'll probably go to the pub afterwards, but I'll head back."

She wished she could stay at the B&B that Jane had recommended, but how could she desert her family? The drive home would be tiring but Richard was rubbish at anything domestic, and she didn't want them to think she didn't care. She'd been let off the leash for a while but had to stay in Richard's good books.

Katy threw her mac over her arm, picked up her new khaki-green handbag and left, whispering, "Bye-bye, Constantine!" to the house. "Look after the kids. I'll be back later." She had a habit of naming houses and cars, then talking to them as if they were people. Richard ignored her. The children thought it was fun at first, but they'd long grown out of it.

The car, Beauty, purred into action, and Katy took off through the manicured streets of Turnham Green, crossing the river and negotiating the metropolis of sprawling South London.

She was compelled to press on with this spiritual stuff, regardless of guilt, seemingly spurred on by the presence of something – like a loving hand gently urging her forward. It felt lately as if invisible tracks kept her fixed to a course that was not hers to determine. Her life had become an unpredictable ride that she had to see through to the finish. She'd spoken to Shanti about it over a soy latte in town. "You're being fast-tracked," she'd said. What did that mean exactly? Shanti always said 'spirit are' like it was a collective that was helping from some unknown vantage point. Surely 'spirit' was singular? It ought to have been 'spirit is' – like the Holy Spirit – a singular entity that permeated everything. Shanti had said, "Spirit are taking you to where you need to be – lining you up for the next step." Whatever that was! Katy was enjoying herself. It was an exciting new game and she was learning the lingo and rules of engagement.

As she approached the M25, she slipped an Eckhart Tolle CD into the narrow slot on the dashboard. A soft, even monotone filled the car. Her mind wandered. She loved her new group of friends. They were the few, she thought, the 'elect' that 'got it'. She fancied they were all part of a parallel world of alternative-minded, conscious people – awake, aware of something more – inhabiting a reality that others neither saw nor recognized. It was like being part of a secret society: The New-Age Masons. No. She didn't want to be associated with the Masons. It was mostly men and weird handshakes, wasn't it? She grimaced, turning her attention to the road for a moment. Eckhart was still talking in the background as she overtook a stream of cars, ever watchful for speed cameras.

A private club, she thought. Now, what would the admission criteria be? You'd have to have heard of the *Bhagavad Gita* – maybe read it, or at least listened to an audio version – and you probably needed to read *Power Versus Force* so you'd know what level of consciousness you were resonating at. And all members would have a pristine copy of *A Course in Miracles* on their bookshelf – even if they'd never studied the lessons or looked at the text. Perhaps they'd have read *A Return to Love* instead and got the gist of it. Of course, they'd all know it was her – Marianne Williamson – who'd penned the famous quote that everyone thought was Nelson Mandela's: 'Our deepest fear is not that we are inadequate…but, that we're powerful beyond measure.' Something like that. Katy thought she'd got it wrong – her own deepest fear really was that she was totally bloody inadequate – a fraud who was about to be found out!

Eckhart Tolle was still droning on in the background. Something about the pain body. Katy made a mental note of her surroundings. Two more junctions till the M23.

They would all struggle to understand Krishnamurti, she thought, picking up her train of thought, and pretend to hate The Secret (but secretly watch it – ha!) What else? They'd all know about the Mayan calendar and 2012 and they'd all pretend to understand what Bruce Lipton was talking about. Actually, epigenetics made total sense to her as a therapist.

Junction 7 was looming. Katy indicated, slowed down to the speed limit, and began to cross to the inside lane. Eckhart was saying something about the past and the future.

Back to her friends. Some of them had seen strange apparitions at night. She wasn't sure how she'd feel about that – it could be scary. She'd sensed the presence of angels but she'd never seen a UFO or anything. Tara and Ben had – they'd shown her a picture of three pyramidal formations of light which they said had hovered over a field near Stonehenge before mysteriously disappearing. Her new associates loved crystals and they could tell you their individual properties: citrine was for abundance; rose quartz was for love. They knew all this stuff, and that brought comfort to Katy. It meant she wasn't going mad. She knew it was odd, a psychotherapist with voices in her head, but it was a single, loving Voice – compassionate, wise, informative – and she was lapping it up.

Katy exited the slip road onto the M23. Eckhart had faded into the background and her thoughts took over again. She'd put her cynicism to one side and decided to embrace this roller-coaster she found herself living. It was fascinating – all these new insights – and she was beginning to share her experiences, one or two even with Richard. Of course, she still worried people might think she was bonkers, but friends like Shanti and Tara helped her to see it was the rest of the world that was mad, not her. Of course, she'd never, ever tell her family – they'd humiliate her, tearing her beliefs to shreds. And she'd never tell anyone about the Voice.

Eckhart was talking about being intensely present. She couldn't concentrate – perhaps it was his tone and the fact he kept repeating himself. How many times had he said, "in this moment now"? Katy's mind drifted to the exquisiteness of the English countryside. The morning light drew her attention from the invariable pitch of Mr. Tolle, and the sporadic traffic that trundled along the M23. A soft bank of late autumn mist spread itself across the South Downs where treetops punctured the low-lying fog, appearing to float trunkless above it. Swallows, their silhouettes darting across the palest blue, swooped and circled before landing on a wire. It arrested her. She was frozen in time at the breath-taking beauty. A car cut in front, sounding its horn, the driver shooting her the customary two fingers. "Fuckwit," she said out loud, swerving across two lanes to a chorus of hooting as she realized she was about to sail past her exit.

Eckhart had stopped and she ejected the CD, replacing it with Handel's Messiah. She hadn't got a clue what he'd been talking about anyway. A crescendo of orchestral sound filled the car. She listened with grim determination. It would raise her vibration ready for the SRT course, she thought, trying to appreciate what she could only think of as bombastic classical. She should have brought Bach's Cello Suites. They were more her style. On the way home, she'd listen to her music, cool music, the stuff her inner boho loved.

As the road ahead cleared, Katy slipped the convertible into sixth gear. Above the strains of the Hallelujah Chorus, her mind raced. She thought about her secret club, her clients, her family, and how much she loved driving the open road, especially unencumbered by children or anyone else for that matter, and especially fast. She'd have made a good Formula One driver – maybe a female Stig – or a 'star in a reasonably priced car' – her name up there on the board with Gordon Ramsey's. Blimey, over a hundred, she noted on the speedometer, she'd better slow down.

Winding through the villages just outside Brighton, her mind was smoothly ticking over. The secret society was like a shoal of bright, spiritual people, tumbling along the same crystal waters. They gathered at seminars, read similar books, discussed metaphysics and mentors, and saw the importance of connecting with nature and sitting in silence. The waterway was peppered with crucial co-ordinates which they swam towards, mysteriously guided by intuitive forces, each following their unique path through the rapids and into deep pools and warm shallows. Not everyone would read the same books or attend the same lectures, but they'd all be led according to their needs. They might swim alone then re-group, only to split and re-join later. Alone, yet in the same shimmering stream, alone, yet part of the shoal – the current carrying them towards the Light, taking them home. It was all about learning, growing, and discovering.

We're never truly alone, she thought, and with that came the realization that everything was connected. She remembered something Thich Nhat Hanh had said: "See this blank piece of paper? Can you see the cloud in it? No? If you look very carefully, you can see. Without the cloud, there would be no rain. Without the rain, there would be no tree. Without the tree, this piece of paper would not exist." We do nothing alone. We're inter-dependent…but we need to be self-accountable, otherwise, we'd become the spanner in the works.

The car stopped abruptly at a T-Junction. Katy had lost track of where she was and had no idea which way to turn. 'Left,' she heard the thought as if it had been planted there, clear and certain. Following the road through, she picked up a sign for a familiar-sounding village and glancing at her hand-written directions, she sped off.

It was dawning on her as she drove that fellowship, sharing and co-operation were more important than grabbing what you could. We need to work together, she thought, but we can't do that until everyone's ready – till we're all consciously aware. You had to be awakened to the bigger picture, to the invisible threads that connected each pearl – had to realize the cloud was right there in the paper! Everybody had to play their part, but many were still stuck in the old paradigm: Pass go, collect £200, buy a better box for yourself. Win, lose, compare and compete.

Katy slowed down, looking for the *Jolly Farmer* sign that Jane had said was about a hundred meters from the entrance to her cottage. Having parked the car, she picked her way along a small, brick path, leading up to a chocolate-box thatch with its half-timbered upper floor and red-brick base. The windows were tiny, the chimney stack tall, the flowerbeds awash with roses, lilac, and lavender. There was a kitchen garden to the side, well stocked with herbs, vegetables and poles on which runner beans must have grown. She took a deep breath before lifting the forged iron door knocker.

A slim woman in an expensive trouser suit, sleek cropped hair and a horsey silk scarf draped loosely over her shoulders, opened the small cottage door. Jane Joyheart was nothing like Katy had imagined. "You must be Katy? Come through to the kitchen and make yourself a drink," she said in BBC-perfect enunciation. "We're just waiting for a few more before we start."

There was a vast choice of herbal teas, a jar of instant coffee and a box of regular tea bags. Katy made herself a ginger and lemon before taking a shortbread finger from a plate of biscuits. She noticed a tray containing various types of milk: goat's, rice, skimmed and organic full cream. One or two of the group were already chatting as the others arrived in ones and twos.

"How was the journey?" said a small, Indian woman. "The one here, I mean." She smiled. "Not Brandon Bays'!"

Katy joined in the pun. "The spiritual journey or the one from London this morning?"

As they gathered in the large kitchen, conversations were struck up. It was as if they'd known each other for years. We're all part of the shoal, thought Katy. She felt connected to them in a way she didn't with the mums at school and her old book circle friends.

"I think we're all here," said Jane. "Let's move into the sitting room."

The group were about to learn the art of dowsing with a pendulum. It was a necessary requirement before moving on to the complex charts, numbers and detailed sheets that formed the core of Spiritual Response Therapy – SRT. Katy diligently took it all in. *Do it with the intention of succeeding beyond expectation, but don't let perfect be the enemy of excellent* – her motto and her hallmark – it won her the results she craved, but at a price. By tea break, she could feel a stiffness in her shoulders.

Lunch was a vegetarian buffet. I'm not sure I belong here, thought Katy, oscillating between a sense of homecoming and a feeling of hovering on the margins. It seemed almost mandatory in spiritual circles to stop eating animals. Katy wasn't sure if she wanted to be part of this club. The last thing she wanted was to be one of those kooky-types that stuck out like a mutt at Crufts – but if she was going to be aware of the cloud in the paper, she'd better start thinking about what she was eating. Her mouth started watering at the thought of succulent steaks, oven-roasted lamb with rosemary, pan-fried seabass with capers. Shanti had told her meat was bad for the colon – it was too dense energetically, she'd said, and you needed to lighten up to become enlightened. Besides, you took on the energetic stress of the animal when you ate it. Katy hadn't taken it too seriously at the time but now she was having second thoughts. Having helped herself to the buffet, she munched her way through raw broccoli with chili and sesame, shredded beetroot and cashew salad, fried tofu in tamari and a generous helping of salad. She felt bloated and full, yet curiously hungry.

"We've decided to go completely vegan," said Jane. "It's the only way to go if you care about the planet."

"And if you're serious about your work!" said a tall, skinny man with a beard and ponytail.

Work? Thought Katy. Surely this stuff's just a hobby – something to keep us from going insane.

"When I was a lawyer in the City," said Jane, "we used to dine out a lot on meat – and a quantity of red." She helped herself to a huge pile of watercress. "We've cut out the meat – but still quaff the vino!"

"What made you quit town?" asked the Indian lady.

"Came to our senses. We realized there was more to life. This cottage, the work I'm doing now, the garden – it's a million miles away from our old London life, and I love it. We've never once regretted leaving."

"We?"

"My husband, Barney and I – and the dogs of course."

"Were you always Joyheart?" asked Katy.

"My maiden name was Hamilton – changed to Joyheart when I married Barney."

Katy could feel the beginnings of a migraine. The stiffness in her shoulders had crept up the right side of her neck to the base of her head. She took two paracetamols.

The group carried plates into the kitchen before resuming.

"Now you've learned the basics," Jane said, "I want you to go through the first eight charts, dowse for blockages and clear them for yourselves. I'll come around and check accuracy as we go."

The group bent over their workbooks, pendulums in hands.

"Remember, we're clearing from soul level! This stuff's been around for aeons. You've all incarnated for hundreds, even thousands of lifetimes."

"Do we have to prep to work every time?" asked a shy young woman.

"Yes. You need to make sure you're aligned with High Self. It's the part that's guiding us – when it can get past the ego – like a puppeteer that's pulling the strings."

"Why High Self?"

"It's the greater part of us that has a higher perspective," said Jane. "Imagine you lived in a block of flats. If you lived on the top floor, you'd see a lot more of the surroundings than if you lived on the ground floor. High Self is on the top floor. You're in the basement."

Katy and the others were rapt.

"The soul picks up discordant energies, vows, curses, blocks, limiting beliefs, programs, patterns, you name it, as it travels its path through different experiences. We're going to clear those blocks – some of which have been around for millennia."

"Is High Self the same as the I Am Presence?" asked a dark, olive-skinned woman with a middle European accent.

Katy could see them coming to blows over semantics. High Self, Soul, Overself, Greatness, Divine Self – were they all the same or different? As a therapist, she'd worked on her 'self' – the person she identified with – me, myself and I. Now it seemed she was to work on a greater Self that was yet to be understood.

By tea break, Katy had cleared 'sexual relationships and love' which had apparently been blocked ninety-five percent at soul level. A swing of the pendulum, a few words directed at High Self – and several lifetimes of thwarted love and sex were done away with. Jane had checked for accuracy, her pendulum confirming one hundred and ten percent clear. "I know what you're thinking," she'd said, "how can it be over a hundred? Well, we're working on different dimensions."

"So is that good?" Katy had asked, "I mean, is it cleared?"

"Yes! It's marvelous! You're spot on!"

Katy beamed. "Powerful stuff!"

"And very high level."

Reflecting on it later as she savored a cup of orange-colored 'builder's tea', she started to wonder about the whole thing. What utter bullshit, she could imagine Richard saying, and he was probably right. All she'd done was waggle a pendulum around. If anything were to happen, like suddenly wanting to jump on her husband and make passionate love, then it had to be placebo. The part of her brain that believed it was cleared would rewire the part that continually recoiled at sex with Rich – and as a result it (and hopefully she) would dutifully perform. Perhaps they should investigate placebo, because it could be the golden panacea the world had been looking for all along. Sham knee operations that worked, the lifting of depression and even the curing of cancer had all been documented under the mysterious 'placebo effect'. Katy felt a pang of guilt as she returned to her original train of thought. She'd lost interest in Richard years ago. Was it her problem or his? The man she'd met had changed, his ideals faded and gone, along with the chemicals of romance. The wall-of-suit that had swept her off her feet had very quickly turned into something else. She'd sensed his steeliness, his fear of vulnerability, his lack of connection, as if he were far away. The foul breath in the mornings, the farts at night, and the glimpses beneath his armor, had eroded her affection. It had happened so slyly that neither had noticed. The charm he'd used to win her over had dwindled once they were married but she'd done what she could to make it work. It was probably her fault – that's what had led her to therapy in the first place. If only she could change, it would be okay.

By the time the group returned for their final session, the right side of Katy's head was starting to pulse as a wave of familiar nausea rose from her stomach. In just a few hours her head would feel as if someone had put a pickaxe through her right eye. The two paracetamols would be about as effective as using a dandelion clock to hit a cricket ball.

The bearded man was having an asthma attack. Everyone dropped what they were doing to help out. "It's past life," said Jane, getting out a set of tuning-forks. "We need to clear it." She placed the tuning forks over his body. "I can't breathe!" he spluttered. Clutching his chest and turning red, he drew a thin, raspy stream of air into his lungs. "I've never had asthma in my life!"

Something was formulating in Katy's mind. "We need to heal him collectively. We were all there – we're responsible for this, it's karmic." The words had left her mouth before she could stop them, her cheeks coloring at her own stupidity.

"Yes," said the Indian lady. "I'm picking up the same thing. We drowned him."

"It was in the Middle-East somewhere," said the shy young woman.

"We're one soul group," said Jane, hovering with her tuning forks. "We've moved through many lives together, sometimes as family, friends, spouses, and sometimes as adversaries."

The asthma attack stopped, and everyone went back to the final clearing of the day.

Katy's 'career and money' was forty per cent blocked. She gulped – she supported Richard and the children emotionally and practically, but it was he who largely supported them financially. The pendulum swung: one hundred and fifteen percent clear.

Jane closed the session. "We're honored to be doing this work," she said. "We're wiping the slate clean, not just for ourselves, but for others. By opening the Akashic Records, we're clearing the negative impact of what happened in the past, for everyone involved in the event. Cause and effect – we're clearing the cause."

Everyone was chatting as they spilled out towards the car park. They were heading for *The Jolly Farmer*, except for Katy, who swung back towards London, her head throbbing, her shoulders sore. Instead of listening to her eclectic music, she sat in silence, accompanied only by her own bubbling thought process. It was guilt, she realized, that made her drive all the way back, only to repeat the process tomorrow. She was anxious about Freddie and Tilly and fretting that Richard might notice the chasm growing between them. If only he'd join her on this adventure, but there was no chance. She knew he disapproved and was bound to laugh at her later. Besides, he was incapable of looking after himself, let alone the children! He might be a big cheese in the City, but he was useless at everything else.

I can't trust him, she thought, he's not part of the group – the Movement of Spiritually Enlightened Souls – M.O.S.E.S – *Moses!* That's what she'd call this secret society she found herself part of! It was safe to be her when she was with them! After all, you couldn't talk to normal people about this stuff.

Katy found a parking space at the far end of Sycamore Road. Her head reverberating with shots of pain, she slid the key into the front door. The smell of lasagna and cabbage hit her before she could see the devastation in the kitchen – pots and pans everywhere, dirty plates on the table, newspapers scattered across the floor, and Freddie's sports bag hanging open on the back of a chair.

"Hello?" Nothing. Turning around, she saw a note on the fridge: *Gone to watch the rugby. Back later. R x*

The phone rang several times before he answered. She

could hear the bustle of people chatting and laughing in the background, the crystal accent of a woman nearby and the chink of glasses.

"Yes?"

"It's me. I'm home. Where are you?"

"Just, err at *The King's Head*."

"When are you coming back?"

"Soonish."

"Where's Tilly and Freddie?"

"Freddie's staying at Tom's and Tilly's gone to a party with Joe."

"I thought they'd split up?"

"Apparently they're back together."

Joe was Tilly's erstwhile boyfriend. Katy could sense she'd outgrown him but couldn't quite let go.

Surveying the damage – tangled beds, towels and clothing languishing in lazy heaps, half-filled cups of cold coffee – Katy maneuvered through the abandoned house. Tilly's room looked like a burglar had rifled through it and left in a hurry. She closed the door, put the towels back in the bathroom, yawned, and rubbed the back of her neck. It had been a long day and she was spent, bankrupt and on the brink of being overdrawn.

Standing on the top landing, she whispered, "Are you there?" In the mirror she saw her face crumple in silence. Wiping away a tear with the back of her green sleeve, she wandered into the office and fired up the laptop. The enquiry form which had been hanging around for eleven days was still unanswered.

Wow! A Harley Street therapist and healer – you always were amazing. Go for it, girl!

He'd written it at precisely 11.11 pm, she noticed. Probably found her when she'd changed her name. He'd recognize Fralinski, but not Stone. An odd sensation rippled through her as she cast her thoughts back to the wild teenager. He hadn't crossed her mind in all those years, not once, until eleven days ago. In the quiet of the house and heavy with tiredness, she wondered what he was like now? What he was up to? She imagined those thighs, that bottom! Of course, he'd be married now, with children, just like her! She was curious, it came with the territory – knowing people's business was her business. She'd reply, telling him about Richard and the kids, about her London life, her career – that would impress him! He'd wonder why he'd left her all those years ago!

They'd been young and it had only lasted a few weeks before he'd ended it for no apparent reason. The fifteen-year-old had told herself she'd been stupid to think that he'd loved her. In the privacy of the family bathroom, copious tears had fallen, but nobody would ever know. It had been her secret. Putting it all behind her, she had moved on, only her closest friend seeing through the cheerful mask. With head held high, she was dating someone else within a few weeks and Tony was history.

"Toast!" she said out loud, smiling at the use of his word. There weren't many people from school she'd like to hear from, but he was one of them.

Tony! What a surprise! How lovely to hear from you! Fill me in on the last 32 years!

Best – Katy.

She hit 'send' and with perfect mistiming, her own voice of reason entered backstage: 'You shouldn't meddle with old flames!' I bet he's a nobody, she chuckled to herself, closing the laptop and making her way to bed. Richard barged in, setting the chimes jangling just as she was dozing off. The thud of his shoes grew louder, the aroma of smoke, booze and something faintly resembling Chanel No.5 followed him into the room. "I'm asleep!" she murmured, as he undressed before slipping into bed. Curling her legs up to her chest, she rolled away.

At around 3.30 am, Katy became aware of something. She'd just cleared sex, love and relationships and had been working with the green Aura Soma – which had been clearing the green heart chakra, the seat of love, and she'd been dressing head to toe in green. Her final, momentary thought before plunging back to sleep, was 'Tony *Verde!* Verde means green! I lost my virginity to that bastard.'

Chapter 10

Katy lay in bed, clinging to the remnants of sleep before the imminent intrusion of the alarm. Anthony Verde! He was one of the cool kids at school: Shoulder length golden hair, wavy and luxuriant like a mane, framing a strong chin which bristled with stubble. A rebellious streak fueled his reckless regard for rules. He was dangerously different. Instead of Donnie Osmond and Slade, he was into Pink Floyd, Led Zeppelin and David Bowie. It was 1977. Even his school uniform looked trendy on him; the puce blazer perfectly complementing his pale skin, the upturned collar rakish, the sleeves pushed up to reveal muscular forearms. The two-year age gap added to the intrigue. He was someone to be admired back then, thought Katy. At fifteen she'd been pretty cool herself – daring, different, with a street cred that belied her polished accent. Tony had joined the sixth form from one of the local schools that stopped at Year Five. He was fresh meat for the older girls, their hormones spilling out along with their cleavages, which he ogled with his cerulean eyes. Katy had studied him from a distance, picking up the gossip in the playground from the giggling geeks in their gingham dresses. They were hopelessly square – shy, girlie, rosy-cheeked, and winsome – blushing at any male attention. Katy hadn't been like that. She'd feigned an interest in rugby just to watch the testosterone-filled figures running up and down the field in their tiny shorts. With zero interest in the game, she'd eye up the bottoms in the scrums, imagining them in the shower post-match. Any decent player had her attention. She couldn't tear herself away from Tony's muscular legs with their curly blonde hairs and the pert bottom that stuck out, fleshy and perfectly formed like a peach. Of course, she'd known it was all hopeless – he was in the upper sixth and she was just a fifth former.

Katy rolled over and opened an eye, peering at the clock. There was still time, she decided, pulling the duvet up around her ears and sinking back to her thoughts.

She'd lost touch with everyone from school after that one disastrous reunion. Of course, it had been the right decision to put it behind her and move on. The event had been dull, the turn-out disappointing and the venue an anonymous hotel furnished with plastic seats and a sticky dance floor. It was the 80s and she was single. Perhaps her old partners in crime and former conquests would show up, she'd thought, but it was the ones she didn't remember that had stood at the cheerless bar or tapped their feet to Wham!

Katy winced as the memory crystallized. She'd made her entrance in a short, tight-fitting vintage number, red wine in one hand, black cigarette-holder in the other, a Camel smoldering in the holder as she sucked at it, her cheeks hollowing, her ruby lips pouting as she sent out coils of smoke. Her nails were painted crimson to match a quilted, gold-chained bag and patent leather stilettoes. She'd stopped abruptly at the sight, through her heavily kohled eyes, of the 'Marks and Spencer brigade' in their tasteful taupe. The evening might have held some sway if Tony or someone engaging had been there, but as it was, there was nothing to do but down her cheap plonk and ask for another. And another. The end of the evening was a blur, just a vague recollection of gyrating her bootie for every single male she could lay eyes on, despite vertiginous heels and mediocre music. That was pre-Richard, she reminded herself. The rebel had acquiesced, the wild woman had been tamed and the demons had been exorcised. You can't be a revolutionary forever. There comes a point when you have to settle down, grow up and train your unpredictable nature. A smart career-woman had replaced the temptress; marriage to Richard had suffocated the hippy, and yoga had taken over from partying.

An electronic alarm brought her musings to an abrupt end and she reached for her gown before braving the chill morning air.

* * *

It was a grey November day and Katy, dressed in scarf and hat, trudged through the sleet for her appointment with Terry.

"Have you been keeping your dream diary?" he asked.

"Yes, but nothing out of the ordinary, except..." she hesitated. Did she really need to divulge this? Terry waited, knowing it was best to let the silence hang if you wanted your client to open up.

"I've been having lucid dreams at night."

Terry leaned forward, his expression deadpan. Katy shifted in her seat, her hand reaching up for her left earring. "It's as if I'm being mentored."

Terry scribbled something down.

She continued. "I think people become preoccupied with their misgivings, then give up on their hopes. Maybe that's the root of a lot of problems." She paused, her mind pulling it all together. "Depression, for example, anger, even. Can I give an example?"

"Please!"

"Say you want to – I don't know – run a coffee shop! Instead of getting on with it, you start worrying that you don't have enough money. You don't know where it should be or how to set it up. Do you get my drift?"

Terry pushed his spectacles up his nose with his index finger and nodded.

"Then your friend tells you there's no money in cafés and it's terribly hard work," she continued. "And your parents tut because they want you to be an accountant. Then you realize you'll never be able to compete with *Starbucks*, and before you know it, you've snuffed out your dream."

"Are you feeling dissatisfied? Unfulfilled?"

Ignoring his comment, she continued, "But if you'd had a bit of faith, you might have made it work. Not straight away, things take time, it's like saying you want a baby!"

"Do you want another baby, Katy?"

"No. I'm just using it to illustrate a point. You can't decide you want a baby then expect it to arrive the next day, can you? It would be impossible! But people don't give up because of that! They try for a baby then wait. Maybe they get pregnant in a month or two, and in another nine, they have a baby."

"And your point is?"

"I think a lot of people give up because they think what they want is impossible or it'll take ages – or maybe it's because they don't think they have what it takes or they're not deserving? But there are loads of examples that prove just the opposite. All sorts of people who aren't that good make it big time!"

"And what is it that you want?"

"I don't even know anymore – but if I did, I'm starting to realize it might be possible."

"Give me an example that proves the opposite?"

"Victoria Beckham! She's living proof!"

"Of what?"

"That if you know what you want," she sang the next bit. "And, as the Wannabe song goes, you have the balls to stick with it, you can make it work! Look at her! A famous husband, a career as a singer – and she can't even sing! Then a designer, without ever going to art college…and that's not all! She's wealthy, she's got kids and she's probably a size 2."

"Are you jealous of her?"

"No!" snapped Katy, her cheeks reddening. "The only thing that's special about her is her dogged ability to stick with it and get what she wants! It's infuriating!"

"Because you don't have what you want?"

"Because I have to toil blood, sweat and tears to get anything, and it all comes to her on a plate!"

"I'm sure Victoria – what's her name? Spice? – I'm sure she didn't just sit back and watch it all materialize! She probably toiled blood, sweat and tears too!"

Katy screwed up her face and a lump formed in her throat.

"Maybe I *am* envious. I suppose even Posh had to see the openings, seize the opportunities, and dare to take them."

"I'm sure she's worked quite hard," countered Terry. "Perhaps it's time to count your blessings? There are plenty of good things in your own life! Comparison always steals your joy."

"Yes, I know." Katy fell silent as she chewed it over. Maybe he'd hit on something, but was Posh being genuine or living a manufactured lie? Either way, she seemed happy. It wasn't fair.

"Where does this envy come from?" Terry asked, breaking the silence.

"Dissatisfaction with my own life?" Her tentative answer surprised her. "That's crazy! I've got everything I've always wanted."

"Have you?" Terry looked at her over his glasses, which had slid down his nose.

Katy stared at the edge of the desk.

"So, what could you do?" prompted Terry.

"I need to reframe – shift the way I view things. Some clients never make progress because they're more comfortable with the problem they know than with the changes they don't."

"True! That's resistance! Change frightens them so they cling to their neuroses."

"I want to make the changes, Terry, even if they are frightening. I've lost sight of who I am and what I want. I feel like a rat in a designer cage on my gilt-edged wheel, and it's going too fast! I've taken on too much! Everyone wants a part of me – Richard, the children, the clients. My life is a constant battle against time!"

"Why?"

Katy stared at Terry, searching for the answer in his kind, wrinkled eyes. "I don't know."

"And if you did know?"

"Not that old chestnut!" she said. "Because if I stop, the whole lot will come crashing down."

"And if you asked for help?"

"It just starts a row and I don't have the energy to deal with it."

"It starts a row because you ask for help?" Terry looked up, frowned slightly, then made a note, circling it for emphasis.

"Yes. I feel like I'm being bull-dozed. No, steamrollered. That's what it feels like. Richard steamrollers over me." She shivered.

"How does that make you feel?"

"Powerless, cornered, angry. And it takes it out of me."

Terry's pen moved across the page. "Is he controlling?"

"Very."

"So, you keep going and keep your mouth shut to keep the peace?"

She nodded.

"Why?"

"I can't face the alternative. I don't have the energy for it."

"Does he use physical violence?"

"No, but..."

Terry waited patiently.

"I feel bullied. Maybe it's just because he's taller than me, but I feel overpowered, manipulated, even. It's scary."

"What does he do that makes you feel afraid?"

"I can't put my finger on it. There's nothing obvious. It's just how he is! The kids' friends call him 'Stalin'! He wears a peaked cap and a long black coat to the rugby and shouts from the side-lines, apparently. He's a very imposing figure, you know, but it's not that, it's his presence, the way he carries himself, the cut of his jib."

"And what would you say to one of your clients if they were in your shoes?" There was a pause while Terry let it sink in.

Katy recoiled slightly, her eyes widening as she stared at a small repeating motif in the carpet. She knew the answer but refused to acknowledge it. Perhaps she'd given the wrong impression or maybe Terry had misinterpreted her.

Terry could see he'd hit a delicate spot and there was no point in pushing it further. He held the silence. The psyche would go to work in its own way and in its own time. Meanwhile, he'd lead her back to the previous issue.

"And what if you stopped and let it all come crashing down?" he said, watching the look of horror on Katy's face. The silence deepened. He glanced at his watch and made a note to address the issue again.

"Let's take a look at where you're spending your time," he said, bringing the session to a close. "I think you may be heading towards burn-out if you don't slow down."

Katy hadn't had time to record her comings and goings, so she'd made something up. She handed the scribbled note to Terry. He studied it, sighed, took off his glasses and pinched the bridge of his nose between his finger and thumb.

On the train back home, Katy was haunted by that final gesture. He'd known it was a fake time-and-motion study, why hadn't she just come clean? She'd been stupid to think she could fool him. Her eyes prickled with tears. All that stuff about Richard and Victoria bloody Beckham. She didn't want to think about it, it was too draining. Staring out of the window, the backs of buildings rushing by, her mind quietened. A stream of thought sprang from somewhere and she reached into her bag, fishing out a notepad and pen to capture it, lest it was forgotten.

It feels as if a compassionate hand is gently taking the reins of my life, steering me towards the next step as it arises. Whoever it belongs to sees far into the distance, timewise. I mean, above the minutia. They seem to be looking from a higher vantage point. Maybe they've already calculated the entirety of my life, and they're able to execute, with military precision, a strategy for me – but they're not letting me in on the plan. Something, or someone, is coordinating hidden points along a path of space and time – taking me along a trajectory I can't see. It's as if the very fabric of creation is being manipulated. Different event horizons are beginning to dovetail with alarming accuracy. Something big is about to happen, I know it, I can feel it in my bones. It's just around the corner, but I can't quite grasp it.

Chapter 11

Richard was sitting on a black chrome and leather sofa in the waiting room of a smart office in the City. He looked across at his colleague, a woman in her late thirties, her honied hair scrupulously tucked into a chignon, revealing a graceful neck. Out of the corner of his eye, he could see the dark-navy fabric of her skirt pulling slightly as she crossed her legs. She pushed back the cuff of her jacket with an index finger to reveal a gold bracelet watch.

"We've got another five minutes at least before the meeting starts," he said. "Are we all set?"

"There was a hiccup with the valuation." She flicked through her papers. "If we hadn't managed to persuade them that their P/E ratio was tickety-boo, we could've lost the deal at the last minute."

"Good work."

"Thanks to your detailed proposal, they were happy to continue negotiations. Acquisitions are always a nightmare."

"I think they were sold by the leverage we could generate with some clever media relations."

"Yes, but the deal itself has to hold water, and it was close!"

"Could've been six month's work down the drain!"

"Due diligence is always a fraught process, but the lawyers are happy, the investment bankers are ready, and it looks like we're going ahead." She tucked a stray hair back into the chignon with a long, French-polished finger. "You'll need to do something about the site closures in the North, if it all goes ahead as planned."

Richard opened his briefcase. "All part of strategic communications," he said, plucking a glossy folder from the top of a fat dossier.

"Their in-house corporate development team are on board, so I think we're almost there, but you never know with M&As, they can drag on forever," she said.

"I'd like to sew it up this side of Christmas," said Richard, frowning at a message on his phone. "Otherwise it'll mess with my corporate communications strategy." Richard winked at her. "The Financial Times was nosing around this morning," he said, leaning in so as not to be overheard. "Had to 'misdirect' them."

"Is that legal?" asked Emma, turning to look him in the eye.

"My lips are sealed."

Emma looked away as she laughed. "Seriously, Richard, I don't want any misunderstandings or surprises, OK?"

"I've already briefed the CEO and the main board members and our message is consistent."

"Media training?"

"The usual rigorous questions. I did my 'Paxo' impersonation."

"*Why is this bloody politician bloody lying to me!*" mimicked Emma.

"*I couldn't possibly comment,*" he returned, smiling. "But seriously, they know what line to tow."

"Do they know about the risks?"

"Absolutely, and they know exactly how to minimize them and focus on market position and growth opportunities."

"And the main print media?"

"We need to delay. Timing is critical at this stage. I need to control who gets what, and when. I'll give them the story I want them to print at the time I want it printed. I don't want anything fueling the rumor mill."

"Shouldn't we be giving them the full monty?"

"We will. In time. There are a few grey areas I need to deal with first, and I don't want anyone else leaking anything before I'm ready."

"For what?"

"The right moment. It's all about nerve."

"Nerves," she repeated, pushing her slender index fingers

into her temples. "Do you have any paracetamol, I'm getting a headache?"

Richard rummaged in his briefcase and produced two white pills, their foil wrapping creased with age.

"Like I said, you've got to have nerve, keep the tension taut then let go at the precise moment, like an archer holding his bow till he's sure he's on target."

Emma frowned, stood up and turned towards the window, perching her willowy frame on the back of the sofa. A small diamond glinted from its fixture, hanging around her neck on a delicate gold chain. The top two buttons of her crisp shirt were tantalizingly open, perfectly revealing the classy piece of jewelry. She was calm, in control, thought Richard, casting his eye over her with proprietorial approval. Her only armor was a flash of lip gloss, a touch of mascara and her Mont Blanc pen. He walked over to join her. "Don't you just love the view from this window?" he said, leaning in close. "If you look carefully you can see the Lloyds Building – through that gap." His left hand was resting on her shoulder, his face almost touching her hair as he directed her gaze with his right hand. She smelled of Chanel and expensive leather.

"The people look like matchstick men from up here!" she breathed.

"Or little worker bees...buzzing home to suburbia. What are you doing afterwards? Dashing off, you busy little bee?"

"No plans actually."

"Fancy a bite to eat – there's a little wine bar round the corner – great tapas."

"Tapas? An offer I can't refuse!" she said, closing her file and laughing.

"That settles it then." He plunged his hand into his jacket pocket. "Sherbet Lemon while we're waiting?" he said, proffering a crumpled bag and watching the dimple on her face as she smiled and reached in with an elegantly manicured finger and thumb.

* * *

In another part of the country, a short, bald man was busy at his computer. He'd just finish up here before heading to the Masonic Lodge. It was a game to him, a charade – the RAF, marriage, the Masons – and he had played valiantly. The life he'd constructed made him feel responsible, triumphant even.

Later he'd be in the mess, downing a bottle of Bordeaux, reinforcing the deception with alcohol-driven bonhomie. His wine-tasting hobby was a stroke of genius, the perfect cover for blotting out guilt and compensating for whatever it was that was missing. He'd be fifty soon. A couple more years and he could retire from the force. A rebel couldn't stay loyal forever, and beneath the imperturbable surface, the outrageous flirt was buried but still breathing, waiting for the right moment, the right woman. He was an officer and a freemason, with a badge of respect, but the challenge had worn thin, the game won years ago. His life had become tiresome and tarnished like any fake. An embryonic craving for something more, something challenging, was awakening in his veins.

He finished the email, hit 'send' and closed the laptop.

* * *

Katy arrived home after her Thursday evening clutch of clients. Wandering into the kitchen, she slid her hand to the back of the refrigerator, taking out a slim bar of eighty-five per cent chocolate. Just one square, she told herself, breaking off two.

Tilly was upstairs, music blaring, and Freddie was just through the archway in the snug watching *Family Guy*.

"Where's Dad?" she called through, the last piece of dark deliciousness melting on her tongue.

"Dunno! Thought he was with you!"

"I've been in Harley Street!"

"Oh. Tilly might know."

"Tilly?" She called, realizing she probably couldn't hear over that thumping beat. Stomping upstairs, she knocked on Tilly's door and stuck her head around, trying to ignore the ramshackle jumble-sale inside. Her eyes met shambolic piles of clothes, books, magazines, and makeup. "Did Dad say anything to you about being late?"

Tilly shook her head. Was she conveying the negative, or was she just keeping time to the music?

"Wait!" she said, suddenly, "he phoned earlier, said he'd be late, something about a deal in the City."

"Thank you!"

Struggling not to spark a row, Katy closed the door, took a deep breath, and returned to the kitchen.

It was eleven o'clock when she pulled herself upstairs to meditate. No sign of Richard. She wasn't going to message him nor be one of those wives who nagged! Passing the mirror at the top of the stairs, she felt a warm, familiar feeling, as if she were being wrapped in the lightest cashmere.

"It'll be okay," said the Voice, and pre-empting her answer, added, "I won't keep you. I can see you're tired."

"Thank you," she thought, moving towards the office just as the windchimes jangled downstairs. Richard was calling to her. "Kit? You still up? Where are you?"

"Coming!" she said, running back down to give him a hug. He smelled of alcohol, garlic and something sweet which Katy couldn't quite place.

"You reek of wine. Did you have a good time? I thought it was some kind of deal?"

"An acquisition. Ended up entertaining the client in the pub."

"Pub? You smell of garlic and..." she sniffed him at close quarters, "Chanel No.5! I thought I recognized that perfume, my mum used to wear it when I was a kid! Made me feel sick in the car!"

"Don't be ridiculous!"

"I'm not! I hate that perfume! I'd know it anywhere!"

"Must have been one of the team. There's a ball-breaker of a woman banker. Could be her."

"Rich, answer me honestly, are you seeing someone else?"

"What the hell do you mean?" he bellowed. "I've always been loyal to you. I've always delivered."

"Rich, what am I supposed to think? You're home late, and you stink of wine, garlic and women's perfume!"

"Is that the sort of level you've sunk to, Katherine? Bloody Hell! I don't know where you get this shit from! Is it one of your clients? Doing the dirty on his wife? Well I'm not like that, and you damn well know it!" His face crumpled as if he were about to cry. "You know you can trust me, you know I'd never do anything to hurt you..." Katy moved in to comfort him. "I'm sorry," she said, "I don't know what came over me."

"You always insist on hurting me! What about me, Katherine? What about *me*?"

"It's okay, Rich. Calm down," said Katy, placing her hand on his arm and stroking it gently. "I thought you might be seeing someone else. I mean, I wouldn't blame you!" She took his hand in hers. "We haven't had a sex life for a long time, and it's my fault." Her heart was pounding as she said the unthinkable.

Richard shook her hand away, turning towards the window and running his fingers through his thinning hair. Moments later, he spun back, jaw tight, left eyelid twitching, his face pale.

She'd hurt his feelings, she knew it. He was fragile. It was his childhood. She knew where the bones were buried, how could she have been so callous, her, a therapist who should have known better! Of course she had to make this work! He was her husband! She'd loved him once, hadn't she? He'd be distraught without her! Always feeling alone and abandoned, that's what he'd told her, after everything that had happened with his mum. "I'm sorry, Rich, I really am," she said, reaching both arms around him and holding him close. "Come on, let's go to bed."

Chapter 12

Katy emerged from the shower, her hair tightly coiled in a towel, turban style, her thick gown tied at the waist. Flinging open the wardrobe, she realized that just as suddenly as it had come to her, it had left: the urge to wear entirely green was gone! Keeping a few choice pieces, olive, linen trousers and forest, boiled-wool jacket, she bundled the rest into a dustbin liner, earmarking it for charity. A craving for lime-green remained, so the yoga top was salvaged, along with a cheap, bright-green hoodie that she'd bought in the sale. She was hankering after magenta now, a color she'd never worn. Foraging through her bedside cabinet, she found an old pair of sunglasses – lime-green frames with magenta inside. She'd bought them ages ago for a fancy dress. It must be the Aura-Soma, she thought, it's telling me to change bottles.

The charity shop took her sack of green with appreciation and while she was handing it over, something caught her eye: A string of magenta plastic beads with matching earrings. She picked them up before spotting a plum-pink and lime-green, check scarf, an acid green designer jacket which, because of the color, was a total bargain, and a mauve and cerise floral skirt with bright spring foliage. She bought the lot. Trying it on at home, with a new *Sugar Plum Fairy* lipstick she'd purchased from the chemist down the road, she looked in the mirror and winced. The lipstick clashed with her skin tone, sucking the color from her face and producing a cold, pinched effect. She eyed herself up and down. "I look like I need a dialysis machine," she muttered.

The dark glasses in the middle of November were conspicuous but gave her something to hide behind. Her bold but finely-honed sartorial elegance had sunk without trace. She was obliged to wear her charity shop outfit, however embarrassing and however much she protested. At least it was Wednesday and the only person who'd spot her, apart from Richard and the kids, was Shanti, who she'd be seeing later. But before that, she'd better buy something a bit more tasteful in lime-green and magenta, if such an outfit existed, or she'd look ridiculous at work tomorrow.

"My God! What are you wearing?" said Shanti, opening the front door, her mouth gaping, her eyes darting up and down.

"It's the bloody Aura-Soma!"

"Huh?"

"The Aura-Soma. Looks like my wardrobe's telling me when to switch bottles!"

"You'd better come inside."

"My clothes are telling me what to do."

Shanti let out a peel of laughter. "What's the bottle after this?"

"Baby-pink and pale-blue," said Katy, turning down the corners of her mouth.

"I'm guessing you're on spring-green and pinkish-red now?"

"Lime-green and magenta. What does it mean, Shanti? This Aura Soma stuff and all these colors. Lavinia said something about chakras, vibrations, and frequencies, but I was too embarrassed to ask her about it. Can I use your loo?"

"Sure. Want a chai latte and some chocolate covered rice cakes?"

Shanti disappeared into the little kitchen at the back of her cottage, and after some clattering, and the sound of a blender, emerged with a tray just as Katy returned.

"Chakra, it's pronounced with a 'ch' like chocolate, not a 'sh' like Shanti, it's Sanskrit," she said, setting down the tray. "Now, Sanskrit is an interesting and complex language because one word can mean different things, depending on context. Did you know that it's one of the five sacred languages? It's Indo-European, and the Hindu Holy Vedas and Scriptures are written in it. That's why we chant in Sanskrit – *Lokah Samastah Sukhino Bhavantu.*"

The last bit was sung in her sweet voice. "It means 'may all beings be happy and free, and may my thoughts, words and actions contribute to that happiness and that freedom.'"

"Very nice, but what does chakra mean?"

"I'm getting to it," she said, sipping carefully at the hot milky drink which she'd seasoned with cardamom pods and a sprinkling of cinnamon and black pepper. "It means wheel, circle, turning or vortex. They're basically energy centers."

"But why magenta? I thought they were the colors of the rainbow – you know, red, orange, yellow, blue, indigo and violet?"

"And green."

"What?"

"Green. You missed out green. You're thinking of the seven major chakras, but there are more – above your head, in the palms of your hands, on the soles of your feet. The ones you're talking about are the ones you see in diagrams of people meditating."

"Yes. Red at the bottom, then one above the other, with violet at the top of the head."

"Correct. They're usually just in front of the spine."

"But what about magenta?"

"It's a higher chakra, above your head!" she said, holding her palm a few inches above her to indicate.

"And lime?"

"Chartreuse or pale olive? True yellow-green would be even higher."

"What do they do?"

"Magenta is for the soul and a higher level of universal love, and I'm not sure about the lime. It could be an aspect of the heart chakra, about letting go of bitterness and sourness."

"What's the significance then?"

"You're being guided by a higher love, being prepared to connect with it."

"Why?"

"Probably to open your heart and mind to universal love so you can link to something much bigger," said Shanti, pausing for thought. "And the green is helping you let go of the past, probably so you can learn to love yourself."

"I'm not sure I like the sound of that," said Katy, nibbling on a chocolate rice cake. "How does it work?"

"The chakras are like energy portals. They turn and open like the iris of a camera, but more like a vortex. Think of them as turning, unfolding like a flower, and spiraling like water eddies, but upwards and outwards. Actually, they're a bit like antennae, sort of transmitters and receivers." Shanti was scribbling a diagram on a piece of paper to illustrate her point.

"The goal is to purify and activate them, so they're functioning properly and in balance with each other. They get blocked, you see, like a drain or a kitchen sink, and you need to unblock them."

"So, the Aura-Soma's a kind of spiritual dyno-rod?"

Shanti let out a girlish laugh. "Yes! It's a big cosmic sink plunger that's freeing you up energetically!" The visual humor had Katy giggling too.

"But seriously," continued Shanti, "You've got to work through them to expand your consciousness and become more aware, more connected."

"But why?"

"The more aware you are, the more connected you become and the more expanded your consciousness!"

"But why do I need to expand my consciousness?"

"Enlightenment, that's the goal, self-realization. It's the very first baby-step on the long path to ascension."

"That's rubbish, Shanti. Nobody 'ascends'."

"You start with self-awareness," said Shanti, ignoring the last comment. She was used to dealing with sceptics. "The chakras are called the seven seals in the Bible."

Katy shot her a glance. Was she serious?

"The book of Revelation," said her friend, "John the Divine's

Apocalypse. You should read it! The seven seals have to be broken before we can graduate to the next level."

"I thought it was all hell and damnation? And anyway, isn't the Bible just a load of nonsense?"

"No! It's a great metaphysical Love letter from The Divine! You just have to know how to interpret it," said Shanti, sitting back in her chair. "Because I'm half Indian, I came at it from a different angle. It wasn't rammed down my throat when I was growing up, it was just another story, like the Mahabharata. Anyhow, the book of Revelation is speaking of the *end times*, which start off with destruction. But when you get further into it, it talks about the thousand years of peace and the new heavens and the new earth. It's an amazing read! You've got to take a look!"

Katy finished her chai latte and reached for a second rice cake. Shanti could talk gibberish at times. "You were telling me about the chakras," she reminded her.

"Each of the chakras is associated with different things – a musical note, a seed syllable like Om, a symbol, a color, a mandala, a system of the body, an emotion." Shanti was counting them off on her fingers. "Each has a vibration and a frequency. That's why the Aura-Soma lady talked about the vibration of your name."

"So, each of these bottles I'm working with is affecting a whole load of stuff that's connected with the chakras?"

Shanti nodded. "And the green was all about love, the heart, the circulatory system and a whole lot more."

Katy picked up the tray, taking the empty mugs and plate to the kitchen while Shanti followed. "Tell me about frequency and vibration and how that's connected to chakras."

"Okay, but let's get settled. We're in for a long afternoon."

"Do you mind?"

"No! I love talking about this stuff. A lot of people don't want to know. They're asleep to it all – like Muggles!" said Shanti, lighting a fire in the small sitting room grate before sinking into a large floral armchair. "I've got blankets and hot cocoa for later if the temperature drops," she said, gathering her thoughts. "Where shall I begin?"

Katy watched the fire roaring. A wisp of incense curled up beneath a brass dancing Shiva on the mantel. Either side of the statue were two white candles which flickered in the draft.

"You already know about the basic chakras," said Shanti. "Red at the base, violet at the top, each one vibrating at a different frequency." She stood up to illustrate. "The red is for survival and being rooted to Mother Earth, orange is the sacral for sexuality, reproduction and creativity, yellow is the solar plexus for confidence, fear and other lower emotions." She placed her hand over each area as she spoke. "Then it's green for the heart, which is love and compassion, turquoise-blue for the throat and communication, indigo for the third eye, which is mental capacity, intuition and psychic ability, and violet at the top of the head for the crown chakra, the gateway to a higher consciousness."

Katy nodded as she leaned forward, eager to hear more.

"Each of those colors has a spectrum or a wavelength. Red has the longest wavelength and the lowest frequency, and violet has the shortest wavelength and the highest frequency."

"Hang on. That's where I get lost. What's the difference between wavelength and frequency and between frequency and vibration?"

Shanti sighed, puffed up the cushion behind her, put her clasped hands behind her head and looked up. "Have you heard of Nicola Tesla?"

"Rings a bell, who is she? Another healer?"

"He. He was an inventor and futurist, dead now, unfortunately. He was a genius really but unrecognized, and I'm sure something dodgy happened because a lot of his work was either suppressed or stolen, but that's another story," she said, unclasping her hands and leaning forward. "He's known for his work on electricity, but I love his theory about the numbers three, six and nine."

"They're my favorite numbers!" Katy chimed in, "Three's my favorite, and I love six because that's my birthday and it's double three, and I love nine because it's three threes!"

"Well, Tesla said those numbers were the key to the universe!"

"Wow!"

"Anyhow," said Shanti getting back on track, "he famously said *if you want to find the secrets of the universe, think in terms of energy, frequency and vibration.*"

"But what are they?"

"All right. *Frequency,*" said Shanti, pulling a blanket over her lap, "is the rate per second of the vibration of a wave. Think of two people holding a long skipping rope, with one person moving their end up and down so the whole thing snakes."

"Got it. That's a wave."

"Correct. It could be a skipping rope wave, a water wave, a sound wave, a light wave, or an electromagnetic wave. It still applies. The frequency is how fast the wave is vibrating."

"Vibrating?"

"Moving up and down. *Vibration* has a sound, like a guitar string vibrating and a movement, like the spin drier shaking. It's the movement of any wave, the oscillation, or the motion back and forth, or up and down. It's the 'snaky-ness' of the rope."

"I think I've got it. The frequency is the rate at which the wave is moving back and forth. It's how fast the snaky-ness is."

"You've got it! And each wave has its own signature, its own frequency and vibration. The bottom string of a guitar is different from the top one because they vibrate at different rates, because of the relative lengths and thicknesses of the strings and how tight they are. In the same way, the base chakra is different from the crown, and red is different from violet."

"And the Aura-Soma is tuning the wavelengths, frequencies,

and vibrations of my chakras, so they're in harmony, like someone tuning a guitar?"

"Exactly!" said Shanti, pushing herself out of the chair to tend to the fire. "Cocoa?"

Katy nodded, and Shanti disappeared into the kitchen before returning with two steaming mugs of hot chocolate.

Katy's mouth widened into a smile of recognition. "So, when they say, 'raise your vibration' they also mean 'raise your frequency?'"

"Yes! The vibration of your name means *the sound wave frequency of the sound of your name* along with its numerical value, its geometry, its wave shape and size, and its color. Your name has a vibration, and that vibration has a frequency and a corresponding sound and a corresponding color and a corresponding form. It's a kind of code, like a computer code."

"I can't imagine the color, I mean, we can't see it, can we?"

"You know dog whistles? We can't hear them, but dogs can. Well, there are loads of sounds the human ear can't hear, and there are loads of wavelengths of light that the human eye can't see!"

"You mean ones that are shorter than violet or longer than red?"

"Colors we've never seen, yes."

All that could be heard was the slurping of hot chocolate as they tried to imagine a new color.

It was Katy who broke the lull. "So, the Aura-Soma bottles are energetically clearing the blocks and limitations, not just in my chakras, but in my life?"

"Yes. They're realigning you by raising the vibration and frequency of your chakras to their original state."

"How do they get out of whack in the first place?"

"They get blocked, sluggish, stuck, that sort of thing."

"How?"

"You should know that, Katy! Trauma, childhood stuff, past-life karma. All the things a therapist deals with like worry, fear, anger, ingrained habits." She took another sip of cocoa. "Then there's environmental pollution, Wi-Fi, mobiles, eating processed food, lack of exercise – all sorts of things can block those babies!"

"Can the bottles clear all that?"

"No. They can only provide the conditions for the gunk to come into your awareness so you can process and release it yourself."

"Then make the necessary changes."

"Exactly."

* * *

"What the hell are you wearing now?" said Richard, as Katy walked through to the kitchen.

"New bottle of that stuff. Lime and magenta for a while, I'm afraid."

Richard rolled his eyes and returned to the newspaper. "I thought we'd have a bit of a splash," he said, turning the page, "and go to your favorite Michelin-starred restaurant, if I can bribe the maître d' for a table." He looked up at his wife. "But on second thoughts, perhaps you'd better spend the money on some new togs."

"Can we afford it? The restaurant, I mean?"

Richard tapped the side of his nose with his index finger, sniffed, returned to the paper and muttered, "Yes. I got a rather large bonus from work."

"I thought they came quarterly?"

"This one came early, just in time for Christmas," he said, snapping the paper shut as if to close the matter.

Chapter 13

Upstairs, in the quiet of her office, Katy flipped the laptop open. Her heart missed a beat as she noticed the email address. Tony Verde had replied. With racing pulse, she tip-toed out to the landing, her ear straining for signs of the family, before quietly shutting the door and scurrying back to her desk. What would he have written, what would he be like now, she wondered? Holding her breath, she opened the mail, but there was something odd about the long, newsy message. Instead of excitement, she experienced a detachment, as if she were reading a letter from a client or an uncle. He was married, with a daughter, had travelled widely and had an interest in the esoteric. Smiling to herself, she noted he was fascinated by the fact that she was a healer as well as a therapist. It surprised her that he'd settled down but there was a maturity to his writing. It must have been the intervening years, she supposed, she herself had grown up, why not him? He had moved away from the area, just as she had, and like her, he no longer saw anyone from school. It was all rather pedestrian in the end, she thought, smiling with relief as she pictured a happily married, older, Tony with a golden-haired daughter. He held no attraction whatsoever. She wasn't a dizzy teenager, and neither was he. Hitting reply, she penned her own version, expanding on her thriving therapy practice, her spiritual interests, and her house in Turnham Green. It was an odd exchange, and once done, she felt a sense of closure and shut the laptop.

Leaving the office, she thought she saw something move in the mirror and turning towards it, she heard the Voice.

"Good evening, Katy!"

"Oh. Hello!"

"You've been learning about vibration and frequency."

"How did you know?"

"Omnipresence. I'm not just here in the mirror, you know!"

"Are you following me?"

"Not at all! Would you like me to expand on the subject?"

"I think I've got it, thanks – vibration and frequency are important!"

"You know that everything in the cosmos is moving? Everything has a vibration and a frequency."

"Even rocks?"

"Even rocks. The cosmos is open-ended – that means there's no beginning and no end!"

Katy screwed up her face, trying to imagine what that was like.

"It keeps expanding, moving, changing, shifting, birthing and re-birthing, creating and re-creating."

"What about dying? Isn't it a cycle of birth, *death* and rebirth?"

"It's not so much *death* as moving into a different cycle, but that's another subject. The soul doesn't die when the body does, it goes on in another format, so to speak. Energy doesn't disappear, it just changes form."

"I see."

"As above, so below, as without, so within."

"Now you're talking in riddles."

"What happens in the higher heavens or the greater cosmos also happens here, because everything is related and connected. What happens on the outside affects the inside. Have you ever been affected emotionally by the environment?"

"Yes! That's basically what Feng Shui is, isn't it?"

"Quite so. Well, as you're changing the frequency and vibration on the *inside*, in the hidden energetic world, you're affecting the *outside* world and how it shows up for you. And similarly, as shifts are taking place in the higher dimensions beyond this world, your world is responding." The Voice paused to let it percolate in Katy's mind.

"The electrons *within* an atom are constantly in orbit around the nucleus, and the world is constantly revolving around your sun. Similar pattern, you see? The sun above shines its brightest at midday, and below, in the recesses of your mind, the pituitary responds. The sun sets out there, and in here," she could sense the Voice was pointing at her forehead, "the pituitary tells the body to make melatonin." There was a pause. "Nightfall above, sleepiness below."

"That's interesting."

"It's by design. Everything's linked, therefore everything's affected by a change in the system. Patterns in nature repeat at different scales and levels, because they're all coming from a Higher Blueprint. There's an infinite space to explore within the inner realms of your mind, because it's connected to the Mind of Creation, which is also *out there*, in infinite space. As the Hermetics said, *the universe is mental*."

Katy laughed out loud. "It certainly is mental! Totally mental!"

Freddie had just emerged from the bathroom below. "You're bloody mental!" he called up, "Talking out loud to yourself like that!"

"It's okay, Freddie! Just thinking something through."

He scampered into his bedroom and shut the door.

"Go on," she urged the Voice.

"The Divine Mind is infinite and everywhere, even in the farthest reaches of space. That's *consciousness.* There's an infinite cosmos to explore out there and an infinite mind connected to what's in here." Katy could almost feel a gentle hand touching her crown as she heard the words 'in here'.

"Your mind is unfathomable, and so is the Mind of the cosmos. You're simply poised right now as a gateway between the two. Because everything is connected, there's really only One grand creation, and everything in the One is a unity of realities which are moving at different rates, from sub-atomic particles all the way up to super-galaxies. Like wheels within wheels."

"Like the cogs inside an old watch? Small ones, large ones,

some inside others, all of them connected, all of them moving at different speeds."

"Not bad. Now, imagine that in multiple dimensions and colors."

"I can't!"

"Imagine one infinite, living, interconnected, constantly expanding and positive existence of LoveLight." The Voice could see Katy was struggling. "What's important for you right now, is that constant change and constant motion is the only constant in the universe. Change is evolution and evolution is change."

"Hmm. Deep."

"I'll bid you farewell with that, dearly beloved Katherine."

"Wait! What about the Aura Soma and the SRT?"

"They're both tuning you into the correct frequency."

"Like me tuning into Radio 4 after Richard's left it on Sports Live?"

"Yes! You're grounding the vibration of your new name by making an energetic pathway for it."

"I'm making it real, making it fit?"

"*Real*izing it. Yes. You're matching yourself to the new frequency, and the Aura Soma and SRT are helping you clear the things that are getting in the way. That, and your sessions with Terry."

"You know about Terry?"

"Omniscience."

"You've been listening in? Is that room bugged?"

"I see and hear everything, and there is no judgement. I see that you're realigning your system to synchronize with the vibration of your new name and its potential. Changing your name has sent out a signal, like a radio signal, and it's been received on High."

"What will happen?"

"You'll be able to receive, carry and transmit the new frequency, extending it into the world."

"What do you mean?"

"The vibration of your name is a carrier wave for your higher purpose."

"And what's that? To teach, like the soul contract said? But how?"

"You're growing into the person you need to be, to carry out that mission. The first step is to clear the things that are blocking your frequency!"

"The sink-plunger... And I have no idea what's going to be dredged up as it plumbs the depths! It could be a slimy matted knot of misery, pain and sorrow!"

"I'm afraid so, but I'll be guiding you through the conflicting emotions, rest assured!"

It wasn't much assurance. A disembodied voice that she wasn't sure was real would be counselling her? Could she trust it?

"Do you feel threatened, manipulated or afraid when I speak?"

"No."

"What do you feel?"

"Warm, joyous, loved." She paused. "Safe, even."

"Have I ever coerced you, forced the issue, persuaded you against your better judgement?"

"No! Never! You've always been very polite."

"Do you ever feel at ease, calm, blissful when you're in my presence?"

"Yes!"

"So, what is your inner knowing, your innate discernment?"

Katy smiled. The Voice was gone, but she could almost feel it smiling back.

"One more thing before you go!" she said, "What are Akashic records? Jane Joyheart talked about them."

She waited in the silence, her ears straining, her mind ready.

Chapter 14

"Helen, come in here a moment," warbled Richard into the phone as he hastily licked sherbet lemon shards from his fingers.

A few seconds later, his secretary came bustling into the office, her face beaming. There was something in her manner that reminded him of a faithful old dog. If you treated someone well, you'd get more out of them, he thought – keep your allies close and your enemies even closer. That's how he'd cemented his most strategic relationships.

"Close the door and sit down," he said.

Helen clutched at a shorthand notepad, pen poised, ready for his dictate.

She was experienced, this woman in her practical black slacks and tweed jacket, but it hadn't always been the case. He'd plucked her from the typing pool, the mother who'd returned to work once the nest was empty. She'd been all fingers and thumbs with the new technology, and something in him had taken her under his broad wing. He'd always been a sucker for the underdog, especially if they showed potential. He'd give them a hand-up if they were willing to work at it. And if they weren't? He'd drop them right back where he found them. He had no time for people who couldn't rally round him.

"I'd like you to take my credit card shopping to one of those fancy jewelers in Old Bond Street," he said, winking at her. "I need two bits of decent bling. Get something gold and dainty, tasteful, maybe with a small diamond," he added, "and something impressive in silver, will you?"

"I don't know if I could—"

"I trust you, Helen. You've got an impeccable track record and I know you'll do the right thing. Here's the pin number, keep it secret, don't write it down and don't give it to anyone." He could change the pin later, and besides, he was covered by insurance, he reminded himself.

"Yeah. Of course. Thanks," she said, accepting the slim plastic card. "What's the budget?"

"Whatever it costs."

"In Bond Street? You sure?" she said, raising her eyebrows.

"Keep the whole lot under £3,000 if you can."

"Gift wrapped?"

"Separately, discreetly," he said, his eyelid twitching slightly, "and be back by…" He glanced at his watch. "Five."

Helen closed the office door as she left. He visualized her taking her thick coat from the stand and that functional handbag from beneath her desk. Listening for the muffled sound of her sensible, flat-shoed footsteps receding down the corridor, he unlocked his desk drawer and removed an envelope, which he zipped into the side pocket of his briefcase. She'd be back in a few hours with the two gift boxes. Stuffing a sherbet lemon into his cheek, he turned his mind to more important matters. He had a few phone calls to make and an 'off the record' comment for the Times diary, which he knew would set a hare running. 'Misdirection,' he mused.

A little before 5 pm, the intercom buzzed. "Mr. Stone – I'm back with the bits and bobs."

She hastened into the office and handed him a turquoise paper bag tied with white ribbon.

"The little box is a pair of gold stud earrings with small diamonds, and the big box is a solid silver bangle, quite unusual."

"Good work, Helen," he said, untying the ribbon. "And the credit card?"

"Oh yes, of course!" she said, burying her hand in her pocket and extracting the prized piece of plastic.

"Thank you, Helen. You can leave this till tomorrow," he said, gesturing to a pile of papers on his desk. "If you hurry, you'll miss the worst of rush hour."

Almost curtseying as she left, Helen closed the door. Richard discarded the bag, locked the small box in his desk drawer and placed the larger one in his briefcase, along with the envelope, and left the office.

Picking up an Evening Standard at the station, he slipped down into the cold, windy subway. With any luck, he'd be home by 7.30 pm.

The cursed wind chimes rattled as he opened the door to number eleven. He knew Katy would be home. It was her admin day, well that's what she called it, more like a day off, he thought. "Anyone home?" he called upstairs.

"Coming!" his wife sang out. "Let me just finish this last invoice."

There was always something more important than him. She should have been dropping what she was doing and greeting her lord and master! God knows, he worked his arse off for this rabble, he thought, thinking of the envelope. The least they could do was acknowledge his home coming. "Tilly? Freddie? I'm home!"

"We know, Dad," said Freddie, sidling out of his room. "What's for dinner, Mum?"

"Takeaway. I haven't had time to cook. Fish and chips?"

"Yay! Tilly! We're having fish and chips – from the chippie down the road?"

Richard rolled his eyes and snorted. "I suppose you expect me to get the bloody things?"

"No! I've been cooped up in here all day. Tilly, Freddie – want to come with me?"

Richard was left alone in the kitchen with his briefcase, which he opened, fishing out the envelope and the gift-wrapped box, and placing them on the shelf next to the television in the snug. His shoes were pinching and he eased them off, carrying them as he headed upstairs. The bedroom dwarfed him, and he shivered, trying to shrug off a feeling of emptiness. The house was silent. He put his shoes on the rack, loosened his tie, hung up his suit and took his shirt off, dumping it on the bedroom floor. It lay crumpled in a heap, dejected, unwanted and alone, with only a pair of dirty socks nearby for company. A freshly ironed shirt was selected from the wardrobe, which he hung on the handle while he searched for a tie and suit to match. The art of war, he said to himself, is to know your enemy, and besides, you only get one chance to make a first and dominating impression.

The fish and chips were served just as he liked them – soggy, with plenty of salt and vinegar. It was a pity these fancy southern chip shops didn't do mushy peas and gravy, but there were some sacrifices he'd had to make in order to rise up the ranks and be somebody. He couldn't let the past catch up with him now. He watched the family stuffing their faces.

I'm the silverback of this troop, he thought, ramming a huge portion of battered cod into his mouth, and licking the grease off his fingers. He could see Katy wincing at him from the other side of the table, her, with her finicky fish knife and fork. Bloody posh Home Counties.

"Stop fussing with that oily paper, will you?" he said as Katy packed the remains into the bin. "I've got something for you." He stood up, reaching through the archway into the snug and returning with something in his hand. "Here you go. Don't tell me I never get you anything," he said, proffering a package.

Unwrapping its white ribbon, fingers impatient, she peered into the box. Her eyes widened. "Richard! It's gorgeous!" She smiled and slipped the heavy silver bangle onto her wrist. "I love it," she said, showing it off in the kitchen spotlight.

"I've come into a bit of spare cash," he said, holding out the envelope. "Here, treat yourself to a nice new outfit. That lime green thing ought to be shot."

Katy took the envelope, hurled her arms around Richard, and kissed his slobbery lips before hugging him close. "Thank you!" she whispered.

"Don't ever accuse me again of seeing someone else!" he said, stroking her hair, a smile creeping across his face.

For once, she decided to stay with him in the snug. He smiled to himself before spotting her laptop. "Put that bloody thing away will you," he said. "It belongs upstairs!" He sank into the settee and picked up the TV remote.

As Katy sprang up the stairs, Freddie seized his moment.

"Dad?"

"What?"

"I'm worried about Mum."

"What is it now?" he said, slamming down the remote control.

"I heard her talking to herself outside her office." Freddie spoke rapidly, his words unclear, his head bowed slightly. "Something about being mental, and I've heard her muttering up there before. I think she's talking to the mirror." His hands were clasped in front of him.

"For fuck's sake," spat Richard, nostrils flaring.

Freddie backed out towards the kitchen. "Just saying, Dad." He was peering at his father from beneath a curly fringe. "Maybe it's pressure, I heard on the television..." He saw the look on Richard's face and his words petered out.

"Heard what? What pressure? A part-time job as a therapist?" Richard boomed, his eyes widening. "Let me know if you catch her again," he said, looking into the distance and squinting slightly, like he always did when he was scheming. "I think her supervisor ought to know about this." His nose wrinkled as if he'd smelled something bad and his eyelid flickered involuntarily.

Chapter 15

Three months later – February 2009

Katy had taken on a clutch of new clients. There was an impeccably dressed City Lawyer who didn't believe in herself. She'd only got to where she was by pure fluke, she'd said, and was worried someone was about to find out. Of course, it was all in her mind, and when Katy explored further, they unearthed an over-critical father who had always belittled her. That evening, Katy had recorded a hypnotic induction for herself, going back into her own childhood and healing old hurts. The same week, she was scheduled to see a Super-Head who'd taken over a challenging school in one of the failing London boroughs. The session was cancelled last minute due to time pressures. The following week, the same woman fell asleep in the chair as Katy probed further. There's way too much on her plate, thought Katy, a ridiculous work schedule, two children and a husband who seemed to do nothing but watch telly. "You can't go on at this pace," said Katy, "or something's going to give." Together they explored the need to be accepted, seen and recognized. Between them, they re-scheduled her week, Katy encouraging her to delegate, drop her standards at home and carve out down-time for herself.

Later, there was a polite gentleman who called and booked a session the following week. He turned out to be a meticulously dressed and urbane museum curator, who refused to let his bullying wife ruffle his feathers. He'd maintained control over his own feelings, pressing them beneath the veneer of his outward appearance and telling himself and everyone else that he was 'fine'. The musculature of his face and limbs were taut and even his clothes were restricting him, with his buttoned-up collar and tightly laced shoes. Katy's teeth were clenched as she took notes, her stomach pulled in beneath a tight belt, her legs neatly wrapped and crossed, but she noticed none of that. Her attention, as always, was on her patient and how she might help him.

There had been a scary session with Terry when he'd told her that Richard had been in touch. "Your husband and son are concerned about you, Katy."

She'd sat frozen in the chair not knowing what to say while Terry had investigated further. She'd felt uncertain. What if it had all been in her mind? Perhaps she'd been hallucinating, making it all up. Strange things happened when people overdid things. Maybe she wasn't as strong as she thought. Terry had convinced her to take time off. He was right, of course.

"I was shocked by your time diary," he'd said.

Sighing with relief, she'd realized he hadn't clicked that she'd made it up! Thank goodness he didn't know the truth, which was far worse!

"Now, what's all this about the mirror?"

The story she told was that she'd been thinking out loud at times, practicing client conversations in the mirror. None of them was going to buy into the notion of the Voice, after all! It took all she could muster to convince herself she wasn't going mad.

"I hadn't realized anyone had been listening," she'd told Terry.

They had closed the subject and begun working through the overwhelm that gripped her every waking hour and the fear that if she stopped, her life would fall apart. It takes time to change an ingrained habit, she'd reminded herself when she felt the pressure mounting. Terry had closed the session by insisting she take a holiday. "Not at home," he'd cautioned. "You'll end up doing paperwork or painting the house. Get away completely, out into the country. Walk in nature, read a book, lose yourself."

Katy had become aware of how often she told herself and just about everyone else that 'she didn't have time' or 'was running out of time' or 'was really busy'. She recalled the Voice telling her that her dominant thoughts were sowing seeds. Struggling to find different phrases, she'd tie herself in knots in an attempt to plant something new, but the truth was, she *was* busy and time starved. "My schedule is quite full at the moment." Trying to find ways to change the empty 'box life' she'd shoe-horned her way into, she'd set aside time to connect with nature by walking in the woods at the weekend. The constant pace of life, like a treadmill that was running slightly too fast, was exhausting, and quite possibly contributing to a slow death. The mounting incidence of chronic illness during midlife had not escaped Katy's notice.

"Dream about what you really want," the Voice had said, so Katy had been spending five minutes each day on the train day-dreaming of a happy marriage, sexual intimacy, connection, support from her spouse and a life filled with joy. There were other joys, she had realized, like seeing clients heal, deepening new friendships, and feeling her way within the Movement of Spiritually Enlightened Souls (MOSES).

Katy was plunging deeper into the unusual and further from the mundane. She had started to notice synchronicities in her life, plans falling effortlessly into place, offers of help coming from unlikely sources, clients having the exact same problem she herself had just faced.

The Voice continued to coach her now and then, helping her with difficult emotions that were bubbling up from the past: an authoritarian boss whom she'd been terrified of, the near loss of Tilly when she was born, her brothers' incessant teasing during her formative years, her father's hurtful put-downs, her mother's lack of maternal love. Terry had suggested she give herself permission to rest, and she had forced herself to find at least ten minutes a day. Life was becoming less of a marathon, less of a battle against time. Even though the monthly migraines were crippling, she smiled more often and was noticing a spring in her step, despite the pressure that remained. There were glimpses of contentment and moments of happiness. It had taken a lot, she reminded herself, to get to this point. She'd had to face down some of her worst demons – being shamed and humiliated by her father, the guilt of feeling she'd not been the perfect daughter and the notion that she wasn't a proper psychotherapist because she hadn't trained in Jungian or Freudian Psychoanalysis. She still didn't think she was slim enough and perhaps would always think she was overweight, despite the fact her BMI (Body Mass Index) was in the lower half of a healthy range. She'd calculated it several times, just to be sure. The strange outfits weren't helping, she told herself, catching her reflection in the mirror. If she were dressed in black, she'd feel better. She waited for the Voice but it wasn't forthcoming. A pile of paperwork was threatening to topple from her desk, but she'd pushed any concerns to the back of her mind. Terry had said she must slow down.

At least the lime green and magenta had been dumped unceremoniously outside another high street charity shop. She'd obviously let go of enough bitter past and opened her heart and mind to something bigger, whatever that was. Maybe it was those mystical moments she'd experienced when she'd walked through the trees on Sundays? One thing she knew for certain, she would never, ever, wear lime and magenta again, and was now sporting baby blue and pink. According to her notes from Lavinia, this bottle was about the inner and outer journey of transformation and finding freedom through embracing change. Ultimately it would lead to the opening of the crown chakra (shake the bottle and the two colors made lilac). Katy grimaced at her reflection in the mirror. The colors weren't entirely flattering at her age and looked pale against her dark, reddish-brown hair and olive skin. Tilly rolled her black kohled eyes in disapproval at the fluffy, pastel-rose, cowl-necked sweater with faded blue jeans and pink ballet pumps. "Mum!" she said with heavy sarcasm before skulking away. Katy knew the Baby Spice look was not only passé but ridiculous. "Bloody Aura Soma!"

she muttered.

Richard was keeping a low profile and hadn't been so vocal in his criticism of her friends and lifestyle. He seemed preoccupied, working hard at the office, and coming home late with bunches of roses. Perhaps he'd softened? Were the visualizations on the train beginning to work? Could there really be a 'happily-ever-after'? He'd given her plenty of spending money, and they'd been to a few posh restaurants over Christmas. She looked at the beautiful silver bangle and felt the weight of it on her wrist. He'd obviously put a lot of thought into it. How silly she'd been to think there was someone else. Richard was right, he'd been telling her for ages he was a good catch. How stupid she'd felt when he'd explained it was his secretary, Helen, who wore Chanel No.5. Dear Helen, with her fussy ways and her sensible clothes and a husband she'd loved for years.

Katy was getting to know Tony better as their light, newsy emails ran to and fro. His experiences seemed to mirror hers. He'd been married twice just like her, had done well for himself, was practical and had an interest in metaphysics. He sounded, from his anecdotes, as if he was a great father. He'd travelled a lot, and certainly knew his red wines! They'd hit it off as virtual pen-pals from the start, quickly finding common ground. The rebellious teenager had grown up and Katy looked forward to Tony's charming, well-written missives. Richard had never written anything more than 'love Rich' in a birthday card or 'I'll be late home' in a text message. It was refreshing to read Tony's accounts of his daughter, his wife, his big house in the country. He was a hands-on father, who'd been there from the offset, taking little Amber to the doctors when she was sick, collecting her from nursery, teaching her to ride a bike. Katy felt a jolt, and clenching her teeth, she looked away from the screen, recalling all too vividly Richard's absence from child-rearing, what with his long hours in the City.

Amber. She must have inherited Tony's thick golden locks. She imagined his long, curly hair, cropped now into a thick thatch of sandy waves with a few greying hairs at the temples. The emails came from an official MoD address, Ministry of Defence. He'd told her it was nothing exciting, just a desk job in the sticks. She figured he was probably a Civil Servant, but she couldn't help feeling he was hiding something. He seemed too confident and polished. Maybe he was top brass, she thought, her imagination running away with her, a Rear Admiral or a Colonel. An officer and a gentleman! She could picture him, dashing in his uniform with the military buttons, the epaulettes, and the square jaw. No, he might have smartened up, but you could bet your last few pennies that Tony Verde would never join the British Army!

March 2009

Meeting Tara for coffee on Wandsworth Common one bright spring-like Saturday afternoon, Katy broached the subject of Tony. She needed to talk it through. Shanti wouldn't understand, being so resolutely single, and it wasn't something she wanted Terry to analyze.

"I feel like I've known him for ages, and in a way, I have!" she said, crossing her legs and squinting into the sunlight. "After all the emails, I was thinking we could meet up." A smile played on her lips as she turned towards Tara.

"Terrible idea," Tara said, setting her mug down sharply on the table. "You're too busy to see half your friends, let alone a stranger!"

"But I really enjoy his emails and he's in town every so often." Katy's eyes were sparkling.

"Do I need to remind you, it's not a good idea to meet up with your ex?"

"But it was all so long ago, Tara, we were just teenagers, and I don't have any feelings for him anymore." She was twirling a chestnut-red lock of hair around her index finger.

"Then why are you emailing him every week?"

"We've got a lot in common, but there's nothing between us, I promise you!"

"Oh yeah? No smoke without fire, that's what I say," said Tara, reaching into her capacious bag for juice cartons and mini boxes of raisins.

"Honestly, there's nothing there! He's married with a kid." Katy's eyes were wide, her palms open.

"And you're married with two kids!"

Tara stood up and beckoned to her children. "Hazel? Jake? Who wants apple juice?" They left their game and came running on chubby little legs towards the café.

"I can't help thinking he holds the key to something."

"What?"

"I dunno, but there must be a reason he's come back into my life. Maybe it's to do with my spiritual journey?"

"Just be careful, Katy," Tara said, pursing her lips and pulling a wet wipe from her bag.

* * *

Sitting at her desk on Monday morning, Katy's pulse quickened when she saw an email pop up from the familiar MoD address. Eager to read the latest instalment, she ignored two client enquiries and a message from her accountant. They could wait. As she read his review of the weekend, all thoughts of work and domestic pressures faded. Her shoulders relaxed, her face softened, and her eyes wrinkled into a smile. At the bottom of the page, there was a PS.

How about meeting for coffee one afternoon in town?

Oh my God! He'd been thinking the same thing. It must be a sign, she thought, staring at the screen. Her fingers hovered over the keyboard, but Tara's words were still echoing in her mind. She'd leave it for now.

Downstairs in the kitchen, she boiled the kettle for a cuppa but couldn't stand still. Ants in your pants, she told herself, pacing from the kettle to the fridge. She absently opened the door and stared at the contents before shutting it. Opening it again, she slipped her hand to the back of the fridge, extracting a prized bar of 90% dark chocolate. I've got to stop eating this stuff, she thought, cramming four squares into her mouth. The kettle had boiled, and she took a mug of steaming Earl Grey into the garden.

There had been so many synchronicities recently that she could no longer call them 'coincidences'. They were more like little miracles of timing. She was always in the right place at the right time or led to the perfect book or the most effective approach for a client. It was as if there was an invisible plan taking shape with little signposts showing her she was on track. Katy sipped at her tea and watched a robin perching on the washing line. Life's running quite smoothly for once, she thought. Money's flowing in, I've got a waiting list, and when I need time off, I get cancellations. It's uncanny. The daffodils were peeping through the borders, she noticed, as the spring sun warmed her face. It felt like the world was waking up after a long hard winter. Something stirred within, a surge of enthusiasm lighting her up. I'm riding a wave at the moment, she thought, but I don't know where it's taking me, and that's frightening. What if I come down with a crash?

Having finished her tea, she went back upstairs. She'd better mull this Tony thing over before replying. Maybe the Voice would tell her what to do but for now there were accounts and enquiries, and a website that needed editing, then clients to see, dinner to cook, post-session notes to be completed and a holiday that needed booking.

* * *

Katy had kept Tuesday clear and decided to use the available time to tidy up the house. Tony's email was still playing on her mind. She wondered what he looked like now as she took a bin liner, polish, and duster up to the office. 'Start at the top and work down,' she told herself. Katy hesitated on the landing. "Hello?" she said, peering into the mirror and waiting. It was never there when she needed it! Emptying the office bin, then polishing the mantelpiece and shelving, she wondered why the Voice didn't answer.

That's better, she thought, straightening the papers on her desk. The char would hoover and clean on Thursday, but Katy had to get the place tidy first! Leaving the office, bin-liner in hand, she stopped again at the mirror. "Are you there?" After pausing, she continued down the stairs. Your environment reflects your state of mind, she thought, gathering up washing, making beds, and putting clothes away. The mess was disturbing her psyche and as she folded towels and replaced toilet rolls, she could feel a dark cloud of resentment drawing itself around her. Neat and tidy would restore her sanity, she decided, folding T-shirts and hanging up jeans. Richard had been out late on another work-jolly the night before, celebrating, he'd said, and the kids were just your average teenagers, their worlds revolving only around themselves. The last thing they were going to do was volunteer to help. Katy returned to the mirror. "It's just that I'd like your advice about something," she said, eyes looking to one side as she strained for a response.

They did as they pleased, Rich and the children, as if the house would take care of itself, and the sock fairy would forever fill their drawers with freshly laundered footwear. They'd left a trail of destruction and expected her to clear up. She was tired, and on top of that, felt guilty because she'd been away so often on courses. It was no use, the Voice clearly wasn't there. I wish the house wasn't so bloody big, she thought, tears beginning to form as her eyes prickled. She'd felt like Cinderella when she was young, helping Mum with the washing and ironing, polishing the wooden floors, making tea and baking scones, and all instead of playing with other children at a nursery! The boys hadn't had to do anything. They were older and at school, and when they got home they went to the park to catch butterflies and fly paper airplanes or climb trees. She wasn't allowed to join them because she was the silly little girl, and besides, she wasn't old enough. It had hurt, and thinking about it so vividly now, the tears were running freely down her red, blotchy face. Blowing her nose on a piece of toilet paper, she sniffed back the sobs, but they started again. She hadn't had any playmates till she got to school and now, here she was, stuck cleaning, just like then.

She sat down on the edge of Tilly's bed and looked out of the large, sash window. A patchwork of lawns with verdant borders ran along the backs of the houses, punctuated by the odd swing or climbing frame. The garden next door housed a huge trampoline. What she'd have given to live here as a child, and what she'd give now to live anywhere else. She hated the middle-class suburb with its monied privilege and narrow outlook. Give me a mixed area with different cultures anytime, she thought, realizing she was no longer that trapped little girl. She was an adult and, as the Voice had said, she was the director of her life and was free to create any ending she liked. She *would* have a loving marriage and a happy outcome if she did a bit more work on herself, and she *would* live in North London.

Having shoved the washing into the machine, Katy stopped to throw together a cheese and tomato sandwich. Radio 4 babbled in the background with the usual news roundup – more fighting in Bagdad, political posturing, a police raid on a drugs cartel in Bristol, floods in Wales, an oil spill in the Atlantic, and a pedophile ring in Manchester. She switched off as The Archer's theme tune started. If you are what you eat, she mused, I'm becoming a sandwich, but there's never time to cook! 'You're not eating properly,' she could hear her mother's nagging voice.

'You won't have enough milk for the baby.' As if she knew, the woman who'd given up and bottle-fed, letting her eldest son feed her new-born daughter while she flirted with her theatrical friends. "It's in the past. Let it go," she said out loud. "Think about positive memories instead!"

Katy slipped an Alan Watts CD into the sound system. It was a recording of some of his better-known talks. She'd borrowed it from the library thinking it might lift the drudgery of housework. The kitchen took the brunt of family life with its large table, bay window, and arched entrance to the room beyond, which was once a playroom when the children were small. It now housed the television, a built-in shelf unit and a lumpy old sofa. Every time Richard called it the snug, Katy would mishear 'smug'. The settee was strewn with newspapers, magazines, and squashed cushions. She folded the papers and plumped up the pillows, finding a half-sucked sherbet lemon stuck to one of them.

This is the real secret of life — to be completely engaged with what you are doing in the here and now. And instead of calling it work, realize it is play, said Alan Watts in his peculiarly educated and English accent. Katy opened the French windows to let in some air. Soon it would be summer and they could leave them open all day, assuming summer would actually appear, unlike last year, which was peppered with overcast skies and cool breezes. Huh. Global warming is such a misnomer, she thought, or did they use the term 'climate change' now?

Normally, we do not so much look at things as overlook them, said Alan.

Katy clenched her teeth and took a deep breath. "Spit-spot," she said out loud. "A spoonful of sugar helps the medicine go down." She slipped her hand into the back of the fridge and pulled out a 70% with orange and spice. Just two squares, she thought, taking three then feeling guilty. She'd be putting on weight at this rate. It had to stop!

The only way to make sense out of change is to plunge into it, move with it and join the dance.

Dance! Thought Katy, stopping Alan in his tracks and replacing him with Groove Armada. Turning the volume up and singing along, she unloaded the dishwasher, tapping her feet and swaying her hips as she put the crockery and cutlery away. Stacking the dirty plates to the beat of the bass, then wiping the stove to the slower tracks, she got through almost an hour of boring housework as if it was fun. It was the nearest she got to dancing these days. Her mind drifted back to her twenties when she'd be out, shaking her booty every weekend, then further back through time, to her childhood. She clutched at the edge of the sink and welled up. She'd wanted to be a ballet dancer. The teacher had said she was excellent, and she'd always got distinctions in her exams. Her face contorted now as the memories came swimming back. Dad laughing at her, his face creasing, and his shoulders heaving. "You?" he'd said. "You'll be the one they send on to test the stage!" She hadn't been overweight, just a typical seven-year-old with a bit of puppy fat around her tummy. Steadying herself, she began analyzing it. Just an abreaction, she thought, it's over now. I'm safe and I'm not fat. She sat at the table and worked through the feelings. Emotional Freedom Technique would be the best way to process this, she thought, her fingers lightly tapping at specific acupuncture points as she gave voice to her emotions. It was over. She smiled. If she'd carried on dancing, she'd be anorexic and smoking 30 a day to keep herself skinny, and she probably wouldn't have met Richard or had the kids. The music had stopped.

* * *

Wednesday was admin day, and Katy tackled the mounting pile of invoices and receipts on her desk, along with emails, client handouts, and another tweak to her website. A young woman rang to book an appointment. She seemed to be in a panic. "I'm getting married in six weeks' time and I can't stop eating dark chocolate!" she said, her voice rising, "Can you help me?" Katy grimaced, her stomach tightening. "Yes. Let's see when we can fit you in."

"Soon, I hope," gabbled the strangled voice, "at this rate, I won't fit into the dress!" The appointment was booked. Katy looked down at her thighs and hips. Thank goodness she didn't have to fit into a wedding dress any time soon.

Having caught up her admin, she decided to spend the evening researching Akashic Records. She hadn't been sure, exactly, of what they were, and had been meaning to find out since the Spiritual Response Therapy course. It turned out they were a kind of energetic, coded library of information, holding records of events in another dimension called the astral plane, which itself was an esoteric term for another realm of existence. It seemed that researching one thing always led to another. This arcane stuff was slippery. Late into the evening she was still poring over websites and rifling through the dictionary and the large encyclopedia that otherwise gathered dust in the sitting room. She'd been reading about the Theosophical Society, which still existed. Theosophy was apparently based on the belief that one could use spiritual techniques to 'experience' God. Perhaps Helena Blavatsky, its co-founder, had coined the phrase 'Akashic records' but Katy stumbled upon references to Rudolph Steiner and Alice Bailey using the same expression. They all seemed to have one thing in common: a belief in another mystical, spiritual world that informed the real world. Interesting though the research was, she couldn't see the significance of it, until she read a quote by Edgar Cayce, pronounced Casey, according to the website, which said that an Akashic record was a dimension of consciousness that contained a vibrational record of every soul and its journey.

Every soul? She read on, skeptical at first. An etheric, *subtle, of the ether*, record, held on another plane of existence, *Astral Plane,* of everything done, said, believed and experienced by a soul. She wondered how many souls had ever existed. The records related to the future as well as the past, were connected and were interactive. She tried to imagine a computer spread sheet with entries of every thought, word, action, deed and feeling there ever was and ever would be. If you changed one thought in the system, then you'd change the system itself, by putting an etheric spanner in the works. The records weren't just held in a static repository, out there on the lip of space. Collectively, they were a dynamic force which had some kind of influence over your daily life! That can't be right, she thought. If I do something to you in a past life, good or bad, it could affect, in this life, you, your family and friends, me and my family, and others on the periphery, like a ripple effect going out through time. The one event would tie together several people and by extension, several records. Maybe that's what karma *the law of cause and effect* was about, she thought. Something I did *or caused* in a past life could affect me in this life. Perhaps that explained why innocent people got caught in the crossfire or died horrible deaths when they'd lived decent lives. The Spiritual Response Therapy had been clearing these records, she realized, the full magnitude beginning to sink in. Imagine the knock-on effect, she thought, it would be like *Back to the Future*, except worse. Change one thing in time and you have a domino effect on your hands.

* * *

Nobody in London wants to see a therapist on a Friday afternoon, so Katy packed up her bags and headed home before the commuter rush. With any luck, she'd have a couple of hours before the kids got back. Changing out of her dusky-pink, wool jacket and muted blue check trousers, she threw on a pink sweatshirt and faded blue jeans. In the kitchen, she picked up the Alan Watts CD. Might as well listen to the rest of it, she thought, slipping it into the player.

I have realized that the past and future are real illusions, that they exist in the present, which is what there is and all there is.

Katy began unloading the dishwasher and reloading it and by 3.30 pm, she was mopping the last spillage from the granite work surface and polishing the glass behind the stove. Her mind was on her clients, the children, what they'd have for supper. She caught sight of herself reflected in the polished glass. I'm done with the past, she said to herself, it's over. She tipped the dirty water away and got the broom out to sweep the floor. I need to count my blessings, she thought, getting out the dustpan and brush, look at what I've got right now! She emptied the dustpan, put away the broom and looked around the gleaming kitchen. She had this fabulous house, her children, her work. She needed to start focusing on that. Maybe she should write a gratitude diary; she was always telling clients to start one! Let's see, she said to herself, stopping for a moment to count three blessings, I've got my health, my figure, and Richard, who provides for us – he's not that bad. I need to heal the rift between us.

What we have to discover is that there is no safety, that seeking is painful, and that when we imagine that we have found it, we don't like it.

Tidying up the snug, Katy wondered if she should get back to Tony, let him know she didn't think it was a good idea to meet up? She was waiting for the Voice. There was nothing in it, she knew that. She'd married Richard for better or worse and the vows had meant something to her, even though Rich had looked away when she'd said them.

The sun had disappeared now, and there was a chill in the air. Tying back the curtains and straightening a picture on the wall, recollections came trickling back, of ex-boyfriends and former times. There was one old flame who'd cheated on her for over a year without her knowing. Her face screwed up as the pain of betrayal shot through her. Collapsing on the cushions she'd just plumped, she galvanized herself. She'd process it with eye movements. Looking from side to side, first at the window then at the archway, her eyes darting, her head resolutely still, she worked through her emotions and thoughts. Thank God I'm not with that scumbag, she said to herself, blowing her nose and wiping away the tears. Why on earth so much was coming up from the past, she had no idea. Perhaps it was the Aura-Soma? Anyhow, the kids would be home soon, and she'd better start thinking about supper.

'Clean Kitchen.' She loved ticking things off her endless lists. If she hadn't been so damned organized, she'd have drowned in the overwhelm. She had to keep going because nobody else was going to pick up the pieces if the spinning plates dropped.

It's better to have a short life that is full of what you like doing, than a long life spent in a miserable way.

Katy turned the CD off. She'd had enough of Alan Watts and went upstairs to research English holidays. Terry had asked her to take a break and it wouldn't be long till Easter. A quaint little cottage in the country would be just the thing. Get away from it all, fresh air, long walks in nature, pub lunches and cozy evenings reading by an open fire. While she was at it, she might as well look at hotels and flights for that spiritual conference in May. Shanti had already booked the tickets and they could travel together. The website had an offer on flights to the Yucatan peninsula, she noticed. In fact, there was a hotel and flight deal. She fancied a holiday with some culture as well as sun, sea, and sand. She'd chat to Richard about it later.

The wind chimes rang out, calling her back downstairs. Tilly's face was thunder, her jaw set. She'd evidently had a bad day at school. Flinging her bag at the newel post, she missed by a narrow margin, spewing books and pens across the hall floor.

"I finished with Joe!"

"Oh!"

"He's so immature! I've had enough!"

Stamping into the kitchen, she slammed the door while Katy picked up the scattered pens and exercise books along with a box of tampons. Clattering sounds were coming from the kitchen. "You alright?" called Katy. "Fancy a cup of tea?"

"No."

"Want to talk about it?"

"No."

Katy left her to it. It was the second time she'd split up with Joe. He was a lovely young man but probably no match for Tilly, who had bigger ideas. Freddie would be home after rugby practice, and hopefully, she'd have calmed down by then, and they could get into the kitchen. At the top of the stairs, Katy halted at the mirror, closed her eyes and breathing slowly and deeply, dropped into a meditative state. Maybe the Voice would show up if she was still, but nothing was forthcoming. Shutting the door to her office, her thoughts turned to Tilly, who'd be seventeen soon, almost an adult. When she, Tilly, had gone to University, she'd probably miss her. She thought of Joe and then the tampons. Tilly had been seeing him for weeks before she'd asked to go on the pill. It must have happened within a loving relationship, she thought, comparing it to her own disastrous experience – a fumble in the dark at a party and a quick but painful 30 seconds of manic pumping. It had been an invasive, empty experience that was over before it had begun. She couldn't even remember who it was, until later when it dawned on her.

Her mother, Ursula, had been useless, impractical and ill-prepared. She couldn't stop giggling about sex, and how Katy was now 'a woman'. She could still hear the girlish laugh. Ursula hadn't even bought her a pack of sanitary pads, and when she did, they were those big, old-fashioned things that her mother had cackled at. "We used to call them bunnies," she'd said, winking, "because they looked like white rabbits hanging in a butcher's shop." Katy's stomach lurched, her face wincing and flushing hot, just as it had all those years ago. She'd had to find out about periods and sex by herself, using condoms and a wing and a prayer until she was old enough to go to the doctor alone. It may have been the liberated 70s, young women burning their bras and overtly eager to lose their virginity, but sex and contraception had been the teenage Katy's secret. It hadn't been like that for Tilly, thank goodness. Katy had been prepared as soon as she noticed the signs of pre-pubescence in her blossoming young daughter.

A tear trickled down her cheek and she brushed it away with her hand. Not another memory to process? Using a visualization technique, Katy went back in time to the teenage self, took her by the hand and led her away, giving her permission to have a mother who was sensitive, mature and supportive. She healed the child inside and showed her what she'd grown into, told her how proud she was of her, how much she was loved now. Having completed the process, she dabbed her eyes, straightened her hair, and opened the laptop.

Tony's email caught her eye. She'd strike a neutral and professional tone, ask about his wife's business trip, give him some advice about child psychologists and fill him in on her week. Only at the end, did she address the idea of meeting up. Her fingers hesitated for a while as she held her breath. There must be a reason for this ongoing friendship, perhaps it was to do with her work? He'd alluded to the fact he was having a few problems with Amber, but she didn't specialize in child therapy! Maybe she should meet him just once to find out what it was all about. Beneath her T-shirt, she could feel her heart beating. What if he was boring and they had nothing to talk about? Why waste her time on him when she was so busy? And besides, if they did click…

PS. It would be great to meet up sometime. Let me know when you're in town. I'm pretty busy, but I could probably find time for a quick cuppa.

If he asked, she could say she had no time, and it wouldn't

be a lie.

Freddie came rattling through the door, knocking the windchimes into a frenzy, carrying his dirty kit bag and an old satchel crammed with tatty books. "Mum?" he yelled up, "I'm starving. When's tea?"

Katy came bounding down the stairs just as Tilly opened the kitchen door. "Flapjack?" she said, shoving a plate full of them at her brother, who took three and wolfed them down. The kitchen was a bombsite of pots, pans, wooden spoons, baking trays and dirty knives. Katy bit her lip and clenched her fists, pushing the nails into her palms.

"Tilly," she said sweetly, the blood pulsing through her temples, "Thanks for making flapjacks."

"S'okay."

"Do you think you could help tidy up?" said Katy, nodding towards the mess and faking a smile.

"I'll do it later, I've got homework," said Tilly, leaving the kitchen and skipping up the stairs.

"What are we having for dinner," said Freddie, rummaging through the fridge. "Anything to snaffle?" He opened some orange juice. "Had to practice in the rain. There was nothing to eat afterwards," he moaned, swigging straight from the carton as he continued to survey the contents of the fridge. "Oh God, Mum, not vegetarian!" He'd spotted supper on the bottom shelf.

"I'm trying to cut down on meat, it's not good for you."

"But you love meat," he said. "You're such a fraud."

"And it's expensive!"

"Don't give me that bullshit, it's since you started that spiritual stuff, isn't it?"

"But Freddie—"

"It's ridiculous! I'm not having those Linda McCartney's, they're nothing like sausages."

"I don't know what else we've got."

"I'm a growing boy, you need to feed me properly!" he said,

his voice rising in panic.

Growing boy? Thought Katy, he was already six-foot tall and filling out. She ran her hands over her flat stomach and small frame, wondering how she'd ever produced her son, who was on the 96th percentile even at birth, all coiled over like a swiss-roll. It must have been Richard's genes.

"A boy could starve round here, you know," said Freddie, a cheeky smile lighting up his face and turning it all boyish and innocent.

"I'll cook onions, mash and gravy, they'll be fine," said Katy, taking the bogus sausages from the fridge.

Clearing away Tilly's debris as well as the dirty supper plates, she wondered how many meals she'd cooked and how many more she'd produce before she died. If she added up the average time spent preparing food, what percentage of her life would that be? If she didn't keep going, she'd be sucked under. And how come Tilly always managed to muck up the house the minute it was tidy? Katy hadn't been like that. She'd helped her mum, didn't dare leave dirty dishes, let alone take over the kitchen. Why wasn't Tilly like that? She knew the answer: Tilly didn't have an unreasonable and demanding mother. Katy sighed deeply as she wiped the table. Freddie was right, he couldn't survive on vegetarian food. She should have made him something separate, but she was already working so flipping hard, and it had been a hell of a week, without her feeling like a bad mother.

After supper, at the top of the house, Katy stood in front of the mirror. "Please!" she said softly, hesitating on the landing before heading into the office. Kneeling on the meditation stool, she closed her eyes. Breath. Hara. She waited for the Voice. "Did I do the right thing?" she whispered, sitting in the silence. Within a few minutes of focusing on the breath, the thoughts ebbed away and were replaced with a warm, blissful stillness that radiated from her core. The top of her head was tingling. The peace that passeth all understanding.

At the end of thirty minutes, she rose, checked the mirror once more for the Voice, and realized she hated the pink and sky-blue ensemble she'd been wearing.

I'll buy myself a new pair of shoes tomorrow, she thought, cheer myself up. I know I've got about twenty pairs, but I fancy some navy-blue ones with white edging.

The final Aura-Soma bottle was dark blue and clear. Clear must mean white, she thought, walking downstairs to the bedroom. Peeling off the pink T-shirt and pale jeans, she folded herself into a white waffle gown before dumping the clothes into the bin.

She'd already jumped into bed and was pulling the duvet over her when the wind chime clattered downstairs. Moments later, Richard tip-toed into the bedroom, swaying slightly and smelling of alcohol and Chanel No.5. "Had to get the proposal finished tonight," he offered. "Last minute changes," he said, unsteadily hopping as he took his shoes off. "Didn't want to work over the weekend."

Katy frowned as he trampled his trousers to the ground and stepped out of them.

"Quick celebratory drink with Helen and the team."

At 3am, a painful throbbing on the right side of Katy's head woke her. It felt as if a stake had been hammered into the inner corner of her right eye and her stomach was lurching and nauseous. She reached for the migraine tablets on her bedside cabinet and lay in the dark waiting for the searing pain to ebb away.

"You've been overdoing it, Beloved," said the Voice. "Running around after other people with never a thought for yourself."

"I have been thinking of myself," said Katy in what was left of her mind's eye, "I did a lot of healing this week, and I booked two holidays."

"Still doing, not being."

"I meditate, don't I?"

"If you want to see changes in your life you have to start altering your mindset, how you think, what you believe, the habits you run."

"I'm trying! I've been visualizing a happy marriage and a quieter life, but it's hard, and anyway, where were you when I needed you?"

The Voice was silent for a moment. "In truth, I'm always with you."

"Then why the hell didn't you answer me?"

"Hell has nothing to do with it. I tell you, I'm there when you truly need me."

"But I needed your advice."

"About Tony?"

"Yes! Why didn't you help me?"

"You're a grown woman, Katy. Autonomous, sovereign, and you have free will. Only you can decide what's right for you."

"But I don't know what's right!"

"Deep down, you do. It's time to discern for yourself."

"How?"

"Follow your intuitive knowing, rather than what you think and feel."

"What?"

"The first thought, the deep knowing, the small voice within, is usually right. People over-analyze what they think they should or shouldn't do, and what they feel, and often, that leads away from the truth."

"But…"

"Your thoughts and feelings are a product of your past experience. You show your clients that, don't you? Show them it's based on childhood conditioning?"

Katy had to concede the Voice was right. The hammering in her head was easing up.

"A new pair of shoes only brings fleeting happiness," said the Voice, "and you're after something more, aren't you?"

Katy rubbed her temples with her fingertips. "Well, yes."

"An exotic holiday, a promotion at work, a nice piece of jewelry, chocolate – that sort of happiness depends on external stimuli and is fleeting."

"Yes."

"People seek happiness outside of themselves because they don't believe it exists within, but the true wellspring of joy is that which you cultivate on the inside and take with you to the outside."

"I think I'm starting to get it."

"On your walks and when you meditate, you're connecting to nature, to the eternal, the mystical, to something far bigger and better than a new pair of shoes and a bar of dark chocolate."

"*There is no path to happiness; happiness is the path.*"

"The Buddha. Quite so. As you release the past, Love, Light, Life can flow again."

"Like unblocking a load of interconnecting pipes?"

"That's one way of looking at it!" chuckled the Voice, "Life-force, like water in pipes, can start flowing again."

"Why do you say it with that emphasis?"

"Light, Love, Life?"

"Yes."

"I'm talking about a superluminal, generative, creative Light, not the sort you see with your eyes."

"Oh!"

"You can feel it. It's the feeling you get at the end of your meditation."

"Mmm."

"The three are connected as a trinity, as all Higher Truths are."

"Like Father, Son and Holy Spirit?"

"Or Brahma, Vishnu and Shiva, or Abraham, Isaac and Jacob! But it's not limited to religious concepts - what about electron, proton and neutron?"

"But how is Light connected to Love and Life?"

"They're three in one. Love is an emanation of Divine Light which generates Life."

"I don't get it."

"You will one day. For now, keep clearing those pipes. Fill them with light, become en-*light*-ened, and love, life and happiness will flow."

Chapter 16

Katy flung open the wardrobe doors and removed every scrap of sky blue and baby pink, except for the dusty-pink, wool jacket, and blue check trousers. Everything else went into a bin liner. At last, a look she could live with! Navy suited her and she loved the jaunty look of blue and white stripes and sailor's collars. There were plenty of things in her wardrobe, no need to buy anything, apart from those shoes she fancied. Selecting a crisp, white, linen shirt and a pair of beautifully cut sailor's style pants, she showered and dressed. The trousers must have shrunk, she thought, straining to button them up. "Bloody hell! I've got to stop eating chocolate," she muttered, discarding the outfit, and donning a dress instead.

Downstairs, in the kitchen, she slipped her hand to the back of the fridge. She'd better throw it away right now, but there were only two squares left, what harm could they do? There was an unopened packet, but it was her favorite brand. Maybe she'd keep it – open it to celebrate getting back into the sailor trousers!

Katy sat at the kitchen table with a cup of fresh mint tea, reading the notes she'd made at Lavinia's. *Finding clarity from the light*, she'd written. *The blue and clear bottle is about transforming suffering, freeing yourself from distractions, limitations, and obstacles. This leads to peace and stillness, and when all is still, you'll find clarity.*

Clarity about what, she wondered as she looked at her diary? The chocolate lady was first up today, then a double session with Seamus, followed by a woman who was 'beside herself' because she couldn't afford to heat the swimming pool at her second home! The final client was the man from the museum who was struggling with the feelings that were being unleashed.

* * *

The small bald man finished his group session at The Priory and hailed a taxi.

"Paddington Station, please!" He smiled.

Sitting in the back of the black cab, he felt better than he had in years. His legs open, feet flat on the floor, hands relaxed, it felt as if layers of guilt and shame were falling away. These monthly group sessions had been good for him. Things weren't perfect by any means, but he knew he could dodge whatever his wife might throw at him. His daughter was settling at school and he'd eased himself off the worst of his habits. Something good was about to happen, something wholesome that would bring him a new lease of life. He could feel it in his bones.

The taxi dropped him off, and after crossing the concourse, he grabbed a Cornish pasty from a stall by the platform. He pushed through the turnstile to his train and found a seat. Having eaten the pie, he dusted the crumbs from his lap and stretched out his legs. The rocking of the carriage as it eased out of London, lulled him, and his eyelids grew heavy. He knew what he wanted, and he knew it would work out, just as it always did. There was a distant stirring in his loins as his eyes closed and surrendered.

* * *

Richard sat at a small table in the corner of a busy Smithfield restaurant, watching Emma as she picked at her roast beef salad, her slender hands holding the cutlery with such poise that he couldn't help reaching out to touch them tenderly.

"I've got something for you," he said. The little box had been in his briefcase for months, waiting for precisely the right moment.

"For all your hard work on the acquisition." He pushed the small turquoise package towards her. Recognizing it immediately, she put down her knife and fork and flashed him that smile of hers, all white, even teeth and glossy lips.

"Oh! You shouldn't have!" she breathed, her eyes sparkling

in that way they did.

"Go on! Open it now!" he said, noticing she was about to slip it into her expensive handbag. Her long fingers picked languorously at the white ribbon, unfurling the bow carefully. She took the box in one hand and the lid in the other, her fingers perfectly placed, as if posing for a manicure advert. Looking him in the eye, her mouth open in anticipation, she gradually inched the top off. As she peeped into the box, she gasped, covering her mouth with a flawless hand.

"Thought they'd go with that necklace," said Richard, eyeing up the small diamond that hung just above her cleavage.

"You noticed!" she said wrinkling her forehead and drawing her eyebrows together. She stood up to hug him. "Thank you!" she breathed. "They're beautiful."

Chapter 17

March 27ᵗʰ 2009

It was almost the end of March and Katy had taken Friday off to deal with mounting paperwork and bills. This new regime of Terry's meant she wasn't keeping on top of the bookkeeping.

Before burying herself in invoices and receipts, she took a quick look at her emails. Anything to delay the inevitable, she thought. The Easter holiday cottage in the Cotswolds had been confirmed, and the company she'd approached about Mexico had emailed a quote. The plane tickets to Barcelona for the Conference for Evolution in Human Consciousness had been sent, and Shanti had forwarded details of the hotel booking. She was about to sign off when a familiar MoD address popped up on her screen. Her pulse quickened.

I'm in town this morning. Leaving Whitehall after lunch. You're probably busy, and it's a bit of a long shot, but fancy meeting up for that cup of tea?

Katy's heart hammered rapidly and she stood up. Shit, she thought, what do I do now? Pacing up and down, a determined look on her face, she weighed the pros and cons. She couldn't, could she? She was too flipping busy, and all this paperwork! But it was Friday and she could catch up tomorrow. No, there was too much, it would spill over into the weekend. A cup of chamomile tea would settle her, help her to think. She hurried down to the kitchen.

Standing in the snug looking out of the French windows, she blew onto the hot liquid. She needed to get groceries later, she remembered. There wasn't any food in the house, and they'd be home later, hungry and expecting dinner on the table. After all, she'd taken the day off to catch up the backlog; they were bound to expect her to cook. Katy flung open the door and stepped into the small, walled garden. The roses were just coming into bud, she noticed. Mug in hand, she walked the length of the brickwork patio. What if it was a waste of time and they had nothing to talk about? If she was honest with herself, she didn't want to go. What if he had the hots for her and she had to wriggle out of it? Or worse, if he didn't have any feelings at all and she did? It could be awkward, and it would be a waste of her afternoon. It was Friday and she was tired, for God's sake. Tara's words came swimming back. *Terrible idea.* That's right, she had plenty of friends she'd rather see. It was one thing to exchange emails, and quite another to give up her precious time to see him in person. Heading back inside and closing the French windows against the cool spring air, she'd made up her mind. She'd stay at home and get the accounts finished.

Up in the office, invoices sorted into piles, calculator out, a nagging doubt persisted. All work and no play, she should go! Have a bit of fun for once! Katy pushed it to the back of her mind and pulled up a spreadsheet. All work and no play. Puffing up her cheeks, she let out a long stream of air and started on the 'income' column. All work and no play. Third time. Reaching for her pendulum and charts, she made space amidst the slips of paper. "Should I meet up with Tony Verde?" she asked. The crystal swung on its fine chain and nodded a definitive yes. She must have worded it wrong. "Is it in my best and highest interest to meet Tony Verde this afternoon?" It moved up and down wildly in an emphatic yes. Pursing her lips and holding the chain between a pinched finger and thumb, she thought for a moment. "Is it beneficial, given I've got all this work to do and I'm tired, to give up this afternoon to meet Tony Verde, the Tony Verde from school that I've been emailing?" Still the crystal swayed to and fro in the affirmative. Katy didn't give up. "How beneficial?" she asked, waving the pendulum over a fan-shaped chart, which ran from zero to one hundred percent. If it were over fifty percent, she'd consider it. The crystal shot straight to a small figure eight on its side, just beyond the one hundred mark.

Infinity? Katy frowned deeply and shook her head. It can't be, she thought. "Is it infinitely beneficial?" she asked of the small object in her hands. Yes, came the irrefutable answer as it rocked back and forth. God knows why it's infinitely beneficial, but that's what I'm getting, she thought. There must be a reason and she'd better find out what it was! He'd be coming from Whitehall and going home via Paddington. She looked at her tube map before replying.

I've taken the day off to catch up paperwork. I could meet you around 2.30 pm. Let me know where. Perhaps Hammersmith? It's about halfway and I don't fancy going all the way into town. My mobile number in case you need it – 07936 611339

There was no response. Maybe she'd left it too late. It wasn't meant to be, and she might as well carry on with the invoices, she thought, sighing with relief. Her phone buzzed.

Hammersmith perfect. Can you make 3 pm?

She wondered if he knew it was a big station with two entrances.

See you 3 pm, Hammersmith.

He'd work it out.

Three hours later, wearing a navy and white striped, tight-fitting Breton jersey with midnight blue, high-waisted, linen trousers under her cream mac, Katy left the house, hair straightened into place, make-up on, new blue and white shoes pinching slightly.

Arriving at Hammersmith station six minutes early, she headed for the main Broadway Centre exit, and looked around in case he was already there. Her hands were trembling, her mouth dry, the blood coursing through her. She shouldn't be doing this! What if they didn't recognize each other? She walked the length of the small mall of shops from the tube to the street exit, looking furtively around. Having noticed nothing out of the ordinary, she trudged back to the coffee shop just outside the underground barriers. Standing with her back to the window, she watched the stream of people passing through. Feeling uncomfortable, she straightened her raincoat, smoothed down a stray curl, then placed one foot slightly in front of the other in a pose. She was pulling her already flat stomach in, lifting her chin somewhat and trying to look casual. Focusing on the ever-increasing torrent of commuters, she noticed that some were jostling for position outside the café. Perhaps they were waiting for loved ones or meeting friends. Katy's eyes were fixed on the gates, waiting for a man with a golden thatch of wavy hair, maybe greying at the temples, a few crow's feet around his startling blue eyes. She envisaged him striding manfully in his suit. Oh my God, last time he'd seen her, she'd had wild, long, curly hair! She'd forgotten to tell him it was straightened, as far as the unruly mop could be, into a tamed, short, choppy bob. The station clock showed 3.03 pm. He was late. Maybe he was the other side, waiting at the wrong entrance? Katy chewed the inside of her cheek and checked her phone before slipping it into her mac pocket and furling her hand around it just in case. Her pulse was racing, and her mouth felt like blotting paper.

Some short, bald guy sporting rather unfashionable gold-rimmed glasses was standing next to her, trying to stretch up on tiptoe to see above the taller woman in front. He was nervously fiddling with his left cufflink, then jangling change in his pocket.

It was nine minutes past now, and Tony was late; her pet hate, given the regimented timekeeping she forced herself into. I knew I shouldn't have come, she grumbled to herself.

Taking an old-style mobile from the pocket of his grey mac, she could see the bald man next to her laboriously tapping out a message with one finger and hitting send. Katy's phone buzzed in her pocket and she snatched at it, her stomach tightening. With mounting horror, it dawned on her. No, it couldn't be. She turned to the stranger next to her. "Did you just text me?" The words shot out before she'd had time to think, let alone look at the message. Why had she said that? The text could have been from anyone! Her heart was thumping now. The bald man turned to her, his blue eyes staring through his glasses as he furrowed his pale, wrinkled brow.

"Are you, Tony?" Katy's mouth hung open as she felt herself stepping back involuntarily. It was a stupid question. She'd obviously made a mistake. "Sorry, my mistake!"

"Yes," came the uncertain answer, the voice small and faltering.

Shit, thought Katy.

"I'm Katy," she said, forcing up the corners of her mouth and extending her right hand.

"I was looking for the hair," he said, feebly offering a limp hand.

Me, too, thought Katy, flattening down her unruly mop. He was nothing like she'd remembered him. She must have been shorter back then because he was definitely taller, wasn't he?

"There's a nice café on Fulham Palace Road," she said brightly, her heart sinking. She could see from the blank expression on his face, that he hadn't got the faintest idea where Fulham Palace Road was. "Shall we?"

Tony seemed to have been struck dumb, his mouth hanging open, his eyes fixed on her. Beads of sweat were forming on his high, bald forehead.

"Any good pubs round here?" he stammered, a lop-sided smirk breaking the gormless expression.

Pub? At 3 o'clock in the afternoon? She supposed she'd have to entertain this short baldy from the shires, so she might as well get on with it.

"Yah, there's a couple of pubs on the Broadway," she said, walking purposefully ahead. This was going to be hard work. She should have said no. Bloody pendulum: why had she trusted it? Hopefully, she could get away after the first drink. Forty minutes should do it. He was a clueless out-of-towner and she could make up some excuse about trains and rush hour.

"After you," said Tony, rushing to keep up with her London stride.

Katy rolled her eyes. How could she have been so foolish?

Holding the heavy glass door open, Tony smiled and ushered her into the pub. Katy walked straight up to the bar and was about to order, when 'Baldy' asked her what she'd like. "A large glass of Rioja, please." She'd need something to get her through this awkward dead-end.

"Make that two." Tony winked to the barman.

"Will that be all, sir? If you want another glass, it'd be cheaper to get a bottle."

"Righty-ho! A bottle of Rioja then," said Tony, extracting a smart, Italian leather wallet from his inside pocket.

They sat at a quiet table nursing their glasses, Katy waiting for him to say something, anything. She took a large swig and jumped in. Somebody had to get the ball rolling. "So," she said, taking a deep breath, "Hammersmith's changed so much since I first moved to London." She was looking around the pub, which had obviously been gentrified.

Tony leaned forward as if to steady himself. Holding the stem of his glass, he swirled the rich, dark liquid.

"It's always so busy on a Friday, people leaving work early," she continued.

He sniffed at the wine then sampled it. "Not bad. Rioja's always a good bet in a pub," he said, his cobalt eyes boring into her.

"You know your wines!" Katy smiled, pushing an errant curl behind her ear and taking the glass in her hands.

"Bit of a hobby." He took a gulp.

"Me too!" Her face reddened slightly as she looked down at the coaster.

The conversation moved on from Hammersmith and wine to school days, mutual friends, old haunts, and how they'd both changed.

"What happened to that girl, whats-a-name, the one with the freckles who got caught snogging your friend Rob outside the Physics lab?"

"I know who you mean," said Tony. "It'll come to me... Linda! She moved up North. Married a bloke that my sister used to go out with, can't remember his name, but I know he's a complete dick. More wine?"

The flow of Rioja was oiling the wheels of conversation. Katy was taking small sips, aware that she hadn't eaten much and wasn't used to drinking more than a couple of glasses. Tony loosened his tie, unbuttoned his collar, and leaned back into the velvet banquette, his left arm extending across the top to reveal a very nice pilot's style watch. "Shall I order another bottle?" His legs were apart and relaxed now.

"I'll get it." She could feel his eyes following her, watching the curve of her hips in the tight-fitting trousers. She still had it, despite her age. He might like what he saw, but he didn't have a chance in hell. She'd make her excuses soon and leave; lesson learned. "Another bottle of Rioja and a large bottle of sparkling water please." The water would slow her down, she was already feeling a bit unsteady and needed to stay in control.

The chat meandered on from school to some of the antics they got up to in their teens. Tony was red in the face laughing. "And I jumped on the ice and you screamed!"

"I thought you could fall through and kill yourself!"

"It was only a couple of inches deep, they'd drained it for the winter."

"I didn't know that, I was stoned, remember?"

Katy had broken her 'three-glass rule' and was giggling. Her hair was returning to its natural state as bits sprung up here and there. She loosened her belt a notch.

"Tell me about the healing," said Tony, leaning in towards her and fixing her with those eyes.

"Oh, it's nothing," she said, "a bit of Reiki and some other stuff that I've learned."

"Wow, how does it work?"

"I'm just the channel, the wire if you like, bringing it through from up there." Her index finger was raised and jabbing towards the ceiling.

"I love that sort of thing."

"Really?" Katy wasn't used to it. Richard, the kids, and most of her colleagues, along with the school mums, didn't have the slightest interest.

"What do you do, I mean I know you're MoD, but..."

"Officer in the RAF!"

Katy covered her mouth and stifled a smirk. "Bloody hell! You?"

"Yep! I'm a freemason as well – hence the interest in your healing," he said, filling his glass again.

"I don't really know anything about the Masons apart from the fact it's a secret society." She shivered slightly. "They're a bit dodgy, aren't they?"

"I think you'd like it." He was winking at her. "Symbols, allegories, sacred numbers."

"Numbers?"

"Yeah, there are special number sequences that mean different things. Three, seven, nine, eleven, they're usually odd numbers."

"What about six?"

"Why six?"

"Nicola Tesla. Three, six and nine. They're my favorite numbers."

"You know about Tesla?"

"I know about lots of things," said Katy, leaning in towards him and cupping her glass in both hands, a broad beam lighting up her face.

"Did you know that today is March 27, 2009?"

"Yep!" She was quietly chuckling now and lolling on her chair as she kicked off her shoes.

"March is three."

"Third month. I know, it's my birthday in March."

"Sixth," he said, staring at her.

Her mouth dropped open. "How did you remember that?"

He hadn't, he'd seen it on a profile somewhere when he was researching her, and it had stuck in his mind. "I dunno!" he said. "Twenty-seven is two and seven, which is nine," he went back to making his point about the date, while she propped herself up on her elbow, which slid away. She downed a glass of water, narrowly missing her mouth so that the first sip dribbled down her top.

"And two thousand and nine, is two and nine, which is eleven."

"So, it's a three, nine and eleven day." The look of concentration on her face made Tony smile.

"Yes," he said, downing the last of his Rioja, "Three of the secret mason numbers."

"My birth year was a nine, so I'm my three favorite numbers! Six for the day, three for the month and nine for the year."

He smiled as she excused herself, tottering her way towards the Ladies', swaying slightly as she moved from table to table. He emptied the bottle into his glass and drank it while he waited for her return.

"Have you read Dan Brown?" he asked, tipping her wine into his glass.

"Not my thing."

"You'd like The Da Vinci Code."

"How do you know?"

"I just know, trust me."

"I don't have time."

"You'll get through it quickly." Tony checked his watch. "Oh shit, it's 9 o'clock! I'd better message Lauren and get out of here pronto."

"What?" Katy had lost track of time. "Flip. I'd better text

Richard, he'll wonder where the hell I am."

Grabbing her mac and bag, she marched precariously out of the pub, Tony at her side, gallantly escorting her to her train. She sat back, watching him wave from the platform as the carriage sidled out. He stayed there till his outline was so diminished it was just a fuzzy figure in a crowd. He fancied the pants off her, but she didn't feel the slightest urge towards him.

Taking her phone out of her pocket, she rang Tara.

"I met him!"

"Who?"

Katy laughed. "Tony. He's nothing like I thought he'd be."

"Oh no."

"Don't worry, he holds absolutely zero attraction!" She was giggling.

"You sure about that?"

"I drank a bit too much."

"I hope you didn't let your guard down."

"He's an old-fashioned, short-arsed, baldy."

"Why did you go?"

"Dowsed and got a yes. He told me about the Masons and Dan Brown."

"Just be careful. I don't have a very good feeling about the Masons, or Tony for that matter!"

The train lumbered into Turnham Green station as she finished the call. Katy rose unsteadily to her feet, grabbing the handrail and recovering her balance as the train jolted to a halt. She hadn't gone shopping. There was no food in the house and Freddie was going to go mad. Wobbling along in her new kitten heels, she weaved through the neat suburban streets, the crisp night air bringing her to her senses. It had been a totally unproductive afternoon. He hadn't even divulged any masonic secrets. All he'd done was recommend a best-selling book she'd so far managed to avoid. The dowsing must have been off.

Katy took a deep breath and bracing herself, plunged the key into the front door. The familiar jangle of chimes woke Richard, who'd been snoozing on the sofa, the Evening Standard slipping off his lap. Jonathan Ross's voice was blaring into the darkness from a flickering screen.

"Where the fuck have you been?" said Richard, blinking into the light that Katy had just switched on.

"Went to meet an old friend from school." She'd never been very good at lying. Better to stick with the truth. "Waste of time, actually."

"Why so late?"

"You know me, made the best of it, had a couple of glasses of Rioja and lost track of time."

"A *couple* of glasses?" Richard was looking at her ruffled hair, the loose belt, her discarded shoes. He wasn't *that* emotionally constipated, even Rich could tell she was drunk.

"Where's Tilly?" she asked, diverting the conversation away from her state of inebriation.

"Staying overnight with that girl from school."

"Eva? She'll probably go into town with her tomorrow."

"Seems to do what the fuck she likes."

"Rich, she's sixteen! That's what teenagers do!" Sweet sixteen. Katy had been off the rails by then, she hoped Tilly would pull through okay.

"What are you doing now?"

"Just going to get out of these clothes before sorting out supper."

"We've eaten. Freddie made some fancy cheese on toast thing."

"Oh. Okay. Did he make any for me?"

Richard grunted and returned to the television while Katy made herself a piece of toast before heading upstairs to change.

Freddie was in his room, listening to music. She knocked.

"It's me. Can I come in?"

The room smelled of socks and teenage boy. His clothes were

strewn across a chair in the corner, his schoolbooks crammed under the bed. His battered guitar was pinning down an unruly pile of papers on the small desk. Freddie was stretched out, his full six feet languishing on the bed, one earphone dangling so he could hear his mum. She didn't want to smother him and knew she needed to back off. A young man needs his father and he couldn't cling to her apron strings. She had to cut him free and let him go, but she missed the closeness, the tenderness, the connection. The innocent little boy was growing up.

"You okay?"

"Yeah. Just a bit tipsy! You?"

"Just chilling. Got a big match tomorrow."

She should go and watch him, but that was Richard's domain, the only thing he contributed, apart from money. Father and son needed to bond, and it was best if she wasn't there.

"Okay. Don't stay up too late then," she said, giving her son a quick hug before leaving him to it.

Alone in her bedroom, Katy slipped off her clothes and wrapped herself in a thick bathrobe which did nothing to stop the chill that hung around her. It would be Easter soon and they'd be going away. Perhaps the break was just what she and Rich needed.

Chapter 18

April 2009

Katy had packed everything for their holiday, including edible paints for decorating boiled eggs, and a hoard of chocolate for a traditional Easter egg hunt. Tara had lent her a copy of 'The Da Vinci Code', which she'd tucked into the side of her bag. She'd left a couple of lights on at home, put a holiday message on her emails and another on the answerphone. Constantine (the house) was tidy and Beauty (the car) was loaded. All Richard had to do was sling his guitar in the back and drive, his usual road-rage spilling over from the offset. Phrases such as, "Decided which lane you're in, beer-bottle specs?" and "For fuck's sake, turning right at Bristol, are we?" peppered the entire journey, along with the frequently used "Twat-monger!"

The pretty stone cottage was half-way down a steep and narrow country lane, overgrown with hedgerows either side. Its leaded lights and stone mullions, mottled with lichen, were framed by wild, rambling roses. There was a picket fence with a gate, bordering a tiny strip of gravel at the front, and a small, mature, and somewhat overgrown garden at the back. It was the perfect hideaway. *Within easy walking distance of two pubs, each serving excellent food and local real ales,* read the information sheet. There were a couple of walking maps, a birdwatching book, a battered old draughts set, a pack of cards and several leaflets for local markets, shops, and places of interest.

Freddie and Richard unloaded the car while Katy hid the bag of Easter eggs and inspected the tiny kitchen. Tilly helped her unpack and organize the food.

Later that afternoon, the country air began to work its magic on Katy as she sat on a rickety bench outside, listening to the chorus of birdsong and the bleating of sheep far off across the valley. Richard sat next to her, reading a novel. The kids were off exploring somewhere and there was nothing to do except give herself up to the warm afternoon. If she got herself relaxed enough, she might be able to initiate something in the bedroom. She'd been working with positive suggestion hypnosis and was confident she could resurrect some intimacy with Richard. He was at his best on holiday when he could unwind and enjoy the fruits of his labor. They'd probably sing along to his guitar-playing later as he rattled through some covers. It was times like these that his old sense of humor would return and have them all in stitches.

As the light began to fade, they returned to the cottage. Katy lit a fire in the hearth and sank into the chintz sofa with her book. She supposed she'd better read the bloody thing.

"Mum, are you getting anything to eat? I'm starving," said Freddie, sometime later.

"In a minute."

"Mum. It's gone 8 o'clock!"

"Hang on, just finishing this page," she said, prizing herself away. "Bacon and eggs?"

The washing-up could wait. The story was hotting up, and she sat feverishly reading into the night while the rest of the family watched a film on the small television.

"You coming to bed?" said Richard around midnight.

Reluctantly putting down the paperback, she climbed the small winding staircase, and missing her footing on an uneven step, she jarred her back. The mattress was hard, and by morning, she'd seized up. The emotion behind back pain, she recalled, was feeling unsupported.

A gentle walk loosened her up and a half pint of real ale eased her aching muscles, but by the evening she'd stiffened up again. "This bloody mattress," she muttered, wedging a pillow under her knees.

The following morning, Katy could feel her mind unwinding. Pub lunches, fresh air, board games and television – it was the perfect retro mix. She needed three months of this: no clients, no emails, no phone calls and no big house to run. Her book was better than she'd expected, and her nose was buried in it for hours.

"Come on, Mum, are you going to read that thing all holiday?" moaned Freddie. "I thought we were going for a walk by the lake?"

She had promised, she supposed. Gingerly leaning forward, she winced and pulled herself out of the sofa before straightening her back. She wished she could stay there, reading, perhaps falling asleep later, on those soft cushions. Taking a deep breath, she pulled on her boots, took her coat from the peg behind the door, and grabbed her bag. "Okay, let's go!"

It was more fun than she'd thought, tramping through the meadows to the lake, then on to The Bell Inn. The leaflet was right, excellent food and great real ales. Katy chose a half pint of local IPA and a confit of duck with mashed root veg.

A round route took them back along the edge of a deciduous forest before dropping into the valley where the cottage nestled. Out of breath from the climb through the woods, they rested for a while. In the stillness of the late afternoon, Katy perched on a fallen log while Richard checked his phone and wandered off to make a call. The children were exploring in the undergrowth and she sat alone, surrounded by magnificent beeches. Clear open skies stretched out beyond the line of trees, and a silver strip of water glistened in the distance. Her life wasn't bad and nor was her marriage. She and Richard got along okay, they knew each other, like a comfortable pair of old friends. The kids were doing alright, nothing to worry about, no drugs, no problems at school. They were pretty well adjusted. She and Rich were a good team, and they were doing a sterling job. She closed her eyes and watched the dappled patterns of color dance over her eyelids as she drew in a deep breath of earthy air, blowing it out slowly through her lips. The corners of her mouth turned upwards and a warm glow ran the length of her body.

Back at the cottage, she picked up the paperback, wondering why she hadn't read it before. Richard had scoffed at how badly it was written. "You know the critics panned it don't you?" he said. He was proud of reading only the classics, novels of literary note, whatever had won the Booker and a handful of modern authors. Despite his overt criticism, she was consuming page after page, the plot driving her forward, the esoteric world of MOSES (the Movement of Spiritually Enlightened Souls) being laid bare in print. He'd written about their world, thought Katy, thrilled by the adventure, fascinated by the symbols, and locked into the romance.

"When's supper?" said Freddie. "I'm wasting away!"

He ate twice as much as Katy and Tilly put together, but never put on an ounce of fat. Wrenching herself away from the action, Katy put the novel down and sloped into the tiny kitchen. Opening the cupboard doors, she stared at the basic stock of groceries. Nothing inspired her. She turned to the minuscule fridge, rummaging through the shelves for a moment before snapping into action. Thirty minutes later, they were eating 'croque monsieur' with rocket and watercress salad. It was a holiday after all, so damn the wheat-free, dairy-free regime.

"Is that all we're having?" moaned Freddie, his face in shock.

"You can finish the last of that crusty loaf," said Katy. "The butter's in the fridge."

He slathered a huge hunk of bread with thick slices of cold butter and chewed through it hastily. Every scrap was consumed before the table was cleared.

"What are we having for afters?" Her son was never satisfied.

"Special treat!" she said, eyes twinkling. "Treacle Tart!" Pulling it from its white paper bag, she smiled triumphantly and placed it on the table. "Got it at the baker's next to the pub." She winked.

After a post-dinner game of Knockout Whist, the family settled by the fire to watch the latest Bond movie. Katy buried herself in the world of Robert Langdon. Every time the story mentioned secret societies or codes, her thoughts would turn to Tony. Dull though he was, there was something electrifying about the mysteriousness of his world: The RAF and the Masons, neither of which were familiar to her. Come to think of it, she'd never had the slightest interest in either until now! She was a hippy at heart, and as for the Masons, she'd only ever heard odd snippets. Perhaps there was a side to Tony that was yet to emerge? Could he be a member of MOSES, because something was pulling her towards him? Maybe it was a spiritual connection because she certainly wasn't interested physically!

It rained the next day, and the family entertained themselves at the small cottage. Around 9.30 pm, Katy read the final page of The Da Vinci Code and snapped the book shut. An empty feeling engulfed her. The mystery was solved, the excitement of the thriller concluded. She reached for her phone.

Finished it! Brilliant. Was familiar with the concepts. Thanks for recommending.

The family were engrossed in a television series that she'd now missed too much of to catch up.

Feeling lost, she poured herself a glass of Montepulciano and stared at the TV screen. Her phone buzzed.

You read it quickly! Let's meet to discuss!

Fingers poised to respond, she looked at her brood, glued to the television, and decided against it. She'd ignore Tony for now and concentrate on the family, welcome this opportunity to be with them.

Later that evening she lay on the hard mattress, her mind full of Paris, symbols, and the sacred union of the Hieros Gamos. The time had come to approach Richard, she thought, willing herself to feel something other than dread. Creating a Daniel Craig, Bond-style fantasy in her mind's eye before rolling over to initiate something, her lumber region went into spasm and stopped the action dead. She took a couple of paracetamols and spent the rest of the night flat on her back and motionless. Was the body saying 'no', she wondered? Two days later, as if to prove her theory, she got a nasty bout of thrush, just as her back was improving and she'd psyched herself up for another attempt. It must have been all that beer and treacle tart, she supposed. She wasn't used to that much sugar.

Chapter 19

Katy wondered if it was worth going away. She seemed to work twice as hard either side of a break. Clients were always eager to cram in an extra appointment before she left, and on returning, she'd have a deluge of emails, post and telephone messages to attend to. On top of that was the packing, unpacking and extra washing. The holiday in the middle seemed like an illusion.

Within hours of getting home, Katy was rushing around, spinning more plates than a Cirque du Soleil juggler. Every so often, she'd think of messaging Tony but quite honestly, she was too busy.

Later that week in the quiet of Terry's consulting room, she broached the subject of Richard.

"I don't know where to start," she said.

"At the beginning."

"I'd only been with him a few months when I got pregnant with Tilly." She cast her mind back to the challenging pregnancy. "I was in hospital on bed-rest for weeks, in danger of losing her. I only read the parenting books once I knew she was out of the woods." She shot a glance at Terry, who was leaning back in his chair, softly gazing at her through his round-rimmed specs. "I was so worried."

"Of course, that's natural."

"It wasn't just the baby, I was anxious about Richard as well. I didn't think he'd be able to cope. Anything domestic was a mystery to him."

"You could say that about a lot of men."

Her heart was thumping as she hesitated. She'd never told anyone before. "I hadn't known him very long and I wasn't sure."

"In what way?"

"He's very different to me. Richard's always been aloof and impractical," she said, staring at the pattern in the carpet. "He's academically bright, but clueless when it comes to ordinary living. He couldn't look after himself, let alone a child!"

"How did you feel about that?"

"Scared! I knew the responsibility rested squarely on my shoulders."

"He didn't help at all?"

"He provided for us financially. I wanted everything to be okay, so I went along with it. I did love him. We became close, but it's more of a friendship than a marriage."

Terry made a note. "Going back to the baby, did you get any help from the family?"

"They all live miles away. My parents are like another pair of children who need entertaining, so they're no help. His parents are in Leeds and we hardly ever see them."

"Did things improve once Tilly was born?"

"She was an unusual child, complex, creative." She paused. "Richard didn't know how to react when I had her."

"To you or to the baby?"

"Both. The situation, being a father. He didn't seem to have the emotional intelligence to deal with it."

"Some fathers connect when the baby's a bit older. Did they bond later?"

"Not really. He went back to work straight away and left me to it." A lump was forming in her throat. "I wanted to be the best mother possible, I wanted to do it all perfectly." Her face screwed up as the emotions came flooding back.

"Which is impossible. You can't blame yourself."

"I know that now," said Katy, sniffing back the tears and composing herself. "It was the exhaustion of trying, and the complicated emotions that came up. That's what led me to therapy. Richard's useless with emotions, and I had to talk to someone." She could feel her eyes prickling.

Terry scribbled something down. "So, you have Tilly to thank for your career?"

"I have her to thank for my marriage too. I'm not sure I'd have stayed if it wasn't for her." Katy could feel her stomach knotting. She'd said too much already.

"Carry on," said Terry, leaning forward, his features softening.

"I'd seen another side of Richard." She looked down at her hands in her lap. "He wasn't who I thought he was. He didn't have many friends, wasn't very sociable, wasn't that close to anyone!" He still wasn't, she realized. "But he was the father of my child, and besides, I was scared of being a single parent."

"And scared of being alone?"

Katy looked up, wide-eyed. She hadn't wanted to admit it. Terry waited until she was ready.

"I was frightened of hurting Richard. He'd have been devastated if I'd left."

"Devastated?"

"He had a terrible childhood and I felt sorry for him. He's very fragile under that tough exterior. I decided to stay and make it work. He's not a bad person, you know?"

"What happened to him?"

"His mother, Janet, abandoned him when his sister was born. She doted on Angela and ignored him. He was only two. Then he was bullied at school, and his dad was quite violent, apparently, though I've never seen him angry. Alan's just a docile old man! Rich says he's calmed down a lot."

"Did he go through analysis?"

"Rich or his dad?"

"Either."

"Richard came for a few sessions of couples counselling, but it was futile. As far as I know, Alan's never had therapy. He's a different generation, different background." Katy frowned. People didn't usually change like that. Terry's fountain pen scratched across the page.

"So, you stayed in the marriage and had your son."

"Richard quips that the last time we had sex was when Freddie was conceived." She'd broached the subject at last. "It's his way of dealing with it. He jokes about anything he can't handle – like emotions."

Terry was still taking notes. "His way of resolving the tension. Better than drinking or addiction. Everyone has their coping mechanism. How do you deal with it, Katy?"

"Keep busy." She stared into the distance, shocked by the truth she'd finally named.

"And what would happen if you slowed down?"

"I'd feel guilty." Her mouth hung open. "And I'd have no excuse because I wouldn't be tired and stressed. I'd have to have sex with Richard, and it would be awkward and impossible."

"Why?"

"I feel disconnected. There's no warmth and tenderness there."

"Have you tried to be warm and tender?"

"Yes. He doesn't respond. *He's* not warm and tender with *me*. There must be something wrong with me!"

"Or with him?" Ventured Terry.

"No. He wants sex, I don't. It's me that has the problem. That's what he says. He tells me I'm frigid, and I am!"

"You have no sexual feelings at all?"

"Not for Richard."

"For anyone else?"

"No, but I do have sexual feelings."

As she left Terry's office, something flashed in her mind as if it had been placed there momentarily, like a subliminal message. She suddenly wanted to send Tony a text saying, "I love you." It was both ridiculous and untrue. She dismissed it and carried on marching down the street towards the tube station. As she boarded her train, another unbidden thought flickered, this one even more absurd. "I want to fuck you." It wasn't even a phrase she'd use, let alone send as a text. Resolutely ignoring it, she stood by the doors of the carriage as the other passengers pushed past, taking all the available seats.

Back home that evening, in the quiet of her office, her mind refused to stop. Breath. Hara. It was no use. She was ashamed of herself and angry with Richard. It wasn't just his lack of support but his incessant joking. A sharp one-liner here and there was fine. He could cause raucous hilarity, lifting everyone with a good rib-tickler. Yep. Richard could always make her laugh, but he could never make her happy. What had the Voice said? You have to seek the wellspring of joy within. She turned her attention inwards, but the thoughts continued. Terry was right, it was Richard's way of relieving the pressure, the underlying angst of living. What people did with their tension was important – fritter it away on an addiction, a mere habit, or harness it and use it? We could learn a lot from mother nature, she mused, casting her mind back to Freddie's birth. It took a build-up of pressure to create life, from an orgasm to labor, from a butterfly emerging from a chrysalis, to a chick hatching from an egg. Tension was a powerful commodity if you harnessed it properly. She'd once heard Dame Judi Dench being interviewed on the radio. "Are you ever nervous?" she'd been asked. "Of course, it's the fuel that gives the performance!" Nerves, tension, pressure, fuel. It had creative power if you channeled it, and was destructive if you didn't. The right amount was important, of course. Too little and you had no fuel, too much and it broke you. Just enough pressure could get you good marks in an exam. Too much would overwhelm you. Breath. Hara. Stillness.

Chapter 20

Katy hadn't heard the Voice for ages, but as her life changed, her intuition sharpened. Shanti told her it was a by-product of awakening to a higher consciousness and becoming more aware. Flashes of inspiration would spring from nowhere, ideas would form, and she'd have moments of clear 'knowing' – a phenomenon that she found difficult to explain. It wasn't a feeling, a gut instinct or even a thought, but something deeper and more fundamental. Sometimes it would be her own 'voice' paradoxically coming from within, yet at the same time just above and behind her, as if swinging from an invisible chandelier inside an extended head. She ignored it at first, but quickly learned to listen. "Turn left," it would whisper while she was driving. She'd ignore it, knowing that 'left' was the long way around, only to find roadworks ahead that delayed her by a good twenty minutes. Damn, she'd think, if only she'd taken notice.

As she learned to trust her innate wisdom, she started following it, not only for herself but for patients too. She'd plan a session in advance but realize, as she sat in front of the client, there was a better way. At first, she'd carry on, making it look as if she'd planned a two-pronged approach. The still, small voice, or the knowing, was always right, and within a few days, she was changing tack as soon as she got an inkling there was a better way.

"I love you" and "I want to fuck you" darted through her mind a second time on the way home from work one evening. Where the hell was it coming from, she wondered? Finding an empty carriage on the train, she called Shanti. She'd already told her everything and knew she could trust her.

"You sure it's not just your subconscious?"

"I don't fancy him, and anyway, my libido's flat-lined."

"Could be a fallen influence?" said Shanti.

"What?"

"Well, your psyche's opened up!" Shanti paused. "The Voice and the intuitive hits!"

"So?"

"If you're hearing the Voice, you could be letting something else in too."

"Do you think it's to do with Tony? Has he done something?"

"Could be. The Masons aren't what you think. They're pretty much fallen."

"What do you mean 'fallen'?"

"Dark. Negative. Not of the Light. Has he given you any secrets?"

"No, why?"

"Just wondering if there are any curses. You could dowse! Use your SRT skills!"

"Clear anything untoward?"

"Yes. Get rid of any contracts, cords, curses, anything that's hanging around, anything that could be influencing you for the worse."

"Do you think I'm being punished?"

"What for?"

"I dunno. Not having sex with Richard and meeting up with an old flame."

"That's not exactly a crime, is it?" Shanti's tinkling laugh made Katy smile.

"Thanks, Shanti."

"Just make sure you protect yourself."

"What, with sex?"

Shanti was giggling now. "No! Protect yourself from fallen entities once you know you're clear!"

"Oh!" Katy chuckled. "How?"

"Imagine yourself inside a huge mirror-ball of light, deflecting anything that comes at you."

"Doesn't sound very scientific!"

"Ask Archangel Michael to protect you then."

The train arrived at Turnham Green and having alighted, Katy strode home through the perfect, tree-lined streets, eager to find her pendulum and charts.

In the quiet of her office, she asked: "Do I have anything to clear?" The crystal swung from side to side, indicating a no. "Any fallen influences, psychic hooks, cords, curses?" No.

Putting the charts away, she paused before finishing her post-session notes and switching on the laptop.

Hope you had a restful holiday. It was lovely to meet and catch up. We must do it again. Would love to discuss Dan Brown! When are you free?

She was never free, she sighed, opening her big, page-a-day diary, the one that Shanti called her 'control freak' one. This thing with Tony had to be knocked on the head. It was too time-consuming, and she wasn't in the mood. Flicking through the pages of rigid one-hour slots, she wondered why she was bothering. A realization was forming: she didn't like letting people down, didn't want to upset them. Tony had been kind and she was aware of hurting his feelings. Something was driving her forward, and she found three alternative dates. That's what she did with clients – offered them a couple of slots so they could choose whichever suited them. He probably couldn't make any of these, she thought, punching them into an email. They were midweek, during the day, and he'd be working.

I've got an appointment in Windsor this coming Tue 21 Apr. Could meet you afterwards for lunch if you can get there? Otherwise, Friday 8 May – no clients booked as yet. Monday 11 May I could meet you in the morning for coffee in town. Let me know if any of those work.

She hit 'send' then ambled downstairs. Tilly and Freddie were on the sofa watching television, and Richard still wasn't home. Her phone buzzed.

I'll be late. Another pow-wow but it'll pay off. Rich x

At around 11 pm, the children turned in, Katy following them for a goodnight hug before trudging up to the office. She'd left the laptop open and was about to shut it, when she noticed Tony's reply.

Can do all three. See you Tues in Windsor. Around 1 pm? Meet you outside the Theatre Royal. It's not far from the castle and handy for the station. We'll iron out details for the other days when I see you.

Oh flip, she thought, he was only supposed to pick one! How was she going to wriggle out of this? She honestly didn't have the time!

"Time is an illusion," said the Voice.

"Oh My God! You made me jump!"

"Did I? I'm so sorry."

"Where have you been?"

"Where I've always been and ever shall be. You were doing well without my counsel."

"Why are you back now, then?"

"To tell you about time. You see, from your perspective, it's the movement of the planet spinning on its axis and orbiting the sun, is it not?" The Voice could tell she was lost. "Do you not measure out the increments of your life by day and night? One revolution is 24 hours. And three hundred and sixty-five and a quarter, or thereabouts, makes up your year, or the *time* it takes for Earth to go around the sun."

"Yes?" What the heck was he getting at?

"What I'm getting at, is this." She'd forgotten he could read *all* of her thoughts. "Tick-tock, the beat of the clock, neat, ordered, controlled. Do the birds or the animals worry? They go with the flow of intuitive time, a time to grow, a time to rest, a time to eat, a time to let go – for everything there is a season. But your world, Beloved, has become dominated by time."

Katy gulped.

"You have no time. It's real for you, isn't it? Rushing down the steps to catch the train, cramming seventy minutes of work into a fifty-minute client session, juggling precisely between your 6 o'clock and your 7 o'clock client, doing everything as fast as you possibly can?"

"Nobody's going to tell me it's an illusion!"

"It's elastic," said the Voice. "Or relative. While you're waiting for a bus in the cold rain, ten minutes seems impossibly long. Getting ready for an evening out, ten minutes is impossibly short."

By God, he's right, thought Katy.

"I am that, I am." The Voice chuckled with such love and warmth that it seemed to light the entire room. "There's a book, a teaching you may want to study. It will come when the moment is right."

"Huh?"

"When your consciousness has expanded and your heart has opened further," said the Voice tenderly. "When the student is ready, the teacher appears, but it's always your choice!"

"What book?"

"The Book of Knowledge, The Keys of Enoch®, by Dr JJ Hurtak."

"Blimey, it doesn't exactly trip off the tongue, does it?"

"You'll remember. But I draw your attention to it now because it describes time as *a measurable period of chronology experienced within the consciousness of the specie on a given wavelength of light.*"

"What the fudge does that mean?"

"It means that your experience of time is connected to your consciousness. The more sophisticated your consciousness, the more complex time becomes."

"Quite frankly, I'm lost. And what about the wavelengths of light?"

"There is one type of light for your sun, and a different light for the moon, and yet another light for the stars, but star differs from star in glory, or light."

"I'm sure I've heard that before."

"Indeed. The point I'm making is, there are wavelengths of Light beyond anything you've seen, and to experience that Light, your consciousness has to expand. Eventually your perception of time takes a quantum leap. Did you know that your mind is able to reach higher dimensions?"

"No! And I don't see how I can experience anything *except* being pushed for time!"

"Never say never. As the good Doctor says, *Man is doomed to perfection.*"

"What about woman?"

"Her too."

"I can't see how this is relevant."

"Time changes with consciousness and also with perception. Add to this the fact your thoughts create."

"And I keep thinking I don't have enough time."

"Precisely. You *appear* to have less time in the day. You have more technology, faster communications, greater access to information, myriad opportunities, and as a consequence, less time. You're working harder and faster to beat the clock and while you're at it, your constant mantra is *I'm in a hurry. Don't know where the time goes. Just so busy at the moment.*"

"How can I change it?"

"Slow down. Do less. Breathe."

"How will I get everything done?"

"Perhaps you don't need to get *everything* done?"

Katy couldn't get her head around that.

"I leave you now in Peace, to meditate, and as you expand into the light, may you glimpse *no-time*, the *eternal now.*"

Chapter 21

Tuesday 21 April, 2009 - A nine day, if you add up all the digits.
2+1+4 (for April)+2+9=18, 1+8=9

Katy had thought about cancelling but she couldn't let him down. Besides, he'd only pester for another date – she might as well get it over and done with. An hour or so for lunch would suffice. She'd have to eat something anyway, so he might as well join her.

The idea of her body saying 'no' had captured her imagination. It dawned on her that the painful eczema she'd been experiencing could be a psychosomatic way of avoiding Richard's clumsy touch. She'd been trying to heal it for ages, starting with a leading dermatologist at the King's College Hospital, who'd told her there was no cure, only relief of symptoms. Disenchanted with the medical approach, she'd researched alternatives. As a result, she'd visited a homeopath in Chelsea, a naturopath in Highbury, a Chinese acupuncture doctor in Richmond and a reflexologist in Muswell Hill. Nothing had done the trick so far, though every session had helped reduce the itching. It was emotional stress, she'd been told, that was fueling the problem. Today was the day she was going to fix it for good. Shanti had recommended a South American form of 'cupping' and she'd tracked down a shaman who was operating from a small therapy room in Windsor.

The appointment was scheduled for 11.30 am, which should leave her plenty of time to get to the Theatre Royal by 1 o'clock.

Hurriedly leaving the house a little before eleven, she cursed herself for taking too long to choose her blue and white outfit. Dashing to the car, she slung a navy tote bag on the passenger seat, pushed Beauty into gear and, with tires screeching, left Sycamore road.

Approaching the M4, she'd had enough of the Tony Robbins CD telling her to take 'massive action'. Rummaging through her music discs, she noticed a Van Morrison album. She hadn't listened to *No Guru, No Method, No Teacher* for years. Mellow harmonies filled the car as she drove. The lyrics were so profound! She'd never noticed it before, but he was singing about meditation, contemplation, and healing! Noticing the time on the dashboard, Katy realized she was going to be late if she didn't get a move on. Pushing her foot flat to the floor, and ever vigilant for speed cameras, she moved into the outside lane. It never seemed fast enough, she thought, contemplating acceleration rates, g-force and the speed of light. Maybe her penchant for driving at speed had come from a distant notion of teleporting. Imagine explaining that to a traffic cop or writing it on an appeals form! Her mind was moving from one idea to the next, as if loosely connecting invisible dots. "The way you do anything is the way you do everything," one of her colleagues, Fran, had once said. "You can make a fairly good assumption about your client based on that." At the time, she'd noticed herself gulping down a mug of tea before rushing upstairs to her consulting room. Hmm. She wrote fast, ate fast, talked fast, walked fast, and drove fast. That was because she had to fit everything into her schedule, she reminded herself, but the Voice had said do less, slow down. At that very moment she noticed a police car in her rear-view mirror and reduced her speed immediately. Van the man was singing about warm feelings and it was making her feel cozy.

Travelling at the speed of light would be useful! Katy recalled dragging Richard along to a *Flower of Life* course, hoping to get him involved in her spiritual world. She had hoped it would paper over the cracks in their marriage. A shared experience could re-ignite the spark, Terry had said, but it had been a disaster! Richard had fallen asleep during the explanation videos then disappeared for the practical session, returning only at the end to take her home. He'd told her categorically he had no desire to hang on to her coat-tails and would be pursuing his own interests from now on.

Ooh, now he was singing about reincarnation! She hadn't realized how spiritual these songs were.

Actually, the whole *Flower of Life* thing had been disappointing, despite its initial promise. She'd read Drunvalo Melchizedek's book and thought his teaching would be useful. The sacred geometry was excellent, but the merkaba vehicle you were supposed to create hadn't lived up to Katy's expectations. Huh, the 'final breath', which had never been demonstrated, was supposed to activate your 'energy vehicle' for teleportation. If only it had worked! It seemed her only chance of getting to Windsor on time.

Casting her mind back, she laughed at her merkaba, a kind of energy field, like an invisible spaceship that she thought she could sense around her. Obviously, she'd just imagined it! Nobody else was going to challenge the teacher, Sakhara, so Katy stepped up.

"What happens when you take the final breath?"

"Oh, you take awf in your merkaba," she said, pronouncing 'off' in that affected manner.

"Has anyone ever activated it and taken off?" There was an uncomfortable shuffling and an abrupt change of subject.

Katy wondered now what her real name was. Nobody's called Sakhara, especially not a sixty-something, middle-aged English woman.

The police car had turned off at the slip road and Katy pressed the accelerator down.

She probably had a dull name to begin with, she reasoned, and as for Drunvalo Melchizedek, what was on his birth certificate, she wondered? Probably something ordinary like Dave Cooper. A Mini Cooper pulled out in front of her and she slammed on the brakes just as a speed camera came into view. She'd have got caught if it wasn't for that Mini!

Despite everything, Katy still believed there was such a thing as a Merkabah, it's just that Drunvalo hadn't nailed it.

For God's sake, why hadn't she left on time? It had taken ages and now she was stuck in traffic. The music was still playing. Windsor certainly wasn't a town called Paradise, so it couldn't be the one that Van was referring to. There was something about the lyrics and that powerful voice that was stirring her. It was incredibly romantic and so spiritual! She'd never understood just how beautiful *In the Garden* was.

The rain was pelting down as she approached the town center. How could she have been so stupid on so many levels? Late for the appointment, meeting a man she didn't care about, married to a man who didn't understand her. She swung into a windswept carpark, hoping for a space. Nothing. It was packed. Asking her invisible 'parking guardian' for an empty bay, and visualizing herself already parked, she waited a moment as the wipers swept rhythmically to and fro. Perhaps the parking guardian was disguised as a Volvo? How else would it hold onto parking spots? As if by magic, someone reversed a few rows down. "Yes!" she said, punching the air. It was a silver Volvo. This stuff worked!

Snatching a brolly from her bag and brandishing it against the rain, Katy darted to the nearest ticket machine, battling to run in her high-heeled boots. Blast, she didn't have enough change. She'd have to buy an hour and a quarter and come back after the treatment. Buttoning her coat against the wind and pushing a defiant curl behind her ear, she noticed her gold hoop earring was missing. Damn! Perhaps it was caught in the folds of her scarf, or got dislodged as she rushed from the car? Tottering back to Beauty, ticket in hand, she retraced her steps, watching the ground for any sign of the earring. Once inside the car, she unfurled her scarf over the seat, checking the upholstery afterwards. Nothing. Peering under the vehicle at the wet tarmac, her heart sank as she realized it was lost. It was a punishment, she was sure. She had to tell Tony she wasn't interested, nip it in the bud and finish it, even though it had been a delightful interlude. She made a bargain with the universe. If she found the earring, she'd meet him for lunch and carry on the friendship. If she'd lost it for good, she must say goodbye. Running her hand under the car seat, lifting up the mat, and checking the leather around the handbrake, she felt a pang of sadness – not about losing the earring but about Tony. Her shoulders slumped with the realization she had to put a stop to it. She'd make her apologies and call it a day.

Out of breath, her cream ankle boots splashed with dirty rain, she arrived at the therapy room at 11.45 am.

"José's running late," said the receptionist, without looking up. "Please take a seat."

"How long?"

"About twenty minutes."

Great, thought Katy, clenching her jaw and sitting gingerly on an old chair in the shabby reception area. She'd rushed like crazy and now he was keeping her waiting. He probably didn't give two hoots. She'd never keep a client hanging on like this. Her heart was still reverberating from half-jogging. Catching her breath, she pulled her phone from her bag.

Running late. Can we make it 1.30 pm instead?

She couldn't just stand him up, he deserved an explanation. They'd meet and she'd tell him face-to-face she had no time for another friendship.

Righty-ho! See you 1.30 pm.

Katy switched the phone to silent and picked up a tattered copy of Natural Health Magazine.

"He's ready to see you, Mrs. Fralinski!" sang the receptionist.

"It's Ms., actually."

"Okay, well he's ready," she mumbled.

The 'cups' turned out to be red hot bull's horns, which the little wizened man had heated over an open charcoal fire before pushing onto Katy's body. They were supposed to draw out toxins. She screamed as the first one seared onto her thigh, leaving a round, purple welt the size of a jam jar lid which oozed pearls of thick, ruby blood. It must be doing her good, there was no other explanation. Why else would anyone recommend this torture? The other thigh, her arms and her upper back were similarly blighted. Clutching at a box of tissues, she wiped at her mascara-stained cheeks, shrieking again with each branding. She was paying good money for this, she thought, blowing her nose for the umpteenth time.

Battered and bleeding, through bleary eyes, she could see the ugly swellings, red and bruised. Putting on her navy and white polka-dot, short skirt, she noticed the hem was rubbing painfully against one of the wheals. She'd been disfigured by a mad Mayan witch doctor. It was another sign. How could she go to lunch now? First the earring and now this. One more bit of bad luck and it would be three in a row, and that could only mean one thing: she wasn't meant to meet him. Hadn't the Voice said there would be signs?

After paying for the session and asking the receptionist for some change, Katy glanced at her watch. The parking ticket had expired nine minutes ago. Oh sh–sugar! The third thing would be a fine, she reckoned as she splashed her way through the rain towards the carpark. Craning her neck at the windscreen, she sighed with relief before striding victoriously to the ticket machine. Opening the door to place the voucher on the dash, something caught her eye between the sill and the white parking line. Her mouth dropped open and her heart pounded. There it was – the pristine, golden jewelry, glinting in the rain! It hadn't even been crushed. Somebody could have taken it, but no! How could she have missed it? Wiping it carefully on a tissue, she hooked it back in her ear before checking herself in the rear-view mirror. Oh, my giddy aunt, she looked terrible! A bit of lipstick and a repair job with a tissue would do, but what about the dull throbbing on her leg? She ran her hand up the inside of her thigh, frowning as she took a closer look. The bump had disappeared, along with the pain, but the light, tingling sensation of her palm brushing softly against her stocking had awakened something.

It was still raining when Katy arrived at the Theatre Royal, three minutes early. Pretending to be disinterested, calm and confident, she tried to fathom out why her heart was beating so wildly. It must have been all that rushing around, unless it was something to do with that bloody José and his weapons of mass destruction! Her pulse was definitely racing and there was a strange feeling in the pit of her stomach. The adrenaline was mounting, her hands trembling slightly, like an addict's do when they're waiting for a fix. She stuffed them into her pockets. It was such a strange mixture of anxiety and excitement, it could only be something the mad shaman had done.

Looking impeccable in an Italian suit, expensive polo shirt and soft, leather shoes, Tony rounded the corner. He was quite dapper, as her mother would say, even if he was short, bespectacled, and bald. It was something about his demeanor, the way he carried himself in this famous Berkshire town, that made him appealing. His clothes enhanced him, as if he'd chosen them as an extension of himself. Richard wore what suited his tribe, but Tony was wearing what suited his heritage.

Katy stopped shaking the minute she saw him, her composure returning, her body relaxing.

"Hello, been waiting long?" he said, leaning in, his arms extending to her shoulders.

"A few minutes."

They did that continental thing, kissing each cheek in turn.

"There's a rather nice bistro round the corner," he said, smiling. "Shall we?"

He was in charge this time, and it was Katy who was clueless. She followed him, her arm close to his, her body turned slightly towards him as she spoke.

"I've just had this ridiculous treatment, actually, more of a *mis*treatment!"

His right hand was casually in his trouser pocket, his left hand in line with hers. He turned to look at her.

"Oh yes? What was it?"

"South American cupping."

"Ouch, I've heard of that! Bloody hell, that's painful!"

"You're telling me!"

"I'm sure a good bottle of vino will help."

They walked side-by-side, smiling, laughing, matching each other's pace, their arms swaying gently in time.

The dining room of the brasserie was brimming with businessmen and tourists. Tony spotted an empty table for two beneath a window at the side and asked the waiter if it was free. They were in luck – another couple had just cancelled, and they could take it.

Scanning the menu, they both stopped at the exact same moment, looked up and said in unison "I'll have the onglet of beef!" Katy laughed: Tony smiled.

"What about wine?" he said, glancing at the list. "How about a good South African Pinotage?"

"Perfect!"

"So, what did you think of The Da Vinci Code?"

"I surprised myself and really enjoyed it."

"I can tell you a lot more about masonic symbols."

As the conversation flowed, they mirrored each other, their heads inclined towards the center of the table to catch everything amid the din of the restaurant. Tony would pick up his glass just as she took a sip from hers. She would cut off a morsel of steak just as he'd popped one into his mouth. Both gesticulated wildly as they spoke, and as the afternoon wore on, they were giggling and swapping stories, the bottle of Pinotage finished.

"Let's have a brandy," said Tony, catching the waiter's eye. "And one of those hot chocolate soufflés on the specials board.

Bring two spoons," he added.

The melted chocolate inside flowed, smooth, rich, delicious, sensual. Katy watched it pool, unctuous and glistening against the white plate. They picked up their spoons, scooping up the warm, exquisite pudding and savoring each delicious mouthful. In the presence of this kindred spirit, she felt recognized and at ease. Not wanting the bill to arrive and break the spell, she lingered over the dessert as long as she could.

"I'm getting this," said Tony, taking a card from his wallet.

"No! You can't! We'll go Dutch!" Katy insisted, pulling out her purse.

As they were leaving, he turned to her. "Let's go for a walk by the river. I love the water!"

Katy beamed and nodded in approval. Her head seemingly had a mind of its own because, actually, she damned well had to get back, and besides, she was wearing cream stiletto ankle boots and they were beginning to hurt. Walking further than a hundred yards was going to finish her off, and if the riverbank were muddy, it would ruin the leather. The wine, or was it the brandy, had made her tipsy. She'd tried to sip slowly and was sure she'd stuck to one glass – she was driving after all. Tony must have had the rest because he seemed to be slurring a bit. His conversation had drifted back to the past.

"I remember seeing you with that Gordon idiot once," he said. Katy let out a small laugh and waited for the rest of the sentence. "And?"

"Oh, nothing."

"No, you've started now!"

"Well, I remember thinking how great you looked in your ripped fishnets and punk gear!"

"Did you, now?" said Katy, flashing him a coy smile.

The banter continued. She could see that Tony was watching her totter along beside him, just as he had back then. Further along the river, she began tiptoeing in an effort not to sink into the towpath.

"Are you okay?"

Her face was wincing with every step.

"Hold onto my arm," he said, offering it. "Just to steady yourself over this rough ground. It can't be easy in those sexy heels."

"They're killing me." Her face reddened as she took his muscular arm, letting him lead her to a patch of tarmac.

"Hold onto my shoulder while you take them off!"

His voice was so tender it took all she had to stop the tear that was forming from brimming over. She could hear Richard's voice in her mind's eye "For fuck's sake, why did you wear the sodding things?" Teetering on one foot then the other, and hanging onto Tony's broad shoulder, she removed the boots.

"Come here," he said, blowing into his cupped hands then rubbing them together to make them warm. He squatted down, caressing one foot then the other, gently massaging them back to life. The tear spilled down her cheek, washing away the last scrap of mascara. She wiped it away with her ring finger before he noticed.

The sun was dipping lower in the sky and long shadows danced ahead of them as they ambled back, she in her muddy, stockinged feet, carrying the boots in her hand. The kids would be back from school and Richard would be home in a few hours. She must tear herself away and drive back to reality. Her feet had recovered, and she stopped at a bench to wipe off the worst of the sludge and ease the boots back on. Sitting next to her, his knee almost touching hers, Tony offered his handkerchief and watched as she grappled with the shoes.

"My train's leaving soon." He turned towards her, his cobalt eyes penetrating.

"That's okay. I've got to get going." Her mouth curled upwards at the corners as she gazed up, lingering a little too long before turning away. They stood up. She could feel herself being drawn closer, as if caught in an undertow. Watching Tony's body language, she felt sure he would lean in for a kiss at any moment. The magnetic pull was palpable. She froze. It wasn't what she wanted, she was married, wasn't she? But she was wrong. Tony stepped back, smiled, and gave her a curt wave as he said goodbye, before disappearing into the crowd.

Katy let go of the breath she'd been holding, her pulse still racing. How could she have misread it so badly? Of course he wasn't interested! He had a wife and kid at home! And she had a husband, and two teenagers. It had been a lucky escape. Drawing in a lung full of fresh air, she tapped her chest with the flat of her palm and traipsed back through the puddles to the car.

Van Morrison was still singing as she left Windsor and headed home. She'd been playing a stupid game, and it was time to stop and go back to Richard. No Guru had turned sour as it reached its last few tracks. She'd forgotten it did that. The M4 was a nightmare, but it didn't matter. It gave her time to pull herself together and take stock. Van the man was singing about obstacles now. It was one of her favorites, this album, with its sweet beginning and bitter end. Life would resume, she knew that. Turning into Chiswick High Road and passing the familiar shops, reality came sharply back into focus as Morrison sang the final song, Ivory Tower. How apt, she thought, listening to the lyrics. By the time she'd reached Sycamore Road and found a parking spot, she'd put the surreal afternoon behind her. She lifted her head high, took a deep breath and trooped up to the house.

Hurtling through the front door, wind chimes reeling from the blast, she called out cheerfully "Everything okay? How was school?"

"Alright. When's dinner?" said Freddie, emerging from his room.

"Soon. Is Dad home yet?"

Richard was outside fumbling with his keys. Moments later

he was standing next to her in the hallway.

"Sorry I'm late. Traffic on the M4," she said.

"Huh?"

"Been to Windsor. Had lunch with an old friend from school." Richard walked past her with a cursory nod, while Freddie retreated and closed the door.

They weren't the slightest bit interested. She could have told them she'd had sex in an alleyway with 007 and they wouldn't have batted an eyelid. After hanging up her coat and pulling her boots off, she ran her fingers through her hair and plodded into the kitchen.

She'd better rustle something up. She used to love cooking, but her heart wasn't in it. Tilly was fussy about red meat, Freddie was pure carnivore, Richard hated anything milky, and she was avoiding wheat – it had been giving her stomach-cramps lately. When had it all become so complicated?

After supper she joined Richard on the sofa, watching the news and current affairs. It wasn't her thing, but she had to reach out to her husband.

"How was your day?" she asked.

"Tiring."

"Any news?"

"No."

"I've booked that holiday in Mexico."

"Good. Will you let me listen?"

There was a chill in the evening air. Katy wrapped herself in a thick, blue fleece. Richard was sitting forward, his elbows on his knees, his jaw set, watching Jeremy Paxman annihilate another politician.

"Might as well get sorted for tomorrow," she said. Richard made a grunting noise and she left him to it. After saying goodnight to the children, she pulled her weary body up the final flight of stairs to the office. She wanted to get close to her husband, but it was like kindling a fire that had long been snuffed out. The wood was damp, rotten – it was never going to catch. Collapsing exhausted onto the swivel chair, she checked her emails and made a list for the morning. The phone buzzed.

Great to see you today. So enjoyed the afternoon. Can't wait for next time. Sleep tight. x

She wasn't sure what to make of the single kiss. It both elevated and troubled her. The thrill of the chase, the prey in sight, the lioness poised, but it was just pretend, just a silly game. She didn't want Tony. He was a diversion, she knew that, an escape from the routine, but that was all. It had to stop before someone got hurt.

Pulling the meditation stool from beneath the couch, she sat, back straight, hands in mudra, and closed her eyes. The real Katy had been under wraps for too long, quashed by her circumstances, unable to express herself. Tony had validated her, reminded her she was a sensual, attractive woman who deserved to be cherished. He'd awakened the dormant sense of adventure that Richard had stifled. She'd been subsumed into her husband's world, lost to his needs, serving everyone else. But what about her? She needed to share the load, be heard, appreciated, acknowledged. Weariness overcame her as she sat ruminating. Breath. Hara. Stillness. A sickening rose up from her stomach and her eyes began to prickle with the heat of her tears. Silently, they flowed, trickling down her cheeks and dropping from her jaw. She didn't even know why she was crying. Breath. Hara. Let it go.

Chapter 22

Wednesday, 22nd April, 2009

Tony walked into the familiar meeting room at the Priory and took one of the seats which had been carefully arranged in a circle. He'd be finishing these monthly group sessions soon, he was sure. Today, he was going to 'share' as they called it. God knows, he'd listened to enough stories, it was time to tell his.

"Hi. My name is Tony, and I'm an addict," he said, placing his foot on the opposite knee. "Except, I think I'm getting over it. I haven't been on a porn site for three months, and it's all down to finding a bit of happiness."

"Once an addict, always an addict," piped up someone from the circle.

"You're never over it completely. I've been coming here for nearly ten years!" said another.

"Would you like to share something today, Tony?" the therapist said firmly, casting her eye around the group.

"Righty-ho!" He took a deep breath and started. "After my mum died, I was lost, didn't really know what to do. I got in my car and drove round the Surrey countryside where I grew up. In one of the villages, there was this imposing house with a big bay window. I recognized it immediately, of course. I could picture the big kitchen."

"Your childhood home?"

"No. Last time I was there, I was seventeen, and I was being seduced by a naughty little minx who told me she just wanted a kiss and a cuddle!"

One of the men in the group was guffawing. Tony waited for him to shut up.

"Exactly, mate, and she was only fifteen! We hid in her bedroom – bloody terrifying with her mother downstairs. She was a right old...well, you know."

The therapist coughed.

"I slipped off her bra, and she unzipped my jeans. Rebel Rebel. I'll never forget it. The song was playing in the background. I always remember the line at the end because it suited her. She was hot and I did love her. I was mad to let her go! That gorgeous arse, and what a dancer! Listened to rock music. She was every schoolboy's dream. I liked her, too, you know, she was bright, easy-going, easy to talk to, even for a tongue-tied teenager!" Tony looked down as he collected his thoughts. He didn't want it to turn smutty, but the memory was arousing him. He had to calm down.

"Are you okay, Tony?" asked the therapist. "Ready to carry on?"

"I decided to track her down, but I couldn't find her, not till she changed her name." He looked up. Most of the group were leaning in, with quizzical looks on their faces.

"Her married name was Stone, but she'd changed it back to her maiden name, Fralinski. It was dead easy after that." He was smiling as he recollected the evening he'd found her. "I'd had a couple of glasses of vino, followed by a particularly good brandy, and gone up to the attic room. That's where I, you know, indulged my habit, but afterwards, I felt guilty. I knew I had to get help. I typed 'Therapist, Central London' into a search engine and bang! I couldn't believe my eyes when her name popped up. My heart was in my throat, I mean, my wife and daughter were sleeping downstairs. It took a couple more brandies before I plucked up the courage, but I did it. I contacted her." He paused.

"And?" said a couple of the group members in unison.

"I didn't hear anything for eleven days, and I realized that was it. Went on a bit of a bender, I have to admit. That's when I had my first session with Dr Watkins."

"So, you never heard from her?" asked the therapist.

"All of a sudden, there it was! I thought she didn't want to know, but she sent an email!"

Tony smiled and let out a small laugh. "I got this warm, cheerful message. She hadn't changed much. I wrote back, and it became a regular thing."

"So, you're pen-pals?"

"More than that! I met up with her in Hammersmith last month and again in Windsor yesterday."

One of the women took a tissue from her pocket and dabbed at her eyes. Tony looked down and smiled, slowly shaking his head from side to side. "I hardly recognized her at first, but she looked fantastic!" His ears were turning pink at the thought. "Radiant! Still had that same dazzling character. Knows her wines, too, she ordered a Rioja!" He was lost in his thoughts for a moment. "I kept thinking she'd leave, but she didn't. It all seems too good to be true, so I'm pacing myself. Don't want to presume too much, just seeing what unfolds. No expectations, but I've had such an incredible time. It's brought back great memories."

"And it's helped with your addiction?"

"Yes. I was unhappy, that's why I'd resorted to porn, but I know it's behind me now."

Most of the group were either sobbing or smiling. The session continued as others shared. At the end, some of them came up to slap him on the back and congratulate him. A few gave him a big bear hug. "Great share, mate!" said one, with a faltering smile. A sour-faced man hung around till he got his chance. "I don't think you understand the nature of addiction. I'm telling you, you'll be at it again soon. People don't just get better because they've fallen in love, you know!" He shook his head, pushing his hands into his pockets as he walked away. Tony knew he was wrong. Meeting Katy had rekindled something. The lifeblood was pumping through him, and he was full of vigor.

* * *

It was almost 6 pm on Wednesday when Katy left the house. Tara had called on the spur of the moment to invite her over, along with Shanti. Ben was away on business, and Tara's children were already in bed when she rang. The three of them would have a good chin wag over a glass of wine and a Chinese Takeaway.

An hour and a half later, they were sitting in Tara's kitchen. Katy told them about Tony. "I'm seeing him again next month," she said, having got them up to speed on Windsor.

"I don't think that's a good idea," said Tara, pursing her lips.

"There's nothing in it. It's just a bit of fun!"

"I'm sure Richard wouldn't think it was fun if he knew."

"He does! I told him I'd met an old friend from school!"

"You didn't explain the extent of the friendship, though, did you?"

"Come on, girls!" said Shanti, pouring another glass of plonk.

"Marriage means something," Tara said, before remembering Shanti was divorced. "Well, it does to most people."

"But I'm not doing anything!"

"Yes, you are. You're being unfaithful. You made a solemn vow to be with Richard in sickness and in health."

"I only went to lunch!"

"That's not the point. You're flirting with another man!" She took a swig of wine. "You think adultery is having sex? You're already betraying Richard, going behind his back like that!"

"I'm not going behind his back! I told him, and besides, we're just friends, we get on. That's all. He's happily married to Lauren and didn't even give me a kiss goodbye!"

"Ah! So, you wanted to kiss him?" She shot Katy a withering look.

"No! I didn't! He's not interested, and nor am I."

Tara made a soft growling noise and turned away to look at the takeaway menu. "What shall we have?"

They scanned the leaflet and Shanti placed the order by phone. "It'll be twenty minutes. They'll deliver," she said. "Come on, drink up, I brought another bottle!"

By the time the food arrived, the conversation had moved on.

"Tell me about the numbers," said Katy. "I want to understand what they mean."

"Well," said Shanti, taking a mouthful of stir-fried tofu, "There's numerology itself, which is the study of the meaning of numbers, then there's gematria, which is a Kabbalistic study of the Hebrew letters and their numbers and meanings." She slurped at a tangle of noodles which hung precariously from her chopsticks.

"Just tell me about numerology," said Katy, chewing at a sparerib.

"It was considered an important precursor to mathematics." The last noodle fell, and she scooped it up again.

Tara picked up a spring roll. "Get to the point, Shanti!"

"It's a pity the scientific world doesn't recognize Sacred Mathematics and Sacred Geometries because that's what the Universe is built on!"

"I know, I know," said Tara, licking her fingers. "They're missing a trick."

"The soul contract uses numerology, doesn't it?" asked Katy, picking out the cashews from the chicken dish.

"Yup. Dinah looks at your date of birth and the numbers of the letters in your name."

"Does that mean I've changed my numerology? I remember Dinah saying something about nines."

"Yes. Nine is considered special because there are only two letters associated with it."

Katy was frowning. "Yeah, Dinah said."

"There are twenty-six letters in the alphabet," continued Shanti. "The letters are numbered from one to nine, then back to one. That means there are almost three rows of letters."

"I don't get it."

Tara fetched a pen and paper from the drawer and wrote the numbers one to nine along the top. Under each number, she wrote a letter, starting with A for number one, B for two, C for three, and continued until the row finished with the letter I under the number nine. A second row of letters began with J and finished with R. The third row stopped short at number eight. "See?" she said, waving the paper at Katy. "Every number has three letters under it, except for nine at the end. Three nines are twenty-seven, and there are only twenty-six letters."

"Your name, Fralinski, has an R and two I's, so it has three nines," said Shanti.

"What about Katy?" she asked.

Tara looked at the grid she'd made. "Let me see." She ran her finger along the middle row. "K is two, A is one, T is two - it's just below K - and Y is seven."

Shanti added it up. "Two and one is three, add two is five, add seven is twelve."

"And twelve is one and two if you look at the digits, which means you're a three!" said Tara, taking another gulp of wine.

"My favorite number!" shrieked Katy.

It took a while to work out the numerology of their respective names, but they got there, despite the wine.

"But what does it mean?" asked Katy.

"I can't remember, you'll have to get a book," said Shanti.

"Give me the gist."

She sighed. "One is for beginnings and independence, two is for relationships and union, three is for fun and creativity, four, what's four?"

"Earth, being grounded, I think, but there's a lot more to it than that, Shanti!" Tara poured out the last of the white.

"I know, I'm just giving an outline. I think four is to do with work and logic. Five is about freedom, six is the perfect number for family love and harmony—"

"And romance. Sixes are the romantics!" Tara chimed in.

"That's right," said Shanti. "Seven is the spiritual quest, eight is abundance, isn't it?"

"And balance," added Tara, opening a bar of chocolate for them to share.

"That's it! Balance and the feminine. Nine's a biggie. It's about serving humanity, unconditional love and spiritual wisdom." Shanti stopped to break off a piece of fruit and nut.

"And completion!" said Tara.

Katy leaned back on the sofa, having taken a second square of chocolate.

"Then there's the master numbers." Shanti nibbled at her chunk of fruit and nut.

"What are they?"

"Eleven, twenty-two and thirty-three. All double digits."

"Come on girls, let's change the subject!" Tara had heard it all before.

"Just let her finish! It's only three numbers!" whined Katy.

"Ok, you carry on. I'll tidy up and make coffee."

"Not for me, I won't sleep!"

"Nor me."

"Chamomile tea?" Tara busied herself with the kettle while Shanti explained the last three.

"Eleven is the first master number, highly spiritual, powerful. Can mean a pair – two ones side-by-side. It holds the one energy of beginnings and the two energy of relationships."

"Why two?"

"Add the digits. One plus one is two, which happens to be the beginning of the Fibonacci sequence."

"What?"

"Oh, Katy, don't you read anything? It's the numbers of creation! It's everywhere in nature!"

"Oh, I remember now! Pinecones and nautilus shells? What about twenty-two and thirty-three?"

"Twenty-two is the master builder, and thirty-three is an extremely significant and powerful number," spat Shanti.

"Come on, you two! Chamomile tea, then I'm going to have

to kick you out. My bed's waiting!"

Passing through Hammersmith on the train home, Katy recollected the afternoon she'd met Tony at the station. He'd told her it had been nine for the day, three for the month, and eleven for the year. Spiritual, fun, and powerful. Ooh, and new beginnings and relationships! And if you added up the whole lot, day, month, and year, it was five for freedom!

* * *

Richard and his team were celebrating the successful conclusion of another takeover bid. They left the office and headed to a local wine bar to toast their victory with a bottle of bubbly. As it was Wednesday, they dispersed early, each taking different routes back to their respective homes. Emma hailed a black cab to her apartment in Docklands, Helen jumped on the number 26 bus, a couple of the younger members stayed for another drink, and one trudged up to Chancery Lane. Richard strolled back to St Paul's tube station and boarded a train. Just after 9 o'clock, he pushed open the door to number eleven. The effing windchimes clattered as usual. "I'm home!" he bellowed, waiting for a response. He noticed a scrap of paper propped up on the hallway table.

Rich

Gone to Tara's. Moussaka in the fridge. Just heat up.

Tilly staying with Eva – school project. Freddie at Tom's – rugby practice early tomorrow.

See you later.

Kit. X

He sniffed, clenched his jaw, and took the note, screwing it tightly before tossing it into the umbrella stand. "Huh," he grunted as he climbed the stairs. In the bedroom he carefully removed his tie, placing it on the rack inside his wardrobe door. The shoes were next. He gave them a quick polish with a cloth that he kept on a shelf, tilting them towards the light to check the shine before setting them carefully down. The suit was meticulously arranged on a wooden hanger. Unbuttoning his shirt, he flung it in the corner, then peeled off his sweaty socks and threw them at the shirt.

A grubby pair of jeans hung over the back of his bedroom chair, along with a T-shirt and sweatshirt he'd worn the previous evening. Plucking a fresh pair of socks from the drawer, he pulled on his casual clothes before stepping into his slippers and shuffling down to the kitchen.

Sodding Moussaka! At least it was home-made, he supposed, not one of those frigging pre-packed things. Taking it from the shelf, he placed it in the oven and stared at the dials. Which one was it? He couldn't remember – he'd have to eat it cold. Taking it out of the oven and finding a fork on the draining board, he sat on the sofa in the snug, flicking through the television channels to see what was on.

Around 10.30 pm, he switched off the TV, deposited the dirty fork and dish in the sink, and locked the front door. He may as well turn in. It would be an early start tomorrow.

Upstairs in the bedroom, he undressed, leaving his casual clothes in a heap. Having cleaned his teeth, he donned an old-fashioned pair of pajamas, heaved himself into bed and fell into a fitful sleep. Even in repose, a worried look was etched upon his face. He was dreaming of the money he was going to make on some shares. Images of fat retirement funds and lavish holidays peppered his fantasy before quite suddenly, it turned into a nightmare. Shadowy men in dark glasses were taking him somewhere for questioning. He managed to get away with it, just. Gift of the gab. He'd smoothed things over, but it was close. He was walking down Cheapside now, but he'd lost his way. It was unfamiliar, jumbled up, so he hopped on a bus which promptly took him in the wrong direction. He was far away in the countryside, somewhere East of London. Getting off the coach, he noticed a newsagent, and picking up a copy of the

FT, his heart stopped. Interest rates had fallen through the floor, and most of his investments had tanked. Richard twitched in his sleep. The nightmare continued. Where had he stashed the money? And who'd confused the pin numbers? He rolled over, shaking off the fear, and the images drifted away. There was a distant sound of windchimes clanging. By the time his wife had slipped into bed, he was too far gone to acknowledge her.

Chapter 23

Thursday 23 April, 2009 – a two day (relationships & union)

Thursday evening was prime time for Katy's City clients who could afford her top rates and didn't want to take time off work. The three sessions were usually booked up in advance, despite the higher fee. This evening, however, there was a networking event at the house in Harley Street. Three times a year, the lavish first-floor reception rooms would be opened up – at Christmas, Easter and again at the end of Summer. Tonight, was the Easter Party and Katy had decided to take the day off. At Christmas, she'd gone straight from client work into mulled wine and tinsel, while her colleagues had taken the afternoon off to freshen up. She wasn't going to get caught out again, and besides, she had a growing mountain of paperwork and unanswered emails. The new schedule that Terry had insisted on left her too little time to keep everything under control.

Her first event had been a challenge, she remembered. She'd insisted on seeing her 6 o'clock client, which was precisely when guests were starting to arrive at the big old Georgian house. Unaccompanied and wearing a sober, brown, pin-striped trouser suit, she'd entered the room to a sea of unfamiliar faces. Struggling to make conversation, she swapped business cards with a handful of others, mostly those who like her, were new to the game. A rather glamorous blonde psychologist had been working the room in her figure-hugging, little black number. That was the way to do it, thought Katy – professional with a seductive twist. It was different now, of course – she'd got the measure of the old boy's network, the new kids on the block, the highflyers and the flirtatious professors. There would be light jazz music, canapés, bubbly, and a host of influential consultants to be schmoozed. She was looking forward to it. In an effort to connect with Richard, she'd invited him along and would be meeting him in Cavendish Square at 6 pm.

Crossing items from her list that morning, Katy was pleased she was making headway. Once or twice, head buried in invoices, she'd feel a strong surge in the center of her chest and wonder what it was. Looking up, she'd see Tony's face in her mind's eye, smiling at her, as if he was thinking of her at that exact moment. The third time it happened, her phone buzzed a split-second later.

Just wondering how your day's going? T x

A broad smile played on her lips before Tara's words came swimming back. Putting the phone on silent and placing it face down, she took a deep breath. She wasn't going to get embroiled. Leaning back in her chair, she clasped her hands behind her head and closed her eyes. There was no traffic on Sycamore Road at this time of day, and she could hear birdsong floating in through the open window. A warm, peaceful feeling rose from within, and the corners of her mouth turned up as she basked in the stillness. In a moment of clarity, she knew that Tony was a distraction. Richard was her husband, and she was proud of him. He'd be his usual charming self at the party, and everyone would see how lucky she was. Her tall, dark, handsome man. She opened her eyes and leaned forward, determined to break the back of the paperwork.

Just after 3 pm, her desk tidy, most of her list crossed off, her laptop closed, she sat back and sighed. She'd better get ready, she supposed, but she didn't feel like it. Relaxing at home on the sofa seemed like a better idea. Huh, that was never going to happen! Dragging herself downstairs and into the shower, she washed her hair, shaved her legs, and brushed her body with a loofah. Hair coiled up in a white towel and donning a navy bathrobe, she stepped out of the en-suite. She didn't want to go. All that dressing up, then the train into town, just to network with people she didn't care about. Letting out a sigh and pushing through the uneasy feeling in the pit of her stomach, she flung open the wardrobe doors and stared at the racks of clothes. Nothing inspired her. "I can't face that navy skirt suit again," she muttered, running her eye along the rail. Maybe the midnight blue shirt-waister with the tiny white dots? She could team it with a chunky belt. Not very sexy, but it could be dolled up with some bling and a pair of high heeled shoes. Her solar plexus tightened slightly as she parted the clothes to take a look at the dress. It was a bit stuffy, and she was fed up with blue, fed up with this constant having to do things she didn't want to do! Oh! The craving for blue and white had gone! That was the last of the Aura-Soma bottles, which meant she could wear what the heck she liked! Casting her eye over some suitable outfits, she realized nothing inspired her.

"Red dress."

She felt sure she heard something, but it was so faint, she must have imagined it. Pulling out a beige and black raw silk ensemble and hanging it on the wardrobe door, she pursed her lips. Ugh. She couldn't be bothered, but she had to make an effort. Fran was expecting her, and besides, she'd invited Richard. Taking the silk outfit from the door and pushing it back among the other clothes, she started methodically again at one end of the rail. Grasping a toffee-colored satin dress, her face lit up before remembering the neckline was a bit too risqué. Back it went.

"Red dress."

There it was again. "Is that you?" she asked, pausing, her eyes darting from side to side. Nothing. She carried on to the end of the rail then started again. Perhaps the putty-grey tailored jacket, with that printed skirt?

"Red dress."

Third time. She heard it distinctly. Taking the classic, hourglass, shift-dress from its hanger, she smiled. Sleeveless, with off-white trim around the armholes and scoop neck, she thought of it as rather Christmassy with its red-and-white nod to Santa and its tweedy woolen weave. "I can't wear that," she said aloud. "It's bright red!" Something made her dig out a pair of matching Italian red-leather heels. "It's Harley Street, not the Dover Street Wine Bar!" The tone of her voice was enquiring, but there was no answer. Just the sound of a car driving by outside. What would the black-and-navy brigade think? She'd stick out like a red sore thumb in an ocean of somber shade! It might not fit, all the chocolate she'd been eating, it could be a bit snug.

Oh, for God's sake, she couldn't wear it to a work do! It would be unprofessional. Was she going mad? Did she honestly think she was going to walk into a networking party in a tight-fitting Marilyn Monroe-style red dress? But the Voice had told her. Three times. Trying to find another outfit was useless. Deep inside, she knew she had to wear that dress.

Slipping into silk undies and teasing on a pair of sheer hold-ups, she sprayed herself liberally with her favorite Penhaligon's perfume before pouring herself into the frock. The zip glided up – just. She felt fabulous. Eyeing herself in the mirror and running her hands over her small waist and down her curvy hips, she pronounced it a success. Wow! She hadn't felt this good in ages! Maybe she was meant to stand out. Perhaps there'd be a celebrity client or a famous professor she had to impress. Whatever it was, she'd learned to trust the Voice, even if the advice seemed irrational. It was probably a Being so advanced that it could see into the future, or could it be creating the future, bit by bit, preparing to reveal its mighty work, a masterpiece no human hand could paint? Katy giggled, what an imagination she had!

Sitting at the dressing table, the cosmetics drawer open, she put on a picture-perfect face in just under ten minutes. She'd been practicing for years and could practically do it in her sleep. As she blotted her red, glossy lipstick on a tissue, the phone vibrated. She'd forgotten to turn the sound back on. It'd be Richard. She'd get back to him in a minute, one more dab of powder on the nose, a quick smile to check her teeth for stray lippy and she was almost ready. Teasing out a few strands of hair over her forehead, she checked herself once more in the mirror. "Looking good!" She beamed at her reflection. She'd scrubbed up well and could still turn a few heads.

Reaching for the phone to answer Richard, her heart leapt.

I know you usually work Thurs. Don't suppose you'll pick this up, but I'm in town! Any chance of a quick drink? T x

Her hands were shaking, her composure gone, her mind blank. Then it dawned on her – at that moment, she couldn't think of anyone else she'd rather meet, dressed up to the nines in a sexy red outfit. Before she could stop herself, her fingers punched out a message, seemingly of their own accord.

At home. Work's do tonight. Have to be there before 6 pm but could see you for brief catch up? Meet you 4.45 at Paddington? xx

Sh-sugar! She shouldn't have put those two kisses. Grabbing a cream, leather bag and a Chanel-style, ivory jacket, she left the house. It was sunny outside and after polishing her Jackie-O-style sunglasses, she slid them onto her face.

* * *

Tony Verde had been sitting on the 16.02 train from Paddington to Oxford. He'd arrived earlier than expected and settled himself into a comfortable window seat. The station announcements merged into the background as he found himself obsessing over Katy. He was such a numpty with these phones, it took him ages to type out messages. Stupid really, he thought, because he knew she worked Thursdays. He pressed send anyway, knowing she wouldn't pick up till much later, then stared at the screen before opening the Evening Standard. If she hadn't replied immediately, she'd be with a client. That was her style. Putting his phone in his pocket and trying not to get sucked into the fantasy that was playing in his head, he turned to the crossword to take his mind off things. It would be a long commute home. He felt his mobile vibrate. Probably Lauren wondering when he'd be back. His pulse quickened as he read Katy's message, and with gasping breaths, he grabbed his briefcase and jacket, jumping onto the platform just as the doors slid shut behind him. The station attendant blew his whistle, the carriages were locked and a moment later, the train shunted away. Two more seconds and he'd have been trapped on his way to the shires.

Hands trembling, he fumbled with the keypad.

Meet you at the clock. What are you wearing? Still not used to the short hair!

He headed straight for the station pub and ordered a glass of Aussie Shiraz. A message popped up on his mobile:

You can't miss me! I'm wearing red!"

He knocked back the glass of wine, then ambled towards the clock.

* * *

Katy stood at the center of the carriage, checking her reflection in the double doors. She swore she could feel people staring before returning to their newspapers or gazing out at the passing houses. Her heart was pumping. It was ridiculous, at her age, like being a teenager all over again. She'd better calm down and start thinking clearly. Reframe: it was just a bald, middle-aged, short friend who she used to know at school. Nothing more.

Yogic breathing. Perhaps that would help. Breathe in for the count of six, slowly out for the count of twelve. Her pulse was still racing. Relaxation Response. Breathe in for the slow count of seven, hold for the count of five, out for the count of eleven, hold for the count of five and repeat. It wasn't working.

Emotional Freedom Technique. Nobody was looking, they were all buried in their books or playing games on their phones. Under her breath, she repeated the words "Even though I have this anxious feeling, I deeply and completely love, honor and accept myself." Surreptitiously tapping at different meridian points on her face and upper body, she'd just started making headway when a lady in a lilac cardigan seemed to have fixed her eyes on her. Was it the red dress or the tapping? Spinning around and flashing her a broad smile, Katy's ivory jacket, which was hanging from her bag, fell to the floor. The woman smirked at her as she bent down gingerly in the tight-fitting dress, catching sight of her own smoldering reflection in the glass.

As the train approached Paddington, the light fluttering of butterflies grew stronger, as if thousands of them were beating their wings in a fury. She'd got this under control, she told herself. Gritting her teeth and hanging onto the rail, she wondered what she was doing. Harmless fun, that's all. They were just friends, so why was her pulse racing like this? Did she want an affair? No, it was morally wrong. What would she say to a client in the same scenario? She couldn't think. Was this about validation and attention, she wondered? At this rate, it would all end in tears, as her grandmother used to say. It was getting out of hand, but she couldn't stop.

The train jerked to a standstill and the doors opened. Katy spilled onto the platform, pushing her glasses to the top of her head. He might not recognize her with them on, she reasoned, sashaying across the concourse towards the clock. Tony was lost in a throng of people, but she spotted him fiddling with his left cufflink, and locked eyes with his. Slow down, just walk normally, she told herself. Part of her was in the scene, the other dissociated as if watching a slow-motion remake of Brief Encounter. All that was missing was the music. She wanted to run and fling her arms around his neck, but she mustn't. Standing a respectful distance away, she stopped, a coy smile lighting up her face as she said, "Hello!"

His face was a picture, his breath taken away momentarily. She could tell he was faltering.

"Well, hello!"

She was an iron filing in his strong magnetic field, forcibly pulling herself back but her legs stepped forward of their own volition, and she found herself face-to-face with the unlikely object of her desire. They did the continental kiss thing again, but he lingered a little too long.

"You smell fabulous!" he said. "Where shall we go?"

He smelled intoxicating, but she said nothing. "There's a little wine bar not far from here."

"Righty-ho! Lead the way!"

Their shoulders almost touching, they glided from the concourse, their bodies gently brushing here and there as they babbled to each other about numerology, Windsor, and wine. A station full of commuters disappeared beyond the intimate bubble they found themselves in.

"We haven't got much time," said Katy, checking her gold dress watch. "I've got to meet Richard at 6 o'clock." She quickened her pace despite the heels. "I'll need to leave by twenty-to, and it's almost 5.00 now!"

Pandora's was an old cellar bar which few people knew. It had been tucked away for a hundred years at least and stocked an incredible selection of fine Port, Madeira, and wine. Descending the steep stairs, her derriere jiggling slightly with each step, Katy was acutely aware of Tony's eyes boring into the back of her butt, the tight dress accentuating every contour and sensual movement. She could feel the silky tops of her stockings slipping against each other as she sat at a small, poky, table and crossed her legs.

"Glass of wine?" said Tony, beaming at her.

"Yes! Red!" She winked. Why had she done that?

The tiny cellar was full, and Tony had to fight his way to the bar. Returning a few minutes later with two large glasses, he handed one to her. "Côte de Beaune," he said, squeezing into the tight corner beside her. "Cheers!"

Cramped for space, his leg was pressing gently against hers, sending a delicious shiver up her spine, the taut muscles beneath his suit flexing slightly as he moved.

"I've got something for you." His warm, sweet breath caressed her cheeks as he spoke, he was so close.

Leaning forward to reach his briefcase, which he'd tucked between his feet, his face was so near to hers that she didn't dare move. Her heart was pounding as he fished out a copy of Angels & Demons.

"Thought you'd like to read his earlier book," he said, handing her the paperback.

His thigh was warm against hers, their knees almost kissing. Neither tried to move away as the conversation flowed above the din of the wine bar. Her libido, which had dried up years ago, began to trickle back. To make herself heard, Katy had to lean right in towards him, her hair brushing his face. "How was your day?" she breathed into his ear. His lips were so close when he answered that she could hear the rush of his breath. As they exchanged stories of their respective mornings, she noticed her thigh was pressing harder against his. Hot passion was mounting powerfully within her, like an oil well that was about to blow.

Glancing at her gold bangle watch, she leaned back and squinted at its minimalist face. It can't be! "What's the time?"

"Oh crikey! It's quarter to six! We'd better dash, or you'll be toast!"

The corners of her mouth turned up at the memory of him saying that in her bedroom one afternoon when she was a sweet but not so innocent fifteen. If your mum catches us, you'll be toast! She hadn't heard it in years!

Slinging on her jacket and grabbing her bag, now bulging from the book she'd wedged in, Katy headed towards the steep stairway, Tony following close on her heels.

"I've got to go too!" he said, dropping behind by another

step. The cheeky monkey, he'd be eye height with her magnificent booty! She wiggled it a little more than she needed, fully aware of the effect it would be having. Up at street level, they walked briskly towards the station. Tony was carrying his briefcase rather awkwardly in front of him. She felt sure he was concealing an erection, and the thought sent a delicious tingle through her body. They had to part ways at Paddington, she towards the Bakerloo line and he across the concourse to the mainline trains.

"Thanks for the drink. It was lovely to see you!" Her smile was a little too broad, the tone a bit too gushing. One large glass of wine on an empty stomach had gone to her head. She smoothed down her hair, convinced he was going to make a move. He pecked her on the cheek, said goodbye and walked away. Damn! She'd got it so wrong! Probably just as well.

Darting down the steps to the underground, pulse still racing, she knew she had to finish this dangerous game, but couldn't. Just as she thought she'd hooked him, he'd walked away. Darn the consequences, she'd draw the line at an affair, but she couldn't stop now – it was kick-starting her mojo! It was good he hadn't kissed her. If she could keep this up, she could use the mounting tension to boost her flagging sex life with Richard. He was her loyal husband, the father of her children, and she'd been trying to sort this out for ages!

Running the last few steps, she managed to jump onto the train as the doors began to close. The carriage was packed. She must have read it all wrong. After all, he talked a lot about Lauren and Amber. Perhaps he genuinely wanted a friendship? When she was fifteen, and he was seventeen, she'd thought he loved her, but she'd been misguided. She could easily be mistaken now. Where was that Voice when she needed it, and what was the universe trying to tell her?

The next station is Warwick Avenue. This is a Bakerloo line train to Harrow and Wealdstone sang the robotic female announcement. Harrow and Wealdstone? Bugger. She was on the wrong train! She needed a southbound one to Elephant and Castle. Oh my God, she'd be late for Richard. The panic was rising now. It must be a punishment for playing away. She'd made a complete fool of herself. Perhaps it was written all over her face because everyone was staring at her. Shameful. Guilty as charged. She scowled back and tumbled off at the next station, running up the steps in her heels to the opposite platform. A heaving train arrived, and she pushed her way through a crowd of young Turks who were jeering and whistling. Turning away from them as best she could, she noticed the entire carriage was full of drunken football supporters with their England flags, their bloated faces painted white with a red cross to match. They were chanting something – "Inger-land". At the next station, a man dressed in a chainmail balaclava, and his friend, holding a papier-mâché dragon head, stood disappointed at the platform. The carriage was packed to the gills. "Happy Saint George's!" said an older lady as she stepped off the train. Katy blushed. No wonder people had been staring! She was wearing a red dress with cream trim and an ivory jacket on St George's Day!

* * *

Tony's train idled out of the station, gathering pace as it eased from the suburbs. His briefcase was resting on his knees. It had been his third meeting with Katy, and it was all he could do not to rip that dress off and lunge at her then and there! Watching her bum wobbling up the steps in front of him had almost sent him over the edge! It had done nothing to assuage the already steamy fantasy that had been brewing all afternoon. Blood was coursing through him now, every jolt of the carriage sending shock waves through his already frazzled system. He had to play it cool. Slowly, slowly, catchy monkey. He had to have her, and he wasn't about to screw it up again like he had at seventeen!

Besides, he'd better get a grip. He'd be facing Lauren in less than an hour. Taking his mobile from his pocket, he dialed The Priory. The answerphone kicked in, and he left a message. "This is Wing Commander Anthony Verde. I'd like to book an appointment to see Dr. Watkins as soon as possible. Please call me on

* * *

Richard Stone stationed himself on a park bench in Cavendish Square and unfurled his newspaper. The weak Spring sunshine warmed his back as he enjoyed a moment of solitude in an otherwise pressing day. Turning to the sports section, he lost himself in the back pages, dropping his hand absently into his pocket and rustling for a sherbet lemon. She'd be along soon, probably got caught in all the St George's Day crap. He'd bide his time and steel himself for the performance. Harley Street would be another productive circle in which to move, and he'd been waiting for Kit to invite him for a while. He'd work the room with his usual charm, cleverly engaging those medical types in conversation, lulling them into a false sense of security. People would tell him all sorts of secrets once their defenses were down. A glass of champers, a winning smile, take an interest in them, and they'd usually start spilling a few beans. He felt a cold shiver and pulled his overcoat around his shoulders. An echo, a shadow of something rippled on the surface of his awareness. Looking at his watch, he noticed she was almost thirty minutes late. Must be busy on the tube, he thought, returning to the rugby.

* * *

Katy's train lurched into Oxford Circus, and a throng of people burst out of the carriage, collectively heading for the ticket barriers. A woman in front had an Oyster card that didn't work, and Katy side-stepped, barging into the queue next to hers. A tourist at the head of the line rifled through his pockets for a rumpled card then stood looking quizzically at the machine. Typical! It was always when she was in a hurry. By the time she got to Cavendish Square, her feet were killing her, and she was almost half an hour late. The frenzy at Oxford Circus and the near jog from there had taken her mind off Tony. Her attention was squarely focused on Richard and the party now. Out of breath, she slowed down to a brisk walk and spotted her husband sitting on a bench on the far side. Lifting her arm to wave and calling "Richard!" she hurried the last few yards and stood in front of him, panting. He finished his article before casually folding The Times under his arm and looking up expectantly with that hang-dog expression of his.

"Sorry, I'm late." She'd caught her breath. "St George's day! Train packed!" He didn't say a word, just rose to his feet and turned towards Harley Street.

"Busy day?" she ventured.

"Yes. The usual shit."

"Got most of my paperwork done."

"Good. Kids okay?"

"Far as I know. I left supper in the fridge, and they've got homework. Shirley next door said she'd listen out for them."

"Shirley? That interfering old bat?"

"Rich! She's actually very sweet, and she cares!"

Richard grunted.

They walked up to the house in silence, he striding slightly ahead as she struggled to keep up in her pencil skirt dress and stilettos. He hadn't noticed her outfit at all. No nod of approval, no pleasant surprise, no eyes fixed on her curves. She was glad when they climbed the broad, shallow steps to the lobby of the Harley Street house. The capacious building swallowed them up as they headed up the elegant staircase to join the party. Fran was already tipsy and chatting up a particularly good-looking plastic surgeon. Katy wondered how much was real. He was too good to be true! She made a beeline for them, helping herself to a glass of Prosecco en route. Richard wandered casually over to a rather smartly dressed Israeli woman in her late fifties, her husband joining them a few moments later with a small tray of drinks. Richard had them eating out of his hand within minutes. Katy saw him from the corner of her eye, working the room with that effortless precision he'd honed. She was proud of him. He was charming, presentable, tall, and attractive. Why would she want anyone else? Circulating in her own way, chatting to almost everyone and graciously receiving their compliments on her outfit, she lost herself in conversation with friends and colleagues. Towards the end of the evening she spotted her husband nearby, engrossed with a cosmetic dentist and his wife. People were leaving, saying goodbye, and she headed over to join him.

"We were just talking about you."

"Oh! Good, I hope?" Katy laughed, and the dentist flashed a perfect smile.

"It seems you're quite the star, my dear," he said.

Katy turned to Richard. "We should think about heading home, the party's almost over!"

"Don't be a spoil-sport!"

"Oh, it's quite alright, we must make tracks too," said the wife, her white, even teeth glinting beneath her fuchsia lipstick.

The whole thing came to a grinding halt as the stragglers were politely ushered out onto a rain-splattered street, where they dispersed in different directions.

Sitting in familiar silence, the train grumbling along the District Line towards Turnham Green, Katy sat opposite her husband. Something flashed across her mind as she watched him nod off. They were living separate lives. Her phone buzzed.

Great to see you. You looked STUNNING in that dress! xxx

Three kisses. Her cheeks flushed as a broad beam lit up her

face before fading. It was time to stop. She moved across and sat next to Richard, reaching for his hand. The sudden touch startled him awake, and he took her hand in his, giving it a quick squeeze before letting go.

Chapter 24

Sitting at her desk on Friday morning, Katy made a radical decision to reduce client work to three afternoons and two evenings a week. It would mean disappointing people, but they could go on a waiting list, or be referred to Fran or one of the psychologists. It seemed the only way of fitting everything in! She had to make time for Richard and the kids, she realized.

Every time Tony entered her head, she'd push him aside. Family, work, and her spiritual interests were the three pillars of her life, and there was no room for anything else. The last thing she wanted was to crash and burn like some of her clients. It would take a long time to recover, if ever. Making a mental note to stick to a new regime of supplements, raw green juice, yoga, and meditation, she was sure she could keep her head above water.

This weekend was free, and she'd spend some quality time with the family. Thoughts of Tony persisted, so she booked an appointment with Terry for Monday. It might look like she was in control, but under the facade, a chaotic mix of truncated thoughts, visions and images were vying for her attention. She needed a trusty sounding-board to put them all in order.

Making a rare appearance at the gym that afternoon, it dawned on Katy that her life was stretched to the limit. The pace was rather like the treadmill she was running on – not fast enough to fall off and hit the deck, but too quick for comfort. Resting between sit-ups, she realized despite her professional insights, the support of her MOSES friends, and Terry's advice, she couldn't get herself back on track.

After a quick stretch and cool down, she hurried back to the changing rooms to shower. The hot water rushed over her and she closed her eyes. Cracks of doubt were splitting open, like a frozen lake giving way to something heavy. She glimpsed the chasm beneath and shivered. Shutting off the water and drying herself, Tony swam back into her thoughts. A mélange of emotions came flooding up like a spring tide, washing away the banks of certainty she'd been clinging to. Caught in the undertow, she was pulled under and disoriented. Saturday tomorrow, she told herself, and she'd spend the morning with Tilly and Freddie. The more she fought to get a grip, the stronger the rising current of feelings became until it tossed her away and she broke down in the cubicle, sobbing quietly into her towel. Waiting for the future hadn't worked, because 'tomorrow' never came. When the babies were older, when she'd established herself, when she'd mastered meditation, when Richard took notice, when she'd changed her name, when they'd had a break, when the kids had left for university. When? Tomorrow was never as bright as it was in her imagination, but it kept her going, took her mind off the present, and kept her busy. Busy was stable, it was forward motion – otherwise, she'd lose balance and tumble. One day she'd get there, wherever 'there' was. Meanwhile, cramming her days full kept her too busy to notice the cracks in her marriage, the broken parts of her life! After blowing her nose, she sighed heavily and forced a smile. Fake it till you make it. That's what they said, wasn't it? She drove home via the supermarket, determined to make her life work. "I choose a happy marriage and an intimate sex life with my husband," she said out loud. "This is my intention."

That night, at around 3 am, heart racing, she was roused from her sleep. Recalling her dream for the diary, she wrote:

New client – charming at first but suddenly turned on me, like a mad dog. Threatened me in the consulting room. Body language scary. Baring his teeth. Told me I was useless, and he was going to report me – have me struck off. Turned nasty. Had to act calm and in control but was terrified.

After closing the notebook and taking a sip of water, she returned to a fitful sleep, only to wake in a sweat a while later.

Recurring nightmare. Third time. Bought a rambling old house – too big and dilapidated to maintain. Every room needs gutting, stripping, refurbishing. No time nor money to do it. Three kitchens merged into one with too many appliances and sinks. Couldn't choose which to keep. Huge ballroom at the back flooded. Doric columns standing in fetid water. Back staircase full of dry-rot – foot went through – toilet at the top has broken bowl and won't flush. Stained crack in the U-bend and water, or worse, dripping onto yellowing lino. Massive Victorian greenhouse in the garden – knee-deep in water. River behind tidal. Every tiny pane of glass cracked/broken. Horrified I've bought the place. Lumbered with it. Overwhelmed.

She put down the pen and tip-toed to the bathroom before returning to bed. Half an hour or so later, in another dream, she was grappling with a somber patterned carpet in the gloomy drawing-room of the neglected house. Tony appeared, his smile spilling warm, golden light into the dark recesses surrounding her. Offering his arm, he led her out of the chaos to an oasis of bright, clear space, where he tenderly kissed her forehead. Holding their palms up, they touched each other's fingertips, then clasped hands before letting go and caressing each other gently. There seemed to be something important about the fingertips but she couldn't work out what. Tender kisses led to more urgent ones until she was caught in an intimate embrace, his tongue darting between her lips. It was the arousal that woke her from the dream. She wouldn't write it down – Terry didn't need to know.

The following morning, Tilly announced she was starting a part-time job at the local café.

"But I was going to hang out with you today!" said Katy.

Tilly scowled. "Mum! I'm sixteen! I don't want to 'hang out' with my mother!"

Freddie giggled. "We're not kids anymore, you know! We've got our own lives!" Lacing up his baseball boots, he added, "I'm off to the park with some mates from school."

"When will you be back?"

"Dunno. I'll text you."

"Will you be home for lunch?"

"Probably not. We're kicking a ball around then going to Tom's." Tucking a battered old football under his arm, he left the house to the sound of the windchimes.

Of course, they wanted to be with their friends, thought Katy, it was only natural. They'd be listening to their music, laughing at the in-jokes, and using their own version of the English language! It saddened her, though, feeling so shut out, but it was part of being a teenager, she supposed. It was normal to reject your parents and find your own way. It was healthy.

"Rich?"

"What now, Kit?"

"Any plans?"

"Apart from lying on the sofa with the rugby and the papers?"

"I thought we could go somewhere?" She was dying to get out of suburbia. "What about the South Bank?"

Richard wrinkled his nose and returned to his paper.

"The West End, then?" She was twirling the silver bangle on her right wrist.

"On a Saturday? You must be joking! It'll be packed." He flicked over the page.

"What about a matinee, or a gallery?"

"For fuck's sake, Kit! I'm in the City all day, and the last thing I want is to get on a sodding train into town!"

Katy's shoulders slumped, her smile vanishing as she tried to muster some enthusiasm. "And I'm stuck inside these four walls whenever I'm not confined to my room in Harley Street. I'd like to go somewhere for a change!" He wasn't taking it on board. She could sense his prickly energy, but she had to try.

"Perhaps we could go for a walk by the river? What about Kew Gardens?" She said it as brightly as she could. His withering expression cut through her, but she wasn't going to give up. "I thought we could do something together, Rich." The calm,

254

measured voice was as much as she could manage. She mustn't show him how upset she was – he hated it if she 'whined' or 'turned on the waterworks'.

"We are together, aren't we?"

He looked up from his paper. "I've had a hell of a week. I want to relax for Christ's sake!"

"Okay!" She was biting her lip and counting to ten. If she said anything, it would only cause another row, and she didn't have it in her. Hovering a little longer she plucked up the courage. "I'll tidy up the house and cook a nice supper. Why don't we invite Ben and Tara over?"

Richard's jaw tightened. "I don't want to spend my evening with your whacky friends."

"How about inviting your friends instead?" It was too late, she'd said it now! She knew he didn't have those sorts of friendships, only contacts, acquaintances, and colleagues. Richard's left eye twitched as his nostrils flared. "I'd have to give them notice. Unlike your rabble, they get booked up weeks in advance!" He buried his head in the Times.

Katy spent the day tidying, mowing the lawn, and cooking, while Richard relaxed with the Saturday papers. The children were out having fun and she couldn't help feeling jealous. She'd tried, hadn't she, but it took two to tango? Having stacked away dirty plates and cleaned up after supper, she called through to the snug. "Just going to meditate!"

Richard grunted.

At the top of the stairs, she hesitated by the mirror before wandering into the office. Positioning her meditation stool, she sat, her throat tightening, along with her jaw. A restlessness took hold as an uneasy feeling churned in her stomach. Walking over to the window, she gazed out over Sycamore Road, her fingers fidgeting with the curtain. Moments later, she was standing in front of the bookcase, plucking out A Course In Miracles. Flipping it open at random, she read:

Perception is a mirror, not a fact, and what you look on is your own state of mind, reflected outward.

"Exactly what we were discussing!" said the Voice.

"Oh! You took me by surprise!"

"You weren't *expecting* me. An interesting notion."

"What?"

"Things are rarely as you expect. Expectation is based on a construct you make in your mind, which itself is formed from old memories – experiences, things you've seen, heard or read about."

"It's the picture in your head of how you think it's going to be that trips you up!"

"It's only what you *think*."

"And not what's real."

"You're getting it, by Jehovah!"

"The rational mind can fool you, can't it?"

"Quite so."

"I tell that to my clients. You thought you saw a snake, but it was only a piece of rope."

"You're not really seeing, just taking in a portion of what is, then comparing it with what you know. The mind is conditioned to see what it wants."

"So, you notice a lawn and think 'grass', but you don't see the beauty and form of each individual blade?"

"Good example! The brain takes in what's general, not what's specific."

"It looks for patterns and matches them to its knowledge base. I learned that when I trained!"

"What the logical mind perceives is rarely objective."

"And sometimes, plain wrong! It can see a black bag of rubbish in the dark and think it's a body!"

"And it can deceive in other ways too. You think you can't, that you won't be able to, that you'll fail. Is that a true reflection of reality or just a thought?"

"I tell my clients a story about perception. If you were attacked by a dog when you were young, you'll think that dogs are dangerous. Now, you'll see a dog and avoid it. If you had a loveable pet labrador when you were little, you'll think that dogs are wonderful. When you see that same dog, you'll make a fuss of it! Same dog, two different reactions!"

"One dog, two perspectives, two different truths."

"Is that why witnesses at the scene of a crime report different things?"

"Yes. It's their perception coupled with their *perspective*."

"I'm looking at the mountain from the South, you're looking from the North. We argue about the best route! Another one I use sometimes!"

"Open-hearted discussion usually works! Listen to the other person and understand their perspective!"

"Yes."

"Rest now. Meditate. Be led by your intuitive mind."

"That's the knowing, the little voice inside? But it doesn't always make sense!"

"Not to the rational mind."

"But it's usually right?"

"*The intuitive mind is a sacred gift, and the rational mind is a faithful servant.*"

"That's Einstein!"

"Yes."

"Then he says something about the fact we do the reverse!"

"*We've created a society that honors the servant and has forgotten the gift.*"

"How do we change that?"

"Be the change you want to be in the world."

"Gandhi!"

"You've got it."

"And we change when we shift our thinking."

"Yes. Become aware. Become conscious. Observe."

"And use hypnotic regression and anything else that re-programs the mind and clears trauma?"

"Yes. Goodnight, dear one."

Katy sat back on the stool, a single soothing thought calming her: *Focus on the breath in the nostrils.*

Chapter 25

Terry ushered Katy into his consulting room on Monday afternoon, wondering what had been so urgent. He crossed his legs and leaned back in the chair.

"I wanted to talk a bit more about Richard," she said, fiddling with her bangle.

"Okay."

"He doesn't seem to want the same things as me." She hesitated. "He spent the entire weekend lounging around with the papers and the television."

"Perhaps he needed to relax?"

"I understand that, but he doesn't help around the house, and he doesn't seem to realize I have my own needs!"

"Tell me more."

"He won't lift a finger at home. I even mow the lawn and take the car for service. He doesn't do any of the things husbands usually do."

Katy's eyes were darting from side-to-side. Perhaps she was putting her thoughts in order? Looking up, she continued. "For a start off, he doesn't care about his clothes. He leaves them in a heap, expecting someone else to pick them up!"

"You?" Hmm. He didn't seem to be taking much responsibility, thought Terry.

"Yes. He looks after his suit and shoes because they're important, but he doesn't give a damn about much else, including me. If it's not relevant to his success, he's not interested."

"How does that make you feel?"

"Used and insignificant!"

"Do you feel like that with other people?"

"No! Not since my childhood."

Terry made a note. "Have you tried talking to him?" He knew it was a pointless question. Of course, Katy had talked to him! She was a therapist who cared about people, and who knew how to communicate her feelings. Most likely, she'd chosen a partner similar in character to her father, but she had to work that out for herself. He felt his temples tighten.

"Yes. He just gets angry."

"Why do you suppose that is?" Surely, she'd see it as dysfunctional.

"I think it's Mummy stuff," said Katy, a far-away look in her eyes. "He longed to be loved by his mum, be mothered by her, but she's, well." Katy stopped short. "He feels second best, discarded, unwanted."

"And now he's making you feel second best?" He could be reflecting her own longings for maternal love, thought Terry.

Katy frowned.

He paused before asking his next question. Which way would he go with this? "What makes you think it's his mother?"

"She rejected him when his sister was born. Angela's a couple of years younger. Janet, his mum, told him how beautiful Ang was, not like her ugly little boy. Poor Rich. From the photos, he looked like a normal kid to me, and he certainly turned into a handsome man."

"And Richard told you this?" His eyes widened as he looked up.

"Yes. He might look powerful in that black coat and shiny shoes, but deep inside he's hurting." Katy took a tissue from her bag. "There's a broken little boy trapped inside, just wanting to be loved." She blew her nose and continued. "I can't believe she sent him away. He was only two, for goodness' sake!"

"Sent him away?"

"She put him in a home for a while. Couldn't cope, he said."

"How long was he gone for?"

"I don't know. He won't talk about it. A couple of weeks, I think."

Terry's brow tightened. Katy was obviously mothering him, replacing the love and support he didn't have as a child. "What sort of home?"

"I don't know, he won't tell me!"

His fountain pen scratched across the page. They could be mirroring each other. Perhaps Katy was rejected too? "Carry on."

"He's a Northerner, Catholic. Why do they have so many kids when they can't support them? They were quite poor. He had to go without – toys, Christmas presents, that sort of thing." She sighed and wiped away a tear. "You wouldn't know he was from Leeds," she continued. "The odd tell-tale sign, the occasional flat vowel when he's tired, but that's all. Otherwise he's the perfect City gent!"

"In what way?"

"The way he acts. Wanted to get away from his childhood and succeed, I expect, so he climbed his way to the top! He's like a bulldozer, flattening anything in his path! Very bright, you see. Got to grammar school, then university. He's quite inspiring, actually. A good leader and manager, a brilliant thinker. Cares about his team at work." The corners of her lips turned up into a smile. "That's why I married him, that and his sense of humor." She let out a short laugh, presumably at some private joke she was recalling.

"Anything else?"

"From what he's told me, he was a good little kid, tried to please his mum, follow the rules, do the right thing."

"And how did Mum respond?"

"I get the impression he was always looking for a crumb of affection. She's a hard woman, not the cuddly type."

"Is that your observation?"

"Richard told me, but I can see it too." She paused. "There's something else." Terry nodded in her direction, encouraging her to continue. "There was another baby before Richard. It was stillborn. I wonder if Janet was in mourning when she had Rich? She's very pragmatic. I can't imagine her talking it over with anyone, even the priest. I can see her stuffing the emotions down and getting on with it. You know? For her, mothering was practical. Change nappy, feed, sleep. If she hadn't got over the death of the baby, she wouldn't be able to open her heart to Rich, would she?"

"That's quite possible, does he show any signs?"

"What sort of signs?"

"You know the kind of thing – lack of confidence, avoiding connection, getting angry, being guarded."

"He isn't good with feelings. He can't stand big shows of emotion, and he keeps a very tight rein on his own. I've only ever known him express anger, depression, and occasional excitement when he's won something big like a bonus. Actually, I think he's afraid of something, but he masks it with anger."

"Does he respond to *your* emotions?"

"He hates me crying. Apart from that, he needs big, bold brushstrokes to get it. I have to tell him what I'm feeling, but aren't all men like that?"

Terry looked up at her. "No!" His gentle voice was calm but emphatic.

"I feel like I can't connect with him."

He wrote on the file. *Richard emotionally unavailable. Doesn't express or respond to deeper feelings. Katy mothering him. Was she also rejected by mother? Was father emotionally cold or abusive?* She was blind to what was going on, he noted. Of all people, she should have guessed. He glanced at the figure sitting opposite him. This woman who could register emotions in others from the slightest movement of their facial muscles, the density of the air around them, the tone of their voice, the way they were sitting. He knew her type. They could cry at a song, the beauty of a sunset, or the joy of children playing. She'd feel other people's suffering and pain.

"What happens if you cry?" he said at last.

"I try not to, but I can't help it. The kids tease me if they see me blubbing at a film! I always cry at Cinderella, it's stupid, but

I don't know why."

Identifies with Cinderella archetype, wrote Terry. "And how does Richard react?"

"I don't let him see."

"And if he did see?"

"He'd be angry or walk away, I expect. I'm afraid to show him. He doesn't think adults are supposed to shed tears. He'd probably tell me not to be so immature."

Terry's eyebrow twitched. Stone by name and stone by nature. This man couldn't appreciate what he had – a sensual woman whose breast heaved at the miracle of creation and the frailty of human nature. That heart of hers must beat with a thousand subtle emotions. Empaths like Katy had a sensitivity so rare they could pick up on the sentiments of others and mistake them for their own. He looked up at his client. There was something she wasn't telling him. What had precipitated all this, he wondered?

"Anything else?" he asked.

"I don't think Richard realizes that he *is* loved, or that he's made of love like we all are! His parents do take an interest. I know they love him in their way, but he doesn't see it. He's built this steel wall around his heart, so he doesn't have to feel anything. I'm so sad, Terry, to think of the pain that's locked away inside him."

Terry pursed his lips. "Perhaps he isn't hurting? Otherwise, he'd show it, in some way, wouldn't he? Perhaps he'd cauterize the feelings with addiction, or he'd seek help?"

Katy stared back at him and fell silent. He paused before changing the subject. "Anything else you wanted to discuss?"

"Only my dream diary," said Katy rifling through her bag and triumphantly emerging with the book in her hand.

Terry listened as she read. "Hmm. I think the client dream is your lack of self-belief. I know you didn't qualify with the Westminster Pastoral Foundation, I know you're not a Jungian Psychoanalyst. Still, you are a conscientious and sought-after therapist. You must know that?" His eyes searched hers. Did she still feel she wasn't enough? "Interestingly, it's a male client," he continued. "Bowing to male authority, even if it's misplaced and dysfunctional. Tell me about your father?"

"What about the house? I've had that dream several times, and it's always the same."

"Yes." Terry paused. She'd chosen not to answer the question. The father was likely the key here, but he'd have to wait until she was ready. "When people dream of a house, it often represents the inner self. In your case, there are so many aspects to explore. The flooded basement, the leaking toilet, the tidal river – these point to emotional overwhelm and loss. The subconscious seems to be at breaking point. All the work that needs doing on this house is a reflection of the overload in your life. You have too much on your plate! There's a level of chaos here which is being suppressed, and a need to make order from it, but you fear you're unable to. The fact it's a large home suggests you're worried about your wider family. The three kitchens. Hmm. The heart and hearth of the family are in disarray. You can't decide." He knew there was something she wasn't telling him. "Between what, I don't know, Is there anything more?" He wanted to say, 'is there anyone else?' but he wasn't sure that was appropriate. She may simply be searching for a resolution.

"No. I don't know. Why?"

"I think your psyche is looking for a source of nourishment but can't find it." He scratched his chin. Yes, it fitted with Cinderella, he thought. "Perhaps you're waiting to be rescued? In the dream, you can't resolve all this on your own. You're trapped, and your inner psyche believes your life is beyond your means to repair." He touched his fingertips together and waited. "But you know that's not true, don't you?"

Katy was looking down into her lap. "It does feel beyond me at times."

"And that's what we're here to work through. You're more

powerful than you think." He smiled, bringing the session to a close and placing his notes on the desk.

* * *

Anthony Verde was sitting in the waiting area, nervously fiddling with his left cufflink. Dr. Watkins noticed him jump as his name was called. It could be an interesting session, he thought, motioning his patient into the plush consulting room.

"Has something happened?" he asked. "You called for an urgent appointment?"

"I'd like to finish therapy," stammered the client. "And I, er, wanted to tell you personally."

"I see, and what's prompted this decision?" His voice was steady and calm.

"I'm cured! You've done an outstanding job, and I know in my bones I'm ready to get on with the rest of my life." The words sprang out, a broad smile lighting his features.

"Well, that's good to hear, and what made you come to that conclusion?"

"I haven't looked at porn for months, and I feel like a new man."

Dr. Watkins knew that addictions didn't clear up that easily. "What's caused this turn-around, do you think?"

"I'm in love. I just needed the right woman in my life. Lauren's too bossy, and well, I just don't love her like I should. That's why I turned to the websites! It all makes sense now!"

The doctor had seen this sort of thing before, and knew he had to tread gently. "Oh! And who are you in love with?"

"An old girlfriend from school. I've met up with her a few times, and I just know."

Yes, of course, like every other love and sex addict, they 'just know', thought Dr. Watkins. "What exactly do you know?" he said, his features softening.

"I know it's my one last chance at a relationship that'll work. I fancy the pants off her, always did, always will."

"Well, that's fabulous!" In the true sense of the word, he thought, fabled. "But may I ask how you know?"

"I just do."

"May I offer something?"

"Shoot!"

He had to word this carefully "It's difficult for people to know what their true, long-term feelings are when they first meet someone. All those chemicals firing off! But couples can always choose to take decisions slowly, while they savor the delights of the moment." His soft brown eyes held his client's gaze.

"But I don't want to take it slowly! I already know!"

"Would giving it more time allow you to explore what you already know?" He paused, giving the patient a moment to get used to the idea. There was no answer. "People find reflection can be very useful when they're making lasting decisions." He leaned back and waited a moment. Addicts mostly focused on the immediate hit, and not the later consequences.

"What are you getting at?"

This was going to be delicate. "Tell me, how long have you known her?"

"Over thirty years."

Dr. Watkins' eyebrows shot up. He immediately composed himself, resuming a neutral expression. "You've known her all that time?"

"Well, er, not exactly."

"How long, exactly, has she been in your life?"

"I went out with her at school, but we lost touch."

"And you've been back in contact?"

He nodded. "We wrote each other emails for a while then met up in March."

"Last month or last year?"

"Last month."

Dr. Watkins considered his next question. "And how long were you together at school?"

"A couple of years."

"That's quite some time for a young relationship!"

"What? No! I was at her school for a couple of years. I only went out with her for a few weeks, but I was a fool to run away."

Dr. Watkins pinched the bridge of his nose and took a breath. "So, why did you?"

"I was seventeen! I had my whole life ahead of me! I didn't want to be tied down, did I? But I knew I'd made a mistake when I saw her with Gordon."

"Gordon?"

"The bloke she went out with after me."

"Was she tying you down? Making demands of you, before you left?"

"Er, no, but she might have!"

The doctor made a note on the client file. *Fear of commitment. Jealousy.* "And she might not have? What stopped you allowing the relationship to simply take its course?"

His patient frowned. "Well, I'm doing that now, aren't I?" His voice had a strangled sound to it.

Dr. Watkins had a feeling there was something else. This man was going back into the past to resolve unfinished business. "And you're no longer worried about being tied down?" He wondered if there was a fear of rejection. There was definitely a problem with low self-esteem.

"I'm happy to be tied down now, not in the sexual sense, you understand!" His ears turned crimson. "I mean, I've been married twice, I'm nearly 50, and I know exactly what I'm doing!" He stopped a moment, seemingly lost in a vision, a broad beam softening his face. "It's my last chance to be with the woman I love! Don't you see? It changes everything!"

"I see that's what you believe, and I'm interested in hearing how you know, after only a few weeks?"

"I love her for Christ's sake!"

"May I offer something?"

"Righty-ho!"

"You're already married, and you have a child. Have you considered the ramifications?"

"Yes! I've been miserable for years. Amber can live with me. My new lady friend will love her and probably help her too."

"What if your wife wants custody?" Did this man think it was going to be as simple as that?

"Nah. She won't. She's only interested in her career! Never really been there for Amber."

"Well that could be true, but still, your leaving is going to be disruptive to Amber, isn't it?" He paused. "And most likely to you, as well as your wife?" He could see the look of confusion on his client's face. "If a friend was going to put himself and his family through a breakup, you'd want him to be sure he was doing the right thing, wouldn't you?"

"Yes of course! I see where you're going with this and I can tell you, I'm doing the right thing!"

"Then the program can support and guide you through the process."

"I don't need guidance! I know what I'm doing."

Dr. Watkins took a slow breath. "And what does your lady friend want?"

"She'll want the same as me."

"You've discussed it?"

"I don't need to."

"May I offer, Anthony, that from a psychological perspective, it takes a while to get to know someone. Studies show that spending time together, discussing hopes for the future, hearing the views of a partner, that sort of thing, helps to cement a relationship." He could see this chap wasn't quite on board from the quizzical look on his face. "Statistically, a couple that communicate their feelings, their expectations, their values, are more likely to create a strong bond."

"We're already strong!"

"In what way?"

"I love her, she loves me, and I told you, we've been corresponding for months!"

"Has she told you she loves you?" Tony cast his eyes down and the doctor continued. "So how do you know she loves you?" Clearly, the man was acting on old impulses, a part of him stuck in his teenage past.

The client frowned, opened his mouth, drew breath, then faltered.

Dr. Watkins carried on. "It takes time for a deep and committed relationship to take root. Could it be that you're in the first flush of infatuation? All those feel-good hormones raging through your body?" He chuckled to himself. Even an old man like him could remember what it was like! "What would happen if you held back for a while?"

"I've waited over thirty years and I'm not holding back a moment longer!"

The softly, softly approach wasn't working. "There's a child at stake and a marriage," he said bluntly.

"My marriage hasn't worked for years, and nor has hers."

"She's married too?"

"Yes, and I'm pretty certain she wants to leave."

"She's told you?"

"Not yet."

Dr. Watkins took a deep breath and sat back. "What if it's not what she wants? The possibility exists, doesn't it?" The patient's face was beginning to flush.

"Don't you believe in love at first sight?"

"We're not here to discuss what I believe." Of course, I do, he thought, just not where love and sex addicts are concerned! "You came here to overcome an issue with pornography and masturbation. Your history suggests it's part of a bigger picture of love and sex addiction."

"It's not an addiction, if that's what you think, it's real!" His client's face was now scarlet.

Dr. Watkins changed tack. "Let's suppose it's true that you love this woman."

"It is!"

"Then what's stopping you taking it slowly, one step at a time?"

"Nothing! I already am!"

"In what way?"

"I've waited over thirty years, haven't I?"

Dr. Watkins wondered at times, why he'd chosen addiction as his specialism. "As you've waited this long, what harm could it do to wait a little longer and complete the program?"

"I told you, I'm cured. I don't need the program."

He stifled a sigh. "Which step are you on?"

"Step three. Handing over to God, and God sent me Katy!"

"It's a twelve-step process. Your group therapy, the meetings, your sponsor, and your one-to-one sessions constitute the program. It's designed to hold you through any possible challenges or relapses right to the end of those twelve steps."

"There won't be any relapses. I don't need it. Simple as that!"

He was acting like a defiant child and needed to be reminded of sober reality. "How will you handle the breakup of your marriage and family?" The man was looking blankly at him. "People find all sorts of things come up as they dismantle their lives." Still nothing seemed to be registering. "Do you know what went wrong, why you're leaving?"

"Yes. I'm leaving to be with Katy."

"And what made you pursue Katy in the first place, when you were already in a committed relationship?" He thought he heard the client mumble, 'for fuck's sake' but couldn't be certain. "In our experience, patients who work through what went wrong in their marriage are better able to build healthy relationships in the future."

The client clenched his jaw and looked down at the carpet, muttering something under his breath before looking up. "I don't think you understand," he said, banging his fist on the edge of the desk. "I'm cured, I love Katy, and I intend to be with her!"

"I understand you have powerful feelings for her."

"You don't believe me, do you?" A fleck of spittle flew from his mouth.

"I believe you feel very strongly."

"Bloody psycho-babble!"

Dr. Watkins took another deep breath. "Have you considered mediation with your wife?"

"What for? We're done!"

"To manage the breakup of your marriage and work out how you'll carry on as a *divorced* family. Amber will always be your daughter, and Lauren will always be the mother of your child. You'll want access, I presume? You'll want to take joint decisions in the future?"

Tony gulped.

"Why rush from one committed relationship straight into another?" Dr. Watkins waited. He could see the look of agitation on the man's face. "Studies show it's better to be single for a while between relationships. How do you feel about living alone for an interim period?" He could see he'd lost his client. "Many of our patients find when they're ready to embark on another relationship, they enjoy good-old-fashioned courting. That's the feedback we get. It gives them time to be clear in their own minds."

"For Christ's sake!" A vein was protruding on the dome of Tony's head which was now turning puce. "I'm crystal clear. I know exactly what I want! I have to have Katy!"

"*Have to* are strong words!" The sort of words an addict might use, thought Dr. Watkins. "We *have to* eat, drink, breathe and sleep. There's a difference between a 'need' and a 'desire'."

"You don't understand! This is real love!" The man's voice was rising, the vein on his head throbbing.

Dr. Watkins shifted in his seat. "In which case, you have the rest of your lives to be together, don't you?" His client's breathing eased, the blood vessel disappearing as his fists unfurled.

"When people chase the thrill of romance, marry quickly and divorce when it all wears off, they don't allow themselves to experience anything deeper." The client looked up. "Evidence suggests that couples who wait a year or two and get to know each other before making any major commitments have a better chance of staying together." He paused for the man to take it in. "It takes a while for the euphoria of infatuation to wear off, and that's when people know if there's a deeper connection. That's when genuine love blossoms."

The patient looked down at the floor, his hands clasped, his ears still burning bright.

"Love and sex addiction are thorny issues," said the doctor. "People can think they're in love with the soulmate of their dreams, and it can turn out to be just a chemical reaction." He'd had to spell it out this time.

"You don't know how I feel!"

"No, I don't." He collected his thoughts. "You said she's married. Does she have children?"

"Yes. Two."

"So that's at least seven people who could potentially get hurt?"

"What?"

"You, your wife, your daughter, your lady friend, her husband and her two children." He was counting them off on his fingers.

His client looked straight at him and spoke evenly. "Meeting Katy has rekindled something."

"What if it's simply the memory of teenage infatuation? You mentioned you regretted ending it?"

"It isn't! I feel alive for the first time in years. She listens to me, appreciates me, understands me."

Oh no, he's going to tell me his wife doesn't understand him, thought Dr. Watkins, rubbing his brow as he collected his thoughts. The patient interrupted.

"Lauren's hard as nails. Katy might look all 'London chic', but underneath she's soft and gentle." He glanced up at the ceiling, as if trying to get a grip on his emotions before continuing. "She's kind and loving. The breath of fresh air I've been gasping for! I know what I'm doing! This has nothing to do with addiction. It's the real deal." He rose to his feet, his jaw tightening, the color draining from him. "Thank you for your time," he said, shaking the doctor's hand. Buttoning his jacket, he turned, took a deep breath, and paced out of the room.

Chapter 26

May 2009

Friday May 8th had been troubling Katy all week. Every time she checked her diary, she'd notice the entire day free of appointments, a diagonal line drawn through the clear page. Her stomach lurched. Cancelling would be the right thing to do. She loved Richard and the children and didn't want to hurt them. Any feelings she had for Tony were probably a hangover from the old days. Several times, she'd started writing an email only to delete it. Too formal, she decided, and anyway, what would she say? She couldn't let him down like that, could she? Perhaps a text message would strike the right tone. Having scrapped several drafts, she realized she'd have to phone and talk to him in person.

On Thursday morning, her heart beating wildly, she dialed his number, then hung up before it rang the other end. She'd left it too late. Anyway, she couldn't stand him up, she'd promised, hadn't she? But what about her promise to Richard at the altar? Maybe a quick lunch, just to tell Tony she couldn't see him anymore? Picking up her phone, she pressed speed-dial.

"Shanti? Thank God you're there! I need to ask you something."

"Yes, I'm very well, thank you!" Shanti's laugh tinkled. "What's so urgent?"

"I'm supposed to meet Tony tomorrow, and I don't know what to do."

"Has Tara got to you? Can't you make your own decisions?"

"No!"

"Why not?"

"I feel like I'm clinging to a life raft in violent seas, tossed this way and that. I'm in the grip of survival."

Shanti laughed. "You're turning it into a drama."

"I'm serious! I don't know where I am! I'm completely

disoriented! I've lost my coordinates."

"You sound like you're at home, to me!"

"Emotionally, I mean. I can't distinguish up from down, left from right, nothing's fixed anymore, and I don't know what's true!"

"For pity's sake, Katy, what are you talking about?"

"Should I see Tony, because I promised I would, and I don't want to let him down?"

"No, see him because you want to. You enjoy seeing him, don't you?"

Katy blushed and swallowed.

Shanti waited a moment. "Don't deny your truth. He's a frothy moment in your otherwise flat day, isn't he?"

"He is fun, I suppose, but I don't want it to get out of hand."

"Then don't let it get out of hand! You're the one who's in control!"

Yes, Shanti was right, she thought, busying herself later with work emails. The phone buzzed.

Looking forward to seeing you tomorrow. Meet 0800 hrs at the clock? x

Her heart leapt, as she instinctively responded. Her rational mind was telling her to cancel, but something else took over. The whole day was free, wasn't it? She might as well see him now she'd turned down clients. Besides, she'd already told the family she was taking a day off to see an old friend from school.

Make it 9.30 am. Paddington Station Clock.

No kiss on purpose. The later time would avoid rush-hour, and besides, they had the whole day, what was the hurry?

* * *

Friday, May 8th 2009 – a six day

Freddie woke with a terrible fever. Beads of sweat were trickling down his pale face while his bare chest flushed in the morning chill. "Mum!" he groaned.

"You okay?" asked Katy, rushing into his room. He could barely speak, his throat rasping as he coughed. Putting her hand to his forehead, she shook her head. "You'd better go to the doctor. Do you feel nauseous?"

"No. My head's killing me, my throat's sore, and I'm hot as hell."

The tension that had been bubbling since she woke up evaporated in an instant. How could she leave her sick child at home and go gallivanting around town with 'Baldylocks'? She'd have to cancel. It would be for the best, she knew it. Everyone kept saying she was being guided, didn't they? Well, this must be the sign she'd been waiting for. "I'd better stay home with you." She smiled and stroked his hair, a steady warmth enveloping her.

"Nah, I'll be alright, Mum."

"It's okay. I can't leave you like this."

"There's nothing you can do anyway. You were going into town, weren't you?"

"It's not important. I can cancel. I'll phone the surgery," she said, scrolling down the speed dial for the number.

"They've given you an appointment at 11 o'clock. I'll take you."

"I can go on my own, Mum, I'm fifteen now, remember?"

"But you're not well!"

"It's only down the road!"

Katy's stomach knotted. The raft she'd been clinging to broke free, and it felt as if she was sinking. Was she the worst mother in the world? "Are you sure?"

Freddie managed a weak smile then flopped back on his bed.

"I'm staying, Freddie!"

"I'm fine, just go!"

Down in the kitchen, Katy filled a jug with water and fresh

lemon slices. Placing it on a tray with a glass, a small bunch of grapes, a couple of digestive biscuits and a slice of buttered toast, she went back to Freddie via the bathroom, where she snatched a packet of paracetamol from the cabinet. "Take a couple of these now and sip at the water. If you feel up to it, have a nibble on the toast. I'll get some throat lozenges. I think there's a pack in my briefcase. Are you sure you're okay?"

"Mum, I'm alright. I'll see the doc and sleep the rest of the day."

Katy ruffled his hair and gave him a hug before retreating into the en-suite. "Oh God, please, tell me what to do! Please look after Freddie. I love him very much and please forgive me for being such a bad person. I'm sorry, I really am. I'll give up Tony and stay home if it's Your Will. Just show me the way. Give me a sign. Thank you, God." Her hands were clasped in prayer as the hot water beat down. "Oh, and Amen." She was out of practice and had forgotten the ending. What was she doing praying anyway? She hadn't done that since she was a child!

Thirty minutes later, she was showered, dressed and made-up with subtle smokey-eyes and a flash of neutral lipstick. There was no restriction on what she could wear now, so she'd selected a pair of skinny jeans with ankle boots, a tight-fitting, cropped jersey, and a red leather biker's style jacket. A chunky silver torque necklace finished off the ensemble. Her pulse was racing as she checked herself in the mirror. She should stay at home with Freddie. It was only right. Popping her head around the door to his bedroom, she called gently. "I can stay, you know! I honestly don't mind!"

"I'm not a kid, in case you'd forgotten! It was my birthday last month and I can handle it."

"If you need anything, anything, just call me." She hesitated, turning her thoughts first to Freddie then to Tony. "If you change your mind, or you don't feel up to it, please, Freddie, just phone me, won't you?" A part of her wanted him to need her, this man-child of hers.

"I will. I'll be okay."

"Are you sure?"

"Mum! Just go!"

Giving him a big hug and kissing him on the forehead, she said goodbye then left, windchimes jingling behind her as she closed the front door. An intoxicating mixture of guilt, anxiety and excitement swept over her. Hands shaking, heart thumping, she gasped at the damp morning air before sitting on the low garden wall that ran along the pavement, her mind darting between Freddie, Tony, and Richard. Covering her face with her hands, she sobbed quietly for a moment before regaining her composure. She took the keys from her bag and marched back to the front door, staring at it, her hand level with the lock.

Her shoulders relaxed and her mind became calm as she drew breath. He'd said he'd be okay. There was nothing she could do, anyway, except hang around and take him to the doctor. He could be asleep now, and she'd disturb him. Dropping her hand to her side, she remembered he wanted to be a man, taking care of himself. She couldn't stand in the way of that, could she? Bowing her head, she zipped the keys into her bag, then turned and headed towards the station. She'd call Shirley next door to let her know. She could keep an eye on him, she thought, fishing out her phone and dialing Shirley's number.

The train slid from the platform as Katy raced down the steps. Damn. She'd be late. Sitting on the bench, she tapped out a text.

Sorry, running slightly late. Missed the train. Will be there asap. x

A pair of pigeons were cooing farther along the platform, and she watched them lock beaks. How strange, she'd never seen that before! Pigeons kissing! An incoming message tore her away from her fascination.

Don't worry, I'll be waiting. xxx

A smile spread across her face as her heart fluttered. Looking up, she noticed a new poster for an online dating site: A happy, smiling couple, arm-in-arm, with the outline of a heart drawn around them in red. The train arrived, and Katy took a seat. She'd better check in with Freddie.

You okay? Let me know if you want me to come back. Shirley next door is home if there's an emergency. Love you xxx

There was still no reply when she got to Paddington. He must have fallen asleep. Zipping up her jacket, she stepped off the train and strutted through the barrier towards the clock. She spotted Tony straight away and made a beeline for him. He was dressed in a suave Italian suit jacket with a plain t-shirt, designer jeans, fashionable leather boots and a chunky belt. Striding towards the slight, bald figure, a smile played at her lips. Her worries relinquished their grip, melting away as he beamed at her.

"You look fantastic!" He seemed to be rooted to the spot, mesmerized and doe-eyed.

"Where shall we go?" She smiled up at him.

"Your call!"

"Café first?"

"Righty-ho. Lead the way."

"There's a lovely place in Little Venice. Follow me."

Marching confidently out of the concourse with Tony by her side, Katy smiled from ear-to-ear, her hair bobbing with the new spring that had found its way into her step. It had been ages since she'd enjoyed a day out in the capital and today was an excuse to visit some of her favorite haunts. As Shanti had said, she was in control.

Sitting opposite each other in the coffee shop, they ordered a pot of Darjeeling tea and a home-made, almond croissant.

"I love the almond ones," he said, cutting it in half.

"Me too!"

"Darjeeling's one of my favorites, apart from Earl Grey."

"Really? Same for me!"

Their faces moved closer as they leaned forward to share the pastry.

"I almost didn't make it!" Freddie still hadn't replied to her text, and she was fretting.

"Oh? What happened?"

"Freddie's not well."

"Oh no! Poor Freddie! Are you sure you want to spend the day with me?" He looked crestfallen. "I know what it's like when your kid's sick. If you want to go home …"

"He'll phone me if there's a problem."

"Are you sure? I don't want to come between you and your son!"

He was genuinely worried, thought Katy, reaching out to touch his fingertips. "Honestly, it's fine. I'm here, aren't I? Let's enjoy ourselves!"

"Where are you taking me, then?" Tony winked.

"I haven't decided yet!" Taking a sip of tea, she watched him over the rim of her cup, knowing exactly where she planned to go.

"Rain's forecast."

"I've got a brolly."

He topped up her cup. "You have the last bit," he said, motioning towards the croissant.

A crumb fell from her mouth as she ate, and he leaned across, brushing it gently from her close-fitting sweater. The intimacy of the moment took her by surprise, and she fiddled with her left earring and then the chunky bangle from Richard. A feeling of guilt shot through her. Rich could come here with her if he liked, but he never wanted to! He was such a suburbanite – never leaving the security of his own patch.

"I thought we could go to Covent Garden. I'll show you round the Freemasons Hall," said Tony.

"Covent Garden? I haven't been there for ages." Because Richard hated Covent Garden, that's why, the same as he hated Camden Market, Islington and Spitalfields. Anywhere with alternative overtones and a creative undertow made her spirits soar, while it made him critical and scathing. Her heart yearned for those sorts of places. It wanted to discover trendy Hackney and Hoxton. If only Rich were more like her.

"Penny for your thoughts!" Tony gently patted her hand.

"Do you know North London?"

"Not really, but I'm game for anything!"

"Let's settle up here and head to Covent Garden first."

"Righty-ho. Sounds perfect." He turned around, raising his hand towards the waitress who came scurrying over with the bill.

"I'll get this!"

"No, you won't!"

"Oy!"

They were laughing, mock fighting for the piece of paper when her hand landed squarely on his. She blushed, moving it aside. "Half each, then!"

"No!" He was pushing her away now, giggling as he handed cash to the waitress.

"I'm just nipping to the loo."

"Me too, see you back here."

Leaving the restaurant, Katy checked her phone. Still nothing from Freddie.

"Just need to call home," she said, dialing the number and letting it ring.

"It's me. How you feeling?"

"Bit better. Been asleep."

"Did I wake you?"

"Yeah."

"Sorry, but it's quarter to eleven, just to let you know. You'll need to head to the doctors."

"Okay."

"Will you be alright?"

"Yep. Don't worry."

"I'll call you again in an hour or so to see what he says. Or you ring me when you're finished?"

Pursing her lips, she slipped the phone back into her bag. Guilt requires punishment, she thought. Something she'd learned at one of those endless CPD courses. She and Tony disappeared into the subway at Warwick Avenue before taking a train to Piccadilly Circus. They could walk from there.

The Freemasons Hall was an imposing building, and she wondered how she'd never noticed it before. Tony waltzed her in, offering his credentials at the front desk before showing her around. Shivering within the bowels of the great halls, she pulled her jacket around her. There was a distinctly odd energy, and Katy could feel her stomach tightening, her jaw clenching, as if making herself as rigid as possible might act as a shield. She was afraid, she realized. The vibration was all wrong, but Tony didn't seem to notice. Perhaps she was mistaken, she thought, dismissing her deep misgivings and pretending to be interested. It was only when they stepped outside into the soft Spring light that she felt relieved of the heavy energy lurking within the halls.

Freddie had left a message.

Tonsillitis. Gave me penicillin, paracetamol & ibuprofen.

Managed a piece of toast and some digestives. xx

He must be feeling better, she reasoned. Thank goodness he was okay. Holding her head high, she aimed a silent prayer of gratitude towards the heavens.

Weaving her way through the labyrinthine streets of Neal's Yard, Seven Dials and on into Soho, Katy soaked up every sound, smell, and sight. "I didn't know this existed," said Tony, trying to keep up with her brisk pace. "You certainly know your way around!"

Boarding a double-decker bus to Camden, they sat at the front on the top floor, giggling like two teenagers bunking off school. The bird's eye view of Oxford Street, Regent's Park, and the elegant buildings along its perimeter, brought a feeling of joy to Katy. She was proud to be a Londoner. Camden Market and Camden Lock could be a bit miserable in the rain, but the street food at the Lock would be perfect for lunch.

The rain stopped as they sat by the canal, eating takeaway Vietnamese food with wooden chopsticks.

"I love it here!" said Tony, slurping up a mouthful of noodles.

"Me too!"

"Lauren can't stand Chinese! It's a real treat, especially Vietnamese! I don't think you can get it in Oxford."

Katy laughed as she picked up a fresh spring roll. "Rich isn't keen on markets. He'd rather go to a restaurant, so it's a treat for me too!"

"There's a pub by the lock – shall we have a glass of wine?"

"Gewürztraminer goes well with Vietnamese, I know it's white, but what do you think?"

"I think it's a pub that sells beer. Shall we have a real ale instead?"

Sipping at their beers and chattering, they hadn't noticed the time. The clouds had parted to reveal a thin ray of sunshine.

"Just going to check in with Freddie," said Katy, hunting for her phone in her bag. "Oh, my goodness! It's 3 o'clock!"

"Bloody hell! Time flies when you're enjoying yourself!"

Freddie was watching television. He'd made himself a sandwich and was evidently on the mend.

Katy tucked her phone away and turned to Tony. "Do you fancy going to the Heath?"

"Why not?"

"Let's go to Parliament Hill. There's an amazing view of London from up there."

Gulping down the last of the beer and depositing their rubbish in a nearby bin, they headed back towards the bus stop to catch another double-decker.

"The top?"

"You bet!"

Katy sat quietly next to Tony, both of them gazing out of the huge front window. They'd been nattering all day about food, wine, beer, music, holidays, Freddie, Lauren, and Richard. Not once had she or Tony said anything that might be considered a flirtatious chat-up line. No, there was nothing in this liaison except friendship. They got on, had a laugh, liked similar things, and that was it! Besides, he wasn't really her type, she thought, glancing at him from the corner of her eye. And they were both married. In any case, it was she who'd made the running, made this day exciting, not him. A day off in London with no responsibilities! What bliss! Leaning back in the chair and placing her feet up on the handrail in front, she decided it was time to treat this thing as the companionship that it was. As Shanti had said, she was in control. "You and Lauren must come over for supper one weekend. It'd be great to meet her! Bring your guitar! You and Rich can jam while we sing the 'doo-ups'!" Whatever it was that Tony said, Katy didn't hear. Stunned by what she'd done, she wasn't sure whether to laugh, cry or feel relieved. Of course, it was the right thing to do, so why did it feel so wrong? Why had it jarred, when all she was doing was bowing out of a silly, little game that would only bring trouble? Just because she'd opened up the tête-a-tête to include their spouses, it didn't mean the enjoyment would stop, did it? Had she just been relishing the game and not the company? Perhaps she was trying to recapture something from her youth? Her head was spinning. The bus stopped outside Kentish Town Station, where two pigeons were locked by the beaks, just like the ones she'd seen that morning at Turnham Green. "Parliament Hill Fields, this bus terminates here," went the announcement. Katy gripped the pole and sashayed down the spiral stairs, fully aware that Tony's eyes were on her derriere. Oh, what did it matter anymore? She'd blown it now, and it was absolutely for the best! Opening her brolly against the drizzle, she pressed on up the pathway to the viewing area. Tony's arms were folded around him, his collar turned up.

"Come on! Share my brolly!" she said, watching him scurry to catch up with her. She was out of breath from marching off the adrenaline that had been lingering in her system all day. Free at last, she smiled. Everything was back to normal and she'd see Richard later and fling her arms around him. "Here!" she panted. "Over here. There's one of those metal things that show you what all the buildings are."

"Wow! I've never even heard of this place!"

"Amazing, isn't it?"

"Incredible. Is that the London Eye over there?"

"Yep. And you can see Big Ben, the BT Tower or whatever it's called nowadays, St. Paul's, the City, and that big one over there with the triangle on top is Canary Wharf."

"It's spectacular. Let me read the legend. Oh yes, all the famous City buildings!"

Katy beamed. "It's one of my favorite views, this, and the one from Waterloo Bridge."

"I can see why! Is this part of Hampstead Heath?"

"Yep! We can walk for a bit if you like?" She could see he didn't want to. He looked cold, his face white and pinched, his body hunched over as he hugged himself.

Hesitating before replying, he looked up. "Looks like it's going to pour down any minute."

The sun was sinking in the pale, grey sky, slipping behind a bank of thick, black cloud. Katy found a scarf in her bag and wrapped it around her. "It's been a lovely day," she said. "Thank you." Looking down at her feet for a moment, she collected her thoughts. "It's half-past five. We'd better head back." It had to end somewhere and right now seemed as good a time as any, even though part of her wanted to linger. She'd had fun playing at tour guide.

"How about a drink before we go?"

Perhaps he'd been thinking the same thing. Saying 'no' would be churlish, wouldn't it?

"Fancy going up to Highgate Village?" She loved it up there and hadn't been for ages. This would be the perfect excuse.

Tony frowned. "Is it far?"

"Just up the hill. Five-minute ride. We can take the C69 Bus. There's a couple of brilliant pubs!"

"Sounds great! Another new one on me!" A big grin broke across his face, and a hint of color returned to his cheeks. "Righty-ho! Let's go!"

"Ooh, you're a poet and don't even know it!"

"My mum used to say that!"

Katy laughed. "So did mine!"

Approaching the bus stop, she noticed two more pigeons locking beaks in a kiss. "That's so weird!"

"What?"

"Those pigeons! I've never seen that before, and now I've seen it three times in one day!"

Boarding the bus, she looked back at Tony, following close behind like a small child on a visit to the park with his Nanny! He was all eyes and wonder, like a kid in a sweet shop.

The pub was relatively empty when they arrived, and they took a seat in the corner.

"They've got real ales here! Do you fancy another beer?"

"I fancy something to eat! Look, there's a chalkboard!"

Tony ordered a pint for himself, a half for Katy, and two Venison Sausages with Onion Gravy and Colcannon. Katy listened to the music that was coming from a prominent speaker on the wall behind. "They're playing some great tunes!" she said as he sat down with the drinks.

"Yeah, I noticed!"

The conversation turned to music, pubs, and the places they'd visited that day. The sausages arrived, and Tony ordered a pair of pints. "You might as well have the same as me, the rate you're drinking!"

"No! I'm not used to it! Just a half!" But the waiter hadn't heard and returned with two, pint glasses. Having sampled their third guest beer, Tony noticed the music was getting very loud as the pub was filling up.

"Let's move to the bar!" he shouted.

"What?"

He cupped his hands around her ear. "Can't hear above the din. We're right by the speaker." He pointed up with his hand. "Let's move to the bar. Might be quieter!"

Katy nodded, slung her bag over her shoulder, and followed him. Sitting on barstools away from the speakers, they were able to continue their conversation above the noise. The pub was turning warm and fuzzy. Katy's speech was slightly slurred. "I love this one!"

"The Pale Ale?"

"No! Yes! I do like the Pale Ale, but I was talking about the song!" She'd drunk far too much.

"Me too! Haven't heard it for years! Lauren hates this sort of music."

"So does Richard."

They discussed who'd seen which bands, where they'd seen them, and when. Tony ordered another beer for them both, just as a B.B. King number struck up. It was the perfect excuse to tell her about his sojourn in New Orleans where he'd learned to play guitar. The music shifted gears.

"Ah! This one's great!" He started to sing along to Wonderwall, slightly out of tune.

Katy was giggling, then joining in as they got to the chorus. An uncomfortable feeling came over her when they sang the line about being saved.

"There was something I wanted to say to you, but I won't!" Tony was stumbling over his words.

"I don't remember that line?" Katy winked. "I thought it went a bit differently to that!" Recalling the lyrics as best she could, she sang it out loud, bursting out laughing as she finished. The craft beer had wobbled all the sharp edges off and loosened her up. "What did you want to say?" She had suddenly turned serious.

"Nothing!" His ears were turning pink.

"No! You've got to tell me now! You can't just leave me hanging!" She was pulling at his lapels and giggling. "Hanging on the Telephone," she sang it in her best Blondie impersonation, chuckling again.

"When we were in Windsor…" He took a gulp of beer.

"What?" She was prodding him with her forefinger and pulling a face.

Tony fumbled with his jacket cuff, then ran a hand over his glistening pate before downing the last of his pint. "I was thinking that I wanted to lean across and kiss you!"

Katy's heart raced. Yes! She knew it! And Right now, she wanted to lean across and kiss him, but a thread of decorum stopped her. Gripping at the bar rail, and swaying slightly, she automatically answered in her best therapist's voice, albeit with a slur, "And what stopped you?" It had sounded professional to her drunken ears, but she'd forgotten to suppress the enormous smile that erupted across her face. A moment later, her foot slipped off the rest, and she lurched forward, steadying herself against Tony, whose ears progressed from a delicate shade of rose to a deep crimson as he helped her back onto the stool.

"Hold your hands up like this!" Katy was holding her palms up to him, her fingers and thumbs spread out and curved like claws.

He mimicked her. "Like this?" They looked like children pretending to be lions.

"Yes!" She was giddy now with exuberance. "I saw it in a dream. If our fingers touch, it'll connect all the acupuncture meridians."

"What'll happen?"

"I don't know!" she shrieked, leaning towards him. "Let's

see!"

Tony's fingertips made contact with hers. Something took over, lifting her out of herself as everything froze. The pub was silent, the people momentarily still. A slow-motion movie unfolded as she watched from beyond her body, watched herself holding her breath, waiting for reality to resume and the plot to roll forward.

A bolt of what felt like electricity shot between them, darting down through her body to the floor. She was back in the noisy, sweaty pub. Tony crumpled forward, pressing his open mouth against hers as she stood up to meet him. A surge of energy powered through her from above, buckling her knees in an instant. Slumping back on the stool, she grabbed Tony, who was holding onto her, his strong arms wrapped around her. Everyone and everything in the pub dissolved. It was just the two of them. There was nothing save this moment: the chemical explosion inside, the magnetic bond and the overwhelming urge to press skin against skin. Tony broke the spell, his hands on the small of her back, his eyes boring through hers. "I love you, and I want you in my life. I want you by my side in this life and the next, and I'm prepared to do whatever it takes. I'm leaving Lauren." It all came out in one go, like lines from an old movie.

Katy's mouth hung open, her eyes blinking into the muted light. The people, the pub, the noises had returned. Was this really happening?

"I love you now, and I loved you then," continued Tony. "I've always loved you."

Katy was too shocked to speak, frozen to the spot, her mouth still gaping.

He carried on. "I ran away because it was too much for a seventeen-year-old, but now I'm sure. I know what I want. I want you, Katherine."

Pulling away and holding onto his elbows, she tried to think, but her mind had seized up. "I, I don't know, Tony." She couldn't get her words out at first. "I'm married to Richard. I've got kids!" The full horror struck her. She didn't want to break up her family or hurt the husband that she cared for. Her eyes were darting from side to side. "It's all happening too fast!"

Breaking free of his grip, she headed to the Ladies. Oh my God, what had she done? Her and her bloody games! Look where it had got her! She sat in the cubicle, dumfounded, gathering herself. Clinging to the rock of what remained of her rational mind and professional training, she staggered back to the bar, but the rock wasn't robust enough, and it slipped from her grip. The beer had made her light-headed, and she was feeling dizzy. It was so stupid to drink, she wasn't used to it. Pushing herself precariously onto the barstool, she took one look at Tony and a thousand teenage memories came back in a single deluge. Lurching forward, she clutched at him, holding on with a passionate clinch, running her hands over his broad shoulders and down his back.

"You know when Katherine Fralinski's touching you," said Tony. "It sends a shock wave right through you." Taking her face in his warm hands, he kissed her tenderly then pulled back, looking her straight in the eye. "You could touch me anywhere, any time, and I'd know it was you."

An old Pink Floyd number banged out on the sound system. They were both singing along to *Wish You Were Here,* the lyrics seemingly echoing their deepest thoughts.

"I think he wrote it about Syd Barrett?" they both said together.

Katy was powerless to stop herself as she nuzzled into him, closing her eyes, losing herself, and kissing him passionately. People were probably staring, but she didn't give a fudge. Coming up for air, she spoke again. "Do you remember when it came out in the 70s?"

"Yeah! I had the album!"

"So did I!"

It had been one of the theme-tunes of their misspent youth, hanging out with the long-haired hippies and smoking cheap hash from Morocco.

"Two souls, lost. That's us!" said Tony.

"Someone with a sense of humor has rigged the playlist!"

"Ah! Remember this one?"

"I haven't heard it for years!"

They sang along to the bits they recalled: "Just the Way You Are!"

"It's Billy Joel, isn't it?"

Song after song rang out with prophetic lyrics, each confirming to Katy that she was doing the right thing. A mysterious supernatural power was showing her sign after sign. Three pairs of pigeons, the poster at the station this morning, and now this playlist. You couldn't make it up!

Tony didn't seem to care who was looking as he enthusiastically smooched her. Katy lost herself further with each impassioned embrace. They appeared to be melting into one another as the evening wore on.

"Come on, let's go!" Tony's eyes were twinkling as he took her by the hand, leading her out into a side street. Staggering across the road, he let go and stopped in a darkened doorway. "Hey!" he called. "If you put your hands down my trousers, I can't be held responsible for what will happen." He muttered something about a fantasy, but she didn't quite catch it. High on endorphins and Pale Ale, Katy was a rebel teenager all over again, plunging her hand down the front of his jeans and squealing with delight at what she found. Two drunken figures collapsed into the shadowy doorway, grinding their hips together and kissing fervently.

"Stop!" shouted Katy. It had gone too far, and she wanted it to end. Her family were waiting for her. "We're going to get arrested!" Giggling now, the alcohol and teenage memories sweeping away the sober thoughts of home, she realized she couldn't stop if she wanted to. Ten years of flat-lined libido had been fully resuscitated. A torrent of arousal, which had been barricaded firmly behind marital dissonance, broke free. Tony was raging out of control as if she'd been the match that set fire to his forest.

"I can't think of anything better!" He laughed. "Getting arrested for indecency at our age!" Thrusting himself frantically against her, he closed his mouth over hers, his tongue pushing. Breaking free for a moment and looking up at him through her eyelashes, she coyly said, "I'm all slippy," before nibbling gently at his earlobe. The seam of her tight jeans was rubbing, adding to the mounting pleasure that was taking her over.

"Come on! Let's go to the heath!" There was a note of desperation in his voice that frightened her.

"No!" She was holding him at arm's length when she noticed his flies were open. "I don't want to!"

"Liar!" he sniggered, jabbing his pelvis into hers and pumping.

"Well I do want to, but not like this! It's got to be right!"

"What could be more right than this?" His hands worked their way into her jeans, and he fondled her peachy bottom before pulling at the top of her panties.

"I don't want to have a shabby bonk in the park and regret it later!"

"You won't regret it, I promise." He lifted her up, and she wrapped her legs around him to steady herself. A quiver of ecstasy shivered through her, and she unfurled herself, jumping to the ground.

"I don't want to have an affair!" Through the beer-haze, she was trying to sober up and make sense of what was happening. Straightening her top, she mustered her thoughts. "If we end up making love, I want it to be special!"

"It will be special!" he moaned. "I have to have you, now!"

"We've got to do this properly!"

"We will. Come on!" he growled. "I'm not sure I can handle it much longer, look at me!" His hands were running over her body, his breathing heavy as he pressed himself against her.

"It has to be above board, Tony," she reasoned, holding him at arm's length. "Not a quickie on the Heath!"

"I agree. Let's go to a fancy hotel. I've got to! Look!" he said, pushing down his boxers to reveal his ardor.

Swept away by the alcohol, the boldness of what he'd done, and the memories of over thirty years ago, she reached out with her fingertips. Gently stroking, and delighting in the reaction, every inch of her wanted to go the whole hog. The forty-seven-year-old woman inside fought back. She mustn't. She was married now, with children. The brakes had to go on right now! "Let's sober up and see how we feel in the morning." Yes. That was the sensible phrase she'd been searching for. "We have to be sure it's what we want in the cold light of day." Thank God, her faculties were coming back. Taking a deep breath, she stepped away and straightened herself up. "If it's real, we need to be careful. People could get hurt." She smoothed down her hair which had curled in the rain and was now looking like a mad, cropped bed head. "We have to think this through with a clear mind."

"Pleeeease!" Tony stamped his foot like a child who'd been told he couldn't go out to play.

"No. I'm not going to upset Richard. If it's true for us to be together, we'll do it when the time is right, but not before."

"Go on, Katy! You want it just as much as I do!"

"I want it to mean something!"

He nuzzled into her neck. "I don't believe in sex without love," he schmoozed. "I love you!" He stepped back and motioned with his hand. "Look how hard I am! That ain't going to go away!"

"Tony! We're in a public place! Put it away, for God's sake!" Glancing at her watch, she shrieked in horror. "Sh-sugar! It's half-past eleven! We're going to miss the bloody train!"

"Shit, I'll be toast if I don't get home!"

A bus was laboring up the hill. If they ran fast enough, they might get to the stop in time. Panting and out of breath, they slumped on the first seat they could find. Tony was gazing at her, a star-struck look in his eyes. He reached for her hand, entwining his fingers in hers, then bringing it to his mouth to delicately kiss the back. A luxurious, liquid euphoria seemed to be oozing through her entire system. Letting go, he placed his warm palm on her thigh and gently stroked with his thumb. A tingling sensation of arousal blended deliciously with her already blissful state. At Paddington, he hugged her tight before running to catch the last train to Oxford. "See you Monday!" he called out behind him.

She'd forgotten about their third appointment. It was going to be a tense weekend. Rushing down into the underground, she was relieved to find she had a few minutes to spare before the train arrived. Her thoughts turned to Richard, and she began to sober up. There was a weak mobile signal on the Circle Line platform, and she messaged him.

Sorry I'm late. Went to a pub with real ale & music. Lost track of time. On my way. x

Thank goodness she'd told him what she was doing. Her husband knew her well enough to believe her. Once she was out on a social, she often forgot about time.

Missing the last train from Hammersmith, she took a night bus to Chiswick High Road. Her phone buzzed. It'd be Rich checking in.

I'm on the train. I don't regret a single thing. I love you. Speak tomorrow xxxxxx

Six kisses. Her face burned hot as she gazed out of the window at the familiar streets which this evening looked so surreal. Her pulse was racing as she walked the last few hundred yards home. Home is where the heart is. Oh my God, what had she done?

The latch sprang loudly as she turned her key in the lock.

"Shh, Constantine!" she whispered. Avoiding the windchimes, her heart thumping furiously, she crept through the door and removed her boots. Tiptoeing down the hallway in stockinged feet, she noticed the snug light was still on. Richard was sprawled on the sofa, the Evening Standard on his lap, the television remote in his hand.

"Sorry!" She smiled weakly.

"Why are you so late?" he said. "Freddie's not well, and Tilly's split up with Joe!"

"Oh no! I thought he was feeling better!" Katy looked puzzled. "And I thought she'd finished with Joe a while back?"

"You should've been here!"

"I'm sorry!"

"Where were you anyway?"

"Went to Highgate with my friend Tony from school."

Richard frowned.

"You know what I'm like, we got nattering and I didn't realize it was so late!"

Richard shoved the paper to the floor and switched off the television. "By the way, Shanti left a message. Can you ring her?"

"I'll call tomorrow. Bit late now."

"Nice time?"

"Yeah! Great music. Loads of real ales."

Richard stood up. "I can see you sampled quite a few! I'm off to bed. You coming?"

"Yep!" She switched the light off and staggered after him, clutching at the bannister as she went.

"Did you ask them to dinner?"

"Yeah. Mentioned they should come over one weekend." It felt like a line in a play that someone else was delivering. Her hands were shaking as she undressed. Everything happened in slow-motion again, as she watched herself from the wings, accompanied by the sound of her heart pounding.

"He's an RAF Officer, isn't he?" Richard was buttoning up

his pajamas.

"Yeah. Wing Commander, I think. He plays guitar!"

"He should bring it with him so we can jam. You can sing the 'doo-ups' with his wife if you like?" He hauled himself into the super king-sized bed.

"Sounds great!" Katy got in on the other side, leaving a gulf between them.

"Night, Kit."

"Night." She switched off the light and lay motionless on her back, staring up at the ceiling. Her husband rolled over, farted, and let out a soft snore. She looked at his outline, a mountain of duvet twice the size of her. They were like Pooh Bear and Piglet. People must have pondered how they ever managed sex. Come to think of it, she wondered herself now, they were so incompatible. Even kissing was a mission. She had to lean her head right back and stand on tiptoe while he bent down to meet her.

Heart still racing, her mind reviewing the events of the day, she realized sleep was evading her. She turned this way and that, and plumping up the pillow, she tried to calm down. Yoga Nidra, the sleep of the yogis, that was bound to work. Pranayama, breathwork. That would do the trick. Drifting down steps to pathways that led through doorways into forests didn't have the right effect, either. It was no use; she was on fire. Maybe she could harness the arousal to initiate something with Richard? Turning her head towards him, she knew at once it wouldn't work. She didn't feel that way about him and hadn't for years. Something had gone wrong and she couldn't work it out. She'd shut down to him, but why? At 3.30 am, she slipped into a satin robe, the fabric soft and sensual against her naked body. Taking her phone from the dressing table, she locked herself in the bathroom, reading the entire message thread between her and Tony. Her eyes closed as she recalled the events leading up to the dark doorway. Lingering luxuriously on the intimate details of the drunken but passionate ending, she found sweet release. Returning to bed, a fitful sleep followed and at 6.30 am, she gave up and left Richard to his lie-in.

Despite not drinking coffee for the last nine years, she decided this morning to swig back a strong espresso. Within minutes she knew she'd made a mistake. Soothing chamomile and lavender tea would have been better. Richard joined her at the kitchen table about twenty minutes later.

"You're up early!"

"Couldn't sleep. Bit of a hangover," she said. "Turning into another migraine."

"That why you're back on coffee?"

"Thought it might help."

"Fried breakfast! That's what you need. Greasy-Joe down the road?"

Her phone buzzed.

"Who the hell's that on a Saturday morning?"

"Dunno," she said, diving for the phone with the fervor of a Rugby player about to score a try. With mounting panic, she stared at the screen. Flip, she hoped Rich hadn't seen the name flash up. "Message from Shanti," she said, her adrenals at full pelt.

While Richard was fiddling with the kettle, she opened the message.

Good morning, Gorgeous! Hope you slept well. I didn't get a wink. Can't stop thinking about you. Call you later. xxx

Three kisses. What the hell was she going to do? Switching the phone to silent, she slipped it into her pocket.

"Café down the road?" she asked. "The kids will want to come."

While Richard was showering and the children were deciding whether to join them or not, Katy pulled out her mobile to reply.

Can't stop thinking about you either. We need to talk. Don't phone today. Family here. xxx

Sitting in the Egg and Spoon with a mug of hot tea, a slice of white toast and a plate of full English Breakfast, Katy felt once more as if she was watching a movie of her life from a distance. It couldn't really be happening, not to her. It was too bizarre. Her stomach lurched at the bacon and eggs, which she pushed around the plate before conceding defeat.

"Not like you, Kit! You love fried breakfast!"

"Must have drunk too much last night. Don't fancy it!"

"It'll make you feel better! Best thing for a hangover!"

"Can't face it," she said, sipping at her tea. Her body twitched as she felt her phone vibrate in her bag. She'd better leave it for now.

Back in the safety of her own home, the family otherwise engaged, she slipped the mobile out.

What about tomorrow? 1500hrs? I'll be out on the bike. xxx

Quickly responding before Richard noticed, she typed out

Okay. Chat tomorrow at 3 pm. xxx

* * *

Tony had arrived home in the early hours, having taken an exorbitant taxi ride from Oxford station. Lauren was already in bed asleep. He tiptoed up to the spare room. It was more than his life was worth to disturb madam while she was slumbering. What a day! It had gone better than he'd expected, and he couldn't believe what had unfolded. There was no stopping him now. He lay awake, naked, in the guest room, staring at the ceiling and recounting the events of the day. She was everything he wanted, and he couldn't get her out of his system. His heart raced at the thought of her. He felt vibrant, vital, and horny as hell. He wanted her, now, and was finding it difficult to concentrate on anything else. This was the longest he'd ever had to wait. Closing his eyes, he ran his hands towards his erection, recalling the details of the evening, and lingering on the episode in the doorway. Still sleep evaded him.

At around 3.30 am, he picked up his phone and re-read the messages they'd sent each other. He could imagine her, in a soft, satin robe, smoothing her hands sensuously up her own thighs, her lips pouting, her breathing heavy as she pleasured herself. By six o'clock, he knew sleep had cheated him. After dressing quietly, so as not to disturb Lauren and Amber, he crept out of the house for an early morning cycle. Having stopped at a café for breakfast, he was finding it difficult to eat. For some reason, he'd lost his appetite. He sipped at a mug of tea and managed some toast but had to leave the bacon and eggs. He wasn't sure what to say later to his wife, but he was positive she'd be mad at him. Picking up the newspaper, he flicked idly through, unable to concentrate on anything except Katy and the constant feeling of arousal that refused to be satisfied. It was 8 o'clock when he reached for his phone. Lauren would be out with Amber this afternoon, and he could talk to Katy then. Her reply came back.

Can't stop thinking about you either. We need to talk. Don't phone today. Family here. xxx

Before leaving the café, he sent another message and waited, but there was nothing. He was halfway home when his phone vibrated in his pocket, and he stopped to read the incoming text.

Okay. Chat tomorrow at 3 pm. xxx

* * *

Katy was restless. Perhaps a walk on the common would help? A bit of fresh air and exercise would do her wonders, and she could phone Shanti without being overheard. Richard's head was buried in a novel, so she slipped out alone, calling her friend as soon as she could.

"You left a message?"

"Just wanted to ask how your day went with Mr. Verde!"

"Wing Commander Verde, actually!"

"Ooh, listen to you! Presume it went well? You weren't home when I rang, and it was late!"

"Oh, my goodness, Shanti, you won't believe what's happened."

Shanti listened carefully as Katy recounted the events of the previous day.

"I think he's your twin flame."

"My what?"

"Look at your SRT notes. It's a reward for all the amazing work you do."

"What work?"

"All the clients you're helping, the spiritual stuff you're doing."

It didn't make sense to Katy. What about Richard and the kids? "Tara would say I'm being unfaithful, and I am."

"That's just guilt talking. Is that how you really feel?"

"I'm not sure anymore. I'm so confused! The weird thing is, I had this strange feeling last night that I was being unfaithful to Tony by sleeping in the same bed as Richard!"

"That's interesting. You need to keep watching the signs."

"But look where the bloody signs have led me!"

"I think they're leading you to the truth. It isn't easy to face, but the truth will set you free."

"I can't eat anything."

Shanti's joyous laugh tinkled for a moment. *"It must be love!"* She sang the words in her sweet voice, just like Labi Siffre.

"Or it could be a heady mix of infatuation, lust, excitement and fear!"

"Why fear?"

"I dunno. Anxious about what will happen. Afraid I'm making a terrible mistake. Fear of losing control."

"All the magic happens outside your comfort zone. It's good to feel scared. As they say, 'feel the fear, and do it anyway'! You're on a hero's journey!"

"A what?"

"Hero's journey. Joseph Campbell."

"Oh, right! I don't know what to do!"

"Follow your bliss."

"I dunno what that is."

"Follow your heart."

"But if I look at it logically, I need to be cautious. I don't want to ruin everything on a whim. I've got eighteen years of shared history with Rich and two wonderful children. Maybe that's where my heart is leading?"

"Yeah, and the big house and the luxury holidays, but are you happy?"

"Yes. No. I think so."

"Why don't you put it out to the universe for an answer?"

"I suppose so."

"And contact Dinah. Get her to look at the soul contracts."

"For Tony and me?"

"Yes. It'll give you an idea of the soul relationship. Might give you a bit of a steer."

"What about Monday? I'm supposed to see him again."

"Go with the flow. You'll know what to do."

* * *

Lauren Verde was on a mission to find out where the hell her errant husband had been this time. His story wasn't making sense, and she assumed he'd gone on a bender and got blind drunk. She'd given him a list of DIY jobs that needed finishing around the house, starting with the dripping tap in the bathroom. Sending him off to the hardware store with Amber on Saturday afternoon, she took the opportunity to log into his emails. Nothing there, but he could be using his MoD account, and that was impossible to hack. What about his credit card? Being a banker, it was she that had set up all the accounts and passwords, and being the higher earner, she was the one with the platinum card. It would be easy to track his spending, and that would give her a clue as to where he'd been. Of course, it would take a day or so for the transactions to show, but two could play at his little game.

Amber had a session with the child psychologist at 3.30 pm, and she was due to go horse-riding herself at 4 pm. It would be better for Tony to take the child. It might keep him out of trouble, and she could indulge in a bit of retail therapy afterwards. Besides, her dear, darling, daughter was such a daddy's girl, she was bound to behave better with him.

* * *

On Saturday evening, the Stone family went out for supper. Katy couldn't eat properly, despite it being one of her favorite Indian restaurants. She'd hardly touched her sandwich at lunchtime, either. Tony was taking center stage in her thoughts. How long had they been emailing? About six months? They'd met up three times and had spent three weeks together in 1977. One and nine were ten, make that one (one and zero), she thought, adding up the numerology, add seven was eight, and seven was fifteen. One and five. A 'six' year. Romance, love, and harmony. Huh!

Tilly and Freddie were sniggering at a private joke which they chose not to share. Her efforts to join in were met with derision. Richard talked to her about his pension and another bonus that was due. He was going to use it to invest in some company or another. Apparently, it would double its value and give them a tidy sum. He was going to buy a small yacht, even though they lived some distance from the river.

"Not a riverboat," he said. "A proper little yacht for the sea!"

"But we live in London, Rich!"

"So what? I used to love sailing! You're always picking fault with my plans!"

The rest of supper was eaten in silence, apart from Tilly's raucous laughter when Freddie whispered something to her. He was obviously back on form and feeling better. Richard tutted. A bit of small talk followed between Katy and her husband, just to punctuate the long, uncomfortable gaps.

Sitting on her meditation stool at the end of the evening, it took Katy over an hour to quieten her mind. Perhaps she should pray like she had yesterday morning. Funny how people only prayed when they were in dire straits. Most people didn't give prayer a second thought unless they were facing some calamity. Shanti had said put it out to the universe. Was that the same thing? "Hello?" she said, listening for an answer. There was a rumble of distant traffic, a bus idling at the lights, a dog barking. Far away, a train rattled over its tracks, and a 747 was following the river towards Heathrow. Where was the Voice when she needed it? Breath. Hara. Some people called the Hara 'Dantien'. Shanti called it the 'Manipura' chakra.

"Please, are you there?" Still nothing except the thoughts that kept tumbling through her mind. How did she know if she'd addressed the right god? Shanti said there were loads in India. Ganesh, Lakshmi, Vishnu. Maybe she should pray to 'The Highest God', that ought to do it. She didn't want to be asking the wrong deity. "Most High Divine Source of all that is." It sounded ridiculous, and she pulled a face. "Please forgive me, for I have sinned. I nearly had sex with a married man in a dark doorway. I'm sorry. Please give me a sign. Show me the way. Tell me what my truth is. I'm lost. Be my shepherd. Guide me to my bliss and tell me what my heart wants because I've got no idea. Thanks." Having waited, ears straining, for at least thirty seconds, which seemed interminable, she remembered. "Oh, and, Amen!" Another five minutes passed.

It was gone midnight by the time she got to bed, and Richard was gently snoring. A herbal sleep tablet, a melatonin which she'd bought by mail-order from the Channel Islands, washed down with a single malt, should knock her out. She had to get some shut eye. Pushing her earplugs snuggly in, and donning an eye mask, Katy slipped into bed.

Twisted plots and strange scenarios crept into her dreams. At one point, she was walking up the aisle of a church, except it wasn't a church, it was a supermarket with rows of tills and queues of people. Terry was her bridesmaid, and the vicar was her client, Seamus. Her old book-circle friends were throwing rotten tomatoes at her bridal gown. Richard was an undertaker sitting in a hearse outside, waiting for the wedding to be over.

Too tired to get up and record it in her diary, she carried on sleeping until 9 am. Thank goodness it was Sunday!

Later that morning, in the quiet of her office, she switched on the laptop. Emailing Dinah wasn't a bad idea. Her eyes were immediately drawn to a message from Tony.

I meant it. I'll do whatever it takes to be with you, Katherine! I love and adore you. Can't wait to talk to you at 3 pm. There's so much I want to say, so many things I want to share. Where shall we meet tomorrow? Shall I come to Harley Street? What time?

Love you for all eternity. T xxxxxx

Six kisses. Her stomach knotted. What was she doing? It was all happening way too fast. Would they find enough to talk about? What would it be like in the cold light of day? If what he'd said were true, it was everything she wanted, but far too late. Why hadn't he contacted her earlier? Before she'd met Richard?

Closing her eyes and taking a deep breath, she did her best to put him to one side and stay on task. Shanti was right, it would be good to get a steer. She needed to be convinced before making any decisions. It would be stupid to act on impulse.

Hi Dinah

Just writing to ask a favor. Could you take a quick look at the soul contract, if any, between me and Anthony Richard Verde? Dob:16 November 1959. Give me the gist. Don't need details.

Thanks

Love Katy xx

At around 2.30 pm, Katy pulled on her jacket. "I'm going for a walk on the Common," she called through to the snug. "Okay, Mum." Freddie was playing X-box, and the color was back in his cheeks. Richard looked up from the Sunday Times. "I'll come with you!"

What? No, he couldn't. "Er, okay, but…" She couldn't think of anything.

"But what?"

"Oh, nothing. Was going to think through some client work."

"Come on, Kit, it's Sunday for fuck's sake!"

"Okay, just nipping to the loo before we go."

"With your handbag?"

"I think my period might have started."

Frantically searching for her phone, she realized she'd left it on the hall table. Damn.

"Just need to text Shanti. Promised I'd get back to her."

"Hurry up then!" Richard hung around outside, his hands in his pockets, jiggling his change as he cast a critical eye over the neighbors' houses. Katy's fingers scrambled over the buttons on her phone.

Change of plan! Richard with me! Will text when I'm free. xxx

She had to walk twice as fast to keep up with Richard's long stride.

"I've been thinking about the yacht, and I've had a better idea. I'll invest the money a bit longer, and if I play my cards right, we could buy a second home in the country. Property's always a good bet. What do you think?"

She thought she'd had enough of his one-track mind. When would he feel like he had enough? They were already better off than most, and they didn't need a second home! Besides, she'd rather spend the time travelling. Why go to the same spot when there were thousands of beautiful places in Europe alone! No point telling him that, though. He never listened. "Okay," she said. "We could do it up and rent it out." If she'd told him what she really thought, he'd take it as criticism and that would only lead to an argument.

"Not a bad idea! Would add to the value, and we'd get some passive income at the same time!"

Richard's phone rang and shielding his mouth with his hand, he garbled, "Not now. I'll call you in ten."

"Who was that?"

"Journalist looking for a comment."

"I don't mind if you want to talk to them?"

"I'll head home and ring him on the way back. Leave you here to enjoy the dog shit and the litter!"

"It sounded like a woman to me?"

"It was. She wanted me to speak to her editor." Richard's eyelid twitched. He walked a bit further, moaned about a gang of kids on their skateboards, then stopped. "I'm off! See you when you get back." Giving her a quick peck, he turned, retracing his steps, pulling his mobile from his pocket as he approached the road.

Katy carried on walking until she found a quiet park bench. With shaking hands, she typed out her message:

Are you free now? xxx

A few seconds later, her phone rang. The conversation was easy. A smile lit up her face, and as she talked, the butterflies stopped beating inside. "I can't eat anything."

"Me neither!"

"What did you tell Lauren?"

"The truth. That I was out with a friend from school and we lost track of time."

"That's what I told Rich."

"You know you said we should see how we felt when we'd sobered up?"

"Yes?"

"Well, I feel the same. I love you, and I want to be with you."

"I want to do this properly. I need to check we're doing the right thing. A lot of people could get hurt."

"I know, but—"

"Can we take it one step at a time?"

"Of course we can."

"Promise?"

"Promise."

"And no hanky-panky till we know what we're doing."

Tony laughed. "I haven't heard hanky-panky since my Gran died!"

"Where are you?"

"Out in the Oxfordshire countryside! Went for a long bike ride. Where are you?"

"Chiswick Common."

"What about our rendezvous tomorrow?"

"Can you get into town by nine-thirty?"

"Yep. I've arranged a meeting at Whitehall in the afternoon, but the morning is reserved just for you!"

"Aww." She could feel her face reddening.

"See you at Paddington?"

"Umm." Katy was mentally working out tube stations, train lines and proximity. "I'll meet you outside the statue of Eros on Piccadilly Circus. It's not far from Whitehall or Harley Street."

"Righty-ho! Can't wait to see you, Gorgeous!"

"Me too. Hope I can manage the pressure till then!"

"You will. Look after yourself. When you're with me, you'll be able to eat!"

"Can we have brunch somewhere?"

"I know the perfect place to take you."

"Where?"

"You'll find out. See you tomorrow. Eros, o-nine-thirty hours. Love you."

"Love you too." Fudge! What was she thinking? What made her say that?

After two laps around Chiswick Common, the butterflies still hadn't subsided. She may as well head home. A surfeit of energy was pumping through her, scattering her thoughts and sending her off-balance. Like a dog chasing its own tail, she wasted the rest of the day on pointless activity like sorting through her knicker drawer, cleaning the hinges on the toilet seats, and polishing the skirting on all three flights of stairs. She should have done yoga instead. Her adrenaline was off the scale.

Later that evening, she dug out her Spiritual Response Therapy notes and read up on Twin Flames, Flames Mates and Soul Mates. The SRT manual didn't say much, but a picture was forming in her mind, and she wanted to share it with someone. Perhaps Ben and Tara? Taking out her pendulum and chart, she asked, "What is the soul relationship between myself and Tony Verde?" The pendulum swung on its chain. Clamping her hand over her mouth she tried to stifle the gasp before anyone heard. She'd better check, just to be certain. Using his full name, Anthony Richard Verde, she tried again. Oh my God, it couldn't be! It must be wrong. She couldn't dowse that sort of thing for herself and expect it to be accurate, could she? After messaging Jane Joyheart, she bundled everything into the drawer and locked it away.

At eleven o'clock Richard announced he was off to bed. Freddie, who was not quite over his illness, had gone to sleep early, and Tilly was in her room. "Lights off soon! School tomorrow!" called Katy.

Meditation was going to be a challenge, but it was the 'sitting' that was important, she reminded herself. Passing the mirror at the top of the stairs, she sensed something.

"Good evening, Katy!"

"Oh, it's you. I called for you last night!"

"You needed to work it out for yourself."

"Why?"

"Sometimes that's the only way to learn. By experience."

"And what are you going to make me experience now?"

"Actually, I was going to talk to you about the heart."

"Can I sit in my room?"

"I'll follow you in."

Katy sat on the meditation stool, back straight, hands in mudra. "I'm ready."

"The heart is the core of your being, not just the organ that pumps the lifeblood around you, but a center of intelligence and the center of love. Did you know that it generates the strongest electromagnetic field in the body?"

"Stronger than the brain?"

"Yes. And its field is a sensitive transmitter and receiver, with a feedback loop to your True Self."

"What are you talking about?"

"We discussed the logical mind before, how it can be fooled, how its perceptions are based on past experience."

"Yes..."

"What you call 'mind' doesn't just reside in the brain. Think of the brain as something that processes thought, rather than generating it. It's like a terminal on a network. That's how you can 'hear' my thoughts right now! Your brain is receiving and processing!"

"Okay. Makes sense."

"But there are neural networks throughout the entire body as well, principally in the heart and the gut."

"Hence gut instinct and follow your heart?"

"That's it. Did you know that your heart can guide you through the power of love if you let it?"

"Or guide you into trouble if you don't think things through!"

"That's why you need to balance the rational with the intuitive, the masculine with the feminine. The heart must not rule the head and vice versa."

"Easier said than done!"

"If you ask your heart, it will give a true answer, providing the logical mind doesn't immediately hijack it by over-thinking! If you sit quietly and turn within, you'll hear what your heart is telling you, or you'll feel it. The heart chakra opens wide like a flower in bloom when it's happy, and closes like a tight bud when it's not. That alone can guide you to what's true."

"How do you know it's right?"

"The heart of the matter. The center. What remains under the layers of personality, conditioning, identity and anything else that you present as a mask to the outside world."

"Oh, like the heart of a lettuce? That sort of heart?"

"That's right. It's untouched by the outer leaves. But the heart is also the seat of love."

"What's love got to do with truth?"

"Love is a guiding force towards truth. The heart reveals what is, the rational mind misleads and questions, and the ego wants approval, and does whatever it takes to get it."

"But we need an ego, don't we?"

"Quite so, but it shouldn't be in the driving seat."

"Who should be driving then?"

"Your True Self, or Divine Self."

Katy looked puzzled. "Is that the same as your deeper Self or your bigger Self or Greater Self?"

"All words to describe a concept that's beyond the limits of your language."

"I experience myself as me. How do I know there's another, greater Self?"

"Have you ever watched yourself meditating, as if you were behind and above?"

"Yes, I have!"

"Who is noticing and who is sitting?"

"Me?"

"Your bigger Self is watching your smaller self."

"So, the smaller self is your ego – the 'you' that you're familiar with?"

"Yes. The one you identify with."

"And the Greater Self is your True Self or your deeper Self?"

"Or Divine Self, yes!"

"Sounds flipping confusing to me!"

"It's all one Self, with a capital S, but in any case, both selves, small and Great, are connected and designed to work in harmony. They're different aspects of you. Different aspects of *consciousness*." The Voice could see that Katy was confused. "Think of it this way, your Greater Self has a higher vantage point. It can see past, present, and future potential. Imagine it sitting above the maze, in which your smaller self is playing out its life."

"Like one of those whizz-kids playing an avatar computer game? It's the kid that guides the avatar through the different levels. He can't physically go inside the computer, so he relies on his alter-ego. The avatar itself doesn't exist without the kid… So, they need each other?"

"Not a bad analogy!"

"Thanks!"

The Voice paused for a moment to let Katy receive the compliment.

"Let's go back to the heart and to love because that's a portal to your True Self."

"Is your True Self also your soul?" Katy was trying to make sense of this complicated subject.

"There are subtle differences, and there are levels of soul, too, and then there's your spirit, but we're drifting off track. Let's stick with 'True Self' for now."

"Okay. True Self."

"The brain might see the logic of love, but only the heart can experience and know it."

Katy's palms were sweating now. "Why are we talking about love?" Her eyes were darting from side-to-side, her breathing shallow. Did the Voice know about Tony? It must do, it knew everything. There was an awkward pause while she remembered it could read all her thoughts.

The loving Voice seemed to deliberately gloss over her private asides, perhaps to save embarrassment. It carried on. "Love isn't simply romantic love or the love you have for your children or the love you have for your pet. It's not just the things you love, either, like chocolate, your favorite song, or the latest fashion collection. Love is all of that, and so much more. It's the essence of Creation! The most important force in the Cosmos! Have you not heard it before? Faith, hope and love, and the greatest of these is Love!"

"Is that in the Bible? They read it at weddings, don't they?"

The Voice chuckled. "Quite so."

"So, love's important? Being loving, loving everything, receiving love?"

"Love conquers all, heals all, endures all. It's the one unifying force that builds bridges between everyone and expands awareness. Love yourself. Love one another. It's Love that illuminates with its Light, revealing truth, bringing joy, peace, harmony, bliss."

"Wow! Love makes the world go round."

"That's another one! Yes!"

"And it's the heart that feels it?"

"And experiences it, knows it, transmits, receives and connects to it, acts as the portal to it."

"Blimey! Why don't we know this stuff?"

"The Ancients did, but the Wisdom is largely ignored nowadays."

Katy was struggling to process all this, but at least it was taking her mind off Tony.

"Your True Self," continued the Voice, "is guiding you through the medium of your heart, and the awareness of your intuitive mind, towards the things you love."

"Is it telling me what to do?"

"Good Lord, no! You have free will. It's showing you, if you wish to follow, your Higher Purpose, your Bliss, that which your soul is seeking! There's a bigger picture, you see?"

"Why so many words for the same thing?"

"Language is limited, and the concepts are limitless."

"What's our Higher Purpose?"

"Now that's a complicated question with many levels of response!"

"What's my Purpose, then?"

"Your Purpose, like everyone else's, is to be Love in action. It's your passion expressed through your inherent skills and talents, in your own distinctive way!"

"Wow! What does that mean?"

"It's you, doing what you really love for the sheer joy of it! And it turns out that you'll be good at it too!"

"Isn't that a bit selfish?"

"Isn't it selfish to be miserable doing something you hate and polluting everyone around you with your bad mood? Joyousness is infectious! Be joyous and infect others with it!" The Voice chuckled. "Besides, your purpose happens to be in service to others most of the time, but that's not why you pursue it."

"What makes you go for it, then?"

"The exhilaration, the fulfilment, the contentment. It fills you up, and you lose your small self in the process, as your True Self flows through you unimpeded."

"Being in flow, being on fire?"

"Yes. Have you ever lost track of time because you were so deeply involved in something you loved?"

"Yes!"

"That's when your True Self is expressing itself through you."

"Hang on," said Katy. "So, your True Self, for example, could paint a masterpiece but must express it through your small self, which holds the brush and knows the painting techniques?"

"And when both selves are in harmony, you're in flow,

you're deeply involved, you've lost track of time, and you're enjoying yourself!"

"That's true!"

"Your true passion, the thing that consistently brings you joy, is your purpose."

"How do I find it then? Is mine being a speaker, like Dinah said? Because if it is, I haven't got a clue how to do it!"

"You've always loved talking, haven't you?"

"Yes, but—"

"Your purpose is something you already know at some level. Follow your heart and listen to the wisdom of your intuitive mind."

"What if it's wrong?"

"That's the small self, speaking! It wants to keep you safe, you see? So it says 'what if'? And that's what sabotages you! What if it goes wrong, what if I fail, what if I'm not up to it, what if I lose all my money? Those are the questions that stop you in your tracks. What if I can't paint the masterpiece?"

"Ah! Like the conditioned patterns in the mind that we talked about?"

"Exactly! The small self is a collection of conditioned patterns. And the more you become aware of those patterns, the more you can change them and live from your True Self. Now you can expand your consciousness until it goes beyond the limitations of your rational mind!"

The Voice gave Katy a moment to catch up.

"How does it go beyond the mind?"

"Rational mind. We go beyond, into the intuitive, connected, Higher Mind!"

Katy was lost. The Voice waited patiently.

"My head's aching."

"Practice harnessing the power of your mind."

"I thought you said it was all about the heart?"

"The heart empowers the thoughts of the mind."

"Huh?"

"Thoughts create, and love is the essence of creation. Learn to choose the right thoughts and the right, love-based emotions. Oh, and visualize it too!"

"How do I know if they're right?"

"What is 'right' for you, is that which serves your evolution and brings true joy. Choose the thoughts and emotions that help you and lead you to your bliss."

"But what if I have doubtful thoughts and fear-based emotions?"

"You will! You're human! Accept what is, but don't give them power! Let go of the thoughts that keep you small, or at least don't give them too much airtime. You mustn't let fear hold you back from your destiny!"

The Voice was gone.

Katy was exhausted and managed a scant ten minutes of meditation before creeping into bed and falling asleep.

She was transported to the wedding dream. In the church that was a supermarket, she noticed Tony waiting at the altar, which doubled as a cured meats counter. Above it hung a poster which read This is a sign. Watch out for more! As she approached the altar-come-counter, she noticed the Reverend Seamus was holding a thick tome, and reading aloud in his Irish brogue: "Every-ting in your life can be guided by a Higher Power – a part of you that's Greater than you'll know. It's connected to everything. You just need to surrender your control of how you tink things should be, and flow with what is."

There was a flash of lightning and the supermarket, and everything in it disappeared. The resulting clap of thunder shook Katy to the core. Standing in a field of white light, Tony by her side, she heard a reverberating voice say, "What God has joined together, let no man put asunder."

Waking in a sweat, the sheets tangled around her, she noticed the rain outside was bucketing down. Behind the curtains, the sky lit up momentarily, and seconds later, the thunder rolled. She must have heard the storm in her sleep and woven it into her dream. Padding to the bathroom she splashed her face with water, the last scene still haunting her. That was the marriage vow! What God has joined, let no man put asunder. There was no point writing it down. It would be better to talk to her friends about it. Making a mental note to organize an urgent catch-up with Shanti, Ben and Tara, she returned to bed, but not to sleep. It would be good to get Fran along, too, get a therapist's perspective without it being Terry's. She'd sort it out tomorrow. Relaxing her body as best she could and observing the breath in her nostrils, she struggled to maintain focus. Somebody told her once that lying motionless was as good as sleep, as long as you could keep both body and mind still. About ten minutes later, she turned over, her mind recounting her earlier phone conversation with Tony. In a few hours, she'd be seeing him again. Her heart skipped a beat, and the corners of her mouth turned into a broad smile.

Chapter 27

Monday 11th May, 2009 – a nine day

Jane Joyheart had replied:

Your dowsing is 120% accurate. As long as you weren't expecting/ wishing for something specific, you can be sure. My pendulum says you're correct.

Katy checked her emails, hoping there would be something from Dinah. Nothing yet. It might be quicker to message her friends about meeting up, rather than call them. Tara and Ben would be thrilled to see Fran again! It was Katy who had recommended her for hypnobirthing when Tara was pregnant with Hazel. Lunch at a restaurant would be preferable. She needed to see them as soon as possible, and on neutral ground.

Need an urgent catch up with you all. Lots happening. I know it's short notice, but can you make lunch tomorrow? I'll pay! Tara – bring the kids if you need to. St James's Café in the Park, 1 pm? Let me know xx

After consulting her diary, she prepared her client files for the afternoon, then showered and dressed. A small square of dark chocolate and a cup of mint tea was all she could manage for breakfast. Her hands were shaking, her pulse racing as she left the house. By the time she got to the station, the butterflies were gathering strength.

As she crossed Piccadilly Circus she spotted Tony, standing near the statue of Eros. He was dressed in a smart suit, his briefcase in one hand, an overcoat slung over his arm. Her heart beat wildly as she rushed towards him. This time there was no hesitation, and they both leaned in for a full kiss.

"Hello, Gorgeous! I missed you over the weekend," he said, pulling her towards him.

Squeezing each other tight, and grinning from ear to ear, they both realized how hungry they were.

"I'm starving!" Katy had lost weight over the weekend, she'd eaten so little.

"Me too!"

"My butterflies have finally gone!"

"So have mine! Let's go!"

"Where you taking me?"

"Surprise! Follow me!"

Katy wondered where they were heading as they strolled arm-in-arm up Piccadilly. It was sublime to be with a short man. This would have been impossible with Richard. Outside a rather grand old building, Tony stopped. "After you, madam!"

It was the Royal Air Force Club! She'd never been inside before and was giddy with excitement. Thank goodness she was wearing her smart work clothes. Tony was the perfect gentleman, opening the door, guiding her to the table, pulling out her chair. Feeling like a princess, she sat, back upright, legs tucked neatly together, trying to recall the last time someone had treated her like this.

Sitting in the sumptuous dining room, they ordered from the breakfast menu. Tony was touching her continually, holding her hand or placing his palm on her back, lightly resting his fingers on her knee, or tipping her chin up towards him, and gazing at her face. They couldn't take their eyes off each other. Katy felt compelled to maintain contact with him, a gesture here, a squeeze there and a soft caress. The conversation flowed effortlessly as they chatted about their weekend, their inability to eat, their respective spouses.

"The only time I feel sane is when I'm with you," he said, fondling her hand.

"I know what you mean."

"I knew I'd be able to eat once you were by my side." Breakfast had arrived, and he was tucking into scrambled egg with smoked salmon.

"I've been on the Tony Verde diet. Kiss him in a pub, and

you instantly lose three pounds! At this rate, I'll get to my target weight in a couple of weeks!"

"You look fine as you are, to me." He eyed her up and down with approval.

"Tony, we need to talk."

"Be my guest!"

"I'm serious."

"So am I!"

Hesitating, she took another mouthful of eggs Benedict. "We're both married, and we've both got kids."

"And we're both unhappy."

"I don't know. Richard and I get on well."

"Oh yeah?"

"I know you and Lauren don't see eye-to-eye. You told me she doesn't like red wine or olives, doesn't like your sort of music, but that's the thing, Richard does! He loves those things, and he's got good music taste, just doesn't like old 70s rock!"

"Listen, if your marriage was great, you wouldn't have done what you've done! You wouldn't be sitting here with me right now, would you?"

"I don't know. Perhaps it's unfinished business from the past?"

"I think you're just papering over the cracks in your marriage, and you have been for a long time. Underneath it's in bits."

Katy took a sip of tea. "I want to be sure of what I'm doing." Setting the bone china cup back on its saucer, she added, "And I don't want to have an affair."

"Nor do I! I want to spend my life with you!"

"That's the thing. It's all happening so fast, and I think we need to be certain before we jump into it, hook, line and sinker."

"I am certain, and it's a bit late now, we're already hooked!"

"I've contacted a friend of mine, Dinah, about our soul contract. It'll give us an idea of our soul relationship, and that'll help us decide if we're doing the right thing."

"I already know I'm doing the right thing, but if you want to get it done, go ahead! Anything that reassures you is fine by me!"

"You'd probably need to go and see her too."

"Okay. How much does it cost?"

"A couple of hundred quid, but I'll pay – it's me who wants it done!"

"Righty-ho! Set it up and let me have the details."

"Thank you." She squeezed his hand. Feeling more settled now, a broad beam lit up her face.

"Tell me a bit more about it. I've never heard of a soul contract before."

Katy explained as he listened, nodding in the right places, and asking relevant questions.

"They have some really lovely rooms here," said Tony, changing the subject.

"No! I told you! I'm not having an affair."

Tony laughed. "Okay! I'm prepared to wait. Let's go for a walk in the park." He signaled to the waiter and settled the bill.

The trees in Green Park had been there for years, their trunks wide enough to hide behind. Tony led her to the edge of the grass and found a suitable old London Plane. Taking her around the side and checking the coast was clear, he grabbed her by the waist and pulled her towards him, kissing her excitedly, running a hand over her breast then squeezing her bottom. Leaning back against the trunk, she tugged at his belt, yanking him closer, her tongue darting into his mouth. He thrust his pelvis into hers, pressing hard against her. A tremble of excitement coursed through her as she held him close. "I can't!" she breathed into his ear, "I've got to go to work!" He was undoing her top and kissing her belly. "Tony!" she moaned. "We've got to stop! People can see!"

Buttoning herself up and straightening her jacket, she ran a hand through her hair. "If I don't leave now, I'll be late."

"Listen, I can't see you tomorrow. I'm at Brize Norton but can get into town on Thursday."

"I'm working from 3 o'clock."

"I'll meet you at eleven hundred hours at the café in Little Venice."

"Okay, see you then! I should have heard from Dinah by then!"

"Here's looking at you, Beautiful! I'll walk you to the station."

"It's okay, I'll walk through the back streets from here. See you Thursday!"

"Have a good one with your clients, Gorgeous!"

Sugar! She'd better get her head around work. After a lingering goodbye kiss, she paced across the park and through the streets of Mayfair, weaving her way towards Harley Street.

Heart still thumping, she wondered how she'd manage her first patient, but as soon as reception rang through the professional in her took over. She'd done her ten thousand hours, and it showed. Sailing through her appointments with laser-like focus, she completely forgot about Tony for six whole hours. For the first time in days, she felt normal. Within thirty minutes, the illusion was shattered, as she walked back into the eye of the storm, lashed by a tumult of emotions.

Turning her phone back on, it lit up like a Christmas Tree. Tara was meeting Ben in town then joining her at St James's Café. She might be a bit late. Her kids were staying with a friend. Shanti had organized cover at the shop and would meet her there, and Fran had moved her 2 o'clock client so she could stay for longer. Perfect! They could all make it at short notice.

There were three voice mails from Tony and three text messages, each one more gushing than the last.

You looked stunning again today, my Gorgeous. Can't stop thinking about you. xxx

Hello, Sexy! Can't wait to kiss those beautiful lips again. xxx

I miss you more than you can imagine. I love you. xxx

Richard had never written anything like that, and he'd majored in literature! No love letter, no songs, no poetic email or gushing text message. The most she'd got was "Happy Birthday Kit xx" His words were usually prompt, to-the-point and business-like. "Running late. Home by 8 pm. x." If only he'd made an effort, perhaps she wouldn't be in this mess! All those songs he'd written, and they were all about himself. Not a single lyric about her. Nothing even dedicated to her. Picking up her phone, she tapped out a message to Tony.

Thank you for a lovely brunch and thanks for being you. Can't wait to see you Thursday at our café. xxx

She had to slow down! Trying to live a secret life was driving her crazy, and it had only been a few days! At this rate, the tension would snap her in two, and they could each have a part of her! After packing her client notes into her bag, she left the office and headed towards Oxford Circus. The thrill of it all was too much, and she decided to walk off the feverishness. Pounding along Oxford Street, her breathing heavy, her legs aching from the effort, she marshalled her thoughts. It had to be handled sensitively. She wasn't going to make any significant moves until she'd spoken to her friends and heard from Dinah. Turning down a side street towards Mayfair, she kept powerwalking. The last thing she wanted was to hurt Richard and the children. Huh! Children! They were nearly adults, for goodness sake. Tilly would be seventeen soon! It would be better to stay with Richard until they were at university. But what if her soul was dependent on her following her truth right now? Anyway, how could she be sure it was her truth? Oh my! Why had she started all this in the first place? It wasn't exactly a walk in the park! That thought brought her full circle to Green Park, which was now on her left as she marched towards Hyde Park Corner. She couldn't get the memory of this morning out of her head, but she had to. Richard and the kids would be waiting at home and they deserved more!

* * *

Katy sat on her meditation stool, staring at the moon that shone through the window, and wondering if Tony was looking at it too. Letting her eyelids close, she could picture his exquisite blue eyes, feel his stubble against her cheek, almost smell his cologne. Lost in her thoughts, time went by unnoticed. Breath, Hara. Focus on the breath in the nostrils. Feel the hara move with the breath. An hour later, still daydreaming, she almost fell off the low wooden seat. It was gone midnight. A large scotch, two herbal sleep tablets and a melatonin would surely knock her out for the night?

Chapter 28

Tuesday 12th May, 2009

The paperwork was mounting up, and she ought to buy groceries, but Katy's priorities were changing. Tilly's room looked like the local mafia had raided it, and the laundry bin was almost full. Normally she'd be on top of it, but nothing was normal anymore. Sitting in the office, she pulled out the relevant client files for her afternoon and evening sessions. Another new patient at 6 pm, she noticed: A woman in her mid-forties who wanted to talk about her marriage. Katy didn't offer relationship counselling. It wasn't her field, and besides, she hadn't cracked it herself, so how could she advise others? This particular woman was the sister of a client. Not wanting to let anyone down, she'd agreed to take the lady on, but only to delve into her personal perspective, and not to advise on the marriage nor see the spouse.

Checking her emails for Dinah's reply, she was disappointed to see there was nothing. Tony had written a romantic message. He was excited about their future. So was she but wanted some assurance. Why hadn't Dinah responded? At least she'd be able to talk it through with her friends over lunch.

* * *

It was a sunny afternoon, and the five of them sat at a table on the terrace, overlooking the park. The waiter took their order, and after the usual pleasantries, it was Fran who asked, "So what's the big occasion?"

"A lot's happening, and I need to run it by you."

"All of us?" said Fran, polishing her fork with her serviette.

"You're my trusted confidantes, and I value your opinion!"

"Shoot!" said Ben, plucking a bread roll from the basket.

"Well…" Katy was searching for the right words.

"It's not about Tony, is it?" Shanti's laugh tinkled.

"Mmm." She nodded.

"I thought you were going to knock it on the head?" Tara was staring at her.

"I was, but—"

"I'm sorry, but it's adultery," she said, pushing her plate away. "I haven't come all this way to talk about your smutty affair. I don't agree with it." Her lips were pursed. "How could you include me and Ben in this, when you know what my feelings are?" Her jaw was set as she placed her palms on the table and stood up.

"Hang on a minute, Love!" said Ben, taking her hand and squeezing it. "Sit down. Let's hear her out, eh?" He smiled as his wife complied. "Katy's invited us for a reason. She wants us here. We're her friends!"

Tara smiled weakly and fiddled with her napkin.

The waiter arrived with their order, and Katy paused until he was out of earshot. "I'm not having an affair. There's been a whole series of events which I don't quite understand, and I think I'm supposed to be with Tony!"

"What sort of events?" said Fran, tucking into her plate of pasta.

"Signs. Coincidences. I don't know when or how it started, but there's definitely something strange going on."

"I knew it!" said Shanti. "You're being guided."

"Maybe I am! I was guided to change my name to Fralinski, then book the Aura-Soma session, and go on the SRT training! I've been clearing chakras, stuff from childhood, things from soul level!" She stabbed at a prawn with her fork. "It's been crazy! And in the midst of it all, Tony pops up, out of the blue!"

"Probably because you changed your name!" said Ben, pointing his fork at her.

"I know, but there's more!" Katy pushed her salad around the plate.

"Like what?"

"His name is Verde, for a start, and he contacted me when I was wearing green, and healing the heart chakra. He was my first, and I replied the evening after I'd cleared 'sex and sexual relationships' on the SRT course."

"I'm not convinced."

"Tony's middle name is Richard, and Richard's middle name is Anthony! Don't you think that's weird?"

"I didn't know that!" It was the first thing Tara had said since threatening to leave.

As they ate, Katy filled them in on the red dress, the pigeons, Freddie going to the doctor on his own, and the playlist in the pub. "And then there's the numbers," she said.

"What numbers?" said Fran.

"The numerology. I haven't worked it out yet, but there's always a three or a six involved. Three things in a row, like text messages or emails, three or six kisses. We met up six months after he first contacted me, and we first went out in 1977, which was a six year."

"Anything else?"

"May 8th, when everything changed, was a six day. I first saw him again on March 27th. Nine for the day and three for the month, so maybe nine's involved too."

"Hmm."

"And I've been setting the intention of having a loving, passionate relationship with my husband."

"What's wrong with that?" said Ben, putting his arm around Tara and giving her a smile.

"Nothing, but I said husband. I didn't specify Richard."

"You could be creating it with someone else. Someone who's *like* a husband," Shanti said, topping up her water glass.

Katy nodded. "And there's something else! My eczema's miraculously cleared up!"

"I told you José was good!"

"It might not have been José," said Fran, dabbing the corners of her mouth with her serviette. "It might have been psychosomatic. She had eczema because she didn't want Richard to touch her. Now she's met Tony, the eczema's cleared up! I've seen all sorts of things heal like that! Especially under hypnosis!"

"And another thing." Katy blushed and twiddled her left earring. "I had this dream about a wedding, and I heard the words, 'What God has joined together let no man put asunder!'"

"Yes!" Tara chimed in. "Marriage vows. The dream's reminding you that you're married to Richard!"

"But I was standing next to Tony. There was a flash of lightning, a crack of thunder, then the words. It doesn't make sense if it's to do with Richard."

"Of course, it does! It's a warning!" said Ben. "It's God telling you not to mess around!"

Tara beamed at him and squeezed his hand.

The waiter returned and cleared away their plates. Katy had managed about half her prawn salad.

"Did you ask Dinah about the soul contracts?" Shanti looked up from the dessert menu she'd been poring over.

"She hasn't got back to me yet."

"Probably nothing to say!" Tara said, scanning the menu. "I think I'll just have a coffee."

Katy ignored her. "I've been doing some research on soulmates."

"Oh, yes!" Shanti launched into one of her soliloquies. "People think they've only got one soulmate, but that's rubbish. We've got hundreds. And they're not all romantic liaisons, either. Most of them are here to teach us. We come across them so we can grow. They can be your mum, your dad, your brother, your daughter." She paused for thought. "Your granny or your best friend down the road, or even your boss at work. At a soul level, you'll have travelled with them through aeons of time, incarnating as different characters, but always turning up in each other's lives."

The waiter took their order.

Everyone leaned in to hear Shanti's quiet voice above the clatter of the restaurant. Wise, introvert, wonderful Shanti, who seemed to know everything about anything alternative!

"Where was I? Oh yes! Soulmates! It isn't all positive, either," she continued. "Sometimes you get a challenge or a bit of a kick up the b."

Katy wondered if 'b' was for backside, bum, bottom or butt. "Like having a histrionic mother?"

"Or a psychopathic boss," said Ben.

Their drinks arrived.

"Exactly. Sometimes they guide you, like the teacher who was strict at school, but you always liked them," continued Shanti.

"I had one of those. Mrs. Schofield." Tara was scooping the foam from the top of her cappuccino.

"And some of them love and support you." Shanti nibbled at the mini shortbread that had come with her tea and sighed. "But mostly they show you what's in your shadow by rubbing you up the wrong way and pressing all your buttons!"

"Why?"

"Because they're the opposite of you."

"Huh?"

"That's how it works. We made soul contracts with them before we incarnated. Deals designed to stir things up so we would learn from the clashes." She was jabbing at the mint teabag with her spoon.

"Spell it out for us, Shanti!" Tara had forgotten she was cross. She loved listening to her friend.

"A true soulmate acts as a mirror. Your soul has chosen to be around them so you can learn something." Picking up the tall glass mug, she blew on the hot liquid. "Look, I don't know exactly how it works, obviously. It's far too complicated when you take past lives and karma into account, and all the different members of your soul family, but I could give you the gist?" She looked up. Katy and Tara nodded, and she continued. "Let's imagine you and your sister are up in heaven as souls." Taking the salt and pepper, she placed them together to demonstrate. "At this point, you're soulmates rather than siblings. She agrees to be a bitch from hell when you both incarnate, so you can learn what it's like to be on the receiving end of emotional abuse." She placed the pepper in front of her. "You agree to be an annoying younger sister who's clever and well-behaved." The salt was moved in line. "She makes your life miserable. You learn to heal yourself, assert yourself, and put boundaries in place." She took a mouthful of peppermint tea. "And you end up helping other people who feel bullied. You become compassionate. You forgive your sister and find out she was a bitch from hell because she was jealous of you!" Sipping at her drink, she paused before continuing. "She never thought she could live up to your standards! She was in competition with you for your parent's love, you see? She felt threatened, and it came out as bad behavior." Shanti shuddered. "She's learning about jealousy and envy, how to overcome it, how to believe in herself."

"Blimey!" said Fran. "Your sister sounds complicated!"

Shanti cast her eyes down, shrinking back into herself.

"So, it's not someone you're with for life?" Ben had been quietly taking it all in.

"No. Sometimes we share the journey with them for a month, a year, a decade – but it can be for life!"

There was a pause, and Katy broached the subject of Twin Flames. "I've been looking at different soul relationships," she began, looking up for approval. "It's all about proximity or how close the souls are." She drank from her chamomile tea. "Imagine a field of daisies."

They nodded.

"The entire field is your soul family. The next field is another soul family. Within your field there's a clump of daisies, all growing together. They're your soulmates, and like Shanti says, they teach you, and they could be anyone that you have a meaningful relationship with – uncles, aunts, cousins, lovers."

"We're probably all soulmates," Shanti added.

"Within the clump, there's a single daisy. All the petals on that daisy are your Flame Mates. So are the petals of the neighboring daisies that touch yours." Katy was sketching out her theory on the back of a paper serviette.

"Flame Mates carry you through life and help you along the way," chipped in Shanti.

"That's right. Freddie and Tilly are Flame Mates, and so are Richard and I. That's why we've been a tight-knit family." She gulped. "Richard helps me financially, and encourages me when I don't believe in myself, and I help him emotionally. I've provided him with the close, loving family he never had as a child."

"And that's exactly why you're meant to stick together! In sickness and in health, for richer or poorer, remember?" Tara wouldn't let it go.

"I know, Tara, but there's more. Each individual petal can be split in two, like the yin and yang, the two halves of the one soul. They're the Twin Flames. The closest you can get." Katy stopped. She felt uncomfortable with Ben and Tara. They probably wondered what their own soul relationship was.

It was Shanti who broke the awkward silence. "It's a highly sacred soul union," she explained. "When Twin Flames meet, there's work to be done, devotional work, in service to humanity and the planet. Together they create the one soul in preparation for ascension. You have to be pretty advanced to meet your Twin Flame!"

Fran almost choked on her coffee. Shanti ignored her. She was used to people reacting that way, and she'd learned to rise above.

"Of course, you can have a perfectly wonderful relationship with a soulmate or a Flame Mate. It doesn't have to be your Twin Flame to make it work, does it?" said Katy, hoping to smooth things over with Tara and Ben.

"How would you know if you'd met your Twin Flame?" asked Ben.

"There'd be fireworks!"

Ben was rubbing his chin. "But how could you be sure? How would you know what your soul relationship was? I mean, there were fireworks when I met Tara, lots of people experience that at the beginning, but it doesn't mean they're with their Twin Flame!"

"You'd have to dowse," said Katy. "Unless you recognized them."

"How?"

"I dunno! Signs? Intense feelings? A magnetic pull?" She wasn't exactly sure, but her explanation seemed to fit.

"So, what's the soul relationship between you and Tony? I take it you've dowsed?" Tara was interested now.

Katy blushed. "It's hard to be objective, but if I had to bet, I'd say we're Siamese Twins. I dowsed several times and got the same answer."

"What's a Siamese Twin? Is that the same as a Twin Flame?" asked Tara.

"Hot flame, big flame, blue flame, flaming heck!" said Fran. "What does it matter? Nobody can really know this stuff! What's important is how two people interact, how loving they are, how respectful of each other, how free they are to be themselves and grow within the relationship!"

"I know, Fran, but—"

"Let's get back to Siamese Twins!" Tara was curious. "What are they, in soul terms?"

"I don't know. There wasn't much about it on the SRT course, and I can't find it anywhere on the internet. It's incredibly close, though! It must be?" Katy looked up expectantly.

"How does that fit in with the daisy theory?" asked Ben.

"You know when two daisies grow so close they touch? I think that's Siamese Twins. When another petal, exactly like yours, is lying back-to-back with you."

"Or where two petals are joined at the base because they haven't split properly!" said Fran.

"I'm sure he's the one, Fran! You just said it's about the couple themselves, and that makes sense!" said Katy.

"Don't give me that bullshit, there's no such thing as 'the one'," said Fran.

Tara reached out to hold Ben's hand. "I don't see how it makes sense, Katy?"

"Of course, it does! I met Tony when we were both teenagers. He turned up at my school but only for the last three years, and he was my first. Then he turns up after all this time! There must be a reason!"

"Not necessarily," said Fran.

"Can't you see? It's all kicking in because I've chosen this path!" Katy's thoughts coalesced as she saw the connections. "Tony only found me because I changed my name, and I only changed it because of the soul contract! I went to Dinah because I wanted to know my soul purpose, why I was here on planet Earth!"

"And you only care about your soul purpose if you're awakening to something bigger!" said Shanti.

"That's right! And Shanti keeps saying I'm being guided, and I am! When I changed my name, it sent out a signal to his soul that it was time! It must be pre-ordained!"

"Yeah. Sure." Fran was checking her phone.

Katy wasn't going to let it go. "We love the same things, we get on incredibly well, he's into metaphysical stuff, and the chemistry is out of this world! You can see how it would work, can't you?"

"But you've only known him a few months, and anyway, you're spoken for!" said Fran.

"I reckon we're already married at soul level. That's why I heard the vow in my dream."

Fran rolled her eyes. "You're basing a major life decision on a hypothetical idea that souls are like daisies! You over-analyze everything. Why not work through your feelings? What do you feel for Richard and the kids? What do you feel for Tony? Is it worth upsetting the apple cart?"

"I've been chatting to Terry about that."

"Your supervisor? Does he know about Tony and all this soul-flame-daisy stuff?"

"No. I didn't tell him. He's not MOSES."

"Who's Moses?" asked Fran.

"M.O.S.E.S." Katy spelt it out. "Movement of Spiritually Enlightened Souls!"

Shanti squealed. "Love it!"

Fran wasn't going to be derailed so easily. "All I'm saying is, be cautious! Step back and think it through with your therapist's mind, not your spiritual one!"

Katy had to convince Fran she was destined to be with Tony. The more she thought about it, the more obvious it became. In her mind, Siamese Twins were even better than Twin Flames because they were joined! "But you have to admit it's incredible when you look back and join the dots?"

"Most people's lives are pretty amazing when they look back and join the dots," said Ben.

Katy pressed on. "I couldn't possibly have known that my first true love—"

"Hang on, you said he was your 'first' – I thought you meant your first sexual conquest?" said Fran.

"I did."

"And he was your first love as well?"

"Well, my first serious boyfriend, then, and my first lover.

How could I have known he was my twin soul? I suppose we had to grow up before we could be brought back together by fate."

The waiter arrived with the bill, and there was the usual scrabble to work out who paid for what. "I told you! My treat!" said Katy, snatching the piece of paper, and taking out her credit card.

"Are you sure?" said Ben.

Katy nodded.

"That's very generous! Thank you!" said Fran. "I'm afraid I've got to love you and leave you." She hesitated. "I don't mean to be a wet blanket, but here's the thing – I don't know anything about Twin Flames and Flame Mates, but I do know that in real life, Siamese Twins are born with huge challenges. One twin is joined to the other, and their lives are at risk because of it. Usually, one thrives at the expense of the other. It doesn't seem very healthy or equal to me. Just saying."

"She's got a point." Ben and Tara were getting ready to leave. "We've got to make tracks too. Take care of yourself, Katy. We worry about you."

"Me too." Shanti hugged everyone. "And I love that MOSES thing! You should organize a monthly MOSES meeting at your house!"

"What for?"

"Meditation, healing, support. It could be a Satsang community where we talk about what we're doing!"

"I'll think about it."

Walking back to Harley Street, two things played on her mind: Fran's comment about real Siamese twins, and Shanti's suggestion that she hosted a regular meeting.

One of the few times Katy felt calm and in control was when she was seeing clients. She could focus one hundred percent on their problems and forget her own, which she had done that afternoon. Tony called her at 9.30 pm while she was walking along Piccadilly towards Victoria. They whispered sweet nothings and caught up on the day's news. He'd already sent three text messages and an email. How they had so much to say to each other was beyond her.

Sitting on the train home, Katy's thoughts turned to her new patient. The six o'clock lady was married to a man who was good-looking and earned a generous salary. There was nothing wrong, exactly, she'd said, but the spark had gone, and she couldn't connect with him. Their sex life was dead in the water, and they had very little in common. There were two teenage boys, both at private school, and she loved them to bits. Whilst there wasn't anyone else, she couldn't help thinking that if the right man walked into her life, she'd be torn. That worried her a lot, and that's why she'd booked the session. Her concern was for her boys, how it might affect them, and for her husband, who'd be left high and dry without her. Her biggest fear, though, was that she'd end up as a single mother. It was the financial struggle that worried her, she'd said, but Katy could sense there was more. The client didn't want to end up as 'an old maid on the shelf'. That was her exact phrase, and it had taken Katy back to her own childhood. Her swimming teacher, Mr. Tompkins, had told her when she didn't want to dive off the board, that she'd end up as an old maid on the shelf! She was terrified of diving at the time, and it must have gone straight into the psyche. For years she was anxious about being left on the shelf. It was only when she went through therapy that she realized Mr. Tompkins meant no harm: he was simply telling her not to be held back by her fears.

Bringing her attention back to her client, Katy had reassured her. "But how would that be possible? An old maid is someone who's never married and never had children!" The woman had smiled weakly, but she hadn't taken it on board. It was as if she needed to be in a relationship. She couldn't bear the thought of being alone! Co-dependence, thought Katy. Keeping a lousy relationship going was more important than her own wellbeing! Or more precisely in this woman's case, keeping the family ticking over was more important than following her truth.

A shiver ran over her, and Katy gazed out of the train window. 'Follow your bliss' would be terrible advice to give someone who was a co-dependent, or an addict, for that matter! Crikey, if her client, Seamus, followed his bliss, he'd create a living nightmare!

At home later, in her office, Katy wrote up her post-session notes before locking the files away. She switched on the computer. Tony would have sent her a little goodnight message, and she was eager to read it. The laptop was taking ages to load. Huh. Fran. She could be stubborn at times. Anyway, she was divorced and resolutely single! What did she know of hot passion and Divine Partnerships? Playing it safe hadn't got her very far, had it? As Shanti always said, 'the magic happens outside the comfort zone!'

Opening her emails, her eyes were immediately drawn to Dinah's message.

Hi Katy

Why did you want to know about the soul contract?

I took a look. Remarkable! Couldn't believe my eyes! Had to check with Head Office. Tree says he's never heard of two individuals mirroring each other so perfectly!

Anthony Verde is without question a Twin Soul! You both hold the frequency of 11 (the Twin Flame). You know we look at the vowels and consonants separately? Well, your first names mirror each other (they are reversed, so to speak). You both have 7 (spiritual quest) for your middle names, and nine (the spiritual path) in your surnames. In fact, you, Katy, have the 22 energy as we discussed. Anthony has the potential of 33, but as you know, few mortals can ground that vibration, so we usually take it as a six (love and harmony).

Overall, you are a 9, and he is a 6. Spiritual love and romantic love. 69 is a very sexy number! You'll find there is an extremely passionate connection but much more. The numbers literally hold each other. The 9 rests in the lap of the 6 if you look at the shape! One is the reverse of the other. Like the yin and the yang. It's an incredibly close, complementary soul relationship. The physical aspect is interesting – there's a karmic lock which means you're locked into each other. You can't get out of it!

I urge you to have a full reading, asap, both of you.

Loving kindness,

Dinah xx

PS - Given the charts, I'm assuming it's a romance? Is he married? If so, I need his wife's dob and full name.

Sitting motionless, Katy could feel the enormity of Dinah's words pressing against her. Reality had broad-sided her from nowhere and all she could do was blink at the screen. Oh, my God! What now? Her head was swimming.

Scurrying to the mirror, she whispered "Hello?" Only the thumping of her heart could be heard. "Are you there?" Her eyes were transfixed as she waited. "Where are you?" She held her breath. A car drove by outside, and she returned to her emails. There was one from Tony. How on earth was she going to tell him? Her fingers trembled as she typed out her reply.

Hello, Gorgeous!

I love your little goodnight emails. You make me feel like a Goddess.

I have something to tell you about the soul contract. We need to see Dinah asap. Let me know what works for you. She needs Lauren's dob and full name. Don't know why, but can you send it to her? Email dinah@Soulcontract.co.uk.

I'll tell you more on the phone!

Can't wait to see you, either! The only time I can eat is when I'm with you. Unless I'm holding your hand or standing within an inch of you, I feel like I've been cast adrift.

Sweet dreams, my darling! Chat tomorrow.

K xxxxxx

Shanti would still be up, and she was bursting to tell someone.

Checking the coast was clear, she shut the office door and dialed the number.

"Wow! I told you! He's been sent to you! Amazing news!"

"I don't want it getting back to Richard. It has to be hush, hush, okay?"

"Of course. Mum's the word."

"And I want to hear the full reading before I do anything."

"Absolutely!"

"I'm going to be careful who I tell. Just my trusted inner circle for now."

"You going to tell Terry?"

"Not yet, but I will."

Shanti changed the subject. "What about the MOSES meetings?"

"I've been thinking about it, yeah."

"Your house is perfect. Easy to get to, fairly central and big enough for a small group."

"I could start in June, after our trip?"

"To the conference? That's not till the end of the month. Why not do a dummy run before we go?"

"Could do. Need to check in with Richard. I'll let you know."

"Okay. If you go ahead, I can help with invites."

"Thanks. Let's chat again soon."

Katy had never felt so alive, riding this roller-coaster of a lifetime, with each twist more thrilling than the last.

The laptop pinged. There was another mail from Tony.

Hi, Gorgeous

Sounds great. Could call you now if you're free? Otherwise, chat tomorrow.

Can do Thurs or Fri eve, or next Mon any time.

Let me know.

Have sent her Lauren's details.

Sweet dreams, Sexy.

Love you. xxxxxx

Thursday was already booked up with client work, so it would have to be Friday. Monday was too long to wait, and besides, it was Tilly's birthday on Tuesday and she didn't want a late night. Her heart was thumping as she rang Dinah. After running her through the reason for the reading, she confirmed Friday evening at 7 o'clock, then emailed Tony to let him know.

Chapter 29

Thursday 14th May, 2009 – a three day.

Freddie had been complaining about the lack of food in the fridge and had left a shopping list. Richard had moaned that morning that his shirts hadn't been ironed, and Tilly had left the kitchen looking like a team of chefs had been competing against the clock. Did they really own that many utensils?

Having passed it by Richard, who had grunted, the inaugural MOSES meeting was scheduled for the following Friday, 22nd May, 2009: A two day (union), with the frequency of twenty-two, the Master Builder, and if you added two and two, it carried the vibration of four, grounded and practical. So far, ten people had been invited, and with Katy, that would make eleven, the first master number.

Before leaving for town that morning, Katy checked her emails and noticed one from Dinah. She and Tony were to have two separate readings, for some reason. Dinah had scheduled one straight after the other.

Just before 11 o'clock, Katy waltzed into the café in Little Venice. Tony was already waiting, and a broad grin stretched across his face as he saw her. She ran towards him, and he stood, scooping her up in his arms, and lifting her off her feet, before planting a kiss on her cheek. "Hello, Gorgeous! You smell divine, and you look hot!"

"Had to run, train was a bit late."

He winked. "I didn't mean that sort of hot!"

They ordered a pot of Earl Grey and a flapjack.

"Dinah's confirmed tomorrow. We need two separate sessions."

"Why?"

"I dunno, but I trust Dinah. We can ask her when we get there."

"I feel like I'm living in two worlds!" said Tony. "And I'm not sure which one's real!"

"I know what you mean. Nothing feels concrete right now! It's driving me insane!"

"A therapist going insane?" He laughed. "You'll be hearing voices next!"

Katy froze for a moment. "Actually, I've been hearing this Voice for a while!"

"Oh, wow! Really? Tell me about it! What does it say?"

Sighing with relief, she filled him in on the details, reassured by his nods and encouraging comments.

"I feel like I'm in a film sometimes," said Tony. "Except the director keeps changing the plot."

"And re-writing the ending! That's how I feel too!"

"I keep thinking I'm going to wake up!"

"And realize it was all a dream!" They were both laughing. The tea and flapjack arrived, and Tony poured while Katy cut the snack in two.

"I'm not sure how it's all going to end," she said.

"Oh, I'm pretty certain I know! It'll be with us, together, living out our lives in the most extraordinary way!" He leaned across and kissed her. "I was in the kitchen with Lauren last night. We were chopping vegetables, and I thought, if that was Katy, I'd walk across and stand behind her, put my arms around her, and kiss the nape of her neck."

Stroking his hand gently, she blushed. "Life is shifting gears in a way I didn't expect. I'm not sure what to think. Everything was so mapped out and nailed down, and now it's being ripped apart and tossed aside."

"Your eyes look stunning when you're being dramatic, like that!"

Looking up at him, she felt herself diving beneath the surface to a deeper world within.

"Fancy going to Tate Modern? There's an exhibition on –

Russian Avant-Garde painting!"

"Do we have time? I'd love to go!"

Tony checked his watch. "Yeah, if we leave now, we should have a couple of hours!"

Leaving the café, he opened the door for her, eyeing her bottom wobbling in the slim-fitting business skirt. "I had a dream about you this morning."

"Did you now?" She turned to give him a sultry look over her shoulder.

"We were sitting at the kitchen table, reading the papers and drinking tea. You stood up, looked at me just like you did then, walked out of the kitchen towards the bedroom, and said 'I'm wet'." His grin widened.

"I can just imagine where that dream went!"

"Can't we go to a hotel?"

"No! I know it sounds old-fashioned, but I don't want to cheat on Richard, I don't want you cheating on Lauren either, and I don't want sex in some crumby hotel."

"It doesn't have to be crumby! I was thinking of somewhere romantic!"

"I want to wait."

"I feel like I've known you forever. We've only been seeing each other a short while, and it seems like months. It's too long to wait!"

"I know. Time's elastic."

They worked out the best route to Bankside and boarded a train.

"Let's see what Dinah says tomorrow. I've confirmed 7 o'clock at hers. Still okay for you?"

"Yep!"

"I'll meet you outside John Lewis at six."

Katy hadn't been to a gallery in ages. Last time she'd visited Tate Modern, the kids had enjoyed it until Richard starting complaining about the pointlessness of modern art. It was so refreshing to be accompanied by someone who was genuinely open-minded. The morning flew by and neither wanted to tear themselves away.

"Got to go. Clients!" she said, gently rubbing his lapels between her thumbs and forefingers.

"Time really is relative! It feels like five minutes since we were in Little Venice!"

"I know. I'll see you tomorrow."

"It'll seem like days till then."

Lingering a moment longer, he held her close, cradling her head against his shoulder. "I hate it when you go. Unless I'm actually touching you, I'm all at sea."

Client sessions went well that afternoon, with Katy managing to focus on something other than her current drama. As she left the building, her phone lit up. Three romantic text messages from Tony and a poetic voice mail. He called her at 9.30 pm, and they chatted until she reached Victoria. The walk had become a regular habit, and with the loss of appetite, she was only a few pounds off her target weight. A regimen of Harley Street, walking to Victoria, meditation in the evenings, and yoga in the mornings, was keeping her from cracking as the pressure mounted.

Her phone buzzed.

Went out for drink with work. Heading home. R x

Oh no, the kids would have been on their own! Ringing the landline, it was Freddie who answered.

"It's alright, Mum. Tilly cooked. We had pasta."

"You're okay on your own?"

"Yeah! We're not kids, you know! We've done our homework and eaten. I cleared up. The kitchen was a bit of a mess."

"Aww. Thanks, Freddie! What are you doing now?"

"Just finished revising English. About to watch telly."

"Exam tomorrow? You in good shape?"

"I think so."

"What about Tilly?"

"She's in her room."

"She okay?"

"Yeah! She's listening to music and painting her toenails black. She's got an art exam, I think."

"Remember I'm out tomorrow evening?"

"Yeah, I know. Your friend who does the contract thingies."

"Dinah, yes. I'm almost home. See you in ten. Love you."

Chapter 30

Tony was waiting outside John Lewis in a pair of expensive chinos, a designer polo shirt, and a beautifully cut suit jacket. Katy wondered why she hadn't noticed how gorgeous he was from the start. Hurrying towards him, he caught sight of her, a broad smile softening his face as he rushed to her side. They enveloped each other, clinging together, holding tight as if they were long-lost twins. He kissed her firmly on the lips, and a warm shiver ran through her.

"Come on! We'll get the tube. It'll be quicker than the bus in this traffic," she said, taking his arm. "How was your day?"

Crammed onto a train, they stood, pressed against each other, canoodling without a care for the other commuters wedged around them. At Seven Sisters, they changed onto the over-ground and headed towards Stoke Newington. Between kissing, caressing each other, and giggling, they almost missed their stop.

Walking out of the station, Tony looked curiously at the dirty, urban landscape. "Not exactly how I thought it would be!"

"There are some lovely Victorian and Edwardian houses on these side streets. Dinah lives in one, well the top floor flat. It's been converted."

Tony followed her as they crossed the busy main road and headed towards Dinah's. Ten minutes later they were standing outside a bay-windowed, three-story, terraced house. Katy rang the doorbell, and a woman's voice scratched through the intercom. The door buzzed and they mounted the steep staircase.

After greeting Katy with a hug, Dinah turned to Tony. "You must be Anthony!" she said, holding out her hand. "How lovely to meet you!" Ushering them into the stark lounge, she offered them herbal tea.

"I've had a look at both your charts, and I've got interesting news, but I want to talk to you separately," Dinah said.

"It's okay, we don't have anything to hide! Go ahead!" Tony took a sip of his ginger tea, as Katy nodded in approval. "Just carry on, Dinah!"

"It's not protocol. I've done a full personal reading for Tony, and I've also looked at his wife's chart. I want Tony to be fully aware of the situation so he can make an informed choice. If you're here, it could influence him unduly."

Katy's heart sank. "Who should go first?"

"It doesn't matter, really."

"Lady's first, my darling. I'll go and find a café back on the High Street." Tony got to his feet. "How long will you be?"

"Should be done in an hour."

After kissing each other goodbye, he disappeared down the stairs.

Dinah opened her folder of papers.

"I want to go over your personal reading, just the salient points, then look again at your contract with Richard. Just so you're refreshed and know where you stand."

Dinah reminded her of the reading she'd had just over six months ago, then pulled out another document. "Okay. This is the chart for you and Anthony. I've looked at his nickname, Tony, as well as 'Katy'. We call them 'overlay' names."

As she was explaining the squiggles and numbers on the chart, Katy's jaw dropped.

"You and Richard had a pretty good contract, but your relationship with Tony is dynamite! It's an incredible match. The sort of thing you don't see very often, in fact, I've never seen it, and I've been doing these charts for years."

Katy almost choked on her tea. Dinah fetched a glass of water from the small kitchen.

"Katy, this man is going to be holding the space for you,

literally holding you while you step into the next phase of life," said Dinah, pausing to let it sink in. "He'll be helping you in a very practical way to ground yourself, to get out of your head and into your body. He's going to support your transition into the life you were meant to live. Oh, my goodness, Katy!" The gravitas of what she was saying needed to be hit home. Her voice was calm, measured, precise. "He's going to help you step into your power and sovereignty, so you can do what you came here to do."

The information was too much for Katy. Her breathing was shallow, and she felt giddy, as if she might faint. "Be careful what you ask for," she said in a monotone. "I've been asking to know my true purpose, and how to fulfil it." She could feel a migraine coming on and massaged her forehead with her fingertips. "And I've been asking for a loving, passionate relationship with my husband, but I didn't specify Richard."

Dinah gave her time. "I can't tell you what to do or advise you either way. If you want a loving and passionate relationship with Richard, it's still in your power to create it."

"Sounds like you were going to say 'but'!"

"But you may not be able to fulfil your purpose, and I'm not sure you'd be able to break free of Tony! There's a karmic lock in the physical. It means you can't get out of it easily."

"Get out of what?"

"I don't know. Something's binding you together."

"Could it be to do with our work?"

"I don't know! It could be, I suppose, or maybe it's designed to make you stay together? But I honestly can't tell."

"Tell me truthfully, Dinah, is my contract with Tony better than the one with Richard?"

"Better isn't really the word. You've got to see the contract as a potential. And yes, the potential is greater, but that's at soul level. Only you can decide what's better for you in your life, at this level!"

"Anything else I need to know?"

"It's a contract. You have to play your part too. You're here to introduce him to a higher spiritual path, a wider understanding, and lead him to his true destiny. He's not on the right path for his soul right now."

Katy was frowning as she tried to pull it all together and weigh it up. "What about Lauren?"

"I'll talk to Tony about her. It's his wife, and it's not for me to divulge, but he can tell you if he wants to."

Katy sighed.

"What you do with the information is entirely up to you," said Dinah. "All I can tell you is the likelihood of two people having similar, mirroring numerology like this, is about a billion to one! This couldn't have happened by chance. You changed your name and it shifted something. The Forces that Be are maneuvering you into position."

"What should I do?"

"Go away and think about it. Talk to someone you trust. Only you can decide."

"It all seems too incredible!"

"It is! It's unbelievable!"

"But it is true?"

"I'm just as baffled as you, but the reading is true. I've double-checked, and so has Tree."

After going over the finer details, the reading was complete. The doorbell rang, and Dinah buzzed Tony in. They could hear his footsteps climbing the stairs before he entered the lounge. "How did it go?"

"Brilliant! I'll leave you to it," she said, giving him a hug and peck on the cheek. "About an hour?"

"Make it an hour and a half at least. Maybe more. I've got two contracts to go through."

Katy disappeared into the street below, heading towards a restaurant she knew, not that she'd be able to eat much.

Sitting at a small table in the French-style Brasserie, her heart was racing. She felt as lustful as the teenager who'd spied Tony in the rugby team all those years ago. A fifteen-year-old's libido seemed to be coursing through her, but she had to hold out. Her stomach lurched as she turned her thoughts to Richard and the children. How could she break up the family she'd loved and nurtured for so long? Dreading what could lay ahead, she forced herself to imagine the scenario. She was petrified of making the wrong decision and hurting everyone in the process. Poor Richard. He didn't deserve this. Abandoned by his mother and now by his wife, well his second wife. He'd left Anita to be with Katy, back in the days when they'd worked together, when she, Katy, had been in human resources. And that was another thing. He'd broken up his first marriage to be with her! She couldn't leave him now, not after he'd risked everything.

The waitress arrived with a bowl of Moules Marinière and a glass of sparkling water. A large cognac might have been a better choice, she thought, her hand shaking as she reached for the drink. On second thoughts, better to be sober when reality was hitting you in the face, no matter how frightening it was.

Plucking a mussel from its shell, the therapist within wondered if it was the thrill of the chase and nothing more. Was she going back into her past to resolve something? Was there such a thing as a mid-life crisis? Perhaps she was going through one? It could all fizzle out, and she'd have lost something precious – her family! What if it was an illusion, just the smoke and mirrors of infatuation? She was a wife and mother, for fudge sake, and a respected therapist. What would people say? Her reputation would be tarnished. No. She couldn't let this thing run away with her. She tackled another mussel and slurped at a spoonful of juice. Three more mouthfuls and she'd managed to eat about half the starter portion she'd ordered. Rinsing her fingers in a bowl of lemon water, she was about to reach for the napkin, when a vision of Tony pierced through her rambling thoughts:

his mesmerizing eyes, his broad smile, that strawberry-blonde stubble over his strong jaw. Of course she was meant to be with him! All this spiritual awakening, all this healing she'd done, it was about finding happiness, wasn't it? Working out what mattered to her? She'd been trapped in an airless life, wanting to break free and soar, but not knowing how to or where to go. Without a doubt, her deeper self knew she was meant to be with her Twin Soul. She imagined them working together, humanitarian work, something that would make a difference in the world. Her heart swelled. It was obvious! Look at all the signs, the soul contract, the way it had happened in a flash!

The waitress arrived and topped up her water. Katy sat back, sipping at the drink and staring at the French-style Moulin Rouge posters on the wall opposite. They reminded her of her honeymoon in Paris with Richard. How could she be so stupid! She couldn't just up sticks and leave the man she'd been married to for almost eighteen years! This thing with Tony couldn't last. She heard her mother's critical voice. It would all end in tears.

Endlessly moving from certainty to uncertainty, Katy picked at a few more mussels. She was caught in a hall of mirrors. What was true and what was illusion? Was she just a worthless sinner? No nobler than a sex addict at the Priory, no more spiritual than the drunken young girls that spilled out of nightclubs, bare legged in their micro-skirts? Calling for the bill, she settled up and left the restaurant. It was almost time to return to Dinah.

* * *

Tony sat on the cream sofa, his legs wide open, his forearms resting on his knees. This dusky-skinned chick, Dinah, had furnished the place with carvings from Bali or India or somewhere. It wasn't his thing. A wisp of incense rose from a filigree silver box, and he wrinkled his nose. Thank goodness he hadn't been seen coming here. What the other officers might wonder, he dreaded to think. Still, he wanted to please Katy, and what harm could it do? This woman didn't know anything about him! He couldn't believe, for one moment, that she could glean anything just from his name and date of birth! It just wasn't possible.

"So! Do I call you Anthony or Tony?" Dinah asked, slipping the papers from his file.

"Tony's fine."

"Good. We have a lot to go through. I'm going to take you through your contract first, starting with the past, the present and the future potential. Remember it's the potential we're looking at? It's up to you to fulfil it!" Tony smiled, and she carried on. "Then I'll talk about your relationship with your wife, Lauren, and how that's playing out, and finally I'll tell you about you and Katy."

"Okay, then." Tony almost laughed. It didn't matter to him; he could fuel his latest Katy fantasy while this woman prattled on. She began reading from the charts, and within a few minutes, Tony's mouth was hanging open. Straightening up and pulling his knees together, he was watching her every move. How could she know all this? Something that disrupted his early school life, a wayward dad, flirtatious and promiscuous in his late teens, a moment of crisis at university, straightening out, possibly by joining the forces, or at least a large organization where there was a clear hierarchy of achievement!

Had Katy told her? She couldn't have, she didn't know half of it herself! He rubbed his temples. "How do you know all this?"

"It's all here in the chart! These readings are incredibly accurate when they're properly interpreted. Were you an addict in your youth? I can see there was a potential, but I'm sure that's all in the past."

Tony opened his mouth to speak, but nothing intelligible came out.

"You have a powerful libido and always have done. It's got

you into trouble in the past."

Sitting up now, and taking notice of everything Dinah was saying, he was becoming utterly confused.

"Any questions?"

"Did Katy tell you any of this?"

"No."

"You've researched my records?"

Dinah laughed. "No!"

His face must be turning pale, he could sense the color draining away. Clasping his hands in front of him to stop the tremor that was forming, he nodded at Dinah to continue.

She took another sheet of paper from the file. "So, let's look at you and Lauren," she said, studying the strange markings and a page of notes she'd made. "Your relationship is strained at best and dysfunctional at worst!" Dinah faltered for a moment. "Is she quite driven? She'd make a good career woman. Strong masculine energy. Probably not that interested in her softer, nurturing side." She turned her head slightly to take a closer look at the chart. "I can see the initial attraction. There were karmic debts that would have brought you together. Do you have children?"

"A daughter."

"And she returned to work almost immediately after having her?"

"How—" He stopped himself. "She works long hours in the City. Commutes from our home in Oxfordshire. Leaves before Amber's up and tries to get back before she goes to bed."

"Who looks after Amber?"

"We had a Nanny when she was little, but my work hours are flexible. I do my bit – take her to the doctors if she's sick, stay up with her at night if she's scared. It was me that took her to A&E when she fell off her bike. She's nine now, so it's easier."

"You sound like a hands-on dad, and that's something for you to consider. You'll want to be with Amber, I'm sure!"

Tony could feel the emotions welling up. He coughed. "I understand her. She's shy, you see. Finds it hard to make friends. She's got a few problems. ADHD and Dyslexia."

"Oh! I'm sorry."

"Lauren's always busy. Would leave her in front of a video all day, but Amber's better if she's out and about. I take her swimming, cycling, to the park. It seems to help." He was grateful that Dinah took a moment to let him find his equilibrium.

"I imagine your marriage showed signs of stress quite early. I could be wrong. I'm only going by the charts."

Tony nodded. "I was away with work, and Lauren didn't like it. Where are you getting all these details from?"

"I'm an intuitive. It's not *all* in the charts, but they provide the sign-posts, the structure, if you like." Dinah looked at her notes. "Does Lauren like to pamper herself?"

"She likes a spa break and a bit of retail therapy."

"It's a comfort thing. There's wounding from childhood. I can see a karmic knot of abandonment. Her fierceness is a shell to protect her vulnerability."

"She's not a bad person."

"No! Goodness, no! I get that. Just emotionally compromised. I'm surprised she had children!"

"It was an accident. Got a bit carried away on our honeymoon and she forgot to take the pill. I wanted a kid and thought it would cement us."

"Did it?"

"For a while, but, well..." He swallowed and looked up at the ceiling. "I started drinking, she started shouting. She slapped me around a couple of times. Just lost it. All cool, ice-maiden one moment, then screaming banshee the next!"

"With your libido, I'm guessing you had great make-up sex?"

"We did at first, but I, I..." He fiddled with his left cuff, coughed, and looked up at the plaster coving. Dinah waited. "I lost interest. She'd dress up in sexy undies, the costly stuff, Coco de Mer, is it? Tall and slim with model's legs, she's stunning but I just couldn't, er, rise to the occasion."

"I see." Dinah looked down and shuffled her papers.

"I, er. When we did, you know, I'd struggle to finish, probably because of all the, er, porn I'd been watching. She'd get upset, then resort to verbal abuse." He swallowed hard and looked down at the floor. "She's hit me a few times. She's quite strong, and she's taller than me." He could feel himself blushing. His ears would be crimson by now, and he buried his head in his hands.

"Can I get you a drink of water?" Dinah went to the kitchen, returning a few moments later with a glass.

"Thanks." He took a gulp.

"Let's move on to your relationship with Katy, shall we?"

He instantly felt the clutches of remorse loosen as the stifling guilt melted away. "I'd like that."

"Your emotional floodgates must have opened abruptly on meeting Katherine."

"This time round, yes. I knew her before, at school. Always liked her, a lot, but it wasn't as intense as this."

"I imagine the sexual chemistry is quite something. You have a 69 energy."

Tony sniggered. It was all he could do to hold himself back. 'Standing to attention' at work had taken on a whole new meaning these past few weeks. Unless he could hide behind a briefcase or a dossier, it was becoming a source of embarrassment.

Dinah went through the details of his soul contract with Katy, confirming what he already felt in his heart. His destiny was somehow tied up with hers. She brought out the best in everyone, and especially in him. There was a sense of something more significant when he was with her. Somehow, she glowed in his presence, and her light elevated him, as the spring sun lifts the spirits after winter. He didn't fully understand 'karmic locks' or 'yin and yang', but it rang true that they complemented each other.

"Katy really gets you, Tony. If you need to express yourself or put your foot down, she'll understand. It won't be like it is with Lauren. Just remember, you can tell her anything, and she's not going to shout and scream or hit you. Okay?"

The doorbell rang, and Dinah pressed the intercom. Katy came running up the steps, iridescent, smiling. He stood up and held her.

"Thank you so much, Dinah!" she said, pulling away and rummaging in her bag. He watched as she counted out the crisp notes, paying Dinah in cash for the readings.

"Keep me posted."

"We will."

A warm unctuous feeling of caramel and cream wrapped itself around Katy as they headed towards the station. "I can't believe our luck!" she said, her arm around his waist. Pulling her close, his hand on her shoulder, he softly kissed her cheek. On the journey back to Paddington they were inseparable. Looking tenderly into his eyes, she felt sure she could see his soul. Something shot through her, just like it had in the pub the previous Friday. It took her breath away. "Will you marry me?" It just came out. She hadn't meant to say it. Squirming in her seat, and clasping her hand over her mouth, she wished she could rewind the last few seconds and edit it out. What the hell was she thinking? Women didn't ask men to marry them! They'd only known each other a few weeks, and they were both already married. Wishing she could fall through a hole in the carriage floor, she desperately tried to think of something.

Tony smirked and squeezed her hand. "Yes! I will marry you!" He leaned across and smooched her. "This calls for a celebration!"

"How about Pandora's? The little cellar bar we went to?"

"Perfect!" he planted a huge kiss on her lips. With the tension gone, they started to laugh as they chattered about the soul contract and what it meant to them.

"Let's not be rash," said Katy. "We'll celebrate tonight." She gave his hand a squeeze. "But next week we'd better work out how we're going to manage this!"

"When are you leaving Richard?"

"Not yet."

"Why?"

"We need to discuss it. It requires careful planning. There are kids involved."

"I think I'll get a motorbike so I can get out of town easily to see Amber."

"One step at a time! We need to tread softly before we get to that stage!"

"Shall I tell Lauren?"

"No!" Katy shrieked. "Not yet. Give me the weekend to think it through, and I'll meet you on Monday. How does that sound?"

"Sounds like a plan!"

Standing in the crowded vaults at Pandora's, Tony ordered a bottle of champagne. "We're celebrating our engagement!" he told the barman. A couple next to them cheered, and a moment later a bucket of ice, a bottle of bubbly and two glasses appeared.

"Here's to us!" Tony raised his glass to hers and they took a swig of fizz. A few of the customers who'd been standing at the bar, toasted them, one or two slapping Tony on the back, and wishing them well.

Finding a dark corner, they French-kissed their way through most of the evening, oblivious to the other clientele.

"Third time lucky!" said Tony.

Katy giggled. "Yep! Me too! I want page-boys instead of bridesmaids." Katy's first marriage had lasted only a couple of years. They were young and had drifted apart, but she'd told him that already. There were no secrets between them.

"We should write a book about this. I mean, you couldn't make it up!"

"I know!"

"You write your side, and I'll write mine. We'll call it *Two Hearts Beat as One*"

"You might have to ask Bono and U2 for that title!" She winked at him before downing her second glass.

"Most people would die to have a soul contract like ours!"

"I know! I can't get over it!"

"All those married couples who think they're happy! They don't have a tenth of what we have!"

Beaming at him, she touched her hand lightly to his face and he took it in his, kissing it tenderly before saying, "I'm going to frame those soul contracts and hang them on the wall of our house for everyone to see!"

"Our house? Where are we going to live?"

"Highgate!"

They polished off the bottle of champagne.

"We'd better get going. It's late," said Katy, glancing at her watch.

Standing behind the information board at Paddington Station, it was evident the bubbles had gone to her head and unleashed something. Passions were at boiling point and keeping their hands off each other was impossible. Pulling at his buttocks, she opened her legs as far as her tailored skirt would allow, pushing her hips forward as she locked her lips to his. Kissing passionately and running their hands over each other, the station dissolved. His breathing grew heavier as he slipped one palm under her top and the other over her backside. A few moments later, he was gently pumping against her, oblivious to the few last-minute revelers making their way home. Tottering on her heels as she leaned into him, her skirt was beginning to ride up, revealing a few inches of thigh. A drunken wag shouted out "Get a bed!"

"He's right!" breathed Tony.

The scruffy young lad turned around and shouted back across

the concourse. "I bet he's got a boner, hasn't he?" Sniggering loudly, he staggered on towards his platform, swigging from a bottle before pushing through the turnstile.

Katy giggled and grabbed Tony's taut bottom, squeezing it with her fingers and urging him towards her.

"Come on! Let's go to a hotel right now!" Tony was pleading, his eyes twinkling.

Perhaps they should. What a soul contract! They were meant to be together, so why not? Something deep inside stopped her. "No! We're going to wait and do it properly."

"Pleeeease!"

"We can't stay out all night."

A station announcement echoed over the PA. "The 23.33 train to Oxford will depart from Platform 9. Departing in three minutes."

"You'd better hurry, or you'll miss it!"

"Shit! I'll be toast!" He gave her one last hug and a quick kiss on the lips before running towards the barrier.

Katy walked down the steps to the underground and jumped on the first train. Frustrated and alone, she wondered why she hadn't let Tony have his way. On the other hand, she felt guilty. Tara would say she'd already been unfaithful and in a way, she had. *Thou shalt not commit adultery.* Her thoughts turned to the family. It was Tilly's party on Saturday. She'd be seventeen on Tuesday. Katy burst into tears.

* * *

Lauren Verde was waiting when her stupid, little husband tiptoed into the farmhouse-style kitchen in the early hours of Saturday morning, smelling of booze.

"I thought I told you to sort out your drinking?" She spoke evenly.

"It was just a half bottle of wine." His voice was strangled.

"Where were you anyway? This is the second Friday you've been out on a bender!"

"So what? And it wasn't a bender!"

"So, you've got a problem, matey, and you need to do something about it!" She stood up and jabbed him in the chest with her long, manicured finger.

"I'm sorry, Lauren!"

"You will be."

"I'll make it up to you!"

"You're in the spare room. We'll discuss your behavior tomorrow. Goodnight." She switched off the kitchen light and glided up the stairs, her excuse-for-a-man following sheepishly behind. She could hear him fiddling in the main bathroom before his footsteps faltered along the landing to the guest room. He was up to something, and she had a fair idea what it was.

Tracking down his credit card payments earlier that evening, she'd noted the places he'd been visiting: a café in Little Venice, a pub in Highgate, and what was he doing at Tate Modern? He hated galleries as far as she was aware!

She hoped he hadn't been seeing some floozy behind her back. If so, she'd have to put a stop to it! She'd confront him tomorrow. How could he? After all she'd done for him! Didn't marriage mean anything to him? She wondered if he could get it up with his bit on the side, and if he could, did he manage to finish the job? Did he pretend to her that he was too tired or feeling under the weather? Even with expensive Agent Provocateur, leather, thigh-high boots and fishnets, her husband rarely rose to the occasion, and when he did, it was mechanical, as if his head was somewhere else. She'd seen the dirty magazines he'd hidden in the loft room; soft, curvy women with big bottoms in compromising positions. No doubt there was worse on his laptop.

Of course, it wasn't the first time his eye had wandered. He'd attempted to stray before, but she'd managed to reel him back in.

He had no choice, really – he'd got used to the lifestyle she paid for! He'd be lost without his pocket money!

Recently, he'd been behaving oddly, like a small child who'd taken a sneaky peek at the Christmas presents under the tree. She was worried, but she needn't be, she reminded herself. Amber was her ace in the hole. He doted on the child, and there was no way he'd leave if he couldn't see his darling daughter. And no way he'd mess around behind her back if she threatened to leave him, daughter in tow!

Slipping into bed, she cast her mind back to the evening she'd first seduced Anthony. The memory of the Oxfordshire pub came sharply into focus. Caroline, his first wife, had gone home early, apparently with a migraine. It was no secret that their marriage was on the rocks, and being Caroline's close friend, she'd heard it first-hand. The four of them had gone out. She was with Howard back then but had always fancied Anthony. Howard was on call, and when his pager flashed, he excused himself and left. She never did find out what the emergency was!

Sidling up to Tony, she flirted with him, touching his forearm as she talked, pretending to pick a piece of thread from his sweatshirt, making eyes at him. A round of drinks later, she started rubbing his calf with the top of her foot, then pressing her knee against his. It was his muscular body that she found so attractive. Running her hand along his firm cyclist's thigh, she'd noticed the bulge in his jeans. The rest was history. It wasn't difficult: he was easily led. And if she could do it, then why not someone else? That thought had always haunted her. His reputation, his past, was no secret to her. He was weak.

Lauren sighed as she switched off the light and turned over. She'd been working in the City long enough to observe how the male of the species operated. He couldn't hide his moves, his childish whims, his little enthusiasms from her! The silly idiot had pretended to be something he wasn't, but she'd seen right through it and married him anyway. What a sap! She could play him like the stock market! If he *had* been up to anything, she'd find out and have him by the balls. Lauren rolled onto her back and folded her arms over the duvet.

Some people said she was domineering, but that wasn't fair. She just had more self-control than most and was able to contain her emotions. Huh! Not like those flappable women who worked for her, crying into their Kleenex at the slightest trifle. She would never allow herself to be exposed like that! She wasn't bossy, she was sensible, measured, tough, but fair. They were just jealous because she was efficient and thrived on pressure. Her mind continued to drift.

She'd always known what she wanted and usually got it. It was just a matter of having your head firmly screwed on, taking a few unpopular decisions, holding your nerve, and waiting for the right moment. Of course, you had to look at the numbers, calculate the probability, weigh the odds. You knew where you were with numbers, they followed the rules and behaved themselves, unlike her husband. Without her, he'd be nothing. Just a washed-up officer in the forces.

Rolling over onto her side, she plumped up the pillow. If she had to, she'd hit him where it hurt. It would be her pleasure! How she'd love to punish him in the bedroom, twisting her spiked heels into his back as he lay face down. The corners of her mouth turned up as she visualized the fantasy. Of course, she'd never let on about her fetish: he could use it against her at a later date, and that would never do! But still, it was her duty to see that he shaped up! Who else was going to stand over him and make him grow up? Hadn't she done everything in her power to keep him on track? And how did he thank her? By repeatedly letting her down! Why on earth did she take him back time and again? For better or for worse, she was hooked, she realized, forever putting up with his broken promises and empty threats. Underneath, she had to admit, she loved him, she needed him.

* * *

Alone in the spare room, Tony lay awake, the details of the soul contract and the celebration at Pandora's playing over in his mind. He didn't care anymore. The bitch from hell could do what she wanted. He'd get a restraining order and make sure he'd have access to Amber. The health visitor and her teacher would vouch for him, and so would the Air Commodore. His record was untarnished, and for once, he knew exactly what he wanted. This was real. The thought of Katy aroused him, but that wasn't all, she made his heart beat with joy. All they had to do was hammer out a few details and make their respective moves. His high forehead wrinkled as he rehearsed what he'd say to Lauren. Turning over, and closing his eyes, a broad smile broke across his face as he imagined himself living in the same house as Katy, their home. They'd be sleeping under the same roof, in the same bed. He'd make love to her every night and it would be perfect.

Chapter 31

Saturday 16th May, 2009

Tilly's party had gone well, considering they were in the middle of exams and they'd deliberately kept it low key. She emerged from the small gathering with a new boyfriend in tow. They looked good together, more suited, thought Katy, watching them from the cover of the car, ready to ferry Tilly and her friends back home.

Was it almost seventeen years since that tiny, premature baby had been placed in her hands?

Look at her now! A beautiful, intelligent young woman, far more confident than she'd ever been! Gosh, Tony was only seventeen when they'd first met! And she'd been just fifteen! Oh, my goodness! Freddie's age! Her children were the same age, or would be on Tuesday, that she and Tony had been when they met! She could feel the color draining from her face. That was young, far too early to be taking relationships seriously. Why hadn't she realized it at the time? She'd loved him, she supposed, and thought he loved her.

Winding down the car window, she turned her attention to Tilly. "Hello! How did it go?"

"Yeah! Great!"

The girls piled into the car, giggling and making the odd comment in hushed tones. Some things never changed! Why was life so confusing for teenagers? At least Tilly had been out with someone steady. Tony had walked away after only three weeks. Huh! Three again. Driving through the back roads, dropping off Tilly's friends, Katy's train of thought continued. Stupid of her to believe he'd had any feelings back then. Why would he have loved her, a fifteen-year-old with spots, bushy hair, and an unfashionable, curvy bottom? How she'd hated her looks back then, and how she'd scolded herself for getting it wrong! She frowned. So why did he tell her a week ago Friday that he loved her, and always had?

Swinging the car into Sycamore Road, it dawned on her. Oh, my God! For the last thirty-odd years she hadn't trusted her own intuition! Tony Verde had dumped her when she'd been sure he loved her. It had shut her down, and she'd lost confidence in her instincts ever since! It was thirty-two years to be precise. That made him forty-nine, like the forty-nine steps of the Bardo! He'd be fifty in November! Reincarnation! Rebirthing to a new era, perhaps? Was this another coincidence, along with the kids' ages? Her head was spinning.

Back home, she said goodnight to Tilly before slipping quietly into bed. Richard was already asleep, thank goodness.

Sunday 17th May, 2009 – a six day

Pretending at happy families the next morning around the breakfast table was more than she could bear. Katy's heart beat wildly every time she caught herself in the lie. Honesty had always been her policy, her heart there on her sleeve for all to see. Hadn't her mother always told her she was an open book? She wasn't used to hiding anything and was rubbish at it! Surely Richard must suspect?

Tilly planned to meet up with her new beau that afternoon, and Freddie was off to Tom's. As Richard sat in the garden reading the Sunday papers, Katy tiptoed upstairs, shutting the office door behind her, before ringing Shanti.

"Dinah said I should think about it, chat it through with someone."

"Good idea."

"But I'd normally talk to Rich!"

Shanti laughed. "What about your supervisor?"

"Terry? I'm not sure. He's old school. Probably wouldn't approve."

"He's a professional! Try him!"

"He doesn't understand the spiritual side."

"See what he says."

Katy paused. She was seeing him on Tuesday and could raise the subject. Feel her way with it. "What do *you* think?" she asked.

"I think you're being guided, and you've got to see what unfolds. Go with the flow."

"But what if the flow screws up my life?"

"It can't really. You'll just pick up the pieces and start again!"

"What about Tilly and Freddie?"

"They're your kids. They love you!"

"They're going to be mad at me."

"They'll get over it."

Katy wasn't so confident. What did Shanti know? She didn't have children. "I can't keep up this double life!"

"It won't be forever!"

"There's no way I could have an affair!"

"You already are!"

"I'm not sleeping with him."

"Yet."

"That's the point! I've got to go one way or the other! I have to decide and it's driving me crazy!"

"Why not wait till after the conference? It's less than two weeks away. You'll be on a high vibration, and it'll give you more clarity. Have you seen who's there this year?"

"I know. It's a brilliant line-up!"

"And with all the meditations, you'll have a chance to think about it deeply, without anyone influencing you."

"I suppose so."

"We can talk about it in the evenings, too, go over all the pros and cons."

"That sounds great. Okay. I'll tell Tony to hold off."

"It'll give him time too! You'll be away for a few days and phoning isn't really an option with the long hours and the cost of overseas calls."

"And the reception there's terrible."

"Exactly."

Katy hadn't had time to think about the Conference for Evolution in Human Consciousness but now Shanti had mentioned it, she was excited. They'd be flying to Barcelona, where they'd meet up with MOSES friends who were staying at the same hotel. It had been booked ages ago. Shanti was right, it would give her an opportunity to step back and make the right decision.

Sitting in the navy, wing-backed chair that was usually reserved for clients, Katy cast her eye over her office with its soft blues and its one indigo wall. The statue of the Buddha seemed to be smiling at her. She stood up to light a joss-stick and three candles. Picking up a small piece of moldavite crystal from the shelf, and holding it in the palm of her hand, she returned to her chair and sat with it. A warmth rose from within and seemed to shine out around her. She closed her eyes, the flickering of the candles casting red patterns against the lids as the smell of incense reached her nostrils. In this perfect stillness, a glowing, peaceful feeling wrapped itself around her. She'd speak to Terry on Tuesday, but she already knew what she wanted. Waiting until after the conference was a good idea. She could talk to Shanti, not about Tony, but about the best way of consciously uncoupling from Richard.

It had been quite a journey, she reflected. At times, it felt as if never-ending fragments of herself had been surfacing. Stitch by stitch she'd sewn them together until she knew who she was, understood what she wanted. A contented smile, not unlike that on the Buddha's face, spread across her features.

Down in the kitchen, she put the kettle on.

"Rich?" she called. "Do you want tea?"

Joining her husband in the garden, she sat next to him on a wrought-iron seat. Her stomach lurched as she took a sideways glance. Their marriage wasn't working, and nor was Tony's. Richard and Lauren might even feel relieved? Perhaps they'd be all too willing to walk away? She just had to work out how to tell him.

Tilly and Freddie would understand, of course they would, and they'd love Tony! He was a great dad, from what she'd heard, probably better than Richard! And Amber would be a little stepsister for them. Doubtless, she'd stay with her mum most of the time, but perhaps she'd visit at weekends? Shifting uncomfortably, she took a mouthful of tea and crossed her legs. Tilly and Freddie would live with her, obviously. That's right. It would all be happy families once everyone realized the importance of the soul relationship and the depth of their love.

Give them a chance to settle, and it would all work out for the best. Even Tara and Ben would capitulate once they understood the spiritual side. The wider family would give their seal of approval as soon as they'd got used to the idea. They'd take their lead from the children. It was just a matter of treading gently and giving them plenty of time. Katy's face lit up as she let go of her fears and focused on the positive.

Richard's phone rang and he jumped up, rushing inside to answer it. Must be that journalist again, thought Katy, watching his eyelid flicker.

Suddenly, she realized something! It was she that had changed, not him. She'd pieced herself back together and felt whole. The sun came out, bathing her face in the warmth of its rays. Lifting her eyes, she noticed the roses were in full bloom. A robin swooped down and perched on the briar, its song ringing out across the garden. Happiness had a habit of wearing off, and her own happiness would bring freedom and joy to others, as well as herself. What was it Shanti had said?

Lokah Samastah Sukhino Bhavantu!

Note from the Author

The copyright laws surrounding song lyrics are stringent. Where one can quote from a book and give the source, or quote a person, one cannot quote from a song.

In my novel, I quote briefly from the late British philosopher Alan Watts, and I use a line from The Book of Knowledge, The Keys of Enoch ® by Dr J J Hurtak. There are small quotes from other people, each one acknowledged.

I would like to have quoted song lyrics that the main character hears, sings along to, and views as prophetic. Copyright laws only allow me to use the song title and the artist.

If you'd like to look up the lyrics online, they are freely available, otherwise, the story can be enjoyed without them.

Chapter 10 -   Spice Girls – Wannabe
Chapter 21 -   Van Morrison – No Guru, No Method, No Teacher
Chapter 22 -   David Bowie – Rebel Rebel
Chapter 26 -   Oasis – Wonderwall
                        Oasis Blondie – Hanging on the Telephone
                        Pink Floyd – Wish You Were Here
                        Billy Joel – Just the Way You Are
                        Labi Siffre – It Must be Love

Blood Profit$
The Lithium Conspiracy
J. Victor Tomaszek, James N. Patrick, Sr.
The blood of the many for the profits of the few… *Blood Profit$* will
take you into the cigar-smoke-filled room where American policy
and laws are really made.
Paperback: 978-1-78279-483-7 ebook: 978-1-78279-277-2

The Burden
A Family Saga
N.E. David
Frank will do anything to keep his mother and father apart. But
he's carrying baggage – and it might just weigh him down ...
Paperback: 978-1-78279-936-8 ebook: 978-1-78279-937-5

The Cause
Roderick Vincent
The second American Revolution will be a fire lit from an internal
spark.
Paperback: 978-1-78279-763-0 ebook: 978-1-78279-762-3

Don't Drink and Fly
The Story of Bernice O'Hanlon: Part One
Cathie Devitt
Bernice is a witch living in Glasgow. She loses her way in her
life and wanders off the beaten track looking for the garden of
enlightenment.
Paperback: 978-1-78279-016-7 ebook: 978-1-78279-015-0

Gag

Melissa Unger

One rainy afternoon in a Brooklyn diner, Peter Howland punctures
an egg with his fork. Repulsed, Peter pushes the plate away and
never eats again.

Paperback: 978-1-78279-564-3 ebook: 978-1-78279-563-6

The Master Yeshua

The Undiscovered Gospel of Joseph

Joyce Luck

Jesus is not who you think he is. The year is 75 CE. Joseph ben Jude
is frail and ailing, but he has a prophecy to fulfil ...

Paperback: 978-1-78279-974-0 ebook: 978-1-78279-975-7

On the Far Side, There's a Boy

Paula Coston

Martine Haslett, a thirty-something 1980s woman, plays hard on
the fringes of the London drag club scene until one night which
prompts her to sign up to a charity. She writes to a young Sri
Lankan boy, with consequences far and long.

Paperback: 978-1-78279-574-2 ebook: 978-1-78279-573-5

Tuareg

Alberto Vazquez-Figueroa

With over 5 million copies sold worldwide, *Tuareg* is a classic
adventure story from best-selling author Alberto Vazquez-
Figueroa, about honour, revenge and a clash of cultures.

Paperback: 978-1-84694-192-4

Readers of ebooks can buy or view any of these bestsellers by clicking on the live link in the title. Most titles are published in paperback and as an ebook. Paperbacks are available in traditional bookshops. Both print and ebook formats are available online.

Find more titles and sign up to our readers' newsletter at
http://www.johnhuntpublishing.com/fiction

Follow us on Facebook at https://www.facebook.com/JHPfiction
and Twitter at https://twitter.com/JHPFiction